THE RIVER SNAKES

a novel by Adam Darby

*Praise for **The River Snakes** by Adam Darby*:

A young man proves to be a quick learner when it comes to killing and drug trafficking in Darby's rural crime novel.

Seth, a Midwestern farmworker, crouches in waist-high corn as he witnesses a stranger kill another man. The fearful young man stays hunkered down for hours, then runs to his truck only to find the killer sitting in it. He demands that Seth drive him first to Kansas City to connect with his cohort Vienna ("Like the sausages") and then, eventually, to Montana. But first, he wants him to help load not one, but two bodies into the truck. Although initially Seth tries to escape from the unnamed murderer, he soon demonstrates a knack for doing his bidding, and he finds that he likes the money that the man pays him. Eventually, the man convinces Seth to permanently lock an associate in a shipping container and, later still, to kill someone. Once in Montana, Seth and the man's other underlings (including Isabel, who's "Indian, maybe a little bit Mexican" and very interesting to Seth) are tasked with traveling the Missouri River for two months in canoes packed with ketamine for a drug deal. For good reason, Seth is wary of his fellow drug traffickers; he also knows the man will kill him, like he killed others, if he disappoints him. Darby excels at describing details, identifying farm weeds as "mare's tail" and "volunteer wheat," noting the "plastic-on-plastic clicking sound" of playing video games, and remarking on the "fuzzy yellow cover on the toilet seat" in a low-rent house. The characterization throughout is strong and the pacing is good, with scenes of violence offset by those of the gang having a few beers, cooking spaghetti sauce, and sharing pizza. The yin and yang of loyalty and betrayal run through the novel until its disturbing end.

A dark, unsettling character study. —***Kirkus Reviews***

To my three girls—for your inspiration and your patience—your love and support—thank you.

1

THE BOY DUCKED DOWN BETWEEN THE NEATLY planted rows and watched the two men—half a cornfield from where they stood—same distance from where he'd left the pickup. The men were on the top of a levee about a quarter mile away—the boy watching them through the swaying leaves of the short, dark green plants—watching them motion with their arms and kick the dirt as they spoke.

The sun was shining and the day had been hot since before noon—little breeze blowing across the field but not strong enough to cool the boy down—sweat soaking through his shirt—pesticide mixture he'd been spraying now sticky on his arms and the back of his neck—hand sprayer sitting on its side behind him—nozzle spurting milky white liquid onto the dirt. It was humid as it always was that time of year—more humid down between the rows of corn where he was crouching.

The boy watched the two men argue for what seemed like a long time—then watched as the man on the right pulled a pistol from behind his back and started to raise it—the other man then reaching out grabbing his arm—keeping the pistol pointed down toward his feet. He saw the unarmed man jump before he heard the gunshot—then looked more closely and saw a little cloud of dust rising at the man's feet—then heard another shot and then another—soon able to see a red dot forming on the unarmed man's thigh—beginning to droop and drip down his blue jeans. The boy saw the man turn and start running down the side of the levee—heard a string of gunshots and then saw the unarmed man trip or collapse and start tumbling down the levee—raising dust and leaving small divots in the dirt as he went.

Crouching even lower beneath the long green leaves the boy lost sight of the fallen man—looked up at the one with the pistol still standing there at the top of the levee—his shaded face staring down at the man he'd shot—eventually taking off his cowboy hat and wiping his forehead with the sleeve of his shirt—then releasing the empty clip into his hand and putting it in his shirt pocket—the boy still watching him as he pulled another clip out of a pocket in his blue jeans—as he pushed it up into the pistol. The boy tried not to breathe as he watched the man standing there staring out over the large, flat field—tried not to move as the man scanned the straight rows of corn—the little patch of still-thriving weeds where the boy was hiding—watching the man shake his head before turning around and walking toward the river—descending the other side of the levee.

Once the man was out of sight the boy tried to calm his nerves—taking deep breaths as he shifted his weight around—taking his hat off and running a hand through his sweat-soaked hair—his feet tingling from crouching so long—his knees stiff.

"What the hell," the boy mumbled to himself several times—moving to a seated position in the dirt—using his hat to swat at a pair of flies.

The boy kept watching the top of the levee—wondering if the man with the pistol would come back and do something with the body—wondering if he could make it to the pickup without being seen—wondering if the man had somehow spotted him already. He kept reaching down into his pockets for his cellphone—remembering each time that he'd left it in the pickup—parked on a little hill in a stand of trees at the opposite end of the field.

The boy sat there in the dirt and tried to think—watching and waiting for something to happen—hiding in the middle of the cornfield as the little breeze made the corn leaves sway and clack together—as the humid, heavy air wrapped around him.

Several hours passed with the boy still sitting there—too scared to move—sitting there sweating as the sun slid down diagonally in front of him—dimming as it got closer to the horizon—dropping until the first sunset colors started streaking across the sky—the boy looking up at the pinks and purples—finally starting to relax when he heard another gunshot—only one and he was pretty sure it came from over the levee. He raised up onto his knees but had a hard time seeing anything in that direction with the sun in his eyes—cupping the bill of his hat and pulling it down low over his forehead—not seeing anyone as he did his best to scan the levee.

The boy waited there as the light continued to fade—as clouds of mosquitoes began to appear and buzz around his ears—eventually getting to his feet but still crouching down—grabbing the hand sprayer and gathering the hose so he wouldn't trip—waiting and listening—watching the levee as the pesticide mixture made a sloshing sound inside the little tank.

"Guy probably killed himself," he said.

The boy raised up—stood there above the waist-high corn—the sun turning orange with half of it already below the tops of the cottonwood trees lining the river. He held the hand sprayer in one hand and adjusted his hat with the other—scanning the top of the levee before turning away—running toward the group of trees where the pickup was parked—holding the hand sprayer out a little away from his body so it wouldn't bounce against his hip—taking long strides so each footfall landed between the rows as he pushed his way through the corn. At the edge of the field he finally stopped to catch his breath—turned and looked back toward the levee but didn't see anything.

Soon he was running again—on through the mosquitoes and a few fireflies—able to hear the cicadas that were starting up. The pickup was down a little dirt path—parked next to a honey locust with clumps of thorns sticking out of its bark.

The boy ran through the little stand of trees—coming to the pickup from behind—tossing the hand sprayer over the tailgate as he continued on to the driver's side door—then squeezing the handle and pulling it open—breathing hard still—sweat dripping down his neck—causing his shirt to stick to his skin.

There was a man sitting in the passenger's seat—brown mustache above his pink lips—cowboy hat on his head—sitting there talking on the boy's cellphone. The boy looked down and saw a pistol in the man's lap—then watched the man hold up a finger like he was nearly finished with his call—sounding lighthearted as he spoke into the phone—bit of an accent that didn't quite seem natural. The man seemed completely at ease—like he and the boy were old friends who'd spent the whole day together—not at all concerned about the pistol in his lap or the dead man at the foot of the levee.

After a second or two the boy took off running in the direction of the highway—another quarter mile along the dirt path to the blacktop but he only got a few steps from the pickup—all the sudden feeling a sharp pain—still trying to run but his body soon refused to move—paralyzed somehow as he stumbled forward—trying to look back over his shoulder but unable to turn his head.

The boy knew he was going down—knew he couldn't stop himself from falling forward—but he wasn't conscious when he hit the ground.

WHEN THE BOY STARTED WAKING UP—HOURS OR minutes or days later—he could hear someone playing music off in the distance—or maybe close by—playing something that sounded like a flute—high-pitched notes played in rapid succession. Later he'd find out the instrument was called a penny whistle.

The boy's eyes were half closed and he was only halfway back—listening to the penny whistle play on—notes becoming more distinct as the seconds ticked by—his eyes soon opening—seeing a few stars and little gray clouds in the sky—wiggling his fingers and toes—his arms and legs. Then the pain started coming from a spot around his right shoulder blade.

"Hello, Seth," the man said—standing a few feet away with the penny whistle held up in front of his chest.

"What?"

"Let me finish—then we'll talk."

The man raised the penny whistle to his lips and started playing the song from where he'd left off—Seth blinking up at the blurry figure—waiting for his eyes to focus. It was hard to see much of anything in the dark—barely able to tell he was looking at the same man he'd seen in the pickup— average height—maybe a little skinny—wearing blue jeans and boots.

Seth watched the man blow into a metal pipe and shuffle around to the music he was making—watched him from flat on his back on the dirt path—the man making two circles around him before coming to the end of the song—then holding his arms out like he was quieting a crowd—the penny whistle in his left hand—eventually folding his arms into his body as he slowly bowed—finally standing up straight again after what seemed like a long time—turning and looking down.

"Seth."

"Who are you?" Seth said as he raised himself to a sitting position—still not ready to try standing.

"I am a man you're going to drive to Kansas City."

Seth didn't say anything—just watched as the man twirled the penny whistle in his hand.

"We better get going," the man said. "Do you have any hand sanitizer, Seth? I couldn't find any in your vehicle."

"It's not mine," Seth said. "I can't drive you anywhere."

The man tucked the penny whistle into his back pocket as he quickly closed the distance between them—putting a foot on Seth's thigh as the boy tried to shuffle backward—then putting his other foot on Seth's chest—somehow keeping his balance as Seth's back slammed down onto the dirt path. Seth felt the sharp pain from his shoulder blade—then felt the man's fists punching down on his face—connecting several times as Seth's vision went black again—relieved when he felt the man quickly jump off his chest—when he saw the blurry glint of the penny whistle as the man pulled it out from his back pocket—when he heard him start playing an even faster song than the one before—hopping away into the darkness.

Seth looked around for the man as he tried to stumble to his feet—taking a long time just to get to his knees—then putting one hand on the ground as he pushed himself up—planting the soles of his boots on the ground and grabbing his knees with both hands—the man still out there some-where playing the penny whistle.

Seth turned and tried to run—this time back toward the cornfield and the levee—getting just beyond the tailgate before he felt a sharp sting in his right hamstring—thinking at first he'd been shot as he waited to hear the sound of the pistol firing—hopping a few steps on his left leg—then falling forward onto the ground—raising a cloud of dust in the dark.

"Get up, Seth," the man said—suddenly nearby. "That one's not nearly as strong as the one I put in your shoulder."

Seth lay there with his face in the dirt—listening as the man opened the passenger's side door of the pickup—as he hopped up into the seat and shut the door. Then everything was quiet.

Seth propped himself up on his elbows—feeling like he might vomit—feeling blood and saliva dripping from his face onto the dirt—pain in his shoulder blade still but now his hamstring hurt more.

After a few seconds he reached back and pulled a dart out of his leg—blinking the tears out of his eyes so he could see the bloody tip—thin shaft and the brightly colored feathers.

2

"DON'T MAKE ME WAIT SO LONG NEXT TIME, Seth," the man said as Seth climbed up into the driver's seat—leg and shoulder still hurting—still covered in dirt, blood, sweat and a few tears.

Seth reached out to pull the door closed—pain shooting through his back from the dart the man had shot him with. He pulled the door toward him but not hard enough to latch it shut—dome light staying on as he glanced over at the man—nail file in one hand as he carefully inspected each thin finger of the other.

"Gotta pop start it," Seth said—grabbing the keys that'd been left in the ignition. "Just so you know what I'm doing."

"Pop start?"

"Yeah—yessir."

"What does that mean exactly, Seth?" The man looked up at him—gestured with the nail file. "You mean roll start?"

"I guess so—yeah—yessir."

"That's the proper term—say it your way again and there will be more pain—do you hear me, Seth?"

"Yessir."

Seth had his foot on the clutch but didn't push down—didn't look at the man or out the windshield—his eyes staring down at the steering wheel—waiting for the dome light to go off—to slowly fade out—then realizing his door wasn't closed all the way.

"My door isn't shut."

"Leave it—you'll be getting out soon."

The man told him to get the pickup started—to roll it off the hill in neutral and then let off the clutch with the gearshift in second—then to turn the pickup around and drive back to the levee. Seth did as he was told—drove slowly over the uneven earth in the dark—dome light still on inside the cab of the pickup. He glanced over once at the man filing away at his fingernails—noticed his blue jeans were pleated—neatly ironed creases running all the way down to his ankles—but his boots were old—gray leather worn and crusty.

"There's a cadaver out here near the base of the levee, Seth," the man said. "Find it."

Seth asked if he could turn on the headlights—the man nodding his head as Seth glanced over again—then turned back to the windshield and started scanning the ground as he drove on—looking for the man he'd seen shot hours earlier.

He soon found the dead man's body—arms and legs stretched out—each bent in an unnatural position.

"Throw it in the back," the man said. "Leave the pickup running."

Seth reversed the pickup until he was close to the body—got out and walked back to the tailgate—turned and looked through the back window at the man in the passenger's seat—working the file back and forth over his fingernails again.

Seth's back and hamstring still ached but he felt the pain wearing off—rubbing the spot where his hamstring hurt as he turned away from the pickup—dim red glow of the brake lights—smell of hot exhaust blowing toward him.

He stood there studying the dead man's body—brown hair and a stubbly beard. All the blood had dried a dark crimson color on the dead man's leg—still red in the white squares of his checkered shirt.

Seth lifted the body—held it up against him in a standing position—then tipped it over onto the open tailgate—trying not to get blood on himself but there were too many gunshot wounds—ending up with a long red slick going down his chest.

The dead man's head hit the metal floor of the pickup's bed as Seth rolled him over—turning away and closing his eyes—trying not to hear the sound it made. Then he grabbed the dead man's ankles and lifted them into the pickup—folding the legs at the knees to get them past the tailgate.

"Very good, Seth," the man said as Seth climbed back into the driver's seat—not bothering to look up as he spoke—rubbing some kind of oil or cream over the knuckles of his left hand. "Do you know what to do now?"

"No—no, sir."

"Try."

Seth remembered the last gunshot he'd heard—near sundown—just a single shot from somewhere near the river—remembered how the two men had been arguing on the top of the levee—how they'd kicked the dirt and wrestled over the pistol. Then he looked across the bench seat—met the man's eyes and said, "Go over the levee—get the other body?"

"Excellent, Seth," the man said—then paused with one hand cupped over the knuckles of the other—looking at Seth and smiling as the dome light was just starting to dim. "You may not be stupid after all, Seth." The cab of the pickup was dark now—slight green glow from the buttons on the dash. "I was sure you were stupid when I first saw you—opening the door with that stupid look on your face—terrified and confused—a stupid, stupid boy."

Seth didn't say anything—just looked at the man and listened—his hands on the steering wheel—pickup's engine rumbling in the background.

"And I thought you'd be soiling your pants after handling a cadaver," the man said—looking down at his hands—massaging his knuckles again. "Why are you so calm, Seth?"

"I won't tell anybody what happened out here if you let me go," Seth said—turning to look out the windshield. "Won't tell what you look like—I'll just say the pickup was stolen—and I won't say a word till tomorrow."

The cab was silent for a while as the man continued with his hands—rumble of the engine causing the pickup to shake almost imperceptibly—green glow from the digital clock and the backlit buttons.

"Maybe I should get rid of you," the man said. "Are you toying with me, Seth?"

"No—no, sir."

"Are you working for someone, Seth?"

"No, sir."

"How did you know about the other body?"

"I didn't. I don't—"

The man shot across the seat before Seth could get his hands up—before he could duck or even tell which of the man's fists hit him first. Then the driver's side door opened and the dome light came on—Seth tumbling out with the man on top of him—covering his head and pulling his legs up against his body—doing his best to avoid the man's fists and boots—dirt soon in his eyes and gritty between his teeth—one of the man's boots eventually finding his stomach—causing him to vomit onto the loose soil—his eyes watering as his midsection heaved—then vomiting again until there was nothing left.

Seth rolled over onto his side and let his head rest in the dirt—still able to see the pickup in front of him—engine still rumbling and the headlights still on—hearing the man somewhere off in the darkness—hearing him start playing a slow, somber song on the penny whistle—playing the sad song as Seth waited to be shot by either the pistol or another poison dart—playing as he moved around but stayed out of sight—sometimes getting closer—other times farther away.

Seth waited for what seemed like a long time—then closed his eyes and either passed out or fell asleep.

SETH WOKE UP A FEW MINUTES LATER TO THE SOUND of his cellphone ringing—opening his eyes and raising his head off the dirt—seeing the man reach in through the passenger's side window of the pickup—grab something off the dash—penny whistle sticking out the back pocket of his jeans.

"Mom," the man said into the phone after glancing at the screen. "He's right here—lying on the ground with tears in his eyes."

Seth raised his head again—blinked a few times to clear his vision—feeling clumps of dirt stuck to the side of his face.

"No no no, ma'am," the man said. "No he's fine, ma'am— he's just laughing." The man was now walking around the back of the pickup. "He's laughing so hard he's rolling around on the ground crying."

Seth watched the man as he started coming closer—as he stared at him with his blank blue eyes—as he pulled the shiny penny whistle from behind his back—then lifted it to his lips to tell Seth to keep quiet.

"I tickled him," the man said into the phone—squatting down next to Seth—poking at him with the penny whistle. "Well I certainly don't identify as such," the man said. "But I'm not sure if your son's homosexual or not."

Seth turned and tried to sit up.

"Well he actually won't be home tonight, ma'am. I suggest you go to the store yourself."

Seth's head hurt now more than anything—pain in his hamstring fading—shoulder somehow not bothering him anymore. He ran his tongue over his teeth—felt them gritty from the vomit and the dirt.

"No, ma'am—no I doubt we sleep at all tonight, ma'am. Yes. No. Alright, ma'am—have a terrific evening." The man touched the screen to end the call—Seth hearing his mother yell something before the call cut off.

"Let's go," the man said as he stood up and started walking toward the pickup.

Seth managed to get to his feet—to take a few unsteady steps—eventually making it to the pickup and opening the driver's side door—resting a second or two before he pulled himself up—dome light on and the engine still rumbling. The man was there in the passenger's seat—cleaning his penny whistle with a handkerchief.

"Your mother's pure trash, Seth," the man said without looking up.

"Yessir."

"A real waste of resources," the man continued—rubbing the shiny metal instrument in his hands. "Imagine if we could simply do away with people like her after they've been given so many chances to contribute—we could save the world, Seth."

"Yessir."

"Drive, Seth—northwest corner of the field—jump out and go over the levee and get the other body—bring it back and toss it in with the other one."

"Yessir."

"Make sure not to leave any of his belongings over there, Seth—and keep the engine running."

They drove on for a few minutes in silence—soon coming to the end of the cornfield—Seth slowing the pickup to a stop—jiggling the gearshift back and forth out of habit—then opening the driver's side door and slipping down to the loose dirt. The man didn't say anything—just kept rubbing the penny whistle with the handkerchief—Seth glancing over at him before he shut the door—seeing the skinned knuckles of the man's hands—pale, delicate-looking with thin fingers and glossy nails—hands you'd never guess could hit so hard.

Seth shut the door and climbed the levee in the dark—stood at the top looking out over the country—moonlight shining on the ribbon of river he could see snaking away in both directions—lines of trees framing fields of soybeans and corn. He turned and looked back down at the pickup—listened to the engine noise mixing with all the insect mating calls—then started descending the other side of the levee—jutting one foot out and down in front of him—careful not to slip. At the bottom he felt the sandy soil shift under his feet—trees spaced far apart—hardly any grass growing between them. Seth looked around for the second body—walking toward the river as he scanned the ground—turning after several steps and walking south along the riverbank—soon spotting the lifeless man—limp body lying face down in the sandy dirt—one of his arms folded underneath his midsection.

Seth stood there and stared at the body for a few minutes—listening to the river and the insects—feeling a headache coming on. He put his hand up to his face and felt dry blood around his mouth—on his cheek and crusted into his eyebrows.

The boy lifted the dead man's upper body by grabbing him under the arms—then started dragging him back toward the levee—lifeless legs making little parallel canals in the dirt—boots slipping off just as Seth was stopping to rest. He dropped the body and wiped the sweat from his forehead—went to collect the boots and remembered the cowboy hat the dead man had been wearing earlier that afternoon.

Seth had to rest one more time before getting the body to the top of the levee—breathing hard and sweating with his hands on his knees once he reached the peak—looking down at the pickup's red taillights—then tipping the dead man's body over and pushing him so he'd go tumbling down toward the cornfield.

After watching the body flip and roll down the levee—watching the dust rise until he finally came to a rest on his back—lifeless arms and legs all stretched out in unnatural positions—Seth returned to the riverbank and started searching for the cowboy hat—first going back to the spot where he'd found the body—then starting south again—scanning the ground just like before. There were a few frogs croaking now—the boy stopping to look out over the wide river—just able to make out the trees and the riverbank of the opposite shore. He stood there for what seemed like a long time—watching the water in the moonlight—guessing where the strongest currents were.

"You'll want to take your boots off," the man said—causing Seth to whip around and spot him leaning against a tree. "Are you a strong swimmer, Seth?"

He looked for the pistol in the man's hands—eyes squinting through the darkness but the man's arms were folded over his chest—his hands tucked against his ribs and out of view.

"I'd wager a tidy sum you're not," the man continued. "Your mother certainly didn't teach you."

"I'm just looking for the man's hat," Seth said. "I saw him wearing a hat earlier and you told me not to leave anything behind."

"You see those whirlpools?" the man said as he walked toward Seth and the river's edge—pointing now with the pistol in his right hand. "That current's strong, Seth—and the water's freezing."

"I know."

The man came close and stared at Seth—studying him—lowering the pistol down next to his hip—Seth watching the man the whole time—still waiting for a bullet or another dart.

"Just following instructions? That it?"

"Yeah—yessir." Seth looked away from the man—looked at the water lapping against the riverbank.

"You might just do, Seth," the man said as he leaned in—almost touching Seth's face with the brim of his cowboy hat. "Might but might not—we'll have to see." Then the man turned and started walking off toward the levee. "I already retrieved the hat," he said—still walking away as he raised the cowboy hat he'd been wearing the whole time—raised it off his head a few inches before setting it back in place.

Seth took one last look at the river—then followed the man at a distance—climbed the levee and then carefully descended the other side. The man was already back in the pickup—in the passenger's seat like before. Seth dragged the dead man's body to the tailgate—lifted it up and rolled it over on top of the other one—jumped up into the bed of the pickup and dragged the two bodies back—positioning them as flat as possible—then looking himself over once he'd finished—seeing blood streaked up to his elbows—front of his shirt soaked through with a mixture from the two dead men—some dry and some still wet.

Seth hopped down—went around and opened the driver's side door—grabbed a roll of paper towels from behind the seat and began wiping the blood off his arms—pickup still rumbling and the dome light stayed on.

"At least it isn't yours," the man said—Seth glancing up to see him examining the pile of bloody paper towels on the driver's seat. "Most of it, anyway."

Seth finished cleaning himself up as best he could—then stuffed the paper towels behind the seat and climbed up into the pickup.

"Buckle your seatbelt, Seth," the man said as Seth shifted into first gear. "Drive five miles per hour below the speed limit—use your blinkers and don't do anything stupid."

Seth started driving—first pulling out of the field and onto the dirt path—then onto the two-lane highway—finally going down the onramp and heading south on I-29—seeing a sign for Kansas City after a couple minutes and checking the clock—checking the fuel gauge—guessing it would be close to daylight by the time they got there—wondering when he should ask about stopping for gas.

"Don't stop for gas," the man said. "It's enough—don't worry." Seth glanced over and saw the man working on his fingernails again. "You know they call it 'petrol' in some countries."

Seth didn't say anything—watched the road and tried not to think too much—kept his eyes on the white and yellow lines. There were a few other vehicles out but not many—mostly semis hauling livestock or frozen food.

"The English do," the man said. "Those arrogant blue bloods."

Seth tried not to listen—tried not to wonder what the hell he was talking about—where they were going and why—what the man might do once they got there.

3

SETH DROVE ON DOWN I-29—ANSWERING THE MAN'S questions—trying to ignore everything else he said. He told the man the pickup belonged to his boss—a local farmer named Mr. Loomis—told him Mr. Loomis would probably call his cellphone early the next morning once he noticed the pickup was missing—then would probably be quick to get the cops out after him if he didn't answer. The man listened but didn't seem too worried—nodding his head as he kept working on his nails.

"When we get where we're going," the man said. "I'll have some things for you to do." Seth tried to look at him without turning his head. "I'm fairly certain you will fail—but there is a small chance you make yourself so useful—so indispensable that I decide to keep you around."

Seth kept driving—making sure to keep both hands up on the steering wheel—to check the speedometer every minute or two.

"Do you understand what I'm saying, Seth?"

"Yeah—yessir."

"Good boy."

As the sun started to rise Seth spotted the big grain elevators and the train tracks as they entered Kansas City—then saw the tall buildings all clumped together downtown—more cars and trucks passing the pickup as Seth stayed below the speed limit—businesses and hotels dotting the sides of the highway now—replacing most of the pastures and cornfields.

"Take the Armour Road exit," the man said. "Stay to your right."

"Yessir."

"It's a beautiful time of day—isn't it, Seth?"

"Yeah—yessir."

"Soft blue light—little hazy due to the moisture in the air." The man shifted in his seat to look out the window. "Perfect temperature now but you know it'll be hot later—bright and hot."

Seth turned his head—looked the man up and down while he stared out the window—guessing the man didn't weigh any more than he did—not an ounce of fat on him, though—little knots and lumps of muscle all along his back—the pistol there too—tucked into the waistband of the man's blue jeans.

"Do you believe in God, Seth?" the man said—Seth turning quickly back to the road—gripping the steering wheel with both hands. "Of course you do," the man continued as he shifted back around to face forward. "Do you think this is all so beautiful—these trees and the dew still wet and cool on the grass and the soft blue morning light—the killing of bad and disappointing men—do you think it's all so satiating because God wants it to be?" Seth glanced over at the man— saw him yawn as he stared out the windshield—little smile forming on his face. "Exit here, Seth."

The man directed Seth past old abandoned brick

buildings and weedy open lots—told him to drive around behind a four-story building with most of the windows boarded up—stopping him in front of an old wooden door with only scraps of white paint left on it.

"Keep the engine running," the man said. "I'll be right back."

Seth sat there as the man opened the passenger's side door and hopped out—watched him jog up to the old wooden door and yank it open—step inside and close it behind him.

There wasn't much else around the old building—empty, broken sidewalks—empty lots behind the pickup and across the street—Seth's eyes getting heavy as he looked out at all the cracked concrete around him—turning eventually and looking down through the back window at the two dead bodies in the pickup's bed—staring at them when his cellphone started ringing—making him jump before he reached over and picked it up off the little ledge above the glove compartment—looked at the screen and saw the number was blocked but he answered it anyway.

"Seth," he heard the man say. "Come around the east side of the building."

The man ended the call before Seth could respond—holding his cellphone up in front of his face—seeing the battery was almost dead and wondering whether he should bother charging it or not—then looking down at the pickup's fuel gauge—little orange stick now covering the last dash on the empty end.

"The hell am I doing?" Seth said—dropping the cellphone onto the seat next to him—then shifting the pickup into reverse.

He backed out onto the empty street—looked over at the cellphone as he paused with the gearshift in neutral—then drove around to the east side of the building—same as all the other sides—dingy red bricks, plywood-covered windows—but then he saw a large roller door going up as he drove toward it—heard the metal panels rattling—heard the pulleys squeaking and the chain tapping the cement floor.

A man stood just inside the doorway—tall and heavily-built—wearing a tank-top and cloth pants—pulling a chain hand over hand as the door kept rising above his head—Seth watching him blink and narrow his eyes as the light hit his face.

Seth slowed the pickup and started turning toward the open door—looking around for the man as he inched forward—checking his cellphone for a missed call—the heavily-built man at the entrance waving him in—leaning out and looking down the street in both directions.

"Where the hell is he?" Seth said to himself—trying to look inside the building but it was too dark and featureless—barely enough light for him to make out the ceiling and the outline of one of the walls.

The man in the tank-top kept waving and checking the street—finally running out of patience as he pulled a pistol from his pocket—pointing it at Seth in the pickup.

"OK," Seth said—raising his hands above the steering wheel. "OK." He slowly lowered his hands and took his foot off the brake—the man waving him in again but with the pistol this time.

"Stop!" the man yelled as he smacked the tailgate—then put the pistol away and started pulling the chain hand over hand again—roller door crashing down behind the pickup— Seth with barely enough time to look back and see it bounce as it hit the cement floor—listening as the man locked the door in the dark—only able to see the outline of the pickup's bed through the back window.

The man in the tank-top came around and opened the passenger's side door—Seth watching him hop up into the pickup as the dome light came on

"Go," the man said. "Keep to the right—slow."

Seth didn't say anything—shifted into first gear and checked the fuel gauge again—then let out the clutch and steered the pickup to the right—headlights shining on a brick wall as he began driving alongside it.

"You ain't been doing this long," the man in the tank-top said. "He shoot you with one of those darts yet?"

Seth looked over at the man—saw him smile in the green glow from the digital clock on the dash—everything else dark except the brick wall and the cement floor—shining crimson and dirty gray in the headlights.

"He give you a gun?" the man said—Seth keeping his eyes straight ahead this time—still not saying anything—feeling the man smile again even though he didn't turn his head. "Hell I bet he even gave them two idiots guns." The man pointed with his thumb at the dead men in the bed of the pickup.

Soon the cement floor turned to rough-cut limestone—Seth slowing the pickup to a crawl—looking over at the man in the tank-top.

"Keep going," the man said—smiling as he kept looking out the windshield.

The front end of the pickup began tilting downward—Seth watching jagged limestone walls rise on each side of them—driving on with his foot touching the brake—both his hands tight around the steering wheel—the limestone walls soon coming together above the pickup to form a tunnel.

"Bet you didn't count on ending up in here this morning," the man in the tank-top said. "Them neither." He indicated the two dead bodies again.

Seth drove on—taking his foot off the brake once the path leveled off.

"Lot harder to make a run for it than people think, ain't it?" the man said—Seth looking over at him but not answering—looking down and seeing the pistol back in the heavily-muscled man's right hand—resting on his leg. "Everybody sits in their living rooms—watching the news. They see some story about a young girl getting herself kidnapped or some terrorist taking a bunch of people hostage. They think, 'Why ain't they running? How come they don't fight back? I'd fight like hell! I'd make a break and get away!' But they don't know—they ain't never been where you're at right now."

Seth kept driving—feeling cold as they got deeper into the cave—his shirt still wet from all the blood and sweat—goosebumps forming on his arms but it didn't even cross his mind to turn the heater on.

It was only another couple minutes before he saw lights and an open space up ahead—large, brightly lit room slowly coming into focus—pickup bouncing over the rough-cut limestone of the tunnel's floor—then stopping at the entrance to the open space.

"Back up to that big pile of salt over there," the man in the tank-top said—pointing to the left with the pistol. "But watch out for the hole. We call it the litter box." Seth looked at the man as he shifted back into first gear—saw him smiling again. "You'll see."

The open space they were now in was a circle maybe two-hundred feet across—ceiling around fifteen feet high with fluorescent light fixtures hanging down a foot or so on chains. It was bright inside the large cave—especially after the darkness of the tunnel and the empty building at the surface.

Seth steered the pickup to the right and saw two shipping containers side-by-side against the wall—then shifted into reverse and began backing up toward the salt pile.

"Stop here," the man in the tank-top said—Seth barely able to see an opening in the uneven limestone floor just beyond the tailgate—a hole maybe ten feet across. "Shut the engine off."

"I can't."

"Why not?"

"Starter quit—I have to pop start it every time."

"Pop start?"

"Roll start—sorry."

The man reached over and turned the key—Seth feeling the engine rattle to a stop—then feeling the man open-hand slap his face—his head hitting the headrest—his eyes starting to water.

"Get out," the man in the tank-top said—Seth already opening the door—sliding out and feeling his feet hit the limestone floor. "Come on back here."

Seth slid his hand along the bed of the pickup as he walked toward the tailgate—blinking and rubbing his eyes—seeing the man in the tank-top waiting for him.

"We'll get you taken care of first," the man said. "Stand over there in front of the litter box." The man raised one muscled arm—used the pistol to point at the hole beside the pile of salt.

Seth walked over—still blinking the tears out of his eyes—looked down and saw an uneven layer of salt at the bottom of the hole—blinked again and saw a shoulder sticking up out of the salt—a knee and the tip of a brown leather boot.

"Plenty of company down there for you," the man said as he raised the pistol.

Seth looked over the man's shoulder—looked across the cave at the shipping containers—metal hinges squeaking as one of the doors began to swing open—the man in the tank-top turning his head when he heard the sound—keeping the pistol raised—his finger on the trigger and the barrel pointed at Seth.

Seth took off running around the pickup—keeping his head down as he heard gunshots—getting to the front tire and crouching down.

"They're already dead, you know." Seth recognized the voice instantly—the strange softness and forced accent—casual way the man with the penny whistle talked. "I thought you'd be able to discern as much on your own." Seth could hear him walking toward the pickup.

"What the hell you talking about?" the man in the tank-top yelled. "I'm after the one you brought alive for some reason."

"I told you already—I don't drive."

"What?" the man in the tank-top said—Seth hearing him sneak around the front of the pickup from the passenger's side—listening as he started taking small steps backward.

"I'm a nobleman—noblemen never drive themselves," the man said—finally arriving near the pickup—Seth hearing his feet stop somewhere close to the man in the tank-top. "Do not shoot my driver."

Seth heard the man in the tank-top turn on the gritty limestone floor—heard him start taking steps toward the shipping containers. "Crazy ass," he said—getting farther away with every step—the man walking with him.

"Oh don't be so agitated—makes you seem simple," the man said as Seth stayed hidden—crouched down next to the driver's side door. "Leave the boy alone—he can be your Halotus for the new sample I brought you."

"What the hell are you talking about?"

"It'll make sense later."

Seth stayed where he was—listening as the shipping container door squeaked again—then hearing footsteps on the container's metal floor.

"Come hither, Seth," the man yelled.

Seth suddenly felt sore all over his body—his face swollen and his shoulder blade hurting again—reaching down and rubbing his hamstring where he'd been shot with the dart—looking down and checking himself for bullet wounds—examining his chest and his dirty pants—feeling the weight of all the blood soaked into his shirt.

Finally Seth stood up and looked around—saw the door to one of the shipping containers halfway open—heavy padlock keeping the other closed. He looked back at the salt pile and the hole—the litter box—then turned back to the shipping containers—light now shining inside the open one. He watched a shadow pass in front of it—then took a deep breath before stepping away from the pickup—walking across the cave toward the light and the two men.

"But I don't think I need something new," Seth heard the man in the tank-top say—listening a few feet from the door.

"But you do," the man said. "This industry is ever-evolving—you know that—therefore you must grow faster than your competitors."

"But I ain't got no competitors round here."

Seth heard the man start laughing—heard the man in the tank-top join in and start laughing too. He took a small step closer—heard one of them stand and start walking toward the door.

"That's a very good observation," the man said.

Seth started to back away but knew it was too late to hide—heard two more footsteps and then he saw the man shoot out of the shipping container.

"Shut it," the man told Seth. "Shut the door and pull the levers down."

Seth stepped forward—put his hands on the door and had to push hard to close it—heard the man in the tank-top yelling and running toward him as he grabbed the levers and tried to pull them down.

"He sounds rather angry," the man said—standing to the side as Seth tried to figure out the levers—twisting the vertical shafts they were fastened to—pulling the handles until the levers loosened and came down.

Then Seth heard gunshots from inside the shipping container—realized the heavy door was vibrating under his frantic hands—the man in the tank-top still running and screaming and shooting as Seth finally secured the two levers and locked the door—as he stepped back and stood there running his hands over his chest and stomach—checking himself once again for bullet holes.

"Well done, Seth," the man said—Seth looking up at him but not saying anything—the man smiling—laughing a little to himself as the man in the tank-top continued screaming—now banging on the shipping container doors. "I suppose we should take his money."

Seth watched the man walk to the door of the other shipping container—heavy chain with a padlock around the levers—the man picking it up and looking down at it—then looking over at Seth.

"Do you think he'd give us the key if we asked?" the man said—bouncing a little as he laughed at his own joke. "Slide it under that door you shut in his face? Think he'd do that for us, Seth?"

Seth looked at the man and shook his head—breathing hard now—bent over with his hands on his knees—then dropping his head and looking down at the rough-cut limestone floor—the man in the tank-top still screaming from inside the shipping container—Seth wondering in a sudden and jumbled rush how he'd gotten there—how he'd become a killer in a cave—accomplice to the strangest, most dangerous man he'd ever met.

The man pulled the pistol out from his waistband—stood to the side and shot the padlock—two ends of the chain breaking apart and swinging against the door—clinking and rattling as the single gunshot echoed off the walls and ceiling—man in the tank-top still screaming and banging on the doors—now starting to scream a few mumbled words about his money.

"Do you think if we left his money," the man said—not bothering to turn around—just standing there watching the swaying chain with Seth behind him. "If we left it sitting in this container and left him to rot in that one—side by side—do you think he'd be a little happier once he finally died?"

Seth didn't say anything—watched the man's back—hands still on his knees—the penny whistle sticking up out of the man's back pocket. "That's avarice," the man said. "Greed."

The man finally stepped forward—pulled the chain free and lifted the levers to open the door—swung it open with the hinges squeaking and popping—then slipped inside.

Seth stood up straight and walked closer—stopped a few feet away from the door and looked inside—the man holding a flashlight as he made his way to the back of the dark shipping container—Seth watching him sweep the light from side to side.

"Come in here, Seth," the man said near the back—pointing the flashlight at something black in one of the corners.

Seth approached the door—looked back at the entrance to the cave—the tunnel that lead up to the real world—then turned back to the shipping container and leaned in—took a step inside and waited for his eyes to adjust to the darkness—still able to hear the man in the tank-top screaming—quieter than before and with more crying—only tapping on the door now.

"Quicken your pace, Seth," the man said as he turned and pointed the flashlight back toward the entrance. "Do you hear me, Seth?"

"Yeah—yessir," Seth said—jogging down the length of the shipping container—hearing the metal booms ring out with every stride—coming to where the man was standing with the flashlight—then looking down and seeing two small black suitcases in the corner.

"Open them," the man said. "Degenerate was spending it almost as fast as it was coming in."

Seth knelt down and opened the first suitcase—saw it was full of loose bills—ones, tens, twenties, a few hundreds—some folded two or three times—a few wadded up into balls.

"Overfed and unconcerned," the man said as he looked down into the suitcase. "Just like this whole country."

Seth stepped over and opened the other suitcase—same array of bills but only half-full. The man told him to drag them both out of the shipping container—then turned quickly and started walking toward the entrance—leaving Seth there in the dark—having to feel for the zippers to get the suitcases closed—standing them up as he tried to find the handles—then looking up and seeing the man approach the doors—wheeling the suitcases now at a fast walk—then lifting them off the metal floor and running when he saw the man step outside the shipping container.

One of the suitcases banged into one of the doors as Seth shot out into the open space—into the limestone cave with the overhead lights buzzing above his head—standing there breathing hard—looking around for the man—hearing the penny whistle after a few seconds—swinging around to see the man sitting on the floor—his back against the door of the other shipping container.

The man played a slow song with a sad look on his face—the man in the tank-top still tapping the door—still crying as he begged to be let out—Seth standing there with the suitcases—waiting until he felt his legs start to wobble—then sitting down on one of the suitcases as he listened to the man still playing the sad song—the man in the tank-top quieting down after a minute or two—only sounds in the cave the long, vibrato notes from the penny whistle—Seth feeling the music lulling him to sleep—his eyes getting heavy as the man neared the end of the song.

"You passed, Seth—good job," the man said after lowering the penny whistle—Seth nodding but not saying anything.

They sat there and listened to the man in the tank-top—crying softly now somewhere near the door of the shipping container.

"It's unfortunate we're living in such evil times—all the deplorable things we have to do," the man said—looking off across the open space—deep in thought for what seemed like a long time—then pinching his nose and squinting his eyes—yawning as he stretched his arms and back. "Put the pickup in neutral and push it into the hole." The man looked at Seth—eyes still watery from the yawn. "Leave your cellphone inside."

Seth stood up from the suitcase and walked over to the pickup—opened the driver's side door and hopped up into the seat—pushed down on the clutch with his left foot and shifted into neutral—then set his cellphone on the seat and jumped out of the pickup—walked around to the front—put his hands on the hood and started pushing. It took a little effort to get it going but after a few feet the pickup's own momentum started carrying it back toward the hole—rear tires dropping over the edge first—pickup's undercarriage dropping and hitting the jagged limestone—front tires lifting off the ground and then it all disappeared—Seth hearing the pickup crash into the salt and the bodies.

He turned around and started back toward the man and the shipping containers—the suitcases full of money—seeing the man still on the ground with his back against the metal door—walking over to him but standing off to the side.

"You're a little disheveled, Seth," the man said—looking up at him—examining his shirt as he started to stand—the man in the tank-top silent now. "Very disheveled, actually. Vienna can't see you like this—there'd be too many questions."

The man started walking toward the tunnel—motioning for Seth to follow him—Seth going over and grabbing the two suitcases—then hurrying to catch up—staying a few steps behind the man—able to hear the man in the tank-top start crying again—smacking the inside of the door as they left the open space.

"Did you understand the reference I made to Halotus, Seth?" the man said.

"No, sir."

"Halotus was a food taster and attendant of the Roman emperor, Claudius," the man said—both of them walking up the tunnel now—not much light from the open space able to reach them—Seth dragging the suitcases over the rough-cut limestone. "He would taste everything the emperor was about to eat—to make sure it was safe. But it's believed that Halotus—after quite some time as a loyal servant—actually poisoned the emperor's food—killing him." Seth didn't say anything. "Do you understand now, Seth?"

"What was I gonna taste?"

The man stopped suddenly—turned around and looked down at him. "We're going to go see a man in the suburbs but first we have to buy you some clothes. I do business with this man, Vienna—same sort of business I used to do with the man you just locked in a shipping container."

Seth turned his head and looked back down the tunnel— still able to hear the man in the tank-top crying and tapping the metal door. "What sort of business?" he said—turning back to face the man.

"A large percentage of the people living in this country today are heavily medicated, Seth—diagnosed with depression, schizophrenia, mania—and like all heavily medicated people with these sorts of diagnoses they want to be even more heavily medicated—teachers, housewives, executives, construction workers, policemen—they're all getting high under the guise of medical treatment."

"You're a drug dealer?"

"Pharmaceutical booster salesman, Seth—all organic— all natural ingredients."

"Boosters?"

"Boosters are sold as a way to increase both the potency and the longevity of psychiatric pharmaceuticals."

"What are they really?"

"Psychiatric pharmaceuticals," the man said—meeting

Seth's eyes and smiling. "You work for me now, Seth. We'll go over all the details later. Come on." He turned and continued up the tunnel—Seth standing there alone for a moment—watching him go—then looking down at his blood-soaked clothes—his hands holding the suitcases full of money—yawning and shaking his head before looking up again—following after the man just as he started to disappear into the darkness.

4

THEY CAME UP OUT OF THE TUNNEL—UP INTO THE dark, empty building at the surface—the man swinging the flashlight from side to side—brick walls and boarded-up windows. Seth walked up and stood beside him.

"What is this place?" Seth said.

"It's an abandoned shoe factory. Before it was built that cave was intended to be a limestone quarry. But for some reason the men of that era changed their minds after digging that big open space." The man started walking toward the far wall. "People in this country used to earn their living, Seth—used to make things that other people needed."

Seth followed the man—the pair soon coming to a boarded-up doorway—lines of sunshine coming through cracks between the boards—Seth walking over and setting the suitcases against the wall.

"Never exit a place the same way you entered it," the man said. "Now be a gentleman and open the door for me, Seth."

Seth was already assessing the boards—heads of the

nails seeming to be in good shape as he stepped closer—wondering how long they were—hoping they weren't ring-shanked as he grabbed the top board and tried to jimmy it back and forth.

"The people that buy our pharmaceutical boosters are not drug addicts, Seth," the man said—walking over to one of the suitcases—sitting down on top of it with one leg crossed over the other. "They lack the courage it takes to be an addict—to live as an outcast. They're just regular people, Seth. Of course all that really means is they're willing to lie to themselves each and every day about what they really want—what they really need. What they really want is to get high, Seth—forget about all their problems—just like an addict. The only difference is normal people aren't brave enough to admit it."

Seth got the first board loose and then wiggled it until it was free—two nails on one end and one on the other—relieved to see they weren't ring-shanked.

"What do they do?" Seth said without turning around.

"Who?"

"The drugs—how do they make you feel?"

"The pharmaceuticals? I wouldn't know."

"You've never taken any?"

"I don't need an escape, Seth. The addicts and the normal people—they're all escaping from something—whether they proclaim their intent to the world or hide it even from themselves—that's all they're doing."

Seth got the second board off and threw it to the side with the other one—looked outside and blinked against the light—sun beaming down without any clouds to get in its way—little windy and already hot—grass and weeds waving low to the ground in the lot across the street.

"Guess I could use an escape," Seth said—standing there looking outside—feeling again like a bullet was about to pass through his body—feeling alive and almost happy but sad about the things he'd just seen and done—sad that his days were probably numbered—maybe even his hours or minutes.

"Then it's a serendipitous arrangement we've come to, Seth—that's just what you'll find as long as you behave appropriately."

After a few more seconds Seth went back to work on the doorway—got the third board off and the man told him that was enough. The man stood up and unzipped one of the suitcases—took some of the bills out and started arranging them neatly in his hand.

"It seems glamorous to have a suitcase full of money," the man said. "But few people think about how filthy these bills are—they're covered in germs."

Seth stood there in the light streaming in from the top half of the doorway—watching the man count the money— watching him stuff it into his back pocket—then wipe his palms up and down on his blue jeans.

"Stay here—inside. I'll go buy you some clothes and come back." The man climbed over the boards still covering the bottom half of the doorway—stood there in the sunlight and looked back into the dark, abandoned building. "You don't have anything to go back to, Seth—might as well see where this takes you." Then the man walked off down the sidewalk.

Seth moved a step to his left so he was fully in the shade—almost stuck his head out the doorway to see where the man had gone—but then turned his head and looked back at the suitcases—turned again and looked out the open half of the doorway—soon started pacing back and forth in the dark—wondering why he wasn't already outside—why he wasn't running down the sidewalk with the sun on his face.

"Drug dealer," Seth said.

He went over and sat down on one of the suitcases—

picked the lighter one up and set it down on his lap. A noise somewhere made him drop it and jump to his feet. He stood there and looked around—then went to the doorway and stuck his head out—seeing the street and sidewalks empty in both directions—only a plastic bag blowing across the broken concrete.

"Buying me clothes," he said—shaking his head as the wind blew through his hair.

The boy soon ducked back into the abandoned factory—walked over and sat on the suitcase again—sat there in the shade for a few minutes—then got uncomfortable and moved to a spot on the floor beside the doorway—rested his head back against the wall and yawned.

SETH WAS STILL ASLEEP WHEN THE MAN STARTED playing the penny whistle—far off in the dark somewhere— Seth waking up and listening to him run around as he played the fast song—standing up and stretching his neck—looking down at two plastic bags next to his feet.

He squatted down and opened the first bag—saw a pack of socks, one of underwear and one of white T-shirts—the other bag containing a folded pair of blue jeans and a plaid shirt—similar to the man's shirt but Seth knew the pattern wasn't exactly the same.

"Just say you got oil on your boots if it comes up," the man said—staying out of sight—then starting in on the song right where he'd left off.

Seth changed into the new clothes—the man staying in the dark somewhere—still playing the penny whistle—notes echoing off the old brick walls—the soggy plywood covering the windows. Seth piled his blood-soaked T-shirt and jeans against the wall—went to the doorway and looked himself over in the light—seeing dried blood on his arms—spitting on his palms to rub them clean.

The man suddenly cut off his song and pushed past Seth into the angled light—tucking the penny whistle into his back pocket as he climbed silently out of the building—Seth quickly following—crawling over the remaining boards that covered the lower half of the doorway—reaching back inside and grabbing the two suitcases—lifting them out and setting them down so he could adjust his belt and tuck his new shirt in. The man hadn't stopped and was already half a block ahead—Seth watching him as he adjusted his shirt and pants—the man walking fast—penny whistle sticking out of his back pocket and shining in the sun—standing up straight as he walked—arms swinging easy down by his sides.

Seth picked up the suitcases and started running to catch up—reaching the man just as they were coming to an intersection—crossing the empty street together with a hot breeze blowing across their faces. Seth had to step into the grass once they reached the other side—the man taking the middle of the cracked sidewalk.

"You killed him, you know," the man said without turning his head. "You—his life ended because of you."

Seth didn't say anything—just looked at the man and waited—tried not to trip as he struggled with the suitcases.

"Are you listening, Seth?"

"He would've killed me."

"No," the man said—now turning to look at Seth. "No, Seth, he would not have killed you. If you had not shut that door I would have killed him. Then I would have killed you."

"Either way," Seth said—looking off across the street.

"True—but details are important, Seth."

They kept walking—temperature rising every minute—dew long gone from the grass and weeds that lined the empty sidewalks—Seth already sweating in his new clothes—eventually stacking the suitcases one on top of the other and carrying them cradled in his arms.

After a while they walked under an overpass and entered a neighborhood of abandoned homes and empty lots—old wooden siding rotting off the walls of the homes—mostly stripped of paint—windows broken—roofs collapsed.

They came to a corner where the man stopped—Seth stopping a step behind him—waiting as the man looked around—standing there as the man turned and grabbed one of the suitcases and sat down on it. Seth pulled up the other suitcase and sat down beside the man—careful not to block his view of the street.

"The people that come here now—to these homes," the man said. "Drug addicts—the obvious kind, anyway—the ones that don't try too hard to hide it—the needle people."

Seth sat there and listened to the man—felt the sun burning the back of his neck—looked around for shade and saw a scraggly maple tree across the street—then looked at the man and wondered if he should suggest they move.

"The needle people could have grown up in these homes," the man continued—staring down the empty street—buckled asphalt and leaning stop signs. "They would have made adequate dwellings at one time—middle class— two parents—block parties. They were normal kids—could have gone on to become pill people or bottle people or McDonald's people like their peers. But—" the man trailed off—turned his head and looked down another street—Seth looking too—seeing a white Toyota Prius turning the corner a block away. "All it makes them is less dependable custom- ers," the man said as he stood up from the suitcase. "That's Vienna."

The Prius pulled up in front of them—Seth seeing a large man behind the wheel—graying goatee and a heavy-looking assortment of bracelets on his left wrist.

The man walked toward the passenger's side door—Seth taking the suitcases to the back of the car and lifting them into the trunk—then getting into the backseat—scooting over to sit behind the man—still trying to figure out his seatbelt as the car pulled away.

"I gotta tell you," Vienna said—his voice somehow not what Seth expected. "This gangster stuff really gets my cookies baking."

"Be sure you don't let them burn, Vienna," the man said.

Seth looked at Vienna—tapping the steering wheel and bobbing his head even though the radio wasn't on—no hair on his muscular arms—Seth spying the bottom of a tattoo below the sleeve of his shirt.

"So," Vienna said. "You, uh, you kill anybody today?" He smiled at the man but the man was looking out the window.

"He did," the man said—Vienna looking up at Seth in the rearview mirror—making eye contact before Seth shifted in his seat so he was out of view.

"Pleased to meet you," Vienna said—holding his right hand up for Seth to shake—palm up with his elbow resting on the center console. "I'm Vienna—like the sausages."

Seth smacked Vienna's palm with his left hand—glanced at the rearview mirror again and saw Vienna with a confused look on his face.

"This is my food taster, Seth," the man said. "He's a quiet boy."

"Oh," Vienna said.

They drove on—Vienna trying to start a conversation with the man but he just kept looking out the window—gave one or two word answers when Vienna asked a question—Seth unable to tell if his eyes were open or not.

The interstate was mostly empty as they drove farther away from downtown—still hardly any traffic when they exited five or ten minutes later—driving down side streets lined with half-empty parking lots, strip malls, banks and gas stations—also fast food places that made Seth's mouth water as he watched people in their cars grabbing greasy bags from the drive-thru windows.

"It's just so raw," Vienna said. "Primal, I guess—what you do—what you both do." Vienna glanced up at the rearview mirror again as they turned and started driving through a neighborhood—mix of two-story homes and duplexes—basketball hoops hanging over the street—bikes with training wheels in a few of the yards. "Every time you call me, man, it's like I'm about to get laid for the first time." They slowed to a stop in front of a split-level home—bottom half brick and the top white siding—yard needed mowing and the roof could've used another layer of shingles. "And that's just the phone call," Vienna said—still talking even though neither Seth nor the man were listening—making a noise with his tongue as he looked at the man—then looked at Seth in the rearview mirror. "Imagine how high my beans are jumping now!"

"Vienna," the man said—turning to look at him for the first time. "Your beans, your cookies—that's all your business. Seth and I are only interested in matters you and I have previously discussed."

"Alright, alright," Vienna said. "I'm just excited, you know?"

"I know—you're motivated and can follow instructions—you're also loyal as a dog. Those are really the only qualifications for your position."

Seth watched Vienna for a reaction—saw him smile and nod—then watched that confused look form on his face again as he stared out the windshield.

"Let's go inside," the man said. "My food taster's tired."

Inside the house the man told Seth to go rest in the basement—Seth nodding before descending the stairs—finding a light switch and then looking around—blankets already laid out on an old couch—dark sheet covering the cushions with a quilt and another blanket on top—a door and a large window across from the couch. Seth stood there and looked at the door—listened to the man and Vienna talking upstairs.

After a couple minutes he sat down on the couch—yawned and then laid his head down on the armrest—pulled the quilt and the blanket over him—kept his boots on and kept listening to the men upstairs—looking up at the bright yellow lightbulbs as he felt his eyelids getting heavy—blinds on the big window still wide open—indirect sunlight finding its way into the basement room—Seth rolling over instead of making the room dark—closing his eyes with his face nearly touching the couch cushions.

SETH WOKE UP WHEN HE FELT A HAND ON THE INSIDE part of his thigh—opening his eyes in the dark room to see nothing but pale white teeth above him—then feeling Vienna's hot breath on his face as he blinked—his heart thumping as he smelled the big man's sour breath—feeling the big hand on his thigh moving and squeezing.

Seth started to fight—grabbing Vienna's hand and trying to pry it off his leg—clawing at the big man's face in the dark—trying to bring his knees up—then feeling Vienna put all his muscled weight on top of him.

"It's alright," Vienna whispered—Seth wanting to scream but didn't at first—kept fighting but couldn't move the heavy man.

"Help!" Seth finally yelled as he felt Vienna undoing his belt.

A few seconds later Vienna flew off the couch and rolled against the opposite wall—Seth seeing a tall figure in the dark he knew was the man—the white squares and the half-white squares of the man's plaid shirt seeming to glow in the dark—Seth watching as he started hammering at Vienna's head with the penny whistle—hitting him at least ten times before he stood up straight and took a few deep breaths—then walked over and turned on the lights—Seth squinting against the sudden brightness—looking over at Vienna—dead or near dead on the floor against the far wall—a gash across his forehead.

Seth stood up from the couch and turned toward the man—saw a smile on his face as they looked at each other—delicate-looking hand holding out the shiny penny whistle—Vienna's blood painted on the last three or four inches. Seth waited for the man to say something but he never did—just stood there taking deep breaths—smiling as he held out the penny whistle—waiting for Seth to take it.

Seth looked down at Vienna—saw the big chest filling slowly—heard a gurgling sound as the chest tried to exhale—then stepped over to the man and grabbed the bloody end of the penny whistle without looking—passed the clean end to his other hand and walked over to Vienna—watching as the big man's eyes started to open—unable to focus as his eyelids kept twitching—spittle at the edges of the big man's open mouth—blood from the gash wetting his gray goatee.

Seth aimed for Vienna's forehead—raising the penny whistle head-high before bringing it down on the open wound—raising it and bringing it down again and again until he felt a crack and then a softness beneath the skin. Then he stood up straight and looked down at Vienna—last breath leaving his lungs—eyes already closed—all the heavy muscles going limp.

"Let's go," the man said.

Upstairs the lights were still on—several empty cans of soup on the kitchen counter—empty water bottles and wet dishes in a drying rack next to the sink. Seth walked out into the living room as the man disappeared down a hallway—saw two small duffel bags by the front door.

"Here," the man said—somehow making it back to the living room without a sound—tapping Seth on the shoulder with a license plate and a screwdriver. "Take the plates off that car and put this one on the back." He smiled as Seth tried to stop his hands from shaking—as he tried to quickly wipe the blood off them—as he wondered suddenly if his face had specks of red splattered all over it.

Seth eventually took the license plate and the screwdriver—took a few deep breaths as he turned toward the door—wanting to go wash his face in the bathroom but too afraid to ask.

"Oh," the man said. "Load those bags in the trunk as well."

Seth looked back and nodded but kept walking—stopped at the door and looked down at the license plate in his hand—saw 'Montana' above the random set of letters and numbers.

After loading the duffel bags and dealing with the license plate Seth went back inside the house—finding the two suitcases they'd arrived with by the door—the man sitting nearby on the floor—rubbing something on the backs of his hands.

"Did you forget the money, Seth?"

"No," Seth said—the man staying quiet—not even looking up from his hands. "No, sir."

"What's in these suitcases, Seth?"

"Money." The man again stayed silent. "Your money."

The man jumped to his feet and Seth barely had time to take a step back—the man grabbing him by the shirt as he tried to retreat—penny whistle held up by his face.

"River trash," the man said. "Can't even keep yourself from being molested." The man looked away—paused with Seth pushed back against a wall—lowering the penny whistle but still holding him by the shirt. "Do not become useless, Seth."

5

THEY WERE ON THE ROAD TEN MINUTES LATER—Seth driving through the dark again—driving Vienna's Prius with the man sitting beside him in the passenger's seat—exiting the neighborhood and coming to the road with all the fast food restaurants—Seth wearing his seatbelt and using turn signals—both hands on the steering wheel as he kept the car below the speed limit—constantly checking the rearview mirrors.

"Do you know where we're going?" the man said.

"No, sir."

"Go to Montana."

Seth wanted to look over at the man but didn't—felt him slouching down in the passenger's seat as the minutes ticked by—thought maybe the man had tipped his hat forward over his eyes but wasn't sure—still unwilling to look over to find out.

Seth kept driving and soon saw a sign for I-29 North—went up the on-ramp—got going and set the cruise control just under the speed limit—finally glancing over at the man—just long enough to see his head bobbing from side to side—his hands held loose in his lap.

There were semis on the interstate but hardly any other cars or pickups—rigs dotted all over with too many orange clearance lights—most with sleeper cabs—Seth even spotting a few with one of those bulb antennas on the back for satellite TV.

An hour later the man moved—readjusted and then settled back into the passenger's seat—Seth watching him as much as he could—half-expecting to be hurt again or killed at any moment—hands still a little shaky—heart still beating in rapid spurts every time a recently formed memory crossed his mind.

Seth tried to focus on the road as he drove on—inspecting the semis—the pickups and cars as they passed him. Then he was just ten miles from his hometown—recognizing the road names on the green exit signs—outlines of the fields he could see in the moonlight. They passed the hospital where he was born—then under the overpass where he used to sit and watch the traffic zoom by underneath—people heading off to untold destinations in both directions—some maybe going all the way to Canada—others maybe to the Gulf of Mexico.

His mother was just down the road—high school he went to and all his friends—his job.

He kept driving—turning the radio on a few minutes later—keeping the volume low—smiling to himself as he finally started to relax—scanning for new stations as the one he was listening to faded to static—wondering what all the semis he saw might be hauling—where they might be going—where they've already been.

As they neared Omaha, Nebraska Seth looked over at the man in the dark—green glow from the digital clock showing him still asleep—his head tilted a little lower now.

Seth knew where Montana was—knew the capital was Helena and that it bordered Canada—knew about its national parks and its grizzly bears. He had a collection of maps and a world atlas in his room at home—was sure of the state's borders and that the Rocky Mountains were piled up on the western edge—that some of the mountaintops held onto snow all summer. But he wasn't sure about the route the man wanted him to take.

He soon came to the exit for I-80 West—flipped on the blinker and tried to remember the interstate map he had sitting in his room—slowed and began to exit. Then the man made a noise—trying to form a word in a dream maybe—Seth jerking the car to the left and accelerating—staying on I-29 North for another ten or fifteen minutes—wondering if he'd done the right thing—if the man was really awake—what might happen if he chose the wrong road.

A while later the car dinged and Seth looked down—saw the fuel tank was nearly empty—looked over at the man but his head was still down—brim of his hat covering his eyes.

Seth exited and found a gas station—careful and quiet as he stopped underneath the bright lights—opening and closing his door without making too much noise—slowly squeezing the handle of the pump and latching it open. Then he leaned over and looked through the passenger's side window—seeing the man's eyes still closed—his chin still tilted down toward his chest.

When the tank was full the latch on the handle released and snapped shut—Seth turning his head away from the window to look at it—then turning back to see the man staring at him.

Seth waited until the man waved him away—went into the station and paid for the gas with his own money—nearly all the cash he had in his wallet—just enough left for a candy bar which he ate right there in front of the clerk in two or three bites. When he got back to the car he saw the man was again dead asleep—climbed carefully back into the driver's seat and started the car—leaving the radio off this time.

Hours later—with the sun just showing signs of rising—Seth started seeing signs for Fargo, North Dakota—looked out the windows and tried to distinguish the features of the land—seeing the gray-green grass first in the dim morning light—in the median and covering the ditches next to the interstate—then the gray-green fields of soybeans, sorghum and a root crop he'd never seen before but thought had to be potatoes. He looked for pastures as he drove on but found none—flattest country he'd ever seen—few trees other than in the towns and along the creeks.

The gray-blue sky came next and there seemed to be more of it than in Missouri—the sun soon rising over the horizon—behind them and to their right—shining in the rearview mirror on the passenger's side door.

Seth wondered how hot it would be this far north.

"Are you hungry, Seth?" the man said—his head still bowed—eyes still concealed behind his cowboy hat.

"Yeah—yessir."

"There's a diner right off exit sixty-two," the man said—raising his head and blinking. "The waitresses are young and pretty if you desire something to look at—breasts and buttocks still defying gravity."

Seth looked at the man and smiled but the man was looking out the window.

"Have you ever been with a woman, Seth?"

"Yeah."

"Well, even if you have, you seem more like a virgin than a rake," the man said—turning to look at Seth—then looking back out the window. "I've never had much interest in any of it."

Seth drove on for another half hour before seeing the exit—neither of them saying anything as the minutes passed—as Seth slowed down and left the interstate.

He parked the car and they walked into the cafe to-gether—the man choosing a booth near the door—large windows looking out at the gas and diesel pumps and the parking lot. Seth ordered a big breakfast—eggs and bacon and biscuits and pancakes—then watched the waitresses as he ate—one or two catching his eye—but the man didn't order a thing—staring out the window as people came and went—semis rumbling off toward the interstate.

When Seth was finished the man paid and they walked out to the car—the man climbing into the driver's seat as Seth walked around to the other side—pulling out of the parking lot and starting down I-29 North again—few minutes later exiting and merging onto I-94 West.

The sun was up now—shining on the left side of the man's face—Seth trying hard to stay awake—wanting to watch the country—to remember the roads they took—wanting to talk to the man—to figure out what was going on—where they were going and why.

SETH WOKE UP AS THE CAR BOUNCED OVER TRAIN tracks—opened his eyes and saw the first structures of a small town—a grain elevator with tall bins right up next to the tracks they were driving over—then a grocery store—a gas station and an auto parts store—then two-story brick build-ings lined up on each side of the street—display windows either cluttered with antiques or nothing at all—faded lines dividing unused parking spaces—a near-empty downtown.

"Where are we?" Seth said.

The man looked at him. "We're home—Wolf Point, Montana—Fort Pike Indian Reservation."

They drove on through the rest of town—Seth guess-ing it was three or four in the afternoon—looking out the window at the small-town businesses—the empty lots—a teenager passing by on a bike.

They drove ten or fifteen miles outside of town—then the man turned off onto a gravel road—headed north as Seth continued looking out the window. The country was flat but not as flat as North Dakota near Fargo—more arid than he was used to—no soybeans or corn or any root crops in the fields they passed—some wheat but mostly he looked out over pasture—trailers sitting off the road here and there with toys and lawn mowers and garbage scattered around the yards.

They pulled off the gravel road and drove down a driveway through a stand of pine trees—then pulled up to a blue metal cattle gate where the man stopped the car.

"Do you remember how to get back to town, Seth?"

"Yeah—yessir."

"Good," the man said—holding a single key out for Seth to take. "Now go open the gate."

Seth stepped out of the air-conditioned car—felt a hot, dry wind whipping through his hair as he hurried around and opened the gate—then stepped back as the man drove through—stretched his legs and yawned as he closed the gate and locked it to the fence post—turning to follow after the car when a large white dog barked and leaped for his face or neck—somehow getting his hands up in time to shove the dog away—but the dog found his footing and came charging back—Seth already running around the right side of the car—reaching for the door handle when he felt the weight of the dog pounce onto his back—claws sliding over his shoulder—the dog turning him away from the car—trying to bite his left arm as they fell to the ground together—stopping suddenly and raising his large head when Seth heard the penny whistle.

"That's his favorite song," the man said—smiling with the penny whistle held in front of his chest—standing back near the gate—watching the giant white dog run over to him with his tail wagging—ears back and his tongue hanging out one side of his mouth. "His name is Titus." The man smiled—petting the dog now with the back of his hand.

"Did you forget about him?" Seth said—still on the ground—sweating and breathing hard—leaning on his elbow as he inspected his right hand—dirt and dark-colored pebbles embedded in his palm.

"Titus guards the property, Seth. He didn't know you but now he does so that won't happen again." Seth nodded—heard what sounded like sheep off in the distance—looked up but only saw hills—behind them more hills and then maybe mountains. "Titus also guards the sheep," the man said—watching Seth as he continued awkwardly petting the dog.

Seth looked at the man and nodded again—then turned his head and saw the sun dropping lower in the sky—saw the gravel driveway winding its way over the hill in front of them.

The man walked back to the driver's side door of the car—Seth watching from the ground as he poured gel into his hand from a small plastic bottle—then rubbed his hands together gently—taking his time—making sure every bit of skin was coated.

The man stepped back into the car and drove away before Seth could get off the ground—drove over the little hill as Seth got to his feet and started dusting himself off—looking around before he started walking—the dog, Titus, walking by his side.

He got to the top of the hill and stopped—looked down and saw a house and a large metal building a few hundred feet away—ten or twelve sheep bunched together in a field—a corral next to the building with weeds growing tall around the perimeter and short-cut grass in the middle. Seth watched the man pull up in front of the house—watched him get out of the car and start walking toward the metal building.

He started walking down the hill and got there a few minutes later—following the same route he'd seen the man take through a metal door cut into the side of the building—a girl turning around and looking at Seth as he entered—standing there so she could study him—trying not to look away as he wondered who she was—where the man had gone—what sort of relationship the two of them had.

"He killed them?" the girl said.

"That's not what I said, Isabel—I said he got rid of them." The man was sitting at a picnic table rubbing the penny whistle with a handkerchief—not bothering to look up at the girl as he talked to her. "They weren't performing adequately."

Seth looked around—saw shiny stainless steel tanks and two or three big boxy machines—polished cement floor with some sort of coating on it—making it shine nearly as much as the tanks—a conveyor belt and what must have been a scale against the back wall—then another door in the back corner.

"He also tastes my food for me," the man said—looking up at Seth with a smile on his face.

"But they're dead, right?" Isabel said. "Ricky and Joe?" She looked at the man but he was busy with the strange instrument he always carried—the weapon he didn't even try to hide—then looked back at Seth as he tried to say something—as he parted his lips and sucked air into his lungs.

They stood there for a few seconds—the man still polishing the penny whistle—Isabel shifting her weight from foot to foot—breathing hard—Seth watching them—taking a step back as he waited for something to happen.

"He tastes my food in order to verify it does not contain poison," the man said. "Do you remember the name of the emperor's food taster, Seth? The one employed by Emperor Claudius?"

Seth watched Isabel—her breathing already starting to slow—her eyes looking more calm—hands relaxing—her feet not moving anymore.

"Halotus," he said.

"Very good," the man said. "If you keep listening this well you're sure to be an adequate replacement." He looked up at Isabel for a moment.

"Is this where you make the pills?" Seth said.

"This is where I manufacture pharmaceutical boosters," the man said—lowering the handkerchief and penny whistle to the picnic table. "Why?" He got up and started marching toward Seth. "Why are you trying to get me to say it?" He walked past Isabel—eyes locked on Seth as he backed him up to the door.

"Just asking," Seth said—raising his hands and leaning back—feeling the doorknob pressing against the lower part of his spine—the man right in front of him now.

"Do they have you wired up?"

"What? Who? No."

"Is that it? Is that what took you so long inside that gas station? Did you meet someone in there?"

"No—no I was eating a candy bar."

"Empty your pockets." Seth pulled out the front pockets of his blue jeans—the man putting his hands in each of Seth's back pockets and the pockets on his chest. "Lift your shirt." Seth lifted his shirt. "Pants down." Seth looked down at the man's hands. "Pants," the man repeated—Seth quickly unbuckling his blue jeans and pulling them down to his knees.

The man took a step back—bent down and inspected his legs—then stood up and grabbed Seth's shoulder and turned him around—Seth putting his hands up against the door as the man pulled down the underwear he'd bought him the day before—Seth feeling the man step back again and bend down.

"Take off your boots, Seth," the man said.

Seth pulled his pants back up—left the zipper down and the belt unbuckled—then took off his boots and turned around to hand them to the man—keeping his eyes on the floor—knowing Isabel was watching them.

"No wire," the man said—dropping the boots to the floor in front of Seth—turning and walking back to the picnic table—wiping the penny whistle again while Seth slipped on his boots.

Seth felt Isabel walking toward him but he still didn't look up from the polished cement floor—got his boots on and stepped away from the door—Isabel walking past him— opening it and walking outside.

"I'll have some things for you to do around here, Seth," the man said as Seth tucked his shirt back in—zipped up his pants and buckled his belt. "Go to the house and meet Benjamin and Bertram, Seth. Bertram insists his name is Spoon but I've improved it for him. I'm going to bed. Tell Isabel I expect dinner no later than nine."

Seth stood there a moment—then went to the door and looked back at the man—still sitting there alone at the table—now pouring a white liquid onto the handkerchief from a small plastic bottle. Seth opened the door and walked outside.

IT SEEMED LATE BY THE TIME SETH STEPPED OUTSIDE the building—looking up at the sunset colors spread across the sky—cool breeze blowing across his skin—surprisingly few bugs for the beginning of summer. A motion-activated light turned on over his head—causing him to look down at his shadow stretched out on the gravel path that led to the house—remembering the dog, Titus, as he stood there—then looking around before he started walking.

As he made his way down the path Seth noticed his shadow shortening—watched it spin around to his right as the path turned—putting his hand up to his chest as he walked—feeling all the sore places where he'd been punched or kicked—his muscles tired—joints stiff—his back still aching in different places—hunger making his stomach growl as he neared the house.

Instead of going in the back door Seth climbed the small hill—walked around to the front of the house and rang the doorbell—waited and then heard a voice and a plastic-on-plastic clicking sound—someone inside playing video games, he knew.

Seth waited but no one came to the door—tried the doorbell again but they just kept playing—making him more hungry and tired with every passing second—standing there outside waiting to hear someone pause the game—finally grabbing the doorknob and opening it himself.

"Why the hell you ringing the doorbell?" someone called over the couch—not bothering to turn around—Seth standing in the doorway now—looking at the backs of two heads—a giant flat screen TV and the video game the pair was playing—knowing they thought he was someone else.

"Shut the door already," the same one said—Seth stepping inside and shutting the door behind him—taking another two steps but they still didn't turn around.

"Which Halo game is this?" Seth said—unsure how to start the process of introducing himself.

The two heads popped up and spun around—Seth hearing the controllers drop to the ground.

"Who the hell are you?" the other one yelled—his partner raising his hands as he started moving backward off the couch.

"Seth—my name's Seth."

"What the hell you doing here? You lost?" the angry one said—stepping back and then starting around the couch.

"No," Seth said. "He made me come with him."

The one coming toward him was a little shorter than he was but stockier—thick arms and wrists—the other one so thin his cheekbones looked sharp and had shadows below them.

"Where's Ricky and Joe?"

"He killed them—one of them, anyway—the other was already dead."

"What?" The stocky one stopped a few feet in front of him.

"He did it—your boss or whatever—I just loaded them into the bed of the pickup like he told me."

The stocky one looked down at the floor—Seth staying quiet so he could think—watching him clinch his jaw muscles—seeing his hands still formed into fists.

The skinny one was still standing behind the couch—Seth turning his head to look at him—about his height but with longer arms—his pants loose around the waist.

"So you the new guy?" the stocky one said.

Seth stood there and looked at them both—felt his heart beating fast as he tried to slow his breathing.

"Yeah," he said. "I'm the new guy."

No one spoke as Seth wondered what was next—only sounds coming from the video game still up on the TV—Seth hearing digital gunshots—digital soldiers shouting through their radios—other players beating and stabbing the two soldiers on the screen that now stood perfectly still—their controllers on the floor.

"OK," the skinny one said—smiling as he flapped his arms once. "Well, I'm Spoon." He walked over and Seth met him in the middle—the two of them shaking hands over the couch. "This box of shit is Benjy."

"I ain't a Jew," Benjy said. "Just the name my folks gave me." He stuck his right hand out and looked back at the game.

"I'm Seth—nice to meet you both." Seth shook his hand.

"Box of shit here's a real charmer," Spoon said. "Better watch out if you ever get yourself a girl." Seth smiled.

Benjy ignored Spoon—walked around the couch and sat back down—reached and picked up his controller—leaving Spoon's on the floor.

"And your wallet sure ain't safe when he's around," Spoon continued—obviously happy to have an audience. "On account of the Jew blood running through his veins."

"One," Benjy said without looking up—still flipping through the video game menu on the TV.

Seth stood in the same spot behind the couch—looking from Benjy to Spoon—watching a big smile form on the skinny boy's face.

"That's what he does," Spoon said. "Starts counting every time I piss him off—says if he gets to three he'll kill me but I know he's bluffing."

Seth nodded—felt his stomach start to growl again.

"Two."

"Oh come on," Spoon said—sitting back down next to Benjy—picking up the other controller and moving his digital soldier again.

"Have you eaten dinner yet?" Seth said—stepping forward and putting his hands on the back of the couch—watching the TV as they started a new game.

"Oh yeah," Spoon said. "There's some burgers and chips in the kitchen—help yourself."

Seth left the living room and found the kitchen—found hamburger patties in a plastic container on the counter—found buns in a cabinet—rummaged through the refrigerator and found ketchup and mustard but no cheese or onions or tomatoes—kitchen looking like it'd been remodeled recently—black and white tile on the floor—backsplash and the wall next to the refrigerator both painted dark purple—appliances all stainless steel.

Seth stood there over the granite countertop and ate

three burgers without warming them up—then started looking around for the chips and saw Isabel standing near the doorway—leaning against the wall.

"I'm Isabel."

Seth finished chewing the last bite still in his mouth. "Hi," he said. "I know—I'm Seth."

"New guy, right?"

Seth nodded—keeping his eyes on Isabel as she nodded back—feeling thirsty after the three burgers—feeling tired after the longest two days of his life.

"Where are you from?" Isabel said.

"Missouri," Seth said—watching her brown eyes—her lips twisting as she looked away—nervous, he thought—or maybe still upset about the two dead men—maybe both.

"I'm from here," she said—stepping over to a wrought-iron table set against the wall. "I'm Indian—could be a little bit Mexican but I'm sure you don't think there's a difference." She sat in one of the chairs and leaned back against the wall—propped one elbow up on the table and the other on the back of the chair—inspecting her fingernails as Seth kept watching—looking down at her T-shirt and cotton pants—her bare feet.

"I know there's a difference," Seth said—standing there with his hand on the countertop—forgetting all about the chips.

"How'd he find you?" Isabel said.

"What?"

"I doubt he posted an ad online asking for resumes." She paused and looked up at him—her black hair pulled back in a pony tail that snaked around her neck and over one shoulder. "Have you done this kind of thing before?"

"No."

Seth walked over and sat down at the table—facing her as Isabel kept facing the kitchen. He folded his arms over the top of the table and leaned toward her—Isabel turning her head finally and meeting his eyes.

"Who is he?" Seth whispered. "What is all this?"

Isabel kept looking at him—Seth tracking her eyes as they scanned his face—as they settled on his chin while she seemed to get lost in her own thoughts—Seth waiting—wondering again who she was.

"You remind me of Ricky," she said—turning back to the kitchen—inspecting her fingernails again. "When he first got here."

"Why'd he kill him?"

"You won't know that until he kills you too."

They sat there for a long time without talking—Seth eventually resting his head on his hands—watching Isabel as she picked and pulled at hangnails.

Just as Seth started dozing off she dropped her hands to her lap—turned and looked across the table at him.

"Come on," she said—standing up suddenly and leaving the kitchen.

Seth raised his head but didn't get up at first—watched her go until she disappeared down the hallway—hearing Spoon and Benjy still playing the same video game—bickering and laughing in the living room.

Seth stood up and stretched—felt his legs weak and his eyes tired—looked down at his bloodstained boots and thought about taking them off but decided against it—left the lights on in the kitchen and walked out into the living room—walked past the TV and all he heard was the video game and the plastic clicking of the controllers—Spoon and Benjy silent as he entered the dark hallway.

There weren't any lights on in any of the rooms Seth found—hallway eventually turning to the right—ending at a stairway that led up to the second floor—Seth stopping at the base of the stairs—wondering if he should go up or turn around—should run out of the house and down the gravel road—maybe try to find that town they'd driven through earlier—try to get away while he still had a chance. Then he heard a door open behind him and turned around—looked through the dark hallway into a dark room—door open but not all the way.

For some reason he remembered the man's dinner—that he was supposed to tell Isabel not to bring it later than nine. He looked around—then walked into the room.

"Isabel," he said—passing through the doorway in a hurry—his hands ready just in case.

The room opened up to his left—turning that way he looked and saw her—barely saw her figure in the small amount of light that somehow made it into the room.

"He wanted dinner before—," Seth said—his voice trailing off as he watched her walk slowly up to him—his eyes adjusting to the darkness—seeing now that she was naked and not looking at him.

Isabel grabbed him by the elbow and led him to a bed in the corner of the room—sat him down as she stood in front of him. He kicked off his boots in a hurry—kicked them nearly across the room—then felt her put her hands on his shoulders and push him back. He lay down flat on the bed and smelled her—trying to see more of her in the dark.

Isabel opened his pants with a cold, soft hand—put her hands on his chest and her knee came down on the bed next to his hip—swung her other knee over him and then was very still for a moment.

Seth waited for her to start moving again—then felt her long hair touching his face—put his hands down and touched her thighs—felt her lifting his wrists and setting his hands down on the bed—then pressing on his chest again—rising up—moving more and more. He knew her eyes were closed—could tell her mouth was open just a little—still trying to see her more clearly—wanting to touch her but keeping his hands on the bed—trying to listen for sounds but she made none.

Afterward Isabel swung her leg back over him and stood

up from the bed—stood there in the dark and didn't move—
Seth suddenly having a hard time staying awake—knowing
she was standing there looking down at him—lying there
with his eyes half closed—wondering what came next but
not really caring—then feeling a blanket float down and
cover his midsection as he fell asleep.

6

SETH WOKE UP IN THE MORNING COVERED IN SWEAT—still under the blanket Isabel had laid on top of him—still in the back bedroom where he'd found her the night before—still wearing the blue and white plaid shirt the man had bought him—his blue jeans and underwear still pulled down below his knees.

He sat up and let his feet touch the floor—feeling the lumpy, tattered carpet—smelling cigarette smoke for the first time—turning his head and seeing a full ashtray next to the bed. He pulled on his boots—looked down at the bloodstains on the leather—then stood and pulled up his pants—tucked in his shirt and pulled his belt tight.

The door was closed and the house was quiet. Seth looked down at the bed—then looked in the closet and saw empty hangers and two suitcases—plaid shirts and blue jeans stuffed into the dresser—a full-length mirror nailed to one of the walls—phone charger plugged into an outlet next to the bed.

Seth opened the door and walked out into the hallway—eventually found a clean, bright bathroom with a piece of yellow carpet on the tile floor—a fuzzy yellow cover on the toilet seat—yellow shower curtain in front of him. He used the toilet but didn't shower—still didn't hear anyone in the house or outside—washed his hands and dried them on the yellow hand towel and left the bathroom.

The video game controllers were on the coffee table in the living room—few empty beer cans and an empty ashtray. He walked past the couch and into the kitchen—countertops wiped down—no dirty dishes in the sink—a single plate on the little wrought-iron table—two pieces of toast and an apple—glass of orange juice and a paper towel.

Seth sat down and ate the toast and the apple—drank the juice—then leaned back in the chair and stretched—muscles sore but already feeling better. He reached up toward the ceiling and arched his back—little aches and pains still—his face still tender to the touch—but he was still alive—memory of the night before still swimming around in his head—the dark room and the naked girl.

He sat in the kitchen and looked around—sunlight angling in through the window over the sink—no sound at all—maybe a water heater ticking somewhere—a bird flapping its wings outside—no one else around.

A few minutes later Seth left the house out the front door—walking out into the warm sunlight—midmorning already judging by the heat and the height of the sun. He stood out in the front yard and looked over at the metal building—seeing the doors all closed—hearing the sheep off in the distance as he remembered the dog, Titus—then remembered about the man's dinner and hoped Isabel had delivered it on time.

The green grass was cropped short where he stood—sheep allowed to graze right up to the house. Seth looked around and saw a fence off in the distance—hills in every direction covered in grass.

He turned and started walking up the driveway—came to the crest of the hill and saw the pasture sloping down to a tree line with a fence set against it—the blue gate he'd opened the day before—the sheep grouped together near it with the dog, Titus, watching over them. The wind was wrong and he hadn't smelled Seth coming over the hill—lying there in the grass as the sheep grazed—but when the big dog saw Seth he rose quickly and looked at him—then looked back toward the sheep—trotted around the flock as Seth watched him.

A white cargo van approached the gate just as Titus was settling back into his spot—writing on the door but Seth couldn't read it from where he was standing—watching Spoon open the driver's side door and step out—watching him unlock the padlock and pull the chain free—then watching him look up and wave.

"Hey!" Spoon yelled. "What's up, loverboy? You sure don't waste no time!" He got back in the van and drove through the gate—hopped out again and locked it with the chain and padlock—then started driving toward the house.

Seth saw Benjy sitting in the passenger's seat—saw Spoon waving again—looking out the driver's side window and smiling as they crested the hill.

Seth turned around and started walking down the hill toward the house—following after the van when he heard a pickup approaching the gate behind him—a blue dually that couldn't have been more than a few years old—camper shell over the bed—windows and the windshield tinted too dark to see anyone inside. He saw the man jump out of the driver's seat and deal with the gate—then hop back in the pickup and start climbing the hill. Seth took a few steps back from the gravel driveway as it passed him and kept going—wondering if anyone else was inside.

He turned where he was standing—watched the two vehicles through the gravel dust—Spoon backing the cargo van up to the large roller door at the front of the metal building—blue dually pickup just pulling up to the house.

Seth started walking again—saw the man jump out of the pickup—someone else opening the passenger's side door. He started walking faster as Isabel came around to the back of the pickup—her hair pulled back and held up in a clip. She opened the tailgate and the back window of the camper shell—revealing packs of water bottles stacked high up in the pickup's bed.

"Seth!" the man yelled. "Come hither!" He waved his arm—then started walking toward the metal building.

Seth changed direction to meet the man—then started jogging—glancing over at Isabel when he was about halfway there—seeing her still behind the pickup—unsure whether she was looking at him or not.

"There's a dolly in here you can use to unload my things," the man said—opening the side door to the metal building and walking inside—Seth following close behind. "Start with the water—I'll show you where to stack it once you return."

Seth stood behind the man a few steps—listening closely to his instructions—then turning to watch Spoon and Benjy unload the cargo van inside the building—walking a large plastic barrel down a ramp at the back of the van—white with handles on the top—Seth able to see a dark liquid sloshing around inside as the sun shone through it.

"The dolly is there, Seth," the man said—pointing to the wall without turning around.

Seth took the dolly and wheeled it outside—pushed it toward the pickup through the short grass—looking for Isabel as he went—finding the tailgate still down but she wasn't there—Seth loading the packs of water onto the dolly as he looked around—still looking as he wheeled it back to the metal building—as he walked it over the threshold—finally giving up as he turned around to find the man.

"This way," the man said.

Seth pushed the dolly toward the back of the building—pushed it between the shiny machines that took up most of the floor space—looked over as he went and saw Spoon and Benjy unloading another barrel.

The man motioned for Seth to wheel the dolly through a doorway—leaning against the wall as Seth entered the dark, windowless room—seeing shelves against the opposite wall with light coming in from the main part of the building—cans stacked on the shelves until they nearly reached the ceiling—Seth looking closer as he stopped the dolly—scanning the labels on the cans as he tipped the dolly forward to a standing position—seeing at least twenty different kinds of soup—organized in vertical columns running the entire length of the wall.

"Over here, Seth."

Seth turned and saw the man pointing toward another set of shelves next to the open doorway—nothing there except for a handful of water bottles—same brand and size as the ones on the dolly.

"Four and one-half trips, Seth—cans there—bottles there."

Seth stacked the water on the shelves as the man watched—then grabbed the dolly by the two handles—turned and looked in a corner of the dark room—seeing two foam pads rolled up—a stack of folded blankets and a pillow.

Seth went back to the pickup but the man stayed inside the building. He made the four and a half trips—hauling the water and the cans of soup to the shelves inside the room—the man staying near the doorway—watching Seth as he came and went—neither of them speaking.

When Seth was finished the man locked the door and walked outside—left without giving him anything else to do—left him to figure it out on his own—to make sure he didn't become useless.

OVER THE NEXT TWO WEEKS SETH TENDED TO THE SHEEP
and any other chores he could find—everyone else spending
their days inside the metal building—never inviting him—
the man never asking for his help anymore.

Every few days Spoon and Benjy would drive away in
the van—Seth able to read what was printed on the driver's
side door one day as they left—Big Sky Spay & Neuter in big
block letters—no phone number—no address—no website.
He tried to ask Spoon about it but the skinny boy would just
go quiet for a little while—then change the subject.

Isabel never left but she hardly ever seemed to be
around—Seth trying to talk to her every time he got a chance
but she was good at keeping her distance—sometimes just
getting up and walking out of the room just as he opened his
mouth.

The four of them shared the big house while the man
stayed in the metal building—in the room with all the bottles
of water and cans of soup. Spoon did all the cooking in the
house—basic things but it was always good—spaghetti,
burgers, grilled chicken and mashed potatoes—only Isabel
able to find something to complain about.

In the morning they'd all get up and Spoon would make
everyone toast—or they'd just pass around a box of cereal
and a carton of milk—sitting or standing around the kitchen
together—Seth trying to ask what they did all day in the metal building—but all three of them would go silent—Spoon
usually the one to change the subject—teasing Isabel about
her clothes or her hair—or he'd complain about how she
never cooked for them—Benjy staring at Isabel while she
and Spoon razzed each other—staring until she told him to
stop.

The weather stayed hot—a storm rumbling through

sometime during the second week—each day Seth trying to keep busy and out of trouble—dagging the sheep with the shears he'd found somewhere—cutting out all the dried feces and mud from their wool—trimming their hooves and giving them some feed every morning—also feeding Titus— even brushing out his thick white coat a couple times.

At night—after the four of them had finished dinner— Seth would watch as Isabel got up from her chair and slipped on her shoes—walked outside and was gone for an hour or two. Then he'd sit on the couch with Spoon and Benjy— playing video games the rest of the night—checking over his shoulder every once in a while to see if she was coming back in the house. Eventually she would come back and march through the living room—go straight to her bedroom without saying anything to the three of them—without even looking in Seth's direction.

In bed at night Seth would remember how Isabel had drawn him into the dark room—how she'd put her hands on his chest—imagining how she must've looked on top of him.

"I KNOW YOU HAD INTERCOURSE WITH HER, SETH," THE man said—walking up to him from behind—making him jump—making him raise his hands reflexively to protect his face.

Seth had been watching the sheep graze at the back of the property—sitting on the ground—resting his head against the wall of a lean-to—nearly asleep when the man came and stood over him.

"It's of no consequence to me," the man continued. "I know you think it is but it is not." The man looked out at the sheep—over the barbed-wire fence at the edge of the pasture—raised a hand to shield his eyes from the sun. "Have you ever piloted a canoe, Seth?"

"What?" Seth said as he got to his feet. "No—no, sir."

The man reached behind his back and grabbed something—Seth watching him closely—raising his hands again and checking his balance—waiting for a pistol or the penny whistle but instead the man pulled out a white envelope.

"I'm giving you this because you've done everything I've asked of you up to this point."

Seth looked at the man and the man looked back at him—smile on his face that could mean anything or nothing—Seth slowly reaching out to take the envelope—opening it and glancing inside—neatly arranged bundle of cash revealing itself—impossible to know how much but it had to be a lot, Seth thought—had to be unless all the bills were singles.

The man turned and walked away—left Seth standing there with the envelope—eventually returning to the lean-to where he sat down and counted the money two or three times.

THAT NIGHT SETH SAT AT THE LITTLE TABLE IN THE kitchen while Spoon cooked dinner—Benjy and Isabel still over in the metal building with the man—still light outside as the long summer day dragged on.

"Why's he giving me money now?" Seth said—facing Spoon who stood over a saucepan—few vegetables laid out on a cutting board next to him. "It's been two weeks since I got here—that how often we get paid?"

"Not really a set schedule," Spoon said—moving from the saucepan to the cutting board. "When you do good work you get paid—and when you don't, well, I guess you know more about that than I do."

"He said he doesn't care about me and Isabel."

"Seems like Isabel don't care about you and Isabel." Spoon set the knife down and stirred the red sauce—then picked up the knife again and went back to chopping.

"She his daughter or something?" Seth said—picking up the beer that had been sitting on the table. "Or his niece maybe?"

Spoon didn't say anything—finished chopping before taking a long drink of his own beer—then lifted the chopping board and slid the vegetables off into the saucepan.

"What's with all the secrets around here?" Seth said.

Spoon turned the flame down on the stove and covered the saucepan—then walked over and sat across from Seth.

"Seems like he's gonna keep you around a while so we can talk about some things," Spoon said. "But there's some topics that just ain't worth the risk."

"OK. What about the pills you're making all day?"

"We ain't making no pills—can't tell you what we're doing but we ain't making no pills."

"OK," Seth said. "What about this canoe business?"

"He tell you about that?"

"Yeah—asked if I've ever steered one or whatever."

"Well you know more than I do. He just showed up with them one day—didn't bother explaining what they were for."

Seth looked at Spoon—then looked off toward the stove and saw the red sauce bubbling—splattering the inside of the glass lid.

"What's your real name?" Seth said.

"Spoon. He calls me Bertram, though. You should call me that whenever he's around." Spoon stood up from the table and walked over to the stove—Seth watching him as he stirred the sauce—as he set a pot of water to boil.

"Spaghetti again?" Isabel said—entering the kitchen through the back door—walking past the stove with Benjy close behind her.

Benjy sat down at the table across from Seth—watching

Isabel walk out of the kitchen—stretching his neck as he tried to track her going down the hallway.

"Jesus," Spoon said—turning toward the little table. "How'd I end up living in Montana with a dumb Jewish ox like you, Benjy?" Seth watched Spoon start shaking his head—wagging the wooden spoon held up in his hand. "Is my spaghetti sauce somehow making you dumber? Some kind of rare allergy maybe?" Spoon laughed at his own joke.

"One," Benjy said—Seth looking at him across the table—watching him pick at his fingernails.

"The threat of violence nearly always does the trick, Seth," the man said from the doorway—Seth whipping his head around to look at him. "But sometimes there is violence—just a part of life—quite often a part of death as well."

The man paused for a long time—then told them they'd be eating dinner in the dining room that night—told Spoon not to fix him a plate—then walked quickly through the kitchen to the living room—the three of them watching him go—seeing the penny whistle sticking out of his back pocket.

Benjy started inspecting his fingernails again—Seth wondering again if he should make a run for it—his hand on the envelope full of cash in his pocket—Spoon tasting the spaghetti sauce at least a dozen times—then fishing one of the noodles out of the pot of boiling water—holding it up and biting it in half—then throwing the two ends back into the pot. Seth watched him—watched him tapping the counter with his bony finger—bouncing a nervous knee up and down—waiting as long as he could before lifting the noodles into three bowls—then spooning the sauce on top.

They each carried a bowl with them into the dining room—Spoon also carrying a container of grated parmesan cheese.

"We are almost ready," the man said—already seated at the head of the table. "Two more days." The three of them stood there with their bowls and waited. "Sit, my boys—please."

Benjy sat down first—choosing a chair next to the man. Then Spoon walked around the table and took the chair across from Benjy. Seth waited—finally taking a seat next to Spoon.

"Using the roads is too risky," the man said once they all had sat down. "Traveling by train—too risky—planes—too risky." They sat there and listened to the man—no one touching their food.

"Each canoe will carry five hundred kilograms of our new product," the man said. "That leaves two hundred kilograms for food, yourselves and all the gear you'll need. There will be twenty drops along the way—I will mark them on a map. There should be a predetermined amount of money at each location—if there's no money you are still to make the drop—we will deal with unsettled accounts at a later time." The man paused—then told them to eat—waiting as he looked around the table at each one of them—watching them pick at their food with a smile on his face.

"You will be on the Missouri River for two months," the man continued. "I will meet you in Kansas City and have a car ready so you can drive back here and repeat the process." They sat there and listened—forks in their hands but none of them went for another bite. "Seth will be in charge. Eventually I plan to employ more disaffected young people—you all will lead your own expeditions. We'll stagger your departures, of course—after a couple years we'll expand into the Mississippi River."

"Seth's in charge?" Benjy said.

The man turned his head and looked at him—smile gone from his face. "Three," the man said—reaching and grabbing the nearest leg of Benjy's chair—pulling the leg and tipping the chair backward onto the ground with Benjy still sitting in it—stepping over at the same time and punching down—reaching up and punching down—dining table blocking Seth's view.

After a few seconds the man stood up—adjusted the sleeves of his shirt—the waistband of his pants. "We'll go over the rest of the details tomorrow," he said.

Seth watched the man walk out of the room—then heard him leave the house out the back door.

THE NEXT MORNING SETH GOT OUT OF BED EARLIER than usual—picked out a pair of jeans and a shirt and waited to hear Isabel leave the bathroom—then carried the pile of folded clothes down the hallway—locking the bathroom door before taking a long shower—drying off and then looking himself over in the mirror—bruises all fading to a green-brown color—scrapes and cuts all devoid of scabs now—showing new pink skin as they healed. He stood there for a long time—twisting his body and lifting his arms—then started to get dressed.

He'd been wearing the clothes he found in the bed-room—Ricky's clothes—left in the closet and the dresser. He stood there in the bathroom and checked his shirt and pants—sleeves and legs a little too long—checked his teeth and tested his breath against his palm—then left the bath-room and walked down the hallway toward the kitchen—joining everyone for breakfast.

"There he is," Spoon said—leaning over the counter-top—buttering a piece of toast. "Guess we'd better start calling you cap'n instead of loverboy."

Isabel was leaning back against the sink—sunlight shining through the window behind her—sipping a cup of coffee—not looking at anyone. Benjy was at the table—Seth looking at his bruised face—the dried blood caked onto his skin—still no bandages on the cuts.

"Morning," Seth said to everyone—taking a seat at the table as Benjy looked up at him. No one greeted him back.

"Word is you're working with us today," Spoon said as he brought over a plate with two pieces of toast on it—setting it down in front of Seth. "Gonna have to take a day off from pounding them sheep."

"You can have at them today if you want," Seth said. "I'll even introduce you."

Isabel set her coffee down and left the kitchen.

"Oh, I don't know, cap'n," Spoon said as he went over to the sink—leaned back and sipped his coffee. "They're liable to have all kinds of diseases if they've been with you." They both laughed—Seth turning in his chair—glancing over at Benjy before picking up a piece of toast—seeing the angry boy staring down at his clean plate. "Let's get a move on, anyway," Spoon said. "Lots to do before embarkation day," He drank the rest of his coffee—set the empty mug in the sink and started for the back door.

The three of them walked over to the building together—went inside where Seth saw the same stainless steel machines as before—Isabel already talking to the man near the back wall.

"We gotta name them, you know," Spoon said to Seth—Benjy walking off to a pile of discarded packaging materials—breaking down a cardboard box—then picking up another.

"What?"

"The canoes—gotta give them each a name."

Seth looked past the machines and saw two long canoes standing against a wall.

"It's bad luck not to," Spoon said.

Seth looked around the building—saw a cutting torch, a MIG welder, some sheet metal with different sized squares cut out of it—also shiny rolls of what must have been aluminum sitting on the picnic table—pair of tin snips beside them—scraps of plywood and a circular saw on the ground close to the roller door.

"Seth," the man said. "Clear that table off."

Seth and Spoon put everything that was on the picnic table in a box—then stood there and watched the man and Isabel walk over—the man waving for Benjy to join them. Everyone sat down—the man placing a stack of laminated maps in front of Isabel.

"I'm in charge of the maps," Isabel said.

"All navigation decisions go through Isabel," the man said. "Benjamin will safeguard the money." Seth turned to see Benjy lift his head—look up from where his hands rested on the table.

"The red canoe will be in the lead," Isabel said. "I'll be in the front with Benjamin in the back. The green canoe will have Bertram in the front and Seth in the back."

"Bertram," the man said. "You will be in charge of any repairs—also water filtration and cooking." Spoon nodded— Seth turning to look at him—seeing his hands in his lap and his head down—whole body bouncing as he tapped his heel on the ground under the table.

"Seth," the man said. "As I said last night, you are in charge. These three have their responsibilities and you are not to interfere with them—but everything else goes through you." The man paused for a moment—staring at Seth—Seth staring back—nodding as he tried not to look away. "That means buying food," the man continued. "Isabel knows the places I've selected. She'll tell you where and when to go."

Seth caught Benjy looking at him—smiling so wide Seth saw a wet spot in the dried blood around his lip.

"Tomorrow morning," the man said as he stood up from the table. "Load everything in the back of the pickup—canoes on top—go and do your work and come back home." The man looked at each of them—then turned around and walked to the back of the building—went inside the room where Seth had stacked all the cans of soup and bottled water—shut the door and started clicking multiple locks into place.

"So how about we talk boat names?" Spoon said.

"No names," Isabel said—gathering the laminated maps and standing up from the table—then marching off toward the door that led outside.

"Oh, come on!" Spoon yelled after her—then turned to Benjy and Seth. "Hey we should paint some hot ladies on the sides like they did on airplanes in World War II."

"No," Isabel yelled without stopping or turning around.

"Good thing Seth's in charge," Benjy said—making sure his voice was loud enough for Isabel to hear—his forehead resting on the table now. "Ask him."

Isabel slowed but didn't stop—didn't turn around as she neared the door—then walked outside with the maps tucked under one arm—just the three boys left in the metal building—sitting at the picnic table together.

"No names," Seth said.

The three of them sat there for a few more minutes—Benjy eventually lifting his head off the table—picking at his fingernails but not saying anything.

They spent the next four or five hours cleaning the stainless steel machines—Spoon taking them apart and handing the pieces to Seth and Benjy—two farmhouse sinks against the wall they filled with screws and small parts—also a drain in the floor where they bent down and washed the bigger pieces with a hose.

Then they got to work trying to decide what supplies to bring—taking into account the space and weight limits they had to work with—first filling dry bags the man had bought with matches and tools and toilet paper—then deciding each canoe would need a small bilge pump and two sponges, a length of rope, a trowel and a roll of duct tape—tube of sealant to share in case the canoes started leaking. They'd carry enough cans of soup to last a few days but hardly any water—filtering the river water each time they stopped to reduce weight.

"You ever been on a trip like this before?" Seth said.

"Not even close," Spoon said. "Before I come here I hadn't been fifty miles away from home."

"Where's home?"

"Front end of that boat's gonna be home for the next two months," Spoon said.

Seth nodded—sat down at the picnic table and looked around the building. Spoon and Benjy came over and sat across from him—each of them leaning forward with their elbows on the table.

"Wonder what he's gonna do with Titus and the sheep," Seth said—waiting for Spoon to respond but he didn't say anything.

"They're just here to make it seem like we're running a ranch," Benjy said without looking up from his hands. "Sheep are going to the butcher—probably get sheered before they get slaughtered." Seth and Spoon both looked at him. "Probably take Titus out back and shoot him—can't risk him running off and somebody finding him and then trying to bring him back here." Benjy flicked a piece of dead skin onto the table—then went back to picking at the same finger.

"Well," Spoon said after a pause. "Guess I better get dinner going." He stood and stretched his hands up in the air above his head—then exhaled and let them fall to his sides. "Big day tomorrow." He smacked Seth on the shoulder and walked off—nearly to the door when Seth saw him look back toward the man's room.

1

SETH WOKE UP IN THE MIDDLE OF THE NIGHT WITH A hand over his mouth—another hand pinning him to the bed. He opened his eyes but couldn't see anything—wasn't all the way awake yet but he knew it was the man. Once he stopped fighting, the man took his hands off Seth's mouth and chest—looking down at him through the darkness— Seth now able to see the whites of the man's eyes—the brim of his cowboy hat.

The man reached behind his back and pulled out a pistol—held it out and motioned for Seth to take it. Seth grabbed the grip and took the pistol—making sure to keep his finger away from the trigger—seeing an extra clip held out in the man's other hand—then watching him reach behind his back again—this time pulling out a cellphone and a small cardboard box.

Seth set everything down on the bed between them— propped himself up on his elbow—the man sitting on the bed in front of him—moonlight or starlight or both leaking in through the parted curtains.

"I'm not abandoning you," the man said. "I'm just leaving—going to Kansas City where I will meet you in two months." Seth watched the man turn his head toward the window—waited until he turned back. "I'm not abandoning you—do you understand, Seth?"

"Yessir."

"Good," the man said. "That's good." He nodded as he turned his head—looking out the window again.

Seth pulled himself up and leaned back against the wall. The man stood up from the bed a few seconds later—told Seth they were to load the pickup and take it down to the river before sunrise—told him Isabel knew the place—then told him to charge the cellphone with the solar charger in the box any time the sun was out—told him the cellphone could only receive calls and that he'd check in periodically—told him to lead the group and that if he succeeded he'd get more money.

The man walked out of the room—Seth hearing the car start soon after—Vienna's Prius they'd driven from Kansas City—parked for the past two weeks on the other side of the metal building. He didn't see any headlights through the window—doubted the other three misfits in the house would have heard the man leave.

After he knew the man was gone Seth scooted back down underneath the blankets with the cellphone in his hand—looked toward the window as he thought about all the things that might happen on the river—as he smiled in the dark and tried to fall asleep.

SETH WOKE UP A FEW HOURS LATER TO THE SOUND OF the pickup starting in the driveway—opened his eyes and saw the headlights shining through the window and sweeping across the bedroom—heard gravel crunching under the tires. He got out of bed in a hurry and started getting dressed.

Outside it was almost cold—only a few insects with enough energy to make any noise—still dark enough to see stars in the sky. Seth hadn't seen anyone inside the house but the kitchen light was left on—coffee pot was still warm. He stood there now in the front yard and looked around—alone without even Titus to keep him company—assuming the other three were already in the metal building—loading the pickup with supplies—with whatever they were selling— whatever drug they'd be trading for cash over the next two months.

There was no wind as he turned and started walking toward the building—seeing the pickup's headlights still on but the engine was off—camper shell and rear tires hidden inside the large doorway.

"Hey cap'n," Seth heard Spoon call out as he swung open the metal door—the skinny boy's voice coming from somewhere on the other side of the building. "Come help me with this thing, will you?" Spoon had one of the canoes by the front end—trying to drag it toward the pickup.

Seth looked around—didn't see any sign of Benjy or Isabel.

"Sure," he said—going over and grabbing the back of the canoe—surprised by how light it was—glad he could probably carry one by himself since he knew there were a few dams on the river—places where they'd have to stop and drag everything out of the water—carry it all down and around to the other side.

"They're getting the lozenges," Spoon said.

"Lozenges?"

"Yeah." Spoon lifted the front of the canoe—pushed it up until the tip rested on the top of the camper shell. "Whole reason we're doing all this."

Seth started pushing the back of the canoe—Spoon guiding it—the pair eventually managing to get it positioned on top of the pickup. Then Seth heard a door open—turned and saw Isabel pushing a dolly with shrink-wrapped blocks stacked up to the handles—watched her push the dolly toward the pickup—looked down and saw an orange color through the layers of clear plastic—then watched as Benjy came out of the room and tried to take the dolly from Isabel—watched her shake him off and keep pushing.

"Good morning," Seth said as Isabel reached the open tailgate—waiting for her to respond as she stood the dolly and slid it out from under the stack—then meeting her eyes as she looked at him.

Isabel raised a hand toward the stack of blocks—raised her eyebrows at the same time—Seth quickly grabbing the top block and transferring it to the pickup's empty bed—shoving it so it slid forward a few feet—then turning around to see her already walking away.

"I'm glad she don't look at me that way," Spoon said—leaning back against the tailgate as Seth loaded the blocks.

"What the hell are you talking about?"

"I don't know—it's too early."

"You can sleep in the pickup," Seth said—loading the last block before turning around—seeing Isabel heading toward him with the dolly and another stack of blocks from the room.

About an hour later they finally had the pickup loaded—lozenges stacked in the bed along with their sup-plies—canoes tied down on top of the camper shell. Seth looked around for paddles as they all started climbing up into the pickup—didn't see any so he asked Isabel who was already in the driver's seat. She looked at him but didn't say anything—then opened the door and hopped down to the polished concrete floor—jogged back to the far corner of the building and lifted a blue tarp—pulled out a crate of black plastic paddles—only halves of paddles Seth figured had to snap together somehow—then walked back to the pickup and tossed the crate in the bed—climbed back up into the driver's seat without saying anything—Seth walking around to the passenger's side door.

They drove down the driveway—through the blue cattle gate and down the gravel road—then turned onto the highway that led to the little town Seth could remember passing through weeks before. After several minutes he looked in the backseat—saw both Spoon and Benjy asleep with their heads bouncing against the headrests—their mouths open.

Isabel turned down a gravel road before entering the town. The sun was just coming up—Seth looking out the window at the pastures and the few cows he could spot—the fences lining the road. They drove on for another few minutes—Seth eventually glancing over at Isabel when there was enough of that blue early morning light—seeing her gripping the steering wheel tight with both hands—her hair down—straight and black—shoulders slumped a little—watching her as she yawned and rubbed her nose—never turning her head.

It wasn't much longer before Seth could see the river far off in front of them—winding its way in each direction—a dark blue ribbon of varying thickness—beyond the last part of the road he could see—no barns or homes or anything else in sight—just the river—a small percentage of the land it shaped along each bank.

Eventually the gravel under the pickup's tires ran out and they continued down a rutted dirt path—Isabel keeping the pickup to one side—staying out of the deepest grooves—going slow but it was still a rough ride—Seth starting to hear Spoon and Benjy waking up—shifting around in the backseat.

"Ain't we gonna get some breakfast first?" Spoon said—Seth turning and looking back—seeing him blink and smile—dig a finger into the corner of one eye.

The path soon leveled out as they continued on—young cottonwood trees now blocking their view of the river—Seth

seeing a turnaround up ahead at the end of the dirt path—
Isabel soon driving straight through it—cutting her own
path through the brush and around the trees—driving
the pickup in a big loop around a dense patch of more
cottonwoods.

Seth looked out the windshield at the game trails
through the grass—wondering all the sudden about grizzly
bears and mountain lions—also wondering if there were
packs of wolves in that part of Montana—wanting to ask
the other three but he stayed silent—waited to see the river
again.

"Hey Isabel," Spoon said. "You're gonna have a pretty
nice view riding in the front of a canoe with this fat bastard
behind you." Spoon paused—Seth watching Isabel look up
at the rearview mirror. "Benjy's gonna tip that thing back so
much you'll be ten feet outta the water." Spoon laughed but
no one else did—Seth glancing back to see Benjy staring out
the window.

"I doubt it," Isabel said. "But maybe your skinny butt
could pull it off."

"Sounds good to me—I'll relax up front while ya'll take
turns paddling me around—be like sitting in first class."

"I sat in first class once," Benjy said—Seth looking over
at Isabel as she rolled her eyes. "That canoe ain't gonna be
nothing like first class on an airplane—I don't care how high
you get in the air."

"Yeah, we know," Spoon said.

"Well I'm just saying—they gave me champagne and a
hot towel—think they gave me two hot towels. I had to look
around at everybody else to know what to do with it."

"Yeah, well he hasn't sent you on anymore airplanes
since then, now has he?" Isabel said—looking up again at
the rearview mirror.

No one said anything for a while as they bumped along
over the uneven ground—sun starting to peak over the

horizon—tops of the trees swaying a little in the beginnings of a breeze. Seth kept himself busy looking out the window—worrying now about all the predators they might encounter.

Eventually they drove over a little hill and saw the river again—within just a hundred yards now—Isabel steering the pickup toward a dense patch of young cottonwood trees and underbrush—then driving through a small gap between the trees—low branches scraping the windows—some heavy enough to twist the rearview mirrors.

"Is he gonna come get the pickup somehow?" Seth said.

"Doubt it," Isabel said without looking over. "We'll probably have to come get it when we drive back up here from Kansas City."

"Won't somebody find it?" Seth said. "That's two months from now." He looked over at Isabel but she didn't say anything—then looked back at Spoon and Benjy but they were looking out the windows.

There was a little clearing inside the stand of trees—Isabel stopping the pickup and twisting the key back—her head dropping back against the headrest as they all sat there in silence—engine ticking as it cooled—hardly any sunlight able to penetrate the trees and the brush—making it dark inside the pickup—dark and quiet inside the little open space—tiny gaps above them showing bits of a bright blue sky.

"Can everybody swim?" Seth said—seeing the three of them turn and look at him but none answering the question. "Best thing to do if you fall in is just get on your back and float—tilt your head back like this—then use your arms and kick your feet to move through the water." He tried to demonstrate as best he could—turning his body in the passenger's seat.

Isabel looked at him—her elbow up on the steering wheel now—hand close to her mouth. "Let's go," she said—Seth watching the three of them open their doors at nearly the same time—dome light coming on as they all hopped down to the sandy soil.

First they carried the canoes over to the river's edge—pushing their way through the thick brush—getting to clear ground that ran all the way down to the water—then transferring the shrink-wrapped orange blocks and their supplies from the pickup to the canoes—Seth keeping the pistol and the cellphone the man had given him in a backpack he'd found back at the house—few extra shirts in there as well—some socks and underwear—also the portable solar panel the man had given him to charge the phone's battery.

It took them another hour before they were ready to leave—sun shining bright now as the morning wore on—shining on their skin as they moved around the canoes—on the sand that sloped down into the river—still cool out but not the time of year for temperatures to stay comfortable for long—time of year when the heat builds early and hangs around after sunset—bubbles up into storms that rage through some evenings and nights.

Seth watched the other three putting their paddles together—decided he should do the same—twisting the two pieces together as he squinted against the sunlight. They all finished with their paddles at nearly the same time—then stood there and looked at each other.

"Guess we're ready," Seth said.

"Let's go," Isabel said—stepping into the red canoe—lower half of the bow already in the water. "Push, Benjy—when we're floating you can jump in but be careful."

Seth watched as Benjy set his paddle inside the stern and started pushing—trying hard to get the loaded canoe to move—Isabel stabbing her paddle into the sandy mud as she tried to help—the pair finally able to build some momentum after a couple attempts—Benjy kicking at the water as he continued pushing—still wearing his blue jeans and boots—same outfit as Seth and Spoon—Isabel wearing sandals and cloth pants that were tied just below her knees.

The red canoe was floating now—low in the water with blocks of lozenges stacked in the middle—Benjy grabbing the gunwale with the water up to his knees—Seth watching the current trying to take the bow of the canoe downriver— watching Benjy lift one leg and swing it over the gunwale— then carefully put weight on it—starting to test his balance as he slid downriver with the canoe—Isabel looking back the whole time—trying hard to paddle against the current. Benjy hopped along on one foot for a few yards—then swung himself up into the canoe—landing with his belly on the seat as the canoe rocked violently back and forth.

"Why the hell are we wearing jeans?" Spoon said. "And boots?" He raised one foot and looked down at it—standing next to the bow of the green canoe—Seth at the stern.

They looked at each other and Seth shrugged his shoulders. Then Spoon pulled out his multi-tool and flipped out the knife—kicked off his boots and pulled off his socks and tossed them into the canoe—then used the knife to cut the legs of his blue jeans off just above his knees.

"There we go," he said—examining the jagged edges of denim looping loosely around his skinny legs—his pale bare feet. "Ain't no sense in getting water-logged like that big dumb idiot."

Seth took the multi-tool and did the same as Spoon—then looked up after he'd finished cutting his jeans and couldn't see the red canoe anymore—saw instead a bend in the river a hundred yards away—stood there staring at the curving ribbon of water—sand and rocks along each bank—trees and spindly bushes beyond the river's glistening surface— surprised Isabel and Benjy were already out of sight.

"Well," Seth said. "I guess we better hurry up."

"Oh relax, cap'n—we got two whole months to catch them."

Spoon climbed into the front of the green canoe—wearing a baggy T-shirt with the neck stretched out—Seth in the blue and white plaid shirt the man had bought him—both of them barefoot now. Seth started to push from the stern but the canoe wouldn't budge—dug his feet into the sand behind him and tried again—forcing the canoe to slide forward a few inches before it stopped.

"Come on, cap'n—I didn't get dressed up just to sit here all day," Spoon said.

Seth pushed again—Spoon stabbing his paddle into the sand and pushing too—the pair eventually getting the canoe halfway into the water—Seth sliding the stern sideways the rest of the way—then holding the canoe steady as he felt the cold water on his feet and lower legs—looking down into the water but unable to see anything past his ankles.

The current started pulling the canoe and Seth had no choice but to go with it—putting one leg up over the gunwale and hopping with the other one downriver—hopping until he had a good feel for the balance of the canoe—then throwing himself into the stern—staying as low as possible—carefully getting himself situated on the seat—putting his hands on the blocks of lozenges as he waited for the wobbling to stop.

"I'm free!" Spoon yelled—trying to sound like a girl with a foreign accent—sitting up straight and holding his hands out wide—one still gripping the paddle. "Free as a bird!"

Seth looked back at the shore—at the stand of trees hiding the pickup—their footprints and the grooves the canoes had made in the sand.

"You ever seen that movie?" Spoon said.

"What?"

"Titanic—ever seen it? That chick gets up there at the front of the ship and pretends she's flying."

"Yeah," Seth said. "I saw it."

"You probably remember more the scene where she's naked on the couch and that guy draws her."

"Yeah."

Spoon smiled as they drifted downriver—turned back around and started paddling. Seth looked for his backpack in all the cargo between them—shrink-wrapped blocks stacked up in the middle with a tarp over the top—camping gear stuffed in wherever they found empty space.

"We'll catch up to them before too long," Spoon said without turning around. "Don't worry, cap'n."

Seth finally found the backpack underneath the tarp—made sure it was dry and then slid it under his seat—picked up his paddle as he looked toward shore again—as he felt the sun warm on his face—felt the cool air coming up off the water.

"Hey," Seth said after paddling in silence for a while—setting his paddle in his lap and touching the water with his fingertips. "Maybe this won't be so bad."

Spoon nodded—smiled and kept paddling. "OK, cap'n."

THEY SPOTTED THE RED CANOE A HALF HOUR LATER—continued paddling hard until Seth was comfortable with the distance between them—then took a break as they watched Isabel drink from a water bottle—Benjy stiffly paddling as he slouched in the stern.

"What the hell you think they're gonna talk about for two months?" Spoon said—paddle in his lap as they floated with the current—Seth trying to learn how to steer—using his paddle as a rudder.

"Doubt they talk at all," Seth said.

"Yeah—maybe not." Spoon twisted around to look at Seth. "Well what the hell are we gonna talk about?"

"You can tell me where you're from."

"Yeah—guess I could." Spoon turned back

around—shaded his eyes with his hand—looked out over the water on both sides of the canoe—then started paddling again. "Guess I could."

After another hour they were pulling up beside the red canoe—wind gaining strength as the sun rose higher in the southern sky—the river clearer than Seth was used to—able to look down and see the bottom in the shallowest places—to stab his paddle down and touch it—even feeling the bottom of the canoe scrape against the silt and pebbles a few times.

The two canoes were side by side as they drifted past the first little town they'd seen all day—Seth resting as he looked up at the few buildings visible from the river—the grain elevator—remembering the town he'd driven through with the man—wondering as he picked up his paddle if it was the same town or another.

"Isabel, you got yourself a motor in the back of that thing," Spoon said.

"What?" she said—turning to look at him.

"That fat, dumb ox back there—he ain't stopped paddling since we started." Spoon pointed at Benjy with his paddle.

"One," Benjy said—sweat dripping down his red face.

"Why you gotta cause so much trouble, Spoon?" Isabel said.

"Chemical imbalance, I guess." Spoon shrugged his shoulders—smiled and looked ahead of them downriver— then started paddling again and so did Seth—soon starting to pull ahead of the red canoe—Seth looking over at Isabel once they were even with each other.

"We'll stop soon," Seth said.

Isabel turned her head—studied Seth's face as they both paddled on. "We should wait till we're farther from that town."

"Maybe," Seth said—keeping his eyes on her as he felt sweat dripping down the sides of his face. "We'll go on ahead—find a place to stop for the night."

Isabel set her paddle down in her lap—sat up straight and turned a little in her seat—then started to say something but stopped herself—Seth watching her as she adjusted her hat—looking down at her neck and arms—her skin shining with sweat and sun.

"First drop is two days from now," she said after a pause—looking behind her toward the little town. "Where we stop in the meantime doesn't really matter."

Seth kept watching her—letting his paddle dip into the water as he waited for her to look at him again—as the green canoe started turning—Seth having to paddle to straighten it as Isabel kept staring behind her.

"Was that your hometown back there?" he said.

"That's none of your business," Isabel said—turning back to face forward—picking up her paddle and scooting to the center of her seat. "Montana's my hometown." She adjusted her grip on the paddle—leaned forward and began pulling hard on the water.

The red canoe quickly pulled ahead of Seth and Spoon— the two of them watching it disappear a half hour later around another bend in the river—Seth and Spoon both paddling hard in the beginning but soon giving up—dropping their paddles and letting the current take them for a while—Seth examining the blisters he'd developed on each palm—cutting strips out of the bottoms of his blue jeans—wrapping them around his hands before picking up his paddle again.

Spoon complained about the sun as they drifted with the current—eventually holding his paddle up in front of his face—scooping water from the river with his hand and pouring it over the top of his head.

They passed fields and pastures and small clusters of cottonwood trees—twice saw anglers standing on the sandy shoreline—Spoon giving each one a big wave and a smile— the anglers pausing for a moment to wave back.

There were no other boats on the river—no clouds in

the sky. Seth smiled more than a few times as the afternoon wore on—tried not to think about all the things he didn't know—all the things he didn't understand.

They were on the river another three hours before they saw the red canoe beached on a little sandbar—thick stand of trees behind them—treeless pasture on the other side of the river. Seth steered toward the sandbar—saw Isabel lying on a towel close to the water—Benjy still in his seat in the canoe.

"Looks like a damn beach—Hawaii or someplace," Spoon said as they got closer.

Seth examined the sandbar—flat and narrow with fine white sand—at least thirty yards long. They paddled until the bow of their canoe ran up onto the sand next to where Benjy sat—head resting in his hands—elbows on his knees in the stern of the red canoe. Spoon jumped out and tried to drag the green canoe up onto the sandbar—Seth stepping out at the same time and pushing—his legs splashing in the water—moving the canoe but not by much—Spoon eventually standing up and wiping his forehead with the back of his hand—Seth watching him as he then reached down into the canoe and pulled out a long piece of rebar—bent into a loop at one end.

"Hey, chubby," Spoon said as he looked toward Benjy. "You got that hammer somewhere?"

Benjy looked up but didn't say anything—reached down slowly and pulled out a hammer and threw it toward Spoon. The hammer splashed into the water a few feet from the green canoe—forcing Spoon to turn away and close his eyes.

"Hold her steady," Spoon said as he went for the hammer—Seth standing there in the river still—holding onto the gunwales as tiny waves rolled against his legs—watching Spoon kneel down and stab his hands into the water—feeling for the hammer as he crawled. "Ain't got no sense—swear to God he ain't got no sense."

Eventually Spoon found the hammer—stood up and pounded the rebar into the sand in front of the green canoe—then retrieved a piece of rope from the canoe and tied the bow to the loop at the end of the rebar.

"Think it'll hold?" Seth said.

"No idea," Spoon said. "Just made it this morning."

Seth took his backpack from the canoe—made sure all the zippers were closed before slipping his arms through the straps—then walked out of the water toward the rebar sticking out of the sand—grabbed the loop and tried to wiggle it.

"We got any more?" Seth said.

"Just one each." Spoon pointed to the front end of the red canoe—Seth turning his head and seeing the same setup as they had with the rebar and the rope.

Seth took a few steps—looking around as he went—down at the water running up against the sides of the canoes—the river stretching and curving out of sight in both directions. "Current doesn't seem that strong," he said.

"It'll be fine, cap'n."

Seth nodded—then turned his head and looked at Isabel—a hat over her face—her cloth pants rolled up above her knees—her chest lifting as she took deep, long breaths—still looking as he walked over to her.

"Hi," Seth said—squatting down a few feet away.

Isabel lifted the edge of her hat and peeked out. "What?"

"Just wondering if we could go over the maps."

Isabel turned her head and let down the edge of her hat. "No."

Seth stayed where he was but finally looked away—looked out over the dark, sparkling surface of the river—put one hand down on the sand to steady himself. "You know if there's any reservoirs upriver from here?" he said. "Corps of Engineers could release some water overnight and we could lose the boats."

Isabel lifted her hat again—Seth able to see both her eyes

this time—two dark circles in the shade—arched eyebrows and long lashes—silent seconds passing between them as he stared at her—as she stared back—unaware of what she did to him, Seth thought—unaware or maybe not—maybe she knew exactly what she was doing.

"They're fine," Isabel said—then disappeared again under her hat.

The sun was still above the treetops and it was hot when the wind stopped blowing. Seth felt a couple mosquitoes buzz by his ears as he looked around the sandbar—as he watched Benjy still sitting in the red canoe—sunburned and still in his boots.

He looked around for Spoon but the skinny boy had disappeared somewhere—gone off to rest in the shade or to gather firewood—not to run away, Seth was sure—too scared of the man and too unsure of himself—probably having too much fun as well.

Seth turned back to the canoes—both still sitting there with the pieces of rebar sticking up out of the sand in front of them. He walked over and wiggled both the anchors—picked up the hammer and sent one of them another six inches deeper into the sand.

"It's fine," Benjy said—Seth pausing to look up at him— seeing how tired he was—his head cradled in his hands and his eyes only halfway open.

"Just making sure," Seth said. "You bring any sunscreen?"

"No."

Seth hit each of the anchors a few more times—then set the hammer down in the green canoe—stood up straight and looked down at the water—the wet sand and his bare feet.

"Come on, you big Jewish ox," Spoon said—Seth turning and seeing him with two small branches in his hands— watching him walk up and drop them on the sand. "Help me get some wood."

Spoon turned and started walking toward a group of

trees a hundred yards away—never getting a response from Benjy—Seth turning toward the stocky boy—seeing his head still in his hands—still sitting in the red canoe. Seth waited a few minutes—then decided to leave him there—walked off by himself after Spoon.

The pair gathered dead branches scattered around the trees behind the sandbar—breaking them apart before carrying the pieces back to camp—making two more trips before they thought they had enough. Then Seth watched Spoon go to their canoe and bring back a small plastic bag—something that looked like dark blue, fluffy cotton inside.

"Dryer lint," Spoon said. "Everything's good for something."

He got down on his knees in front of the pile of wood shavings they'd made with their pocketknives—Seth getting down as well to help block the wind—feeling how much cooler it was now that the sun was going down—how many more mosquitoes were coming out—feeling the skin on his face tight with sunburn as he moistened his dry lips.

Spoon lit the dryer lint with a lighter he pulled from his pocket—Seth smelling burning hair as he hovered over the flames—watching them die out just a few seconds later—some of the shavings charred but nothing continued to burn—Spoon laying down more lint and trying again with the lighter—taking three attempts before they had flames coming off the wood—Seth and Spoon staying hunched over the tiny fire for a long time—breathing in the smoke—their hands and their bodies shielding the small embers from the wind.

When they were confident it wouldn't go out they stood up—stared down at the flames for another couple minutes—sun nearly gone now—both of them having a hard time seeing once they finally looked away from the fire—Seth spotting Isabel near the canoes—blinking as he watched her eat a protein bar—her hat gone and her hair loose—wearing a sweatshirt now as the temperature continued to drop. Seth turned and saw Benjy still sitting in the same place and same position in the red canoe—saw his face still red even though he was now in the shade—his head still in his hands as Seth walked over to him.

"You alright, Benjy?" Seth said—leaning over to try to look at his face.

"I'm fine."

"You still feel hot?"

Benjy looked up at Seth. "I'm fine."

"OK," Seth said—standing up straight again. "Wanna come over by the fire?"

Benjy jumped out of the canoe—started to run toward Seth before he slipped and fell in the sand—Seth jumping back but Benjy had fallen at his feet—reached out and grabbed Seth's ankle—Seth falling backward as Benjy scrambled to his feet and started coming toward him—Seth rolling out of the way—Benjy trying to pivot but he slipped and fell again—giving Seth enough time to stand up and start backing away—holding his hands up with his palms out.

"Stop!" Seth yelled—trying to calm the stocky boy down—sand stuck to his bright red face as he panted on his hands and knees.

Benjy stumbled to his feet and came at him again—Seth still retreating as Benjy spit on the ground between them—sand coating his forearms and sprinkled in his hair—breathing hard with his front teeth gnashed together. Seth kept his hands up—hoping he'd stop but knowing there was too much anger in his glassy eyes—Benjy running forward and gripping Seth's shoulders—taking them both to the ground—the two of them rolling together in the sand—Benjy clumsily trying to land punches—Seth dodging and blocking as he waited for Benjy to tire himself out—fight that lasted maybe a minute before the stocky, sun-sick boy was exhausted—out of breath as Seth stood up and left him on his back—Benjy soon rolling over to vomit in the sand.

Seth turned his head and looked toward the fire—saw Isabel and Spoon sitting there with their backs to him—on the ground together laughing—a small pot and some cans laid out on the sand next to them—Isabel with a water bottle in one hand. He looked back down at Benjy but had a hard time seeing anything—nearly dark now with the sun fully beneath the horizon—brightness of the fire forcing his eyes to adjust when he looked away—watching Benjy roll over and drop onto his back—his narrow eyes partially open— looking up and smiling—still breathing hard with his hands on his chest—sunburned face looking almost purple in the fading, flickering light.

"I'll get you sooner or later," Benjy said.

Seth stood there a while longer—looking down at Benjy's swollen face—still sporting that smile. Then he turned and looked out over the water—river as calm as a pond—nothing and no one in sight—raised his gaze to the steep incline of the opposite bank—saw a few trees off in the distance but he had a hard time making them out.

"YOU TWO DO YOUR FORNICATING INSIDE A TENT NEXT time—so we don't have to see it," Spoon said a few minutes later—looking up at Seth and Benjy as they walked over to separate sides of the fire—ten feet apart with sweat and sand still coating their skin. "I didn't think you two would pair up for at least the first few days," Spoon continued—smiling as Seth sat down on the other side of the small fire—Benjy lying flat on his back near Isabel.

"Idiots," Isabel said.

"Benjy don't look so good," Spoon said—inspecting the stocky boy's face as he leaned forward.

"Too much sun," Isabel said. "You white boys all think you're invincible."

"He sure ain't," Spoon said—still looking down at Benjy.

"Why the hell didn't any of you bring a hat at least?"

"I'll get some," Seth said—looking up at the dark sky. "When I go for food I'll buy some hats—sunscreen too."

They sat there around the fire for another hour or so—drinking bottles of water and eating a can of soup each—taking turns heating their food over the flames in the same small pot. Spoon passed out metal bowls and spoons—gave Isabel the first soup he heated up—then made Benjy's and then passed the pot to Seth. Seth didn't bother reading the can—just opened it and poured it into the pot—then set the pot in the fire and kept hold of the handle.

Isabel was already finished eating—sitting there staring at the fire with her hair hanging loose around her face—Spoon and Benjy finishing their meals not long after.

A few minutes later the three of them got up and walked to the canoes together—leaving Seth sitting there by himself—wanting to turn around and watch them but he didn't—wanting to yell and ask them what they were doing but he stayed quiet—ate the lukewarm soup and watched the fire.

Soon he could hear the three of them assembling their tents near the river—then turned where he sat in the sand and ate his soup—heat from the fire warming his back as he watched Spoon position his tent nearest to him—deftly locking into place the support rods—pulling the tent material taut and making sure the screens were zippered closed.

They all climbed into their tents before Seth had even finished his soup—standing up a few minutes later as the fire started to die behind him—walking down to the water slowly—alone and in the dark—rinsing out his empty bowl in the river and stowing it away with the others—then finding his tent and sleeping bag in the green canoe. Having watched Spoon it didn't take him long to get the tent assembled—fastening the rainfly down and then checking everything over.

"Goodnight," Seth said—hearing their mumbled replies in low, tired voices—then seeing a flashlight click on inside Isabel's tent.

Seth pulled his backpack into his tent and closed the door—got himself zippered into his sleeping bag—felt the sand lumpy and uneven underneath him—used his hands to smooth it out—then tried to sleep.

THE SUN HAD RISEN A COUPLE HOURS BEFORE SETH woke up—opening his eyes to the bright spot a quarter of the way up the wall of his tent—listening for the other three but not hearing anything. He unzipped his sleeping bag—then unzipped the tent door and crawled out—still barefoot as the hot sun hit his sunburned face.

"There he is," Spoon said. "The Nazi." Seth looked over and saw the three of them sitting in the canoes—Spoon turning toward Isabel. "Get it? He beat up a Jew so that makes him a—"

"Yeah," Isabel said. "Got it."

"I didn't beat him up," Seth said.

"Hey come on and get some breakfast," Spoon said—turning back to Seth.

Seth walked over and stood in front of them—took a peanut butter sandwich Spoon held out for him. "Thanks," he said—glancing over at Benjy in the back of the red canoe—seeing a cut above his eyebrow from the man punching him two nights earlier—dark brown scab still covering it—rest of his face bright red.

"You alright, Benjy?" Seth said—taking a bite of his sandwich.

"He's fine," Spoon said. "Probably gonna give you the silent treatment for a while."

Seth looked at Benjy again—bright red color showing even on his neck and hands—eyes staring down at the floor of the red canoe—black plastic paddle resting in his lap.

They were all soon finished with their sandwiches— Spoon walking off toward the trees by himself—Isabel opening a book—Benjy just sitting there in the sun.

Seth walked back to his tent—stretched his sore back and stiff legs—then crawled in and opened the backpack and pulled out one of the clean shirts he'd brought—scooted back out onto the sand and ran back to the canoes. "Here," he said—standing in the water holding the shirt out to Benjy. "Wear this one—it's got long sleeves and a collar. You can dunk your T-shirt in the water and wrap it around your head."

"I'm fine."

"No," Seth said. "If you get sick and can't paddle that makes things harder for all of us."

Benjy looked up—hesitated but then grabbed the shirt and laid it down over the side of the canoe—then moved to take his T-shirt off—Seth walking back up out of the water— looking at Isabel as he went—seeing her raise her eyes from her book—not high enough to make eye contact though.

A half hour later they packed up their tents and got ready to leave the sandbar—Seth tucking his backpack under his seat—seeing Benjy stare at it as he sat in the stern of the red canoe—water dripping down his red face from the wet T-shirt.

Isabel and Benjy paddled out first—making it fifty yards downriver before Spoon and Seth even got their canoe off the sand—paddling out to the middle part of the river as they watched the red canoe pulling away—Seth laying his paddle in his lap so he could look under the tarp for a waterproof bag—finding one and then quickly pulling the contents out—roll of duct-tape, a box of matches that rattled in his hand and some twine—dropping everything to the floor of the canoe before pulling out the pistol, the cellphone and the little solar panel from his backpack—stuffing them into the waterproof bag—squeezing out the air as he sealed it—then slipping the bag inside his backpack and zippering it shut again.

"You gonna help at all back there?" Spoon said—turning to look at Seth over his shoulder.

"Yeah," Seth said as he picked up his paddle—pushed the backpack under his seat with his heal—then submerged the paddle's plastic blade and pulled hard against the water—torquing his body and feeling the canoe lurch forward.

The rest of the morning they paddled without taking any breaks—slowly catching up to Isabel and Benjy—watching Benjy remove the T-shirt from his head a few times and dunk it in the water.

The river was still shallow in many places—Seth often able to look down and see the bottom—to feel the pebbles and sand with his paddle—but shallow or not the river was always moving—its speed and power surprising Seth—always winding its way toward the ocean.

They saw more fields as the morning wore on—more small groups of cottonwood trees—more sandbars.

Around midday Seth spread a piece of his blue jeans over the tarp in front of him—one of the lower legs he'd cut off the day before—ripped it so it opened up into a flat square of denim—placed the fabric on the top of his head—then carefully wrapped a piece of twine around his head to hold the piece of denim in place—able to see two of the corners hanging down around his eyes when he was finished.

"What the hell's all that about?" Spoon said—turning

around in his seat to face away from the sun. "You look like a hippie."

"You should do it too," Seth said. "You're looking pretty red."

"I'm using them scraps for my hands." Spoon showed Seth his paddle—the two pieces of his old blue jeans wrapped around the handle—fastened to it by thin strips of duct-tape.

"Here—take my other piece for your head."

"Sure." Spoon reached out for the fabric.

"I'll do it," Seth said—pulling the denim apart with both hands—then searching for a long-enough piece of twine—both of them quiet as Seth worked on the head covering—Spoon looking off over the river.

"You think Benjy's gonna try to kill me?" Seth said—holding out the denim and the twine.

Spoon kept his eyes on the river—squinting as Seth looked at him—squinting so hard against the sparkling water his eyelids looked like they were shut tight—so hard his yellow teeth were showing. "Maybe," he said. "But he's so stupid he might just forget all about it."

"That'd be nice."

"Yep."

"How long you two been friends?"

"Oh, I ain't so sure we're friends—more like we're forced to live together—then we just got used to it." Spoon looked at Seth. "Guess that makes us family."

"You been living in that house a long time?"

"Three or four years."

"That's a long time."

"Yep."

"What about Isabel?"

"She was there before I came along." Spoon laid the piece of denim over his head—wrapped the twine around and pulled it tight. "So was Benjy." He finished making a knot behind his head—turned around and picked up his paddle.

They stayed close to the red canoe through the rest of the afternoon—Seth making sure they stopped paddling every hour to rest—that they ate some of the protein bars and drank plenty of water.

Late in the afternoon they pulled up beside the red canoe and started to pass it—Seth watching Benjy and Isabel—both paddling hard and sweating—Benjy wearing Seth's shirt—his T-shirt wrapped around his head—Isabel with her hat pulled down low against the setting sun. They passed them in silence and went on down the river—Seth starting to look for a place to stop for the night.

He spotted a place where high water had carved out part of the south bank—a large tree partially buried beneath the sand—smooth wood sticking up without any bark left to cover it—cracked and dead and gray. Seth could tell the current didn't reach into the little inlet—feeling it suddenly stop pushing and pulling the canoe as they paddled out of the main channel toward shore—a clump of cottonwoods just above the sand on the dry ground.

"I'm gonna sleep like a dead dog tonight," Spoon said as the bow of their canoe hit the sand—Spoon already starting to stand up—sticking a leg out and dropping it down into the shallow water.

"Yeah," Seth said. "Me too."

Seth jumped out of the canoe and started pushing from the stern—both working together to slide the canoe up onto the sand as far as they could—Spoon grabbing the rebar anchor as Seth found a heavy rock nearby and hammered it into the sand—Spoon making sure the rope was secured to the canoe.

"Why don't you take it easy," Seth said. "I'm gonna get some firewood."

"You're the boss—think I'm due for a nap anyhow."

Spoon lowered himself into the water next to the canoe—Seth watching him lie back and close his eyes—drifting slowly to a place where just his face was out of the water.

Seth turned and started walking up the sandy bank toward the cottonwood trees—found the highest point and stopped there—turned around and looked out over the river—watching as the red canoe pulled into the little inlet—as it approached the green canoe—still watching as a splash of water washed over Benjy from behind—Spoon diving out of the way and swimming hard as Benjy turned and swung out with his paddle—standing up in the stern of the red canoe as he twisted around—losing his balance and falling backward onto the tarp and the pile of shrink-wrapped blocks underneath.

Spoon stopped swimming once he'd gotten far enough away—looked back as he started to stand—laughed hard as he tried to run with the water still up to his waist.

"Spoon, you idiot!" Isabel yelled—stepping out of the canoe with the rebar anchor in one hand—coiled rope and the hammer in the other.

Seth hurried back down to the canoes—took the rebar anchor from Isabel's hand—took the rope and the hammer—then watched her turn around and lift her tent and backpack from under the bow seat.

"You mad about something?" Seth said—Isabel stepping past him without lifting her head—without stopping.

"Nope," she said—making her way up toward the dry sand. "Mosquitoes are gonna get bad with all this still water." She kept walking—Seth turning to watch her as she found a patch of shade where she dropped her things—as she knelt down to unpack her tent.

"Hmm," Spoon said—Seth turning around to see him on the other side of the canoe—sitting down in the water with his hair wet—arms out wide just beneath the surface. "Wonder what's on your mind right about now, loverboy."

"I thought you were gonna take a nap."

"Too much entertainment."

Seth turned again to find Benjy—saw him sitting in the

stern of the red canoe—eating one of the protein bars with a bottle of water in his hand—seeming stronger—not quite as exhausted as the day before.

Seth walked back up to the little stand of trees and started gathering firewood—not finding much that was dead and dried out so he looked around for anything else—finding a spot fifty yards farther from the river where there was another group of cottonwoods—several branches on the ground with their bark mostly peeled away.

Seth squinted against the setting sun as he made his way to the trees and dead branches—felt his sunburned feet hot inside his boots—jeans cut into shorts and the square of denim still tied onto his head—smiling at the way he must've looked.

Most of the wood he found was rotten—crumbling into dust and spongy splinters in his hands. But he kept walking and eventually found the hard, cured pieces he'd been looking for—breaking off and gathering as many dry sticks as he could carry with one arm—then grabbing the end of a large branch and dragging it backward.

"Thought you'd walked off," Benjy said from behind him—Seth dropping the branch and turning around—then dropping the sticks that'd been cradled in his arm. "I'm surprised you made it this far, to be honest."

"Why?" Seth said as he looked down at a pistol in Benjy's right hand—his head still wrapped in the wet T-shirt—his face still red and swollen.

"He brings you home just a couple weeks before we're set to leave—all you do is fiddle with the sheep all day. You ain't really a part of this—you don't really get what we're trying to do." Benjy raised the pistol and extended his arm.

"So why'd he put me in charge then?"

"You ain't in charge—that was just to make you cooperate—but I knew you wouldn't."

"Alright," Seth said. "You're in charge then—I'm just getting wood for a fire—just like you told me to."

"Yeah?"

"Yeah. And I'll get in that canoe tomorrow and paddle my ass off—do whatever you tell me to do—because you know this job don't get done without all of us."

"Oh yeah?" Benjy looked around—shook the pistol in his hand—his left leg rattling with his knee jutting in and out. "Yeah he wouldn't kill you yet—not just yet."

Seth waited—saw the sun shining on the side of Benjy's face—smelled the grass and the earth—felt a breeze blowing at his back.

"That's why he gave me this, you know." Benjy pulled the pistol back toward his face—twisted the barrel skyward and looked at it. "In case any of you get out of line—think about sabotaging the mission—that's what this is for." He lowered the barrel—extended his arm and pointed the pistol at Seth again.

"OK," Seth said. "Alright I hear you—I'm just gathering firewood—just doing my part." He bent down and slowly extended his hands—started picking up the sticks he'd dropped—keeping his eyes on Benjy.

"Yeah." Benjy lowered the pistol. "Then we're gonna go back there and tell everybody who's in charge—OK?"

"OK."

Benjy put the pistol in his pocket—walked over and lifted one end of the heavy branch—pausing as he watched Seth stand up with the pile of sticks back in his bent arm. Seth waited until Benjy nodded his head toward the other end of the branch—then bent over and lifted it with his free hand.

Seth walked backward as they returned to the canoes— hearing Spoon and Isabel laughing as they got close—also a fire popping—feeling mosquitoes buzz his ears and land on his neck.

The sun was nearly gone now—streaks of purple in the sky as Seth turned his head.

"Nice log you boys got there," Spoon said—Seth looking

over his shoulder—seeing a fire going with a few logs already stacked next to it. "Now was going and getting that wood just an excuse for you two to sneak off together?"

No one said anything—Isabel and Spoon laughing—sitting on logs opening cans of soup—the pot sitting on the ground between them—Seth and Benjy walking over and dropping their log on the other side of the fire—Seth also dropping the bundle of sticks he had cradled in his arm.

"Seth's got something to tell you," Benjy said—looking over the fire at Isabel and Spoon.

"What—gonna let me decide where we stop from now on?" Isabel said—smiling at Spoon as he slapped a mosquito on his arm.

"It's in her blood, cap'n," Spoon said.

Seth looked at Benjy. "Benjy's in charge."

"Right," Isabel said.

"I am."

"OK," Spoon said. "That's fine—whatever." Spoon started opening one of the cans of soup.

It was nearly dark now—Seth able to see the fire flickering on their faces—stars and contrails as he looked up at the sky.

"I am," Benjy said again—pulling out the pistol this time—holding it up to show them.

Spoon froze with the can of soup half-opened in his hands—looking up at the pistol.

"Seth has one of those too," Isabel said—picking up the pot and taking the can from Spoon.

Benjy turned to Seth—looking surprised and angry as he pointed the pistol at him—Seth putting his hands up—taking a step back—wondering if he was about to die—if he should turn and run away into the darkness—run until he found somewhere else to be—until he found something else to do—some other girl to chase, maybe—maybe one who didn't mind getting caught.

"Give it to me," Benjy said—taking a step toward him—Seth able to see his teeth and the whites of his eyes—left side of his face glowing orange from the fire—right side dark and blue from the shadows.

Benjy took another step—held the pistol up close to Seth's face—Seth still standing there with his hands up—watching as Benjy put one leg forward and flexed his knees—as he pulled the pistol back and started to swing it forward. Seth put his arm out and braced himself to block the pistol—then grabbed Benjy's arm with both hands and tried to wrestle the pistol away from him.

They shuffled together in the sand—Benjy squeezing off a shot—fighting to twist the barrel while Seth's ears started ringing—squeezing off another shot but Seth barely heard it. Eventually they went to the ground together—the pistol falling out of Benjy's hand. They rolled on top of each other—threw distracted, no-look punches as they both kept searching the sand for the pistol.

Seth looked up at one point as he rolled on top of Benjy—as Benjy started punching up at his ribs—looked up and saw Isabel just a few feet away—reaching down and picking the pistol up out of the sand. Then Seth felt himself being rolled over onto his back—losing sight of her as he twisted his head around—as he felt Benjy on top of him—trying to punch down at his face. Seth kept his hands up—blocking Benjy's blows as he looked for Isabel—finally spotting her near the river—watching her reach down into the green canoe.

Then one of Benjy's punches finally landed—everything going limp and dark in an instant.

SETH WOKE UP A FEW SECONDS LATER—OPENING HIS eyes to see Isabel's bare feet—then Benjy's boots—the two of them walking toward the fire. It was brighter than it was before—Seth wondering why as he tried to raise his head—realizing his ears were still ringing.

Spoon came over to help him up—Seth slowly getting to a sitting position in the sand—blinking and waiting for the world to come back into focus. A minute or two later he could hear people talking—could look at the fire without being blinded—could control his legs well enough to try standing up.

Seth and Spoon walked over to the fire together—both of them sitting down in the sand across from Isabel—Benjy sitting a little farther from the flames.

"You tough guys have any more weapons?" Isabel said—looking at Seth and then Benjy—Spoon pulling the pot from the fire and stirring the soup. "Give me your pocketknives." Isabel held out her hand—one of the pistols raised in the other.

Benjy reached into his pocket and pulled out his pocketknife—tossed it so it landed near Isabel's feet—Isabel leaving it in the sand as she looked at Seth and motioned with her open hand.

Seth fished around inside both pockets before he found his pocketknife—looking down and seeing the second pistol tucked into the waistband of Isabel's pants—then throwing his pocketknife toward her feet where Benjy's had landed.

"We're not gonna get through this without all four of us," she said. "So no more guns—no more fighting—no more mosquito-infested campsites. From now on I decide where we stop—not making myself the leader because we don't need a leader—we each have our responsibilities."

They sat there and passed around the pot to heat their soups—Spoon heating Isabel's for her—then setting her bowl down in her lap—Isabel somehow eating with the pistol still in her hand.

"I'll get that back sooner or later," Benjy said—sitting

on a log by himself—lifting his first spoonful of soup to his mouth—Seth looking up from where he sat next to the fire—heating his soup as he felt the swollen places around his eye.

"No you won't," Isabel said—sipping a bottle of water.

"He meant for me to have it."

"Well he meant for you not to be such an idiot, too," Isabel said.

Seth looked over at Spoon—saw him sitting in the sand behind Isabel now—following their conversation with a pensive look on his face.

Benjy started to laugh—lifted another spoonful of soup to his mouth—then looked up at Isabel. "You deserve every bad thing I'm gonna do to you," he said.

Seth watched Isabel raise the pistol—braced himself for the gunshot as he leaned away from Benjy—as he felt the heat from the fire on his arm and shoulder.

"We need him," Seth said—slowly setting the pot on the ground and sliding it away from the fire. "Don't kill him—at least not till we're through with all this." Spoon and Isabel both looked at him—Isabel keeping the pistol pointed at Benjy. "I'll do it," Seth continued. "We get to Kansas City and you still want him dead—I'll do it."

"Like he did Ricky," Benjy said—laughing again as he ate—some soup slipping out onto his chin.

Isabel turned her head back to Benjy—Seth able to see her teeth—the pistol shaking now in her hand—breathing hard as she stood up and walked over to where Benjy sat—lowering the pistol as she raised the water bottle in her other hand—then slinging the rest of the water out of the bottle and onto Benjy's face.

Isabel kept the pistol in her hand—kept the other in her waistband—didn't say a word or look at any of them—just turned and walked slowly around the fire—finished setting up her tent and then crawled inside.

SETH WOKE UP EARLY THE NEXT MORNING—SUN NOT even up yet—blue-gray haze creeping into his tent—creeping over the sky and masking all but the brightest stars. He crawled out the little doorway—stood up and stretched—walked over to the fire and saw Isabel sitting there on one of the logs.

"Morning," he said.

"Morning," she said without looking up—poking the fire with a stick—then pulling it out to watch it smoke—tip of the stick turning from hot red to black.

Seth sat down on one of the logs.

"What're you doing up so early?" he said.

"We're behind already," Isabel said—turning from the stick to look at Seth. "We're supposed to make the first drop today—then tomorrow you need to go for food."

"OK," Seth said—nodding his head as Isabel looked back down at the fire.

Meadowlarks were starting to whistle from the trees behind them—the blue-gray light starting to change to an amber color—a breeze starting to blow that made Seth think it would be windy later on.

"We'll make it," he said.

"We have to," Isabel said. "Has he called?"

"No."

They sat there a while without saying anything—Seth wondering when Isabel had first learned of the cellphone—wondering if she'd known about it all along—even wondering if it'd been her idea.

He looked down at his bare feet and the sand covering them—then up at the sky—long lines of dark gray clouds—still a few stars to the northwest—brightening blue sky to the southeast.

"You wanna switch canoes?" he said.

"No."

"OK."

They sat there—Seth watching the sky—the long clouds turning pink and purple—then looking down at the fire until he felt a light suddenly shining on the side of his face—first part of the sun rising over the horizon.

"You know," Seth said—turning his head toward the sun. "That first night at the house—night we met—"

"Oh God," Isabel said—standing up and walking toward the river.

Seth watched her go—wondering why things were different now—why she'd pulled him into that dark bedroom—why it seemed so unlikely to ever happen again.

He sat there on the log near the small fire as the sun rose—watching Isabel as she pulled a waterproof bag from the red canoe—as she pulled a towel and a few other things from the bag. Seth suddenly sat up a little straighter—swallowed as he watched her start taking off her clothes—her shirt and sports bra—then her pants and underwear.

She grabbed something else from the bag before walking out into the river—steam coming off the water—trees on the opposite bank now shining in the sunlight. Isabel dropped down and disappeared below the surface—her head coming up a few seconds later—eyes looking to the sky—wet hair falling back and dipping into the water.

Seth watched her wipe her face—then drop back down so the water was up to her chin—watched her as she moved and made little waves—wondered what she was doing under the surface—then stood up suddenly and ran over to the canoes—got his shirt off before Isabel turned around and saw him.

"What are you doing?"

"I thought—"

"What?"

Seth stood there with his shirt in his hands—looking at Isabel as she turned to face him—seeing bubbles floating all around her in the sun-dappled river—a bar of soap she raised out of the water.

"I don't wanna have sex with you in the river, Seth—that's disgusting."

Seth didn't say anything as Isabel rolled her eyes and swam away—just turned and started walking back toward his tent—crawled inside before putting his shirt back on. He sat there a while—checking the cellphone—brushing the sand off his feet and ankles—few minutes later hearing water splash and drip as Isabel left the river—then Spoon and Benjy getting out of their tents—someone throwing more wood on the fire.

THEY GOT AN EARLY START THAT MORNING—STRONG wind blowing from the west—river snaking north at times—then south—but always making its way to the east. It was hot with high clouds in the sky—hawks riding thermals with their rigid wings—always watching the ground for their next meal.

Isabel kept both pistols with her as she traded places in the red canoe with Benjy—sitting in the stern while she kept him busy paddling from the bow—Seth making sure to keep them in sight—working hard to keep up while Spoon mostly watched the hawks.

They saw a group of anglers in the morning after being on the river only thirty minutes—some waving or nodding their heads as the canoes passed by—saw the group's passenger van parked up on the riverbank—then saw no one else for hours.

"So what the hell's Benjy's problem?" Seth said around noon—Spoon twisting around to look at him.

"Good question."

"Well, what do you think? You'd know better than me."

They were both quiet for a minute or two—Seth paddling as he kept his eyes locked on the red canoe.

"He's been with him so long," Spoon said. "Cooped up in that house or doing stuff like this—getting his ass kicked one minute—then told he's something special the next—and he ain't exactly the sharpest guy around."

"Yeah," Seth said—setting his paddle down in his lap— letting their canoe drift with the current. "So what made you hang around all this time?"

"That's another good question," Spoon said. "I guess when you got nowhere else to go—other than back to the place you come from, that is—and that place is even worse than where you are—you just decide to stay put—see what happens."

"Makes sense."

"Plus it's a whole lot of fun—what he had me doing."

"What's that?"

"All them machines you seen in the shop—know what they was for? How they worked?"

"No."

"Neither did I—neither did any of them—including him. It was my job to figure them out—get them working."

"For what?"

"To make all this." Spoon used his paddle to tap the tarp covering the shrink-wrapped blocks between them.

"So what the hell are they?"

"They're ketamine lozenges—formulated to release just the right amount over a thirty-minute period—so you just get the feel-good—not the hallucinations."

"Pharmaceutical boosters," Seth said—staring at the stack of shrink-wrapped blocks—paddle still resting on his thighs.

"You got it, cap'n." Spoon smiled—then turned around and started paddling.

Seth looked up and saw a few clouds overhead—dark gray with white tops that seemed to be boiling up higher and higher into the bright blue sky. He looked back down as a gust of wind blew the canoe slightly off course—saw shadows starting to flow over the river—surface of the water stirring as the wind swirled.

"How come you finally decided to talk?" Seth said.

"Guess he don't scare me so much out here," Spoon said—twisting his head to talk over his shoulder. "We got bigger problems right now anyway."

Seth started to paddle—watching Isabel in the stern of the red canoe—her figure getting smaller as she and Benjy pulled away—paddling hard through the choppy water.

They paddled another hour or so—following the red canoe around a large sandbar in the middle of the river—past fields and groups of trees—Seth looking out over the fields of wheat and oats as they passed by them.

The clouds continued getting thicker—some patches solid enough to block the sun for several minutes—Seth at one point feeling the wind suddenly die down—air suddenly cooler than before—cool and shady enough for him to take his blue jean hat off and toss it into the bottom of the canoe—turning toward the west and looking up—studying the clouds and the breeze—looking down at the ripples in the water.

"Think it's gonna rain?" Spoon said.

"Not sure—seems like it to me but I'm not from around here."

"Where you from?"

"Two hours north of Kansas City."

"I-35 or I-29?" Spoon said—referring to the two interstates.

"29."

"You know the river around there?"

"Not really," Seth said. "Some, I guess."

"That where he got you?"

"Yeah."

They paddled on until Seth saw the red canoe turn sharply toward shore along the north side of the river—then watched Isabel set down her paddle as Benjy jumped out of the canoe—watched her pull one of the pistols from her pocket—holding it near her knee as Benjy pulled on the bow of the canoe—trying to get it farther up onto the sandbank—yanking on it a couple times before giving up—Seth watching him retrieve the rebar anchor—tie the rope to it before pounding the rebar into the wet sand—sound of metal hitting metal not quite matching the hammer strikes until Seth and Spoon were within twenty yards or so.

"Do you really need to keep that gun out all the time?" Spoon said—smiling as he coasted past Isabel—Seth paddling hard behind him until they hit the sand—then grabbing the rebar anchor and jumping out—splashing through the water as he walked to the bow of the green canoe.

"Just until you stupid boys show me you can behave yourselves," Isabel said.

"I'm behaving myself," Spoon said—Seth looking up and seeing the smile still on his face—then looking over at Isabel—seeing tan lines curving around her chest and arms—smile on her face as well.

"Yes you are."

They set up camp there on the north side of the river— wind still blowing—still cool out with clouds now covering the sun completely—choppy little waves on the surface of the water—little birds playing in the wind nearby.

Spoon got a fire going while Benjy went for more wood—driftwood tangled together a few yards down the sandbar—dead, gray branches with wide cracks running lengthwise.

Isabel set up her tent far away from the fire—crawled inside almost as soon as they got there—zippered the little door closed and clicked on her flashlight.

"Make sure you get a big ole ribeye steak when you go for food tomorrow," Spoon said. "Potatoes too."

They were sitting in the sand next to the little fire—Benjy having just stacked his last load of firewood—Spoon pulling out cans of soup, bowls, spoons and the single pot.

"Not even sure where I'm supposed to go," Seth said.

"Maybe Culbertson," Benjy said. "There's a pizza place there." Seth looked across the fire—saw Benjy's red face studying the river. "Used to be, anyway—could rent DVDs there too—pizza and DVDs."

"Well hell then, bring back a pizza while you're at it," Spoon said—throwing his hand up into the air. "Toppings don't matter to me—I'm only picky about my women."

"They got a grocery store?" Seth said to Benjy—waiting for an answer but not getting one—Benjy in some sort of trance—staring out over the water.

The three of them sat there in silence for a while—waiting for the fire to heat up enough so they could warm their soups.

"You know many places close to the river down where you're from?" Spoon said—breaking the silence as he looked at Seth—Benjy breaking the trance he'd been in as he turned toward them.

"Not really."

"I'm not talking about grocery stores—bars or anything? Dancing places? Benjy over there loves to shake his big ole rump."

"Where're you from?" Benjy said—Seth able to see his eyes just above the flames.

"North of Kansas City—close to the river. You?"

"Minnesota—outside Minneapolis."

Seth turned his head—looked at Spoon as the skinny boy stuck his finger in the pot—steam rising as he stirred the warming soup.

"Chaud, Louisiana," Spoon said. "Means 'hot' in French."

They sat there and stared into the fire—Spoon pouring the soup into a bowl and handing it to Benjy—opening another can and pouring it into the pot.

"I do know one place," Seth said. "Not far from the river. If we could catch a ride it'd only take ten or fifteen minutes to get there." He saw Spoon smile—nod his head as he set the pot on a pile of hot coals—saw Benjy scooping soup into his mouth with a serious look on his face. "I've been there a couple times—went with some guys I used to work with."

"What's it like?" Benjy said.

"It's an old house—way the hell out in the middle of nowhere—back off a dirt road at the foot of a hill. They got a stage set up in the living room—tore out a wall that used to separate off the kitchen and made that the bar. All the other rooms just got a bed in them—you can take one of the girls in there if you got enough money."

"What if you want two?" Spoon said.

"You better rob a damn bank."

Seth and Spoon both laughed—Seth turning his head and looking over the fire—raising up a little to see over the rising flames—watching Benjy set his empty bowl down on the sand—seeing him frown as he rested his head on his hands and stared at the burning logs.

The light was fading as the sun set behind the thick layer of clouds—dark gray with lumpy sections reaching down toward the ground—wind weakening as Seth thought about how much cooler it was than the previous evenings—standing up and walking away from the fire—walking to the water and standing by the green canoe—watching the river as he heard Spoon opening another can of soup—wishing he'd brought a fishing pole as he heard Isabel unzip the door to her tent and climb out—listening from where he stood as she walked over to the fire and started talking to Spoon.

Seth wanted to reach into the canoe and grab the backpack under his seat—wanted to check the cellphone—see if it had any battery left—if the reception was any good or not. He didn't, though—wanting to keep the phone hidden from Benjy and Spoon for as long as he could—so he stood there instead—watched the sky darken—looked for any gaps in the clouds.

After a while he turned around and went back to the fire—flames seeming brighter now in the almost-dark—flickering over the ripples in the sand—surprisingly few insects buzzing around or singing their evening songs.

"Hey, cap'n," Spoon said as Seth took a seat in the sand. "We're trying to figure out where Isabel's from."

"She's from here—somewhere close by," Seth said—looking at her as she looked down at her feet.

"Really?" Spoon said—exaggerating the shocked look on his face—getting Isabel to glance up at him and smile. "I always figured you was some kind of Asian girl—from Thailand or Vietnam or someplace."

"You did not—idiot," Isabel said.

"I always knew you was native," Benjy said—staring at the fire still—eyelids drooping and his shoulders slouched.

Seth grabbed the empty pot and the last can of soup—noticed the stack of three dirty bowls next to the log Spoon was sitting on—opened the can and banged it against the side of the pot—then looked up at Isabel again.

"We better go," she said—standing up and wiping the sand from her legs. "Benjy, Seth—go get two blocks each."

Seth looked up at her from the ground—held up the cold pot and the empty can. Isabel pulled one of the pistols out from behind her back and pointed it at him—then pulled the other one out and pointed it at Benjy.

"Gonna point those things at us for two months?" Benjy said—putting his hands on his knees and standing up.

"Whenever I need to," Isabel said—watching Seth set the pot and the can down before standing up as well. "It's kinda fun."

"Tell me about it," Spoon said—still sitting on the same log. "That's how I feel every time I take a piss."

"Shut up," Isabel said. "The hell does that even mean?" She motioned with the pistols toward the canoes—Seth turning and walking away—feeling Benjy close behind him.

Seth slipped on his boots that had been sitting at the bottom of the green canoe—felt his sandy, bare feet against the dry, cracked leather—then pulled back the tarp from the pile of blocks—took two of them from the stack and started walking back to the fire. Benjy did the same with the blocks in the red canoe.

They walked past Spoon without stopping—past the warm fire—their tents and sleeping bags—then climbed the riverbank—started making their way through the dark trees—Isabel staying behind them with a headlamp strapped to her forehead—lighting up the ground and the trees on either side of them—Seth watching his shadow dance from one side to the other.

Isabel kept the two pistols in her hands—telling them where to go—guiding them with the beam from her headlamp. After a while Seth heard her put one of the pistols away and pull something out of her backpack—then heard the wobble of one of the laminated sheets and knew she was checking one of the maps.

"Keep going," she said. "There should be a road not too far away—keep an eye out for a purple flag."

Seth kept walking—behind Benjy now as he tried to follow the light from Isabel's headlamp—bright, wide beam scanning from side to side over the uneven ground—shining on the lonely tree trunks. He shifted the blocks from one arm to the other—then held them cradled in front of his midsection.

They crossed a field with some shrubs and short grass growing—Seth not seeing any signs of livestock—no fences, terraces or wells—nothing planted. Eventually they found the gravel road and Isabel had them stop—checked the map again and had them move down the road fifty feet or so—then backtrack through the same field going toward the river. Seth scanned the dirt and the thin, patchy grass—following the light from Isabel's headlamp.

"There," Isabel said—Seth stopping in front of her—looking over the illuminated ground. "To the right—keep going."

They found the purple flag with a circle of loose dirt next to it.

"Go ahead, Benjy," Isabel said.

Benjy kneeled down—tried to stick his hand through the dirt—hit something just a couple inches below the surface—found the edge and lifted a piece of plywood with soil piled on top of it—then reached into the hole and pulled out a small black case. Seth watched Benjy unzip it and look inside—watched him smile wide as he pulled out two banded bundles of cash.

"We'll count it back at camp," Isabel said—Seth seeing the beam of light swing to their right—then to their left as Isabel looked around. "Let's go."

They tossed the shrink-wrapped blocks of ketamine lozenges into the hole—slid the plywood back over it—Seth kneeling down to spread the dirt out on top of the wood—to make at least some attempt at concealing the hole—then seeing Isabel and Benjy already walking away when he stood back up.

Spoon was asleep in the sand when they got back. He'd thrown most of the wood on the fire already—flames nearly six feet tall as the wood crackled and hissed.

Seth watched Benjy take the money from the small case and transfer it to a duffel bag he'd been carrying—then watched him walk over to where Spoon was sleeping and throw the empty black case down onto the skinny boy's face—Spoon screaming as he tried to get to his feet—Benjy

laughing hard as he doubled over and grabbed his knees—
holding tight to the duffel bag.

Seth looked over and saw Isabel with one of the pistols
raised—pointed at Benjy—her angry brown eyes staring at
him as he continued laughing—as he casually stepped back
to the other side of the fire—plopping himself down in the
sand with the duffel bag across his lap. She kept the pistol
on him as he pulled out the money and counted it—as he
refused to tell her how much there was.

9

IT WAS RAINING THE NEXT MORNING WHEN SETH woke up—staying in his sleeping bag as he yawned and stretched—his eyes still closed—listening to the rain hit his tent—feeling the cool air on his face that blew in through the vents—squeezing the sleeping bag tight around his neck.

After a few minutes he reached up and felt his hair—thought about how long it'd been since he'd washed it—rubbed his sand-covered ankles together at the bottom of the sleeping bag.

He lay there a while just listening to the rain—opening his eyes and blinking until his vision cleared—watching the drops coalesce and drip down the sides of his tent. Finally he unzipped the door to his tent and looked around—saw Benjy's and Spoon's tents still closed up—Isabel's tent nowhere nearby—saw the fire was out—still smoking a little up through the rain—coming down now in a light mist.

He crawled out and stood up—felt the rain soaking his hair and running down his cheeks—felt the cool breeze gaining strength as he turned toward the river and saw Isabel—sitting in the front seat of the green canoe.

Seth walked over and stood next to her—a clear poncho draped over her head and huddled body—sweatshirt and long pants underneath—one of the pistols in her lap—her head tilted with the poncho's hood pulled down low—eyes staring down at the barrel. Seth waited—watched her gently move her hands over the grip—eventually looking up at him—squinting as he saw the mist hitting her face and eyelashes.

"This is still the reservation," she said—turning suddenly to look out over the trees and the sand around their camp. "The edge of it."

Seth didn't say anything—just stood there letting the mist soak his shirt until it started clinging to his back.

"I was sixteen," Isabel continued. "Sixteen." She paused—looked down at her hands. "I used to watch TV all night—waiting to see my picture pop onto the screen because somebody was looking for me—then years passed—so much time I thought they'd have to include one of those drawings of what I should like all grown up—but nobody ever looked—so then I just stopped—gave up." She raised her head and looked downriver—turning away from Seth as he stood there above her—crossing his arms and shifting his feet in the wet sand.

"Nobody's looking for me either," Seth said. "Or if they are it's just because they think I stole my boss's pickup."

Isabel looked up at him—almost smiled but instead she looked away again—stood up and stepped out of the canoe—Seth holding out his hand but she didn't take it.

"Hey," Seth said—Isabel already walking away. "Can I borrow your soap?"

She turned and smiled. "Sure—just make sure to buy some more when you go shopping later today."

SETH WALKED UP OUT OF THE WATER AFTER WASHING himself—cold as he saw Isabel getting another fire going—huddled over the smoking bundle of twigs in her plastic poncho. He wrung out his wet blue jeans as best he could—then walked up onto the sand and slipped them on—still no sign of Spoon or Benjy as he looked around.

Seth rolled up the ends of his cut-off jeans to above his knees—then tightened his belt—went to his tent and took a dry shirt out of his backpack—checked the cellphone and saw the battery was dead.

He put on the dry shirt—crawled out of his tent and walked over to the fire. It wasn't raining anymore—sun had been up for a couple hours but remained hidden behind heavy clouds—Seth looking up to see if there were any patches of blue sky visible—any sunshine breaking through—shining somewhere nearby.

"Here," Isabel said from the log she was sitting on—holding out a cup to Seth—steam rising off it.

"Thanks," he said—taking the cup as he stepped closer to the fire—leaning over the flames with his free hand stretched out—lifting each foot over the hot coals around the edges.

"Did you bring a jacket?" Isabel said—looking up at him as he shook his head. "Sandals? Those boots of yours are just about useless out here." He shook his head again—still hovering over the fire. "You bring another pair of pants at least?"

Seth took a drink from the cup—feeling the hot, bitter coffee coat his throat—no milk or sugar—shaking his head again—again without looking at Isabel—holding the cup in both hands—keeping it close to his mouth.

"Those two idiots did't bring anything either—you'll have to buy it all in town today."

Seth stood there looking down at the fire—taking hot gulps of coffee every couple seconds until the cup was empty—then stood up straight and turned around so his back faced the fire—looked up at the sky again—finding a small patch of blue this time—off in the distance to the south.

"OK," he said. "I will." He looked down at Isabel—saw her knees dancing up and down—her eyes staring into the fire. "But all that stuff's gonna be heavy—you wanna come with me?"

"I can't carry much with this in my hand." She held up the pistol under the poncho. "Plus I'm not sure how he'd feel about two of us going."

Seth nodded—turned slowly back around to face the fire.

"OK," Isabel said.

Seth stared at the jumping flames—felt the hot, wet denim sticking to his legs and smiled. "OK."

The clouds started to break apart later that morning—Seth eating a protein bar as they all sat around the fire—then opening another an hour later while Spoon filtered water into plastic bottles.

They packed up and started paddling several hours before noon—Seth keeping Isabel and the red canoe within sight just like the day before.

"He call you yet?" Spoon said as Seth opened yet another protein bar. "Isabel told me about the cellphone."

Seth looked at the back of the skinny boy's head—tried using his teeth to tear open the wrapper—his paddle in his lap. "No."

Seth let the canoe float down the river as he ate the protein bar—then pulled the cellphone and the solar charger out of his backpack—connected them and laid the solar panel out on top of the tarp—canoe starting to twist around just as he sat back in his seat—Spoon unable to control it by himself—Seth forced to start paddling again from the stern.

"Had any service yet?"

"Nope," Seth said—looking around at the riverbanks and the trees—the fields he knew stretched out on both sides—then looking ahead of them at a bend in the river—watching the red canoe slip around it and out of view.

They paddled hard for a few more hours—pulling close to the red canoe as they neared a long sandbar on the north side of the river. Seth didn't see any trees around as he watched Isabel pulling toward it—didn't see any driftwood they could build a fire with—nothing but sand—a steep bank and empty expanse beyond.

"Ain't the most cozy spot," Spoon said—hesitating with his paddle out of the water as he looked around.

"It'll do," Seth said—spurring the skinny boy to paddle harder—to build some speed to help carry them up onto the sandy shore.

They pulled up next to the red canoe—coming to a sudden stop as they both jumped out—pushed and pulled the green canoe as far as they could—Benjy still hammering the red canoe's rebar anchor—dropping the hammer to the sand once he finished. Seth walked over and picked it up—hammered in the other anchor and tied it to the green canoe—then walked up the sandbank to where Isabel was setting up her tent.

"You sure this is a good place?" he said—looking down at Isabel where she sat in the sand—fitting together the poles for her tent.

"Yeah," she said—looking up at Seth—brown eyes squinting underneath her hat.

Seth moved to the side so she wouldn't be facing the sun. "Seems a little out in the open."

"Yeah," Isabel said—raising her eyebrows and nodding her head—still working on her tent—standing up and brushing the sand from her pants—then unfolding the fabric and fitting the poles through loops spaced a foot or so apart.

"There's a road right over there," she said. "We'll go to town and get back before dark."

"OK," Seth said. "Culbertson?"

"Yep."

"OK."

They soon finished setting up camp—forming a square with their tents. In the center they dug a little pit in the sand—then went searching for scraps of wood—sticks and a few pieces of driftwood they found hidden in a little cove a few hundred yards downriver.

Seth stood next to his tent and looked around—sweating in the afternoon heat—the lack of shade on the sandbar— hot wind making his shirt flap—lifting the frayed edges of his blue jean hat.

"We're going to the store," Isabel said. "We'll be back before dark."

"You're going too?" Spoon said—all of them standing around the makeshift fire pit—Benjy still with the T-shirt wrapped around his head—Spoon standing there bare-chested with his ribs all poking out.

"We need to pick up a few extra things—he can't carry it all by himself."

"Well," Spoon said—shrugging his bony shoulders. "As long as you get me that ribeye—don't matter to me."

Benjy didn't say anything—went to his tent and took off his boots—then crawled inside and zippered the door shut.

Isabel slipped one of the pistols inside her backpack— then swung it around and stuck her arms through the straps. Seth went to get his backpack from the green canoe—made sure everything was still there—then put the cellphone in his pocket and hurried back to the little pit at the center of their tents.

"Benjy thinks you're gonna run off," Spoon said—lying on his back in his tent with the door open—his hands behind his head and his eyes closed. "Together."

"I said we'll be back before dark," Isabel said. "So we'll be back before dark."

"I know," Spoon said.

ISABEL AND SETH WALKED AWAY FROM CAMP TOGETHER —climbed the steep riverbank and looked out over a barren field. Seth stood behind Isabel a step or two—looked down and saw a pistol grip sticking out of her pocket—saw bandages all over her hands—skin of her arms darkened by the sun—darkest at the tops of her shoulders—thin line of pale skin showing at the edges of her shirt.

They started walking again—perpendicular to the river and straight through the field—sand quickly turning to dirt with thin patches of grass—sagebrush and a few trees way off in the distance.

Seth saw a field of what looked to him like sorghum as they approached a thin tree line—leaves of all the stunted plants a light green color. Then he saw the road.

"How far is it?" Seth said.

"Maybe a couple miles."

"You ever been there before? To Culbertson?"

"Maybe when I was little," Isabel said. "Can't remember ever being there—but it's possible."

Soon they stepped onto the gravel road that led into town—each taking one of the ruts where tires had packed and pulverized the rocks. It was still sunny with no shade along the road—hot with a constant dry wind blowing gravel dust and dirt all around them.

Isabel took a bottle of water from her backpack and drank—then passed it to Seth.

"What about you?" Isabel said as Seth finished what she'd left him in the bottle. "Wrong place wrong time? That how you ended up here?"

"Yeah—I guess so."

Seth looked up at the sky—round, bubbly clouds lined up almost in formation—the two of them walking on for a few minutes in silence.

"You know how ridiculous you look, right?" Isabel said—looking him up and down.

"What?" Seth said—spreading his arms wide—turning toward her with a smile on his face. "It's not so bad—more of a functional look, I guess."

"Like those boots?"

"Well," he said. "I didn't really have a choice."

"Ricky should've had some tennis shoes in the closet."

"I didn't find any."

They walked on down the road—Seth glancing over at Isabel after a while—seeing the smile gone from her face.

Soon they came to an intersection without any road signs—heavy fence posts marking the corners of two pastures—barbed-wire fences stretching as far as they could see. Isabel turned left and Seth followed—walking beside each other down another gravel road—wider than the first and in better condition.

"So you two were together?" Seth said.

"Yeah," Isabel said without turning her head. "I guess."

They walked on—an old pickup passing them a few minutes later—in a hurry going back the way they'd come—forcing them both to step off the road into the shallow ditches on each side—standing there as the pickup slowed—windows down and the body rusting away from the bottom up—an older man behind the wheel—glaring at them as he passed.

"I'm sorry about what happened to him," Seth said—resuming their walk down the road—waiting for the pickup's dust cloud to clear.

"It's alright," Isabel said—again not turning her head. "You didn't do it."

The gravel road soon turned into a paved highway—

yellow centerline faded and missing altogether in places—the town of Culbertson just up ahead. Seth wiped a few drops of sweat from his face—took his blue jean hat off and stuffed it in his back pocket—looked down at his cut-off jeans and his boots—the bared, cracked skin of his kneecaps between.

"He was from California," Isabel said. "Always talked about us going out there once we had enough money saved up."

Seth stayed quiet—not sure what to say—whether or not there was something he could or should say.

They were silent the rest of the way into town—kept walking and soon they were on sidewalks—surrounded by buildings and parking lots. The buildings were mostly empty—two and three stories high. They looked in some of the windows—stopped at corners and looked in all directions—Isabel saying they had to find a place that sold clothes before going to the grocery store.

"Here," Isabel said—hurrying across an empty street.

Seth had to jog to keep up—his feet hot and sweaty inside his boots—at least one blister already starting to form on each heal.

He followed Isabel through a glass door—triggering bells above their heads—then stood there letting his eyes adjust to the indoor light—feeling a fan blowing on him but he couldn't tell where it was coming from—turning to his right as Isabel stepped forward—seeing a middle-aged woman sitting behind a counter—a cash register and a small fan on a shelf behind her. Seth could smell her perfume in the air—blowing across his face as she smiled at him—looking at his face and his hair—then down at his bare shins.

"Here," Isabel said—Seth turning again—seeing her coming up to him holding a few shirts on hangers—picking one out and pressing it against his chest. "Try this one on."

"Oh yeah," the woman behind the counter said. "Nice shirt—that one's a nice, nice shirt."

Seth grabbed it—looked around and then started taking off the shirt he was wearing.

"No," Isabel said.

"It's fine—fine—it's fine," the woman said—waving a pudgy hand behind the counter.

Isabel pointed to the fitting room near the back of the store—giving Seth a playful shove and a smile—making eye contact before he went and tried on the shirt—hurriedly walking back out to show her how it looked.

"Oh yeah," the woman said as he came out of the fitting room—leaning over the counter now—talking to Isabel. "Nice shirt. I believe that come from the pile John Travolta brought in years and years ago. Nice, nice shirt—movie star shirt."

"Really?" Isabel said—turning toward Seth—raising her eyebrows and smiling again.

"Oh yeah. He wore it in all his movies—favorite shirt of his for a long time, what he told me."

"So it's used?" Isabel said.

"Well—"

"I don't think we want it if it's used."

"No but he'd only wear it for one scene—then have somebody come by and take it and he'd just sit there or walk around without a shirt. He did that—went around shirtless a lot—come in here shirtless even."

Seth walked up and allowed Isabel to inspect him—felt her turning him and tugging on the shirt—smoothing out the shoulders—taking her time. It didn't fit quite right, she said—telling him to go back into the fitting room and take it off—Seth hearing her start to haggle with the woman about the price as he walked away.

He came out of the fitting room in the same sweaty shirt he'd walked into the little shop wearing—carrying the Travolta shirt on its hanger out in front of him as he walked toward the counter.

"Here," Isabel said—tossing him a pair of light blue slacks. "You can put the shirt back on—I think it goes with those pants."

"What?"

"They're your new clothes," Isabel said—waving him back to the fitting room. "Go on."

Seth came out a couple minutes later wearing the new pants and shirt—still wearing his boots with no socks. They said goodbye to the woman behind the counter—left the store with a plastic bag full of more clothes—Seth taking the bag from Isabel once they were outside—looking inside at a few pairs of slip-on shoes, long-sleeved T-shirts and athletic shorts—three baseball caps with logos for local businesses and two pairs of sunglasses.

They walked down the sidewalk as Seth examined the items in the bag—stopping at the next corner where Isabel made Seth spin around for her—clapping her hands as he struck a pose. They both laughed as the sun dipped behind the tallest buildings—shading parts of the empty streets— both of them still laughing as they talked about the funny woman behind the counter—as they recounted the John Travolta story she'd told them—still laughing as they started walking again.

For a few blocks they just walked—walked through a town together—feeling the hot day just starting to cool—mirage of possibilities briefly seeming real—feeling young and strong and free—capable of anything. It wasn't until they were almost out of town that they remembered about the groceries—turning around and walking back—looking for a grocery store as they retraced their steps.

"You hungry?" Seth said—looking at Isabel as they hurried along a sidewalk close to where they'd bought the clothes—trying to slow her down—to recapture that feeling of freedom.

"Yeah," Isabel said—her eyes darting all around—still

trying to locate a grocery store. "But we should hurry if we're gonna make it back before dark."

Seth looked up at the sky—shielding his eyes from the sun. "We got time," he said. "Come on." He cut in front of Isabel—making her stop as he held his hand out for her to grab—waiting as she looked down at it—as she looked around at the empty storefronts.

"This is a bad idea," she said—grabbing his hand and following him across the street—hurrying down a sunlit alley that cut between two brick buildings.

Seth led them through town without any idea where he was going—somehow finding the pizza place Benjy had talked about—walking in and seeing shelves of DVDs along one wall—cash register in the middle and a few tables near the big front windows. Seth stood beside Isabel as she ordered—then leaned forward and paid before she had a chance.

"This isn't a date, you know," Isabel said—slipping off her backpack as she walked to a table in the corner.

"I know."

"We need to hurry if we're gonna get back before dark."

"I know," Seth said—smiling as he sat down across from her—Isabel turning to look out the window.

They sat there and waited—a girl bringing out their pizza a few minutes later—Seth going to refill his soda—then returning to the table to find a slice of pizza already on his plate—the two of them eating three slices each without talking—both hungrier than they'd realized.

"You never told me how you got mixed up in all this," Seth said—leaning back as he lifted his paper cup off the table.

Isabel finished chewing—looking down at her plate—then out the window again. "I grew up in a bunch of foster homes—on reservations it's a law that Indian kids have to be placed with Indian foster parents." She leaned back in her chair—rubbed her forehead as she kept staring out the window—Seth noticing how tired she was. "Sometimes they didn't feed us—sometimes it was four to a bed—never bought us shoes—stuff I'm sure you never had to deal with."

Isabel took another bite of pizza—Seth sitting there watching her chew—waiting and staying quiet—still hungry but he left the last two pieces on the platter.

"So one day I'm walking home from school," she continued. "And he pulls up—tells me to get in the car—really nice car I remember—red Lexus."

"He just told you to get in?"

"Yeah—just stopped in the middle of the road and rolled down his window—even knew my name somehow."

"Why'd you get in?"

"Nothing to lose, I guess." Isabel shrugged her shoulders. "Some of the things that happened—growing up like that." She kept looking out the window—pausing before she took another bite of pizza—then chewed slowly before swallowing. "It didn't matter to me where I went—what I did—who I ended up with."

Isabel made Seth finish the last two slices—then asked the girl who'd brought their pizza where a grocery store was—slipped on her backpack and left the restaurant— walking in front of Seth as they made their way down the sidewalks.

It was still hot outside but the shadows were getting longer—sunlight more golden in color now as it bounced off all the brick buildings. Seth rolled up the sleeves of his new shirt—carried the plastic bag with the other clothes inside—watched Isabel and tried to match her pace—her angry, silent march through a near-empty town.

They found the grocery store a few blocks away—Seth pushing a cart through the sliding glass doors—following Isabel around the aisles—fluorescent lights overhead and cheap, dirty tiles underfoot. Isabel stacked cans of soup in the front half of the cart—then protein bars, sunscreen and toilet paper. After the cart was full she led Seth to the back of the store—spent a few minutes inspecting steaks at the meat counter.

"Get one for each of us," Seth said. "I got the money."

"I know," Isabel said—peering through the curved glass at the different cuts—labels with hand-drawn prices at the bottom. "It's gonna be a long trip, though."

Isabel asked the butcher for two of the cheapest steaks—watched him wrap the two cuts of raw meat in waxed paper before handing them to her over the counter. She set the steaks on top of the cans of soup—then rushed off to the other end of the store—Seth pushing the heavy cart after her—cans of soup bouncing and shaking—one of the steaks nearly falling to the floor. He found her looking at bottles of body soap—her hair hanging down around her face as she read one of the labels.

"You boys stink," she said—setting the bottle back on the shelf—looking at him as she reached for a larger bottle near the floor. "Better get the big one."

They paid and wheeled the cart outside—Seth lifting the plastic bags out of the cart and setting them down in the parking lot—sun setting in front of them as they tried to decide how to carry everything—stuffing their backpacks full to start—then Seth stepping over to pick up the rest of the bags still on the ground—stopping suddenly as Isabel cut in front of him—watching her as she picked up half the remaining bags and walked off by herself.

They started down the highway toward the river—no cars around as they left the small town—sun nearly gone as it burned big and golden in the western sky—Seth looking to the east and seeing the moon rising—then looking back toward the setting sun—cicadas jumping and buzzing in the soft evening light—playing together in the grass at the edge of the road.

"We should've bought bug spray," Isabel said as she inspected the back of her arm.

"Maybe next time."

"Yeah," she said—looking at Seth in the fading light—then looking away. "We'll have to be a little more organized next time."

"I guess so," Seth said. "But I've been having fun doing it this way."

They walked on—another twenty minutes and they could see the river—leaving the gravel road as the first batch of stars started shining—winding their way through the fallow field—birds flying up into the sky together when Seth and Isabel passed by a heavy clump of sagebrush—watching from above as the pair continued on toward the river—then coming down to settle themselves back into the thick branches.

10

IT WAS DARK BY THE TIME SETH AND ISABEL REACHED
the steep riverbank—descending carefully as the dirt
quickly turned to loose sand—hands still gripping the grocery bags—heavy backpacks still hanging from their shoulders. They looked up toward the fire and their tents once
they reached the bottom—still walking but stopping when
they saw an old man—sunburned with a gray mustache
and cowboy hat—holding a pump shotgun where he stood
near the stack of firewood. Seth followed the barrel down
to Spoon and Benjy—their heads down as they sat side-by-
side on the sand—the old man turning his head to look at
Isabel—then Seth.

Seth could hear Isabel breathing beside him—could
hear the river and the crackling fire—birds in the fallow field
behind them—bickering inside the sagebrush. He stepped
forward after a few silent seconds had passed—lifted the
grocery bags slowly with each hand—then started walking
toward the old man—watching him turn and back up a

couple steps—swinging the shotgun away from Spoon and Benjy—pointing it now toward Seth's midsection—Seth still watching the man's blue eyes—his hand and fingers wrapped around the trigger—still walking until he was within four or five feet of the old man—setting the grocery bags down once he finally stopped.

"You hungry?" Seth said—taking a slow, casual breath as he wiped his forehead—smiling as the old man glared at him.

"Get off my property," the old man said.

"We were planning to leave in the morning."

"Just think of it as a head start then."

Seth looked down at the old man's hand—thick with short fingers—skin dry and cracked with red and white knuckles.

"OK," Seth said—raising his hands slowly—taking a careful step forward. "But how do we know this is your property?"

"It's mine. You just stay right there or it won't matter noway."

"OK." Seth backed up half a step—raising his hands a little higher. "You married?"

"What?" The man lowered the shotgun an inch or two— cocked his head to the side.

"Do you have a wife?"

"Just get the hell outta here before I shoot you." The man looked back over his shoulder at Benjy and Spoon. "All of y—"

Seth sprang forward—grabbed the barrel of the shotgun with both hands—ripped it away and to his left—knowing Isabel was behind him to his right. He felt the old man lose his grip—then brought his hands together near the bottom of the barrel—stepped forward and used the shotgun as a club to hit the old man across the shoulder. The old man fell to the ground—his cowboy hat tumbling a couple times in the sand. Seth again stepped forward—put his foot on the old man's chest—pointed the shotgun down at his weathered face—almost touching the old man's nose.

"Don't, Seth," Isabel said—close behind him but he didn't look back. "Seth."

Seth pulled the trigger—heard the gun click but not fire—looked down at the old man's face—wet eyes and open mouth—chest rising and falling.

"Seth!" Isabel yelled.

Seth turned his head and looked at her—then felt himself fly backward—felt his limbs fly out loosely in all directions—then felt his body hit the sand with someone on top of him.

"Shoot him, Isabel!" Benjy yelled—flipping Seth over— then trying to pull his hands together behind his back—one of his knees pressing down on Seth's spine. "Shoot him—he ain't gonna listen—not to any of us," the stocky boy said— softer now as he looked up at Isabel—Seth struggling to breath—feeling his ribs ache as he tried to free himself. "Shoot him now before he gets one of us killed—we'll manage without him."

Seth raised his head and saw Isabel picking up the shotgun—made eye contact with her as she stood up straight— as she stared down at him—holding the shotgun tight now with both hands—letting it point down to the ground.

"Sorry, sir," Spoon said—hurrying over to the old man.

Seth tried to roll over but Benjy kept him pinned to the ground—struggled against the weight of the stocky boy until he gave up—laid his head down in the sand—trying to catch his breath as he looked up at Isabel—at the full moon behind her—craters and strange lines that covered the lunar surface—the brightness of it lighting up the sandbar—Seth twisting his head to see Spoon helping the old man to his feet.

"He's got some mental problems," Spoon continued.

"Twerp almost killed me!" the old man said—bending down slowly to pick up his hat.

"Yeah that's right, sir—that's right," Spoon said. "But you did point that scattergun at him first. Now with him being crazy and you putting that thing in his face like you did, I think this turned out pretty well."

The old man stood there breathing—putting on his hat and adjusting it constantly—looking down at Seth where he was pinned to the sand.

"I'm calling the police," the old man said—then turned to Isabel. "Gimme that." He started walking toward her.

"Well, now, wait a minute," Spoon said. "Everybody, let's just hold on—I'll cook up some steaks. Isabel, y'all got steaks, right?"

Seth felt Benjy suddenly release his hands—felt him stand up and then saw him running toward the canoes. Seth stood up as he turned to watch the old man walking toward Isabel—as Isabel pumped the shotgun—as she pumped it again and looked inside the chamber—Seth still watching her as she started shuffling backward—finally taking a step but stumbling in his new slip-on shoes—recovering and then running toward the old man as he saw Benjy coming back from the canoes.

"Benjy!" Spoon yelled.

Seth saw Benjy with the hammer in his hand—running up behind the old man—lifting the hammer as he got close.

There was a hollow thud—a cracking sound as the old man's body leaned to one side—as his head came down in the sand near Seth's feet. Seth looked down at the old man's gray hair—saw crimson-colored blood spattered down his neck—a white spot of skull—something pink inside the open hole.

The old man's cowboy hat was resting in the sand a few feet away—speckles of blood on the brim.

"Not good," Spoon said—shaking his head and looking all around—breathing hard. "Not good at all." He put his hands on his head—took a step or two in one direction—then turned and started off in another.

Seth looked at Benjy—standing there holding the hammer—looking back at Seth with a strange smile on his face—breathing hard and sweating. Seth looked down at his hand—saw his knuckles white as his stubby fingers gripped the hammer—dancing the head of the hammer up and down as he flexed his thick wrist.

"Drop it," Isabel said—ditching the shotgun and raising one of the pistols.

"Benjy," Spoon said. "Don't do it, man—don't do it don't do it don't do it—" He kept repeating the phrase as he paced back and forth—hands running constantly through his hair.

"Drop the hammer, Benjy," Isabel said—Benjy turning his head to look at her. "Drop it."

Benjy turned back to Seth—strange smile still on his sweaty red face. He underhand-tossed the hammer as hard as he could without winding up—wooden handle hitting Seth in the arm before falling to the sand—then walked off toward the smoldering fire—Spoon hurrying to catch up to him—dropping his hands to his sides finally—talking to Benjy but Seth couldn't make out what he was saying.

Isabel walked over to Seth—pistol still in her hand—watching Spoon and Benjy as they threw wood onto the fire together. After standing there a little while she stuffed the pistol into the waistband of her pants—looked down at the dead old man—thick pool of blood slowly draining into the sand—then looked up at Seth and studied his eyes and cheeks—the specks of blood on his new shirt—sand on his pants and in his hair.

"You need to clean your face," Isabel said—then turned and started walking toward the fire—new flames reaching skyward now as Spoon carefully arranged more sticks on top.

SETH STOOD THERE WATCHING THE THREE OF THEM—each taking a seat on a log—forming a circle around the fire—talking quietly together as he stood there alone—dropping his head after a few minutes to look down at the old man's body—at the matted gray hair—remembering the old man's face—angry, scared eyes that had stared at him over the shotgun just minutes before.

Seth looked away—up at the stars—over at the scarred riverbank—then started walking toward the river.

The full moon shined across the river's surface—shined on Seth kneeling down in the wet sand along the shoreline—lifting some water in his cupped hands—splashing it over his face—wiping his cheeks and his forehead—then wiping his mouth and chin on his shirt. He looked out over the river—the steep bank on the other side—tops of the few trees along the horizon.

"Seth," Isabel called—Seth turning around—seeing her looking at him—firelight illuminating her face—her log a little farther from Benjy's than it was from Spoon's.

Seth walked over and stood above them—watching Isabel's hands in her lap—her knees bouncing up and down—goosebumps on her bare arms.

"We need to figure out what to do," she said—looking up at him as Seth nodded. "The old man's pickup is over there." She turned and pointed.

Seth stood there and waited—looked over at Benjy keeping his eyes on the ground—Spoon snapping bits off a stick and throwing them into the fire—then turned back to Isabel and watched her rubbing her forehead with her knuckles—her hair still pulled back even though she was cold.

Seth walked around to the other side of the fire—took a seat on the ground where he could still see everyone—listened to the small fire hiss as they all tried to think.

"The gun," Benjy said—breaking the silence. "Why don't

we put that shotgun in his hands—set him up like he killed himself?"

"No," Isabel said. "Anyone could tell he was hit with something."

They were all quiet again for a few minutes—Spoon grabbing another stick to break apart—tossing the small pieces into the dwindling fire.

"What about the river?" Spoon said. "Put him in the pickup—sink it out where the water's deep."

"Not deep enough," Isabel said. "Plus whoever comes looking for him will see the tire tracks."

"We could rake the sand," Benjy said.

"No," Isabel said. "They'll be able to tell his pickup was here—go out and check the river first thing."

Seth watched Isabel as she stared into the fire—elbows on her knees with her hands still rubbing her face—pressing hard on her forehead until her skin turned red.

"Do you think the pickup we drove to the river is still where we left it?" Seth said.

"Should be."

"Two of us could drive up there in the old man's pickup—leave the body in the cab and park it in the same place in those trees. Then we could drive back here and pick up the canoes and everything—drive down the road a ways making whatever drops we need to along the way—get back on the river once we thought we were far enough away from here."

They sat there for another few minutes—everyone staring at the fire without saying anything—Spoon snapping the last bit off the stick he'd been working on—Benjy somehow still sweating—still flashing that strange smile every once in a while.

"Good," Isabel said. "But we'll have to meet downriver somewhere—too risky to come back here." She looked up at Seth before continuing. "You and Spoon go in the pickup—me and Benjy will get the canoes back on the water tonight."

Isabel stood up and walked past Seth—kept going as he turned to watch her—still watching as she walked past the old man's body and started up the crumbling bank—seeing above her the dark outline of a pickup—then watching her disappear behind it. He stood up as he heard a door squeak open—few seconds later the engine started—headlights came on and the pickup lurched forward—turned to descend the sandy riverbank.

"Nice plan, cap'n," Benjy said as he stood up—then walked around Seth with that smile on his red face. "This oughta be fun."

Benjy hurried over to the pile of firewood—picked up as many pieces as he could and carried them to the river—Seth watching him throw the pieces of driftwood out past the canoes—water splashing up in the moonlight as little waves rippled out.

"Let's get moving, boys," Benjy said as he started back toward the fire and the woodpile.

Seth turned his head and watched Isabel back the pickup up to the body—watched her get out and stand there ready to shut the driver's side door—looking at Seth as she held the door open.

Benjy walked in front of him with another load of broken branches—heading toward the canoes—Seth watching him march to the water's edge—then turning and jogging toward Isabel and the pickup.

"What the hell are you doing?" Seth said.

"Help me with this," Isabel said—indicating the old man's body lying face down in the sand.

"Why do you wanna go with Benjy?"

"I don't."

Seth waited for her to say something more—explain what she was thinking but she stayed quiet—looked off over the river.

Seth walked back and opened the tailgate—noticing

how old the pickup was—bench seat and short bed but the tailgate was in good shape—Seth looking down at the glossy paint—then bending down and grabbing the old man's shoulders—Isabel squatting to grab the feet—lifting the body onto the tailgate together—Isabel articulating the knees to set the legs down.

"Why'd you volunteer to take one of the canoes?" Seth said.

"Spoon can't make it," Isabel said—putting her hand down on the tailgate—finally turning to look at him. "I know how he gets—and you saw him back there."

"Why don't I go?"

"He'd kill you."

"Maybe I'd kill him."

"Yeah," she said. "Maybe you would."

Isabel pushed the old man's legs past the tailgate—Seth rolling the body over once before lifting the tailgate and slamming it shut—brake lights glowing red across their faces.

"I just don't want you to be out there with him alone," Seth said.

"Would I be safer with you? Driving around with a dead body in the back of a stolen pickup?"

Isabel walked around him—climbed back up into the driver's seat—Seth hearing her put the pickup in gear—seeing the tires start crawling forward through the sand—then turning his body to watch her drive toward the canoes—few seconds later hearing her shut off the engine before hopping back down to the ground—Spoon still sitting nearby on the same log—staring straight ahead without moving.

Seth looked up at the sky—saw the stars blinking in whites and yellows—one or two that seemed to give off an orange or even red color. When he looked back down Spoon wasn't sitting on the log anymore—wasn't near the old man's pickup or the canoes—Seth just starting to worry when he saw him walk back into the firelight a minute or two later—wearing some of the new clothes.

"What do y'all think?" Spoon said—showing off a pair of gray pants and a long-sleeve shirt—smiling as he held out his long, skinny arms.

Seth watched him march around in his new clothes—sticking his legs out and adjusting his belt—watched him smile and wondered how his mood could change so quickly.

"Better than before," Isabel said—carrying a stack of the shrink-wrapped blocks back to the pickup.

"Well I'm handsome in just about any attire," Spoon said—smiling still as he inspected his pants. "This'll sure do a better job of blocking the sun."

"What?" Benjy said—standing near the water still—only a couple sticks left in his hands.

"When we're paddling, dumbass." Spoon motioned with his arms. "Still got basically two months to go."

"Well you're not gonna get much sun in that pickup these next couple days," Benjy said—walking up to join the group. "Should've saved your fancy outfit."

"Oh I ain't going with Seth." Spoon squatted until he was nearly sitting on the ground—bounced a couple times and wiggled his legs—nodded as the new pants passed yet another test.

"Yes you are," Benjy said—turning to look at Isabel.

"You're liable to do something devious if either one of them goes with you—but since I already know all your tricks they won't work on me."

"You OK, Spoon?" Isabel said.

"Yeah I'm fine—great actually."

"No," Benjy said. "No—you're going with Seth."

"No I'm not—wouldn't be any help out there on the road if something happens—can't shoot a gun or even drive a stick shift—plus it'd be way less suspicious being a girl and a guy rather than two guys."

No one said anything after Spoon finished talking—Seth walking over and leaning against the side of the pickup—glancing at Isabel and Benjy.

"He's right," Isabel finally said—Seth seeing Benjy turn his head toward her—Isabel putting her hand on the pistol grip sticking out of her pocket. "We need to get going," she said—turning around and walking toward the driver's side door of the pickup.

Seth moved a couple steps down the side of the pickup—getting between Isabel and Benjy—watching the stocky boy clinch one hand into a fist—taking unsure steps as his face seemed to get redder and redder—trying to decide what to do.

"I'll drive," Isabel said—stepping back with the keys in her hand. "We all on the same page?"

"Yeah," Seth said.

Benjy didn't say anything—just looked at Isabel with his hands balled up into fists. Isabel leaned back against the pickup—casually pulling the pistol out of her pocket—holding it down by her side.

"Check out the look on her face, Benjy," Spoon said—walking up and putting his hands on Benjy's shoulders—pausing his inspection of his new clothes. "She means business—yes she does." Spoon stepped around Benjy and did a lunge between everyone—hands on his hips as he resumed testing the new pants. "Business, business, business," the skinny boy whispered to himself—still stretching—his toes now buried in the sand.

Seth kept watching Benjy as he walked over and picked up the dead man's hat and shotgun—watched him as he went to the canoes and got his and Isabel's backpacks.

Isabel told Benjy and Spoon they'd have to paddle the canoes solo into North Dakota—current slowing down to almost nothing once they got to Lake Sakakawea, she said. The plan was to meet there—outside a town called Williston.

Then Isabel told Seth how many more of the shrink-wrapped blocks they needed—Seth going back and forth loading them in the dead man's pickup with an eye on Benjy the whole time—making sure to take the blocks from the green canoe so Spoon had less weight to deal with.

11

ISABEL DROVE UP AND OVER THE STEEP BANK ONCE everything was loaded in the pickup—Seth turning to look back at Spoon and Benjy from the passenger's seat—his head sticking out the open window—suddenly exhausted as he swayed with the soft suspension of the dead old man's pickup.

Isabel stopped once they found the gravel road they'd walked down earlier—Seth getting out to unlock the two front hubs—Isabel shifting the pickup back into two-wheel drive. Then Seth hopped back up into the pickup and they drove on—picking up speed as Isabel switched on the headlights.

"What time is it?" Isabel said.

Seth pulled the cellphone from his backpack. "10:45," he said—checking the battery level before turning off the screen.

They drove out to an intersection and turned left—try-ing to avoid driving through the little town they'd visited earlier—Culbertson. The gravel road went on for a mile or so—Isabel driving slow as Seth tried to keep his eyes open—the road eventually making a sweeping curve to the left—eventually leading to a dead-end. Seth and Isabel looked through the windshield at the river in front of them—both well aware they'd just driven in a circle—were now just a hundred yards or so from where they'd tried to camp—where they'd met the old man—his lifeless body now lying all twisted in the bed of his own pickup.

Isabel turned the pickup around—no choice but to wind their way through town until they found a highway heading west.

"So who came up with the idea of making drops along the river?" Seth said. "You or him?"

"That's a stupid question."

"I just thought maybe you came up with it together."

"He doesn't usually go to other people for advice—or for anything, really."

Seth looked out the window—out at the moonlit landscape of sagebrush and sandy, barren soil—up at the stars too bright for even the full moon to hide. There were no lights in the cab of the old pickup—no green glow from a dash full of buttons and dials—nothing but moonlight to help him see Isabel's face when he turned back.

"You two seem to spend a lot of time together," Seth said.

"Right," Isabel said—chuckle in her voice as she steered the pickup around a curve. "And we have sex every night after dinner—that what you think?"

Seth didn't say anything—turned and looked back out the window.

"He's never tried anything like that," Isabel continued. "I'm not sure he likes girls—or guys, even."

"I just mean you seem to know him better than the rest of us."

"Right. Well, I guess I do—but he just likes to talk at night—to hear himself talking while I sit there and pretend to listen." She looked over at Seth. "Almost like he's trying to be a real person."

"What's he talk about?"

Isabel thought for a minute—adjusted her hands on the steering wheel—shifted a little in her seat.

"I don't really know," she said. "Everything, I guess—anything. I think it's sort of a way for him to put himself to sleep—just pretending to be a normal person exhausts him. He's usually asleep a few minutes after finishing one of those cans of soup."

They drove on—looking out at the edges of fields and pastures—barbed-wire fences and little groups of skinny trees—everything lit up by the pickup's headlights and the full moon. A small car passed them at one point—two spare tires on the right side—swerving over the yellow line once it got in front of them—then speeding off and over a distant hill.

"You can sleep if you want," Isabel said.

"I'm fine."

"It's gonna be another hour."

"That's all?" They looked at each other—Seth able to see Isabel's cheeks in the moonlight—her lips and her tired eyes—shape of her hair around her face. "Seems like we should've gone farther than that in three days."

"Yeah."

Seth looked back over his shoulder but couldn't see anything in the bed of the old man's pickup—no blood or blocks of ketamine lozenges—no old, contorted body.

"Has he called yet?"

"No."

Seth pulled out the cellphone again and tapped the screen—saw there were no missed calls but he finally had a good signal—saw there was enough battery for a while—then made sure the ringer was on before stuffing the phone back into his pocket.

They kept driving over the dark, empty road—Seth feeling his head drifting back every few minutes—feeling his eyes start to close before snapping his head forward—forcing his eyes open as wide as they'd go.

"You ever think about doing something else?" Seth said—trying hard to stay awake—looking over at Isabel as she cocked her head to the side.

"What do you mean?"

"I mean working someplace—getting a normal job."

"Oh," she said. "I guess so."

"What would you do?"

Isabel looked at him. "What would you do?"

They each shrugged—smiled as they stared out the windshield—then drove on in silence for a while.

Soon they pulled off the highway onto a gravel road—few minutes later leaving the road at a place where tire tracks could just barely be seen—Isabel turning the headlights off—driving slow over short grass and between clumps of sagebrush—then around a large group of trees—Seth spotting the little passage through the cottonwoods and the underbrush—grass worn down in a curved line leading out of the trees to the river.

Isabel parked next to the dark tunnel that led through the trees—shut the engine off and looked around.

"Are the keys in it?" Seth said—peering into the tunnel— trying to see if the blue dually pickup was still parked inside.

"Should be."

Isabel reached down and picked up one of the pistols from the floorboard—held it out to Seth across the bench seat.

"Here," she said—looking through the back window now.

Seth took the pistol—keeping his eyes on Isabel— watching her as she turned to look out the windshield—long hair covering the side of her face—tears forming in her eyes as she held back a yawn.

"Back the pickup out of there," she said—still not looking at him. "We can load everything here."

"Sounds good."

Seth jumped out of the old man's pickup and started for the trees—glancing over at the moonlight shining on the river—dry pasture on the other side covered with the angled shadows of more cottonwoods and brush. He came up to the trees and looked down—just able to make out the tire tracks from three days before—stepping over them as he entered the tunnel—unable to see anything after just ten feet.

He pulled the cellphone from his pocket—found the phone's flashlight and turned it on—continued walking but faster now that he could see where he was going—seeing cottonwoods rising up on each side of him—coming together fifteen or twenty feet in the air—grass quickly disappearing from the ground—Seth shining the cellphone's flashlight down on bare dirt—walking alone in the silence and the dark.

He saw the cellphone's screen light up before it started ringing—vibrating in his hand as he stopped and stood there on the dry dirt—looking down at the screen—letting it ring for several seconds—taking a deep breath as he let it keep ringing until he almost missed the call.

"Hello."

"Hello, Seth," the man said—then paused for a moment—Seth standing there with the cellphone up to his ear—his hand partially covering the flashlight. "You know people kill themselves every day, Seth," the man continued. "Sometimes they even kill other people before terminating their own existence. I've never understood that."

Seth stayed silent—walked forward a few steps in the dark—moved his hand and cocked his head to the side— shining the cellphone's light down the path.

"Are you there, Seth?"

"Yeah—yessir."

"It's important, Seth—what we're doing is important. We're helping people—you understand that, don't you, Seth?"

"Yessir." Seth stood there—walked in a little circle in the dirt and waited.

"That's good—good, Seth." The man paused—breathed into the phone. "Have you had intercourse with Isabel since leaving the house?"

"No. No I—"

"You will—be patient and you will. She seems to like that sort of thing."

Seth didn't say anything—inching his way down the path toward the blue dually pickup—waiting for the man to finish talking.

"And what of Benjamin and Bertram? No major issues?"

"No—no, sir."

"Good," the man said—then paused for what seemed like a long time. "It's not easy, is it? Leading an expedition such as this."

"No, sir."

"Constant pain is the only way to really live, Seth—remember that—pain denotes growth. Lavoisier said nothing truly new is ever created—therefore everything you want you have to take from somebody else—money, power, freedom, people—we all have to be thieves—and being a thief can be quite painful."

"Not everybody's like that."

"No—that's true, they're not—but those are the cowards, Seth—the ones that exist only as podiums for the rest of us to stand upon."

"That why we killed all those people in Kansas City?"

"You killed those people, Seth—because you're not a coward—not anymore."

Seth kept inching his way closer to the pickup—shuffling his feet over the sandy soil. He felt his foot kick a pile of dry leaves and jumped—then bent down and held the cellphone out to make sure there was nothing on the ground.

"I will call you again, Seth," the man said before hanging up.

Seth looked at the screen—watched the call end as he heard the cellphone beep—then watched the screen fade out before pointing the flashlight down the tunnel again—seeing the pickup just twenty feet in front of him.

"WHAT THE HELL TOOK YOU SO LONG?" ISABEL SAID— standing near the old man's pickup—Seth looking back at her out the open driver's side window of the blue dually— still backing out of the tunnel of trees and brush.

"He called."

Seth hopped down out of the driver's seat—walked back to the old man's pickup and grabbed the handle to open the tailgate—Isabel moving a couple steps to give him space— Seth reaching into the bed without looking at her—lifting two of the shrink-wrapped blocks and turning around.

"What'd he say?" Isabel said as she leaned in beside him—grabbing two more blocks before turning and following Seth to the blue dually.

"Just asked about the weather—gave me some updates on how the baseball season's going."

"I still have one of the pistols, you know."

"He just rambled mostly—something about people being cowards."

"What'd you tell him?"

"I told him everything was fine."

They finished loading the ketamine blocks—then went back and rummaged through the cab of the old man's pickup—grabbing their backpacks and searching for anything they might've left behind—then walked around to the tailgate.

"I'll do it," Seth said—lifting and slamming the old tailgate shut.

Seth handed Isabel the backpacks—made sure the pistol she'd given him was still in his pocket—then went around and climbed up into the driver's seat of the old man's pickup—drove through the tunnel of cottonwoods and parked it at the end—turned off the engine and sat there—looking down at the empty bench seat beside him.

Seth felt his way in the dark to the back of the pickup—pulled the old man's body out of the bed by the ankles—turned it and wrapped his arms around the soft stomach—leaned back and took the body's weight—surprised by how much heavier it seemed than the bodies he'd had to carry that first night in Missouri—straining as he carried the dead old man around to the open passenger's side door—then dropped the body face down on the bench seat—picked up the legs and pushed them inside—shoved the body forward along the seat—then slammed the door shut.

He used the cellphone's flashlight again as he jogged back out of the tunnel—lighting up the uneven ground littered with branches and piles of dead leaves—looking up and walking once he saw the blue dually—seeing Isabel already in the driver's seat—gripping the steering wheel with both hands—Seth turning off the flashlight as he went around and opened the passenger's side door.

"Let's go," Seth said—breathing hard as the dome light slowly faded—as he pulled the seatbelt strap across his chest—making sure his door was locked and his window was up.

They drove through the dark night—clouds now covering the full moon and most of the stars—drove over the empty roads toward the house—just enough time for Seth to start relaxing before they were pulling into the driveway—driving past the open gate.

The wind was blowing when Seth opened the passenger's side door—pushing it open as he gripped the handle tight—stepping down onto the gravel before fighting the door closed. He looked up but couldn't see any stars in the sky—full moon barely visible through the thickening clouds.

"It's gonna rain," Isabel said—standing in the driveway between the pickup and the house—her hair flipping around in the wind.

Seth grabbed their backpacks and went inside—searched the living room until he found a cellphone charger—plugged the phone in and set it on the coffee table—then went to the kitchen where he saw Isabel standing on the countertop—looking through the cabinets for food.

"Don't tell me all we got is cans of soup."

"No," Isabel said. "I think we can make something work." She looked down at Seth and tossed him a bag of rice. "Know how to cook?"

Seth smiled up at her before stepping over to the stove—dumped the rice into a pot of water and set it to boil. He found two potatoes and a pack of hot dogs in the refrigerator—took the cutting board and a knife and sat down at the little kitchen table to chop them up.

Isabel climbed down from the countertop—came over and sat across from him—setting an open can of peaches and a beer on the table in front of her—fishing a peach slice out of the can with her fingers—closing her tired eyes as she chewed—juice dripping down her chin.

"You don't cook?" Seth said—watching Isabel open one eye and shake her head. "Did you cook before you got here?" She shook her head again but with both eyes closed this time.

Seth cut the potatoes into cubes—cutting out a few bad spots—leaving the skin on—then sliced up four of the hot dogs and carried everything over to the stove on the cutting board—realizing too late there wasn't enough room in the pot for everything—boiling water sloshing onto the stove-top as he started looking around for a bigger pot.

"There's a drawer under the oven," Isabel said—Seth turning to see her finally open the beer.

He transferred everything to a large pot he found in the drawer—cleaned up the stove with a roll of paper towels—then started searching for spices he could add to the make-shift stew—finding a small box with a picture of a chicken on it—several foil-wrapped cubes inside. He unwrapped two of the cubes and tossed them into the pot—standing there as steam wafted past his face—watching the cubes until they started breaking apart—then added more water before covering the pot with a lid.

"Where'd you find that beer?" Seth said as he bent down with his hand gripping the refrigerator door—scanning the illuminated shelves.

"In the bottom drawer—Benjy doesn't think anyone knows about them."

Seth opened the bottom drawer—saw bags of yellow and red onions—some with green sprouts shooting out their tops. He moved the bags—uncovering a six-pack with one beer missing.

"He doesn't like to share?"

"Nope."

Seth pulled out three beers and walked over to the ta-ble—sat down across from Isabel—setting one of the beers in front of her.

"How come he keeps Benjy around?" Seth said. "Spoon figures all the machines out—seems like you take care of everything else."

"He's simple—loyal." Isabel took a sip of the beer. "He's like a dog."

Seth opened one of the beers—took a long drink as he suddenly realized how thirsty he was—set the can down and looked over at the stove—bubbles popping up against the glass lid. He got up and walked over—lifted the lid and stirred the food in the pot.

"Seems to me like he's more trouble than he's worth."

"Yeah," Isabel said—touching the condensation on her beer can—not bothering to look up.

Seth put the lid back on the pot—came back to the table and sat down again—watching Isabel as he sipped his beer.

"You ever kill anyone before you met him?"

"No." Seth took another long drink of his beer—finishing it—tipping the can at different angles to get every last drop. "What the hell's his name, anyway?"

"I don't know."

Seth turned in his chair to face Isabel—put his elbows up on the table—felt the alcohol lifting his head—felt tired and hungry but somehow happy.

"We should come up with one for him," Seth said.

"Oh yeah?"

"How about Voldemort?" Seth cracked open another beer—watched Isabel look up and smile.

"Sounds about right," she said.

They sat there and drank without talking for a while—Seth getting up eventually—going over to the stove to taste the makeshift stew—deciding it needed a little more time.

"Do you like it here?" Isabel said before taking a sip of her beer—keeping the can raised as she swallowed. "I mean living this way—like outlaws—you like it?"

Seth watched her—still standing at the stove with a wooden spoon in his hand.

"I think so," he said. "Beats what I was doing before."

Isabel nodded—turned her head and looked off toward the back door.

"What'd you do before?" she said—turning in her chair to face Seth—leaning her head back against the wall—raising her beer to her mouth.

"Nothing."

Seth turned down the heat on the stove—watched the bubbles through the glass lid as he remembered the cornfield—the hand sprayer spurting out the milky white pesticide as he crouched down in the dirt—the gunshots.

He set the wooden spoon down on a paper towel—returned to the table and sat down.

"He made me shut some guy in a shipping container." Seth took another long drink of his beer—reached over and grabbed the open can of peaches. "We left him there—in this cave underneath some abandoned warehouse." He chewed the peaches. "He was banging on the door and screaming—and we just left him there."

Seth looked at the stove—felt Isabel's eyes on him but he refused to turn toward her.

"Then we went to this other guy's house," Seth continued—washing down the peaches with another sip of beer. "He made me bash his head in with that little flute he's always playing. We left him on the floor in his own basement—then stole his car and drove here."

"He made you do it."

"Yeah." Seth finally looked across the table at Isabel—her eyes just as tired as his—just as cold and closed-off as they always were.

Seth got up and turned off the stove—tasted the stew and decided it was done—then started searching the cabinets for bowls and spoons.

THEY ATE AT THE KITCHEN TABLE—BOTH GOING BACK FOR seconds as they drank the rest of the beers—flashes of lightning outside as they shared another can of peaches—sound of thunder always following a few seconds after—never too loud—only a few raindrops hitting the little window that faced the backyard.

"It looked like a clown car so we knew it didn't weigh too much," Seth said—sitting across from Isabel—last two beers in their hands as he told her a story from when he was in high school. "So we picked it up in the parking lot—eight of us—and carried it over to the outfield fence of the baseball field."

"Whose car was it?"

"The principal's."

"You stole the principal's car?"

"We didn't steal it—just moved it," Seth said—both smiling as he scooped the last peach into his mouth—Isabel resting her head on her folded arms. "So we made our way over to the fence. My buddy Michael fell down at one point and we almost dropped the car on him." They both laughed—tired and a little drunk—relieved to be indoors during the storm. "We eventually made it over to the fence and opened the gate. Then we carried the damn thing all the way to second base."

"What'd you do then?"

"Just left it there—shut the gate and went back to class."

"Did he find it?"

"Yeah." Seth drank the last of the beer he had in his hand—tipping it up and rolling it around—shaking it until the last drips slipped into his mouth—then set the empty can with the others against the wall. "It took him a while. We all hung around the parking lot after school to see what happened. Eventually he came out and saw that his little car was gone. He walked around the parking lot for a while with his keys in his hand—looking all around—getting himself worked up. Then he called the cops. He thought somebody stole it."

"You did steal it."

"No we just moved it. Eventually a cop showed up and talked to the principal—looked around and spotted the car in the middle of the baseball field—pointed it out to the principal and actually started laughing. We all started laughing too—hiding in our cars watching. Then we got the hell out of there."

They laughed—Isabel taking a sip of her beer—pausing with the can held up in front of her mouth—looking at Seth with something on her mind. After a few seconds she tipped her head back—raised the can and finished her beer in one big gulp.

"Come on," she said—dropping the empty can as she stood up from the table.

Isabel leaned forward and grabbed Seth's wrist—making him stand up—his chair sliding back on the tile floor as he stepped around the little table. They walked out of the kitchen together—Seth looking out the living room window at the wet gravel as they turned down the hallway—darker as they left the light from the kitchen—Isabel sliding her fingers along the wall as she dragged him to his bedroom.

She pulled him inside and shut the door—pushed him toward the bed and started unbuttoning his shirt. Seth put his arms around her—laid his hands on her lower back—then felt her wiggle away and disappear somewhere in the dark room—coming back a few seconds later—undoing the last two buttons before pulling the shirt down off his arms.

Seth grabbed her shirt and held it tight—pulled it up over her head before she wiggled away again. He tossed the shirt down and walked forward—held out his hands until he found her. She let him touch her arms—move his hands slowly up to her shoulders—let him touch her hair as she unbuckled his belt. His pants dropped to the ground and he kicked them off—kept one hand up by her hair as he moved the other down and placed it on her hip. She slapped it away—disappeared again to the other side of the room.

"What?"

"Don't."

Isabel came back and pulled down his underwear. Seth

moved toward her—grabbed her upper arm—turned her around as she tried to pull away but he held her tight—wrapping his other arm around her waist—shoving his face into her hair—kissing her cheek and lifting up against her.

"Don't," Isabel said as she tried to get away.

Seth released her waist—tried to spin her back around to face him but she pulled free. He heard her run to the door—open it and run out of the room.

Seth stood there for a while—naked and alone inside the dark room—heard Isabel walk down the hallway to the bathroom and lock the door. He stayed there in the middle of the bedroom until she came out—then walked to the door and grabbed the handle—turned it but kept the door closed—heard Isabel walk past him and keep going—heard her open her bedroom door and shut it behind her—then heard it lock and everything went quiet—thunder softening as the storm moved off to the east—rain slowing down as he listened to the water draining off the roof.

12

ANOTHER ROUND OF STORMS WAS PASSING THROUGH the next morning—waking Seth just after sunrise—drawing him out of bed and and over to the window—standing there with his underwear twisted around his hips—adjusting himself and yawning. It was light enough outside to see the trees whipping back and forth—green leaves being ripped off branches—lightning flashing into the room and thunder shaking the house. Seth got back into bed—pulled the blankets over him—lay there and watched the storm.

"You up?" Isabel said through the door.

"Yeah."

"Time to go."

"Let's wait for the storm to pass." Seth twisted his head around on the pillow—looked back toward the door. "We got anything for breakfast?"

He heard Isabel standing there—saw the shadows her legs made beneath the door—moving a little as she didn't answer—eventually walking off down the hallway. He heard a door open—then a clap of thunder drowned out the sound of it closing.

"What the—" Seth said after he heard the pickup start—jumping out of bed and going to the window again—seeing the blue dually's headlights on and the windshield wipers going. "She won't leave," he said—turning around to search the bedroom—trying to find his shirt and his shoes—turning back to the window as he pulled on his pants and felt for his belt. "Damn," he said as he watched the pickup start pulling away from the house—going down the driveway and over the little hill.

He stood there at the window and finished with his belt—left the bedroom without his shirt or shoes—went out to the living room and looked around. There was a lightning strike and a loud bang of thunder. Seth heard the cabinets rattling in the kitchen—saw the lights flicker but stay on—noticed the screen of the cellphone flash on and off—still sitting on the coffee table plugged into the charger.

He walked over and pulled the cord out of the cellphone—checked for any missed calls or messages—then stuck the phone in his pocket and looked around again—eventually going back down the hallway—stopping in front of Isabel's bedroom door. He turned the knob but it was locked—went to the living room window that faced the driveway and looked out—storm still blowing and the pickup was still gone. Then he went back to Isabel's door and kicked it in.

There was a dresser beside the window—a bed in one corner and a desk in another—a large mirror on the wall next to the closet. The bed was made—no clothes or anything else on the floor—desk cleared off except for a mug with pens and pencils and highlighters inside of it.

Seth walked over and opened the dresser drawers—lifted the bras and T-shirts—looked under the bed and found only a cardboard box full of sweaters—then went to the closet and opened the doors—found more shirts hanging up—more boxes full of clothes on the top shelf. He slid the hangers along the rail—found a cotton dress hanging against the wall—gray and soft between his fingers—stretchy and small—so small that at first he thought it was just another shirt.

He pulled it out of the closet and held it up—found a plastic bag tied to the hanger—ripped it open and a few plastic containers fell to the ground. He picked them up and opened them—makeup containers only half full—some with powders and dusty brushes—two tubes of lipstick and a few bottles of fingernail polish.

Seth sat down on the bed and put everything back in the bag—tied it up as best he could and hooked it back onto the hanger with the dress—then just sat there with the dress draped over his legs—looking around the room. The curtains were still closed over the window but he could tell the storm was letting up. He sat there for a while—then lay down and folded the bedspread over his body—tucked in the edges so no air could get in and soon he was asleep.

"GET OUT OF MY BED!" ISABEL YELLED—SETH BLINKING the sleep out of his eyes as she stood over him—two white paper bags in her hands. "Are you still naked?" she said—making a face before turning to walk out of the room. "I'll be in the kitchen."

Seth watched her walk out into the hallway—rolled over and stretched under the blanket—feeling the colder air from the room creeping in around his body.

The dress and the bag of makeup were still next to him. He sat up and held them in his hands—looked at the window and didn't think it was raining anymore—sun shining brighter through the curtains—shadows of the bushes not whipping from side to side like before.

"You broke my door," Isabel yelled from the kitchen—crumpling sounds of the paper bags in the background.

Seth stood up from the bed and walked to the doorway—trying to smash down the hair that was shooting up from the side of his head.

"Sorry," he yelled down the hallway. "Didn't think you were coming back."

Seth went back to his bedroom and found his shirt—put it on and then used the bathroom—wet his hair from the faucet and tried to comb it down in front of the mirror—then walked to the kitchen where he saw Isabel with fast food wrappers opened in front of her on the little table—also four paper cups with lids and straws in a cardboard drink holder—an unopened paper bag sitting in front of the empty chair.

"That's yours," she said.

Seth sat down—turned the bag onto its side and dumped the food onto the table. They sat there and ate in silence—Isabel sipping orange juice between small bites—Seth quickly giving himself hiccups from eating too fast.

After they finished eating they leaned back in their chairs and drank their coffees—both adding several little cups of cream and packets of sugar.

"Thanks for breakfast," Seth said.

"You're welcome."

"Couldn't just tell me you were hungry? Going out for breakfast—be back soon?"

"I thought you were asleep," Isabel said—smiling across the table.

"You were talking to me," Seth said—tipping the paper coffee cup until all he got was air.

"Some people talk in their sleep." Isabel shrugged her shoulders—leaning forward to search one of the food wrappers for crumbs.

Seth shook his head—sat there and looked around the

kitchen. The sun was shining now—steady breeze making the house creak and moan—raindrops sparkling on the window over the sink.

"You ready to go?" Isabel said.

"Yeah."

They left the house without saying much else—drove out to Highway 2 and went through Wolf Point. Seth saw the fast food place their breakfast came from—sun shining on the metal roof—all the big windows and bright colors. He looked all around the town as they drove through it—trying to recognize the place from when he and the man had been there.

After another hour they passed through Culbertson again. Seth looked out the window—down to where he knew the river was—lifting a hand to feel the side of his face—remembering how swollen his cheek had been—how bad his back ached after those darts the man used on him in the beginning.

"Why would you grab a gun like that?" Isabel said—Seth swinging his head around to look over at her—catching her glance at him with a worried look on her face—then turn her eyes back to the road. "The shotgun he had pointed at you—why'd you grab it?"

"I don't know," Seth said—turning a few seconds later to look back out the window.

"I'm serious," Isabel said. "Why?"

"I've always been careful—always tried to follow the rules—do the sensible thing." Seth adjusted the vent in front of him—directing the stream of cold air to hit his chest instead of his face. "But being careful never got me anywhere."

"So you just decided to do the complete opposite?"

"I guess so."

They drove on—Seth keeping his eyes pointed out the passenger's side window—watching the wind blow through the grass and over the hills in the distance. He looked for the river—for a train to pass by on the railroad tracks they were driving beside.

"Where'd you wanna go?" Isabel said.

"What?"

"You said it never got you anywhere—being careful or whatever—so where'd you wanna go?"

"Oh," Seth said. "Maybe the moon—maybe Mars."

They looked at each other—Seth raising his eyebrows—Isabel flashing a sad, closed-mouth smile.

They drove on for another few minutes. Then Isabel turned off onto a gravel road—started driving south with the sun in their faces—both flipping down their visors—leaning to keep their eyes shaded. Water was still standing in puddles next to the road from the previous night's storm—gravel a dark gray color—not much dust able to rise out of the dampness.

"Can you check the map?" Isabel said—pulling a laminated sheet from under her seat and handing it to Seth—her eyes never leaving the road.

"Sure," Seth said as he took the map and held it up in front of him—then rotated it forty-five degrees and looked at it again.

"It's the red dot," Isabel said.

It was a satellite map without many labels—giving Seth trouble as he tried to find the highway they'd been driving down—finding the railroad tracks first—then rotating the map again and looking out the windshield.

"Turn left down there," he said—waiting as Isabel slowed the pickup—watching her glance around before she made the turn. "Looks like you just follow this road for a while—then turn right."

A couple minutes later they saw the river—brown and sparkling in the sun—little cutouts in the opposite bank where the rainwater had drained down out of the fields.

"Right?" Isabel said as they came to another intersection.

"Yeah—then it looks like the road runs out—so we'll have to walk."

Isabel turned the pickup—drove on down the gravel road—Seth watching her check all the rearview mirrors—watching her as she drove slow and careful—still not raising any dust on the wet road.

"You think Spoon's alright?" Seth said.

"Hope so."

They came to the end of the gravel road a few minutes later—Isabel turning the pickup to the left—inching over rocks and the soggy, sandy dirt—driving toward a group of trees twenty yards away—then circling around to the far side—making sure the whole pickup was behind the trees before shutting off the engine—Seth watching her pull the key out—sit back in the driver's seat and yawn.

They could just see the river over the edge of the muddy bank—full and moving fast—going around a bend to their right.

"Here we are," Isabel said.

"We'd better wait till dark," Seth said. "Looks like the money's only a hundred yards or so back that way." He pointed out the back window with his thumb.

"Good idea."

Isabel already had her eyes closed when Seth looked over at her—feeling for a switch on the side of her seat—finding it after a few seconds—holding it down as she slowly started reclining—Seth listening to the electric motor as he turned to look out the window.

"You wanna climb into the backseat with me?" he said—knowing Isabel wasn't likely to respond—turning after a few silent seconds to look at her—seeing her eyes were still closed—hands folded over her stomach—chest rising and falling with deep, slow breaths.

THEY WAITED THERE THROUGH THE REST OF THE afternoon—Isabel sleeping away the first couple hours—Seth studying the maps she'd brought—then reading the manuals for the pickup he found in the glove compartment.

They shared a protein bar after Isabel woke up—drank a bottle of water each and talked—Isabel telling Seth about the Indian reservation—about some of the foster homes she'd been in—Seth talking about his mother—about all the dead-end jobs he'd had since finishing high school—working sixty-hour weeks for an old farmer—still unable to afford to move out of his mother's house.

They got out of the pickup once the sun started setting—contrails and clouds showing pinks and purples. They leaned back against the front bumper—drank another bottle of water each—mosquitoes buzzing around Seth's neck and ears—causing him to shake his head as he slapped at the insects.

"Here," Isabel said—laughing as she held out a small spray bottle.

"What's that?"

"Bug spray—take it—they like you more than me."

"Thanks." Seth took the bottle—closed his eyes tight and sprayed it all over his face—around the back of his head and all over his neck.

"Why do they like you so much?"

"Because I'm sweet." Seth held the bottle out and smiled.

"Right." Isabel nodded—smiled back before looking down—taking the bottle and making sure the cap was on tight.

They stood there and watched the sun—watched the light on the river change from yellow to orange to a shade of red—then watched all the bright colors disappear as the sun slid below the horizon—stars coming out and blinking in the blue-black sky—cicadas singing to each other from every direction.

"That's actually a planet," Seth said—pointing up as he looked over at Isabel.

"Oh yeah?"

"It's Venus." He smiled and scooted over next to her. "Brightest star in the sky."

"Thought you said it was a planet."

"Well yeah," he said. "I mean it is—so I guess I should say it's brighter than any star in the sky."

"Ahh."

They both looked out toward the west—dim blue ark sitting on the horizon where the sun had disappeared—getting smaller and smaller—more and more stars coming out until the night had fully set in.

"She was Greek," Seth said a little later—looking over at Isabel again—watching her turn toward him—watching the blue light bounce off her face—her hair and lips and neck. "Venus—she was a goddess in Greece."

Isabel nodded—tilting her head back so she could see the sky directly above them.

"Why isn't she a goddess anymore?" she said.

"Oh, I guess it's just an old story—you know, mythology."

"I'm sure there's somebody out there who still believes in her—not mythology to them."

Seth stood there looking down at the ground—wondering if that was true—if anyone still believed in Venus—what the point would be.

"My grandmother told me an old Indian story once," Isabel said—still looking up at the sky. "She died before I got taken away. She told me about two sisters who married two stars. They went to the sky to live with them."

"Then what happened?"

"I don't really remember. I know they got homesick

and wanted to come back to Earth. They went on some long journey—trying to escape." Seth watched Isabel drop her chin—look off with her face scrunched up. "Then they had to marry some old man I think—both of them. He broke their legs or something so they couldn't run away."

"That's depressing."

"Yeah."

He looked at her again—her forehead and cheeks shining blue in the dark.

"Let's go," Isabel said—turning suddenly and walking around the pickup—opening the driver's side door—causing the pickup to start beeping and the dome light to come on—Seth turning to watch her but all he could see was the top of her head.

They packed four of the ketamine blocks into Seth's backpack—started walking north with Isabel in the lead—wearing her headlamp but not turning it on yet—carrying one of the laminated maps under her arm.

"We looking for a purple flag again?" Seth said.

"Yeah."

They continued walking through the dark—Isabel stumbling over the uneven ground a couple times—eventually turning on her headlamp—switching it to the red light.

"It's nice out here," Seth said.

"It rained—usually nicer after it rains—cooler, anyway."

A few minutes later they stopped and Isabel checked the map—shined the red light from her headlamp down onto the laminated paper—then raised her head and looked around. Seth stood back and waited—watched her look down again and shift her feet—then walked over and stood next to her.

"If that's the bend in the river," he said—placing his index finger down on the map. "And that's about where we parked, I think we need to go that way." He lifted his other hand behind her—waving it toward the west.

Isabel looked up at him—shrugged her shoulders and flapped her arms. "Sure," she said.

They turned and walked west—going slow as Isabel scanned the ground with her headlamp—Seth touching her arm after a couple minutes and asking for the map—the two of them checking it together before he pointed to the right—then walked off ahead of her as he looked back and smiled—seeing Isabel roll her eyes. About ten steps later they spotted the flag.

"Lucky guess," Seth said—the two of them looking at each other with the flag between them—Isabel's red light shining in Seth's eyes.

Isabel nodded—then bent down and pulled out the purple flag. They'd forgotten the trowel so she used her hands to dig a little hole in the dirt.

"You feel anything yet?" Seth said.

"No."

Seth got down on his knees in front of her and scanned the ground—told her to turn her headlamp to the brighter white light—both of them kneeling there without talking—inspecting the illuminated soil with their heads nearly touching.

"Here," Seth said. "This is it." He outlined a spot in the sandy, settled dirt with his finger—then stood up and looked around—Isabel shuffling over to the spot as he searched for something to dig with—already pulling at the dirt with her hands.

Seth walked a few yards away—picked up a flat rock about twice the size of his hand—brought it over and knelt back down next to Isabel.

"I got it," he said—stabbing the edge of the rock down into the dirt—Isabel sitting back on her feet—mud on her hands as she tried to keep the light from her headlamp on the hole.

"I'll get the blocks," she said after a few minutes—standing up and stepping over to where Seth had dropped his backpack.

Seth shoveled dirt with the flat rock until he began uncovering a slab of plywood. The rain had drained down into the soil and there was still mud a few inches under the surface—plywood shiny and wet as he pulled the thick mud off it—dark in color when Isabel came back and shined her light down into the hole.

"These people are being a little too careful, I think," Seth said.

"Must be a group of teachers or grandmothers or something."

"Yeah."

Seth kept digging until he found an edge of the plywood—then dropped the rock and tried to get his fingertips underneath it.

"Maybe they're cops," he said with a strained voice—teeth showing as he lifted the plywood—heavy, wet clumps of mud from the edges falling into the dark hole—Seth tossing the sheet of plywood to the side and looking down—breathing hard with sweat coating the sides of his face.

"I'll get it," Isabel said—already reaching into the hole—lifting a clear plastic container with the money visible inside—bills tightly stacked and bound with rubber bands.

They dropped the blocks of orange lozenges into the hole—Seth placing the plywood back over it—covering it with the mud he'd piled up—then tossing the flat rock away and looking down at his pants—his knees and shins stained dark—hands black and a few smudges on his shirt.

"Let's go," Isabel said—already walking away when Seth looked up.

They got back to the pickup a few minutes later—Seth rinsing his hands off with a bottle of water—doors open and the dome light on—Isabel on the other side of the pickup—washing her face with her hair pulled back—Seth unable to keep from looking at her through the open doors.

"We'll stay here tonight," Isabel said. "I can take the front seat if you want the back."

"No that's OK—you take the back."

"You sure?"

"Yeah."

Isabel looked up with soap bubbles dotting her face—hands on her cheeks moving slowly in a circular motion.

Seth found a pair of shorts in his backpack—changed into them as he leaned against the side of the pickup—then left his shoes and dirty pants outside as he climbed up into the passenger's seat—lifted the middle console and tried to stuff in the seatbelt buckles—giving up a few minutes later—scooting over and reaching out to shut the driver's side door—then flattening himself out on the uneven seats as he tried to find a comfortable position.

A few minutes later Isabel climbed into the back—shut the doors as Seth heard her yawn—only able to see her hair sweep by above the seat as she maneuvered around.

The dome light soon faded out—everything dark or barely reflecting light from the stars and moon—everything quiet except the insects and the frogs.

"Do you need a light?" Seth said.

"No," Isabel said. "I'm OK."

Seth lay there across the front seat with his eyes open—still hoping she'd invite him into the backseat—give him another chance after their false start back at the house. He lay there listening to Isabel twist and turn—fold and pack something over and over again—probably her backpack, he thought—trying to use it as a pillow.

The pickup swayed a little as she moved around—went still once she finally got comfortable.

"Goodnight," Isabel said.

"Goodnight."

They lay there in the dark—both still awake—Seth listening to Isabel breathe—trying to quiet his own breathing so he could hear her better—trying somehow to slow down his heartbeat.

"Are you OK?" Isabel said.

"Yeah."

Seth stayed still and waited to hear something—unable to give up hope just yet—hearing Isabel scratch her arm after several minutes had passed—then hearing her breathing get slower and deeper.

His own breathing slowed down after a while—eventually rolling onto his side—folding his arm up under his head.

Soon they were both asleep.

"JUST BE STILL," ISABEL SAID.

"What?"

"Don't talk."

She'd climbed over the seat while Seth was still asleep—lying naked on top of him now—pulling on his shorts as he lifted up to help them slide down. He heard her make a little noise—blinked and tried to see her face in the dark—her head tilted back—teeth flashing as she opened her mouth. He moved so her leg could slip down between his hip and the seat—still watching her—feeling her put her hands on his chest—her long hair sweeping across his face. Then she tilted her head back again—making another noise as he put his hands on her—finally able to see the features of her face—looking down at the rest of her in the dim blue light.

ISABEL WAS STILL ASLEEP THE NEXT MORNING—HEAD resting on Seth's chest with a blanket covering her body—same blanket she'd pulled from the backseat the night before—wrapping herself in it before dropping her head onto

Seth's chest—asleep almost immediately as he curled his arms around her in the dark—smelling her hair and looking at the stars out the windshield.

Seth looked down at the top of her head—sunlight shining through the windshield now—headrests yellow in the morning sun—rest of the seats still gray in the shade—sunlight slowly moving down the fabric—Seth watching it hit the first seem and keep going.

He hadn't slept very much—one of the seatbelt buckles stabbing him in the ribs all night—another pushing into his hamstring. His right hand had fallen asleep but he knew he couldn't move it without waking her—instead letting it tingle till it went numb—lying there without moving—feeling her limp body breathe.

The sunlight kept dropping along the gray seats—Seth watching it as he felt his stomach start to turn over—wondering what time it was—where they could go for breakfast.

He turned his head and saw drops of water on the windshield from a heavy dew—sparkling as they combined to form bigger drops—then running down the slanted glass in jagged lines. He smiled—moved his hand and felt it start to tingle again—felt the places on his back that ached the most.

Soon Isabel's head started moving—her hand coming up to her face—scratching her nose as she yawned. Seth didn't know if her eyes were open yet or not.

"Hey," he said.

"Hey."

Isabel rubbed her eyes but kept her head down on Seth's chest—his shirt twisted and tight around his ribs.

"Can I treat you to breakfast?" Seth said.

"Sure."

They stayed like that for a while longer—Isabel blinking and rubbing her eyes—stretching her legs under the blanket—Seth watching specs of dust floating in the air—watching them float in and out of the sunlight that was shining through the windshield. Eventually he reached up and touched Isabel's hair—pressed down and felt the back of her head.

"We better get going," Isabel said as she raised up—wrapped the blanket around her front—dipped her head so her hair covered her face—then crawled backward and opened the passenger's side door.

"Yeah," Seth said.

Isabel stepped down out of the pickup and shut the door. Seth sat up and found his shorts down around his ankles—reached and pulled them up as he closed his eyes against the sun—then adjusted his shirt before lying back down. He could hear Isabel making her way around the pickup—heard her open the back door and start going through her backpack—put on her clothes and brush her hair—listening as he watched the line of sunlight creep down the driver's seat.

They drove out to Highway 2 and turned right—crossing the border into North Dakota a half hour later—noticing more traffic as they got closer to Williston—more houses and driveways and gravel roads—then a city limit sign and the houses were soon more bunched together.

"What are you hungry for?" Seth said.

"Breakfast," Isabel said—keeping her eyes on the road.

They drove into the center of town—turned at one of the stoplights and found a cafe on the next corner—Isabel parking the pickup on a side street in front of an abandoned building—both of them looking around at the empty sidewalks and boarded-up windows.

They got out and started walking toward the cafe—Seth looking over at Isabel as they navigated the uneven pavement—tapping her on the shoulder—finally getting her to turn and look at him. He smiled but neither of them said anything—stepping over cracks in the broken sidewalk—Isabel walking with her arms crossed against the cool morning—Seth still wearing the shorts he'd slept in.

They sat in a booth at the front of the cafe—only a few other customers eating breakfast by that time—country music playing quietly in the background. Isabel asked the waitress for coffee before they even sat down—Seth nodding when the waitress turned and looked at him—indicating he'd take a cup as well.

Isabel slid onto the polyester seat—rested her forearms on the table and held the menu up in front of her. Seth kept looking at her but couldn't think of anything to say—sat there stacking little plastic containers of jam—trying not to smile as his mind drifted back to the previous night in the pickup.

After a couple minutes he reached over the table and flicked the back of Isabel's menu—using his thumb and middle finger to pop the flimsy vinyl sheet out of her hands.

"What the hell?" Isabel said.

"I'm just messing with you—sorry—I just—"

Isabel went back to the menu.

"I had fun last night," Seth said—leaning forward over the table.

"OK." Isabel leaned back in the padded seat—kept the menu in her hands and didn't look up.

After a while Seth started looking around the cafe— finding a chalkboard with a list of daily specials above a long counter near the kitchen—scanning the words but not really reading them—letting his eyes linger over the careful handwriting—the white-chalk sun beaming down from a corner of the board.

Soon the waitress came over with their coffees—pulled a pen and pad from her apron to take their orders. Isabel asked a few questions—then ordered scrambled eggs with bacon—Seth waiting until the waitress turned to him—then told her he just wanted white toast with butter—more coffee and some of those little cups of flavored creamers—watching her jot down their orders before walking away.

Two cops walked into the cafe while Seth and Isabel were

waiting for their food—walked over and sat down in a booth on the other side of the glass door—local cops wearing dark blue uniforms—the town's name on their shoulders—Seth watching them over Isabel's head—not bothering to tell her they were there.

"So what the hell's your deal?" Seth said—elbows jutting out on top of the table—fingers interlocked as he held his hands close to his chest.

"What?"

"Why do you act like you don't know me after we have sex?"

Isabel didn't say anything—just shrugged her shoulders and let her head drop back against the padded seat—then turned and looked toward the kitchen door.

"I just wish we could act like we're together," Seth said. "Like you're with me and not somebody else—like we're dating or whatever."

"We're not," Isabel said—looking across the table at Seth—then quickly looking away again. "It's not like I want it to be this way."

"Then don't let it be this way."

"It's not that simple," Isabel said—leaning over the table with tears forming in her eyes. "This is serious, Seth. We're paddling down a river dealing drugs—for two months!" She held up two fingers with one hand—brushed her hair out of her face with the other—Seth looking over her shoulder at the two cops as she raised her voice. "And we're either gonna get arrested—one or both of us is gonna die—or we're somehow gonna make it all the way to Kansas City—then have to turn around and do the same thing all over again!"

"Well," Seth said—almost whispering as he leaned forward. "Let's quit." He watched Isabel roll her eyes—sit back and cross her arms. "We have the money we got last night—I have quite a bit left from what he gave me back at the ranch."

Isabel lifted her hand to her mouth—chewed a hangnail

on her thumb. "I'm not running from him the rest of my life," she said—scooting out to the edge of the booth—then standing up and walking past Seth—tears sparkling in her eyes.

Their food came a few minutes later—Seth sitting there by himself with the two plates on the table—turning his head constantly to see if she was coming back from the bathroom yet. He drank another cup of coffee and ordered a glass of orange juice—taking one sip when the waitress brought it over—then setting it next to Isabel's plate as he continued waiting.

Soon he saw the cops look up before he knew Isabel was coming back—the one facing Seth pointing her out to his partner. Then she was passing him and sliding into the booth—her eyes still wet—open wide and red around the edges—wiping her nose with a paper towel she'd brought with her from the bathroom.

"They saw me," Isabel whispered.

"It's alright—just eat."

They ate without talking—Seth eventually pointing at the glass of orange juice with his knife—Isabel raising her eyebrows as she took a drink—wiping her nose a couple more times—then wadding up the paper towel and setting it on the table behind the little packs of jelly.

Seth saw the cops stand up over Isabel's shoulder—both adjusting their belts as they laughed at something one of them had said. He looked at their holsters and all the different sized pouches—made eye contact with one and saw them both start walking—passing the door without leaving—waving at other customers without stopping.

"Hi there," one of them said—both now standing at the edge of the table with their hands on their hips. "Everything alright over here?"

"Yessir," Seth said.

"You OK, honey?"

Isabel nodded. "Yeah."

Seth watched the two cops—nodding as they kept their eyes on Isabel for a long time—then turning to Seth as they moved closer—gentle, fatherly expressions gone from their faces. He smiled and nodded—took a sip of his coffee.

"Let me impart a little knowledge thirty-two years of marriage has taught me," one of the cops said—putting his hands on the table and bending down. "Whatever it is, it ain't worth it." He lifted one meaty hand from the greasy table-top—unfurled his index finger and pointed it at Seth. "And that goes double for you."

Seth started nodding again—smiling wide enough to show his teeth—waiting for what seemed like a long time—the cops finally turning and walking out of the cafe.

They sat there for a few minutes without talking—Isabel picking at her food while Seth drank another cup of coffee—sitting back and glancing out the window—looking up and down the street.

"Let's get a hotel room," Seth said.

"What?"

"Let's get a hotel room. We got the money—and we're not meeting Spoon and Benjy till tomorrow."

Isabel looked at him—tossed her fork onto her plate and sat back. "OK," she said—shrugging her shoulders as she turned toward the window—sunlight hitting her face through the blinds—shadows striped over her eyes, nose and chin—still sad but more relaxed than before—relaxed or maybe just tired, Seth thought.

Seth waved the waitress over and pulled out his wallet—asked her the total without looking at the bill—then had her stay at the table while he counted out the money—handing it to her and telling her to keep the change. Then he scooted to the end of his seat and stood up—stepped over and held out his hand for Isabel. She grabbed it and felt him dragging her toward him—then felt him pulling her up off the seat and suddenly they were outside—walking down the sunny side

of the street together—Seth trying to hold Isabel's hand—
laughing every time she pulled away.

13

THEY DROVE OUT TO THE MAIN ROAD AND FOUND A Walmart—Seth saying he wanted to get some supplies—also something for dinner so they wouldn't have to go out again after they checked into their hotel room.

"This is where we come sometimes," Isabel said as they walked through the parking lot. "For all that canned soup and bottled water."

"Is that all he ever eats?"

"Yep—too worried somebody's gonna poison him to eat anything else—also why he only drinks bottled water."

As they approached the store a pair of glass doors slid open and they walked through—a blast of cold air blowing down onto their heads—carts lined up to their right with an old woman standing there—smiling in a blue vest.

"Hi there," the woman said as she pushed a cart toward them.

"Hi."

"Thank you," Seth said as he took control of the

cart—pushing it ahead as he started scanning the signs hanging from the ceiling—steering the cart to the back corner of the store while Isabel tried to keep up—Seth finally spotting the sign for camping supplies and turning down the empty aisle.

"What are you looking for?" Isabel said.

"We're gonna need more fuel for that little camping stove," he said—looking at the sleeping bags and flashlights—picking up a multi-tool and some water purification tablets and dropping them into the cart. "Also gonna need some gloves and moleskin." He crouched down in front of the fuel canisters.

"I already have all that."

"Well," he said—still scanning the shelves. "You bring enough for everybody?"

Isabel turned and walked away—returning a few minutes later with three pairs of gloves, two rolls of toilet paper and a package of moleskin.

"Anything else?" she said—tossing everything into the cart—Seth looking up from the fuel canister's label—smiling as Isabel raised her eyebrows.

They went around the store and picked up a few other supplies—raincoats and warm jackets—toothpaste and mouthwash.

Then the cellphone started ringing as they were making their way to the grocery aisles—causing Seth to stop the cart in the home furnishings section—he and Isabel looking at each other as the phone vibrated in his pocket.

"Meet you outside," Isabel said as she grabbed the cart—pushing it forward and disappearing around a corner—leaving Seth alone in an aisle of lamps and little end tables.

"Hello."

"Hello, Seth."

A family walked past him—two children trailing their mother—both smacking at each other but only the younger one yelling. Seth covered the phone and turned away—walked out of the aisle toward chest-high racks of women's shirts.

"Have you lost any of the lozenges?"

"No—no, sir."

"Good," the man said. "People's lives depend on them, you know."

"Yessir."

"You don't want to turn on the television one day and see reports of the mentally ill and under-medicated suddenly committing suicide, do you?"

"No, sir." Seth rested one arm on the top of a clothes rack—row of hangers pressing into the soft skin under his forearm.

There was a long pause—Seth looking around the store while he waited—almost expecting to see the man marching toward him with a cellphone pressed to his ear—waiving as if they'd planned to meet there all along.

Instead he saw a woman pushing a cart toward him—coming too close so he moved off to the line of fitting rooms.

"That's good, Seth," the man said. "Now, tell me why you went back to the house two nights ago."

Seth didn't say anything—stood there and listened to the man breathing—tapping something on a table or maybe a wall—someone nearby shuffling through shirts or pants hanging from a clothes rack he couldn't see.

"Be truthful, Seth—a food taster is worthless if they are not completely honest."

Seth walked between the racks of clothes—no one around now—only a few carts squeaking down aisles within earshot. He started around one of the racks—then stopped and looked down at a little girl standing there in front of him—maybe four or five—looking up at him holding a toy still in its box—holding it up to her chest as she stood there without making a sound.

"Seth."

Seth turned around suddenly and started walking away. "Benjy killed someone," he said. "Some farmer whose land we were camping on."

"I see," the man said—Seth stopping again—waiting for him to continue. "And you had to clean up his mess?"

"Yeah—yessir."

"I see." The man paused for a few seconds—still tapping something but slower now. "And what of the pistol I gave him?"

"I got it now."

"You have it, Seth—have it," the man said—then sighed as Seth drifted off toward the back of the store—the fabric counter and the crafts section. "I don't think Benjamin is suited for this life. We'll dispose of him once you reach Kansas City."

Seth was passing by the baby section now—dresses, little sailor outfits and bibs hanging from the rack beside him.

"It's good you told me, Seth—good to hear you're handling things." The man paused again—yawned or maybe just took a deep breath. "Makes me almost proud—the role I've played in you becoming such a captain—such a man."

Seth heard the phone beep as the man ended the call—stopped and looked down at the screen—waited until it timed out and went black—put it back up against his ear to make sure the man was gone—then checked the battery percentage—looked around as he stuffed the phone back into his pocket.

Before walking out into the sunny parking lot Seth stopped at the arcade games between the two sets of sliding glass doors—stepping around a group of wheelchairs as he heard carts rattling over the pavement behind him. He stood there in front of the crane machine and scanned the stuffed animals through the Plexiglas—spotting a small blue pillow with a cartoon face on it—perched in the back corner so Seth moved over to the side of the machine to look at it—then pulled a dollar from his wallet and fed it through the front of the machine—grabbed the joystick and watched the time start ticking down—felt the little crane jerk to life and then guided it toward the pillow.

"HERE," SETH SAID AS HE CLIMBED UP INTO THE PICKUP— holding the blue pillow out to Isabel in the driver's seat.

"What is it?"

"I won it for you."

Isabel looked at him as he pulled the passenger's side door shut—studied his smile and his eyes as he looped the seatbelt over his chest.

"Let's go," Seth said.

Isabel set the pillow down on the seat between them— making sure its smiling face was in the right position—then started the pickup and pulled out of the parking lot.

They drove out to the main road and headed south to- ward the river—passed a few hotels but kept going—several car dealerships along a stretch of the road—then bars and restaurants and hardware stores.

"Where can we leave the pickup?" Seth said.

"Not sure."

Seth watched her squinting with the sun on her face— driving with both hands on the steering wheel—her hair held back and up off her neck in a chunky plastic clip.

"Think we can leave it at the hotel?"

"Wouldn't hurt to ask, I guess."

They kept going and soon the town started to spread out—lone houses and entrances to neighborhoods—the road eventually going down to two lanes.

After another mile or so Isabel turned suddenly into the

parking lot of a Motel 6—still accelerating as they passed the empty pool—braking hard as she pulled into a spot in the back corner of the parking lot next to the dumpsters—making sure they were out of view from the road. Then she hopped down out of the pickup without saying anything—without grabbing her backpack or any of the grocery bags—walking toward the office without looking back. Seth jogged after her—passed her and opened the glass door so she could enter first.

"Hello," Isabel said to the man behind the counter—pale and clean-shaven—hair on the top of his head gelled and slicked over to the side.

The sun was coming in through the windows of the small room—a table against one wall with pamphlets for local attractions and self-serve coffee.

Seth stayed behind Isabel as she walked toward the counter.

"Hi," the man said after looking them both over. "Need a room?" He started pulling out sheets of paper.

"Yeah," Isabel said.

"Gonna need your IDs," the man said as he placed two clipboards on the counter—pushed the sheets of paper up underneath the metal clamps—then slid the clipboards forward. "Fill these out."

"Oh," Isabel said. "I actually left my ID at home." She scrunched up her face—then smiled and shrugged her shoulders.

There was a pause as the man behind the counter looked at them again—his hands still on the clipboards.

"I have mine," Seth said—stepping forward as he pulled out his wallet—his Missouri driver's license sticking in the clear plastic sleeve—causing him to try several times before getting it out.

The man took it and looked it over—looked up at Seth yet again—then over at Isabel.

"We're married," Isabel said. "On our honeymoon."

"Right," the man said—putting Seth's driver's license down on one of the clipboards and sliding it toward him.

Seth filled out the paperwork and paid for the room in cash—then asked the man about leaving the pickup in the parking lot. The man said they could only park there as long as they were guests—told them the airport had long-term parking but you had to pay for it. Then he handed Seth the keycard and they turned to leave.

Isabel scanned the numbers on the blue doors as they walked back outside toward the pickup—Seth watching her—smiling as he remembered her saying they were on their honeymoon.

They got back in the pickup and started driving around to the other side of the hotel—Isabel scanning the doors until she found their room—only three or four other cars in the parking lot. They parked right in front of the door to their room on the first floor—single window looking out at a thin stand of trees and a ditch.

"What's for dinner?" Seth said—turning and nodding his head toward the backseat.

Isabel turned off the engine—gathered a few things before looking over at Seth.

"Chicken," she said—opening the door and stepping down to the parking lot.

Seth carried the groceries and his backpack inside their room. Isabel had propped the door open for him and was already ripping the bedspread off the bed—her backpack on the dresser next to the TV.

"Why do you wanna do it on the floor?" Seth said—looking down at the bedspread—then up at Isabel with a smile on his face.

"Shut up," she said. "Those things are disgusting."

They sat down at a little table tucked into a corner of the room—Seth pulling a rotisserie chicken and two six-packs of beer from the grocery bags—feeling the heat from the chicken through the plastic container—then pulling out a container of mashed potatoes, a smaller one of gravy and a bag of salad.

Isabel opened one of the other grocery bags—pulled out paper plates and plastic utensils—took the wrapper off a roll of paper towels and set it on the edge of the table.

"Did you wash your hands?" Isabel said—glancing up at Seth—his fingers peeling the brown-black skin off the chicken's breast. "Go wash your hands."

Seth smiled—shoved the long, thin strip of skin in his mouth—then stood up and walked over to the sink and washed his hands. He was still chewing as he returned to the little table—drying his hands on his pants as he sat back down in his chair—then immediately started ripping off one of the browned chicken legs.

There wasn't much left of the chicken once they'd both finished—pile of bones and sinew. Seth offered Isabel the last of the mashed potatoes but she shook her head—waved her hand and sat back in her chair. Seth scooped them out onto his paper plate—held the container of gravy above the potatoes—tipped it upside down and waited until the solid brown stream became individual drops—then tossed the empty containers into the grocery bag they were using for trash.

Isabel drank the last of her beer and went for another—Seth already halfway through his second. He put down his plastic spoon and took a drink—watched Isabel as she stared out the window—unopened beer on the table in front of her—her head turned toward the dirty glass and parted curtains—still light outside but shadows had overtaken most of the parking lot.

"What'd he have to say this time?" Isabel said.

"Not much." Seth grabbed his spoon again—went back to the pile of mashed potatoes and gravy on his plate. "He knew we went back to the house."

"What?" Isabel turned to look across the table—her head dipping forward—forehead wrinkled with worry.

"He didn't seem too upset about it," Seth continued—still eating but glancing up at Isabel as he spoke. "I told him about Benjy killing that old man."

There was a pause as Isabel sat there thinking—Seth watching her as he finished his second beer—setting the empty can back down on the table—listening to the hollow sound it made.

"You're cellphone," Isabel said. "That's how he's tracking us."

Seth stared down at the table as he scooped up the last of the potatoes—full spoon suspended between his plate and mouth for a moment.

They sat there without talking for a while—both looking out the window—Seth eventually tossing his plastic utensils and paper plate into the grocery bag with the rest of the garbage—then sitting back with another beer in his hand.

"What'd he say when you told him about Benjy killing that guy?"

Seth looked at Isabel—then down at his beer—tapped the aluminum can on the table and waited before answering.

"He just started off like he always does—said if we didn't get these drops made on time there'd be a lot of sick people that might kill themselves—said we'd probably see it on the news."

"What'd he say about Benjy? Did he say anything about any of us?"

"No—no he didn't really have much to say beyond that."

"What else did he say?"

"Nothing—just said it was good that I told him every-thing. Then he went silent and hung up the phone like he does."

They sat there until it was dark outside—Seth finishing his beer and opening another—Isabel leaving the unopened can in front of her on the table as she stared out the window.

"Get anything for dessert?" Seth said.

"No."

"I still think we should make a run for it—you and me—like Bonny and Clyde."

"I know you do."

They sat there for a few more minutes—Seth drinking as Isabel looked down at her greasy paper plate—leathery chicken skin and dark gray bones. Then Isabel stood up and walked to the bathroom—shut the door and started the shower—Seth listening as she opened the little box of hotel soap—as she pulled the shower curtain closed.

He went over and sat down on the bed—turned on the TV and started flipping through the channels—holding the remote in one hand and a beer in the other—listening to the shower as he kept the volume turned down.

SETH WAS ASLEEP WHEN ISABEL CAME OUT OF THE bathroom—opening his eyes to see her digging clothes out of her backpack—wrapped in a white towel—her hair hanging down wet around her shoulders. She gathered a pile of clothes in one arm and went back into the bathroom—shut the door without looking at Seth—then turned on the blow dryer a few minutes later.

Seth was sitting on the edge of the bed when she came out again—a baseball game on the TV—another beer in his hand. Isabel went over to the bed and pulled back the blankets—Seth turning to watch her slip underneath the sheets—then place one of the pillows next to her running down the middle of the bed.

"That's your side," Isabel said—Seth nodding his head as he watched her try to find a comfortable position—lifting the beer to his mouth but freezing when he saw her look up at him. "I'll make you a deal," she said—Seth turning his body toward her without losing eye contact—lowering his beer as he waited for her to continue. "If we make it to Kansas City—if all four of us make it and nothing happens to us while we're there." Isabel looked toward the window and the door—flowery pattern of the curtains—patchy white paint on the wall. "If nobody dies—I'll run away with you—wherever you wanna go."

"Yeah?"

"Yeah." She turned back to Seth—looked into his eyes but seemed far away—seemed scared and unsure as she stared at the space between them.

"I'm gonna go take a shower," Seth said—remembering what the man had said about Benjy during their last call—wanting to tell her but deciding not to—not yet, he thought—not while she had that look on her face.

He stood up slowly from the bed—stretching as he watched Isabel turn away from him—flip her hair back over her shoulder as she laid her head down on one of the pillows. He finished his beer as he walked toward the bathroom door—looked back at the bed as he heard Isabel turn off the lamp—seeing the blue light from the TV flicker over the blankets—over the table in the corner by the flower-patterned curtains.

He took a long, hot shower—letting the bathroom get steamy as he sat in the tub—water streaming down onto the top of his head—rolling off his shoulders and down his back. There was still a little bottle of shampoo on the counter and an unopened bar of soap. He used them both—then set the unused portions on a shelf in the shower.

When he was finished he turned off the water and brushed his teeth in front of the sink—wrapped a towel around his waist and went back out into the room. The lights were off and so was the TV—Seth looking toward the bed but unable to see anything in the dark—inching his way past the long dresser—feeling around for his backpack—finding it and pulling out a pair of shorts—putting them on underneath his towel and adjusting the waistband—then tossing the towel into a corner of the room—turning and stepping carefully over the old carpet—leaning forward with his hands out as he tried to find the bed.

14

SETH WOKE UP ON HIS SIDE—FACING THE TABLE and the window—dim light glowing behind the thick curtains. He blinked and yawned but stayed in bed—lying there listening to all the early morning sounds—something buzzing outside and down the walkway—vending machines or maybe an air-conditioner—few birds calling to each other from the trees at the edge of the parking lot. He listened for Isabel but she didn't move or make a sound.

After a few minutes Seth rolled onto his back—folded his pillow to prop his head up—then looked around the rest of the room—dark in the corner where he'd tossed his towel the night before—even darker near the bathroom door where the light from the parking lot couldn't reach. He turned back to the window—to the rectangle of light around the edges of the curtains.

"We should get going," Isabel said.

"Yeah."

"What time is it?"

"Five or six," Seth said—twisting around to look at the back of Isabel's head—her hair fanned out on the pillow between them. "You hungry?"

"No."

Seth got out of bed and put on his clothes—packed his backpack and then sat down at the table—picking at the chicken carcass still in its plastic container—watching Isabel sit up and stretch—still watching her as she stood up and walked to the bathroom—hearing the toilet flush a few minutes later—then hearing the shower start as he leaned back in his chair.

He pulled the cellphone out of his pocket and checked the time—then started scrolling through all the apps on the phone—searching for the one the man was using to track them—eventually finding it near the bottom of the list. Seth opened the app's settings—let his thumb hover over the disable button—looked up toward the bathroom and listened to the shower—sitting there trying to think—trying to convince himself that the man would never find them—that he wouldn't kill Spoon—that Isabel wouldn't be upset.

After a while he looked back down at the cellphone—lowered his thumb to the home button—pressed it to exit the app—then turned the screen off. He put the phone back in his pocket and leaned forward—started picking at the chicken again.

Isabel came out of the bathroom a few minutes later—Seth watching her cross the room—wrapped in a short white towel—using another to dry her hair.

"Are you sure you don't wanna just run away right now?" Seth said.

Isabel kept drying her hair as she glanced up at him from underneath the towel—then bent forward and started going through her backpack that was still sitting on the long dresser.

"I'll leave the cellphone here on the table." He pulled

the phone out of his pocket again—set it down next to the rotisserie chicken container. "Then we can hop in the pickup and start driving—go anywhere you want."

"You think it's that simple?"

"Can be."

"No," Isabel said. "It can't—not with someone like him." Isabel pulled on her pants under the towel—turned away from Seth and let the towel drop to the floor—then slipped on a sports bra and a long-sleeve shirt. "Let's go," she said as she turned around—swinging her backpack over her shoulder—Seth looking up at her from the little table—leaning back in his chair.

"I'll wait till we get to Kansas City," he said. "Like we talked about last night—I'll get us there—all of us safe and sound—rich and sunburned." Seth smiled as they looked at each other—Isabel raising her eyebrows—then marching toward the door. "Then we'll go somewhere far away—Florida or Hawaii maybe." Seth hopped up out of his chair—grabbed the cellphone off the table and followed her outside.

They left the Motel 6 with the sun still low in the sky— making long shadows over the road—already hot enough for them to turn on the pickup's air-conditioner—already windy without a cloud in sight. Isabel drove back toward the Walmart—Seth sitting in the passenger's seat looking out the window—daydreaming about beaches and palm trees— Isabel in a bikini—frozen drink in his hand.

Soon they started seeing signs for the local airport and Isabel turned off the main road—steering the pickup through town—following the airport signs—eventually finding the parking lot and pulling into an open spot off by itself.

Seth went around and climbed up into the bed of the pickup under the camper shell—stuffed the blocks of ketamine lozenges into both their backpacks—gathered all the supplies they'd bought the day before—then handed Isabel her backpack over the tailgate and jumped out.

"I'll get the rest," he said—reaching for his backpack and several plastic grocery bags—Isabel taking a step back—looking down at the number painted on the pavement—then turning and walking away.

There was a little office in the middle of the parking lot—blinds all closed with an air-conditioner sticking out of one window. They walked inside and asked the kid behind the counter about parking. He'd been watching something on an old computer and seemed startled—clicking the mouse and stabbing at the keyboard when they walked in—yanking a pair of bulky headphones off his ears.

Seth stepped forward and told the kid how long they wanted to park the pickup in the lot—watched him trace a finger over a spreadsheet pinned to the wall—then told him to check again when the kid told him how much it would cost—watching him slowly trace his finger over the laminated sheet of paper one more time—Seth leaning forward and squinting at the numbers just above the kid's dirty fingernail—then shaking his head as he pulled out his wallet—paying with most of the cash he had left.

He told the kid to call them a taxi—then followed Isabel outside to wait on a bench against a wall of the tiny building—letting the sun shine on their faces—Isabel sitting there with her eyes closed—her arms and legs crossed.

Soon an SUV pulled up in front of the little office—the driver rolling down his window—asking if they were waiting for a taxi. Seth said they were—then jumped up and gathered all their bags—lifting them off the pavement before Isabel had a chance to help.

They got in the backseat and Isabel told the driver they needed to get to the river—the driver looking at them both in the rearview mirror but no one said anything—shrugging his shoulders eventually—then shifting the SUV into gear.

They drove past the Motel 6 and out through the south side of town—past a farm equipment dealership with tractors and combines parked in a grassy lot—then a grain elevator and a few other industrial buildings. Isabel told the driver where to stop and they got out of the SUV—Seth paying for the ride with some of the cash he had left—then watching the SUV drive away as they stood there in the road—the town to their left and train tracks up a gravel embankment to their right.

"Is it because of them?" Seth said.

The hot sun was making them sweat with no shade nearby—dry wind blowing hard across their skin—through their hair and tugging at their shirts. Isabel had pulled out one of the laminated maps from her backpack—stood off to the side of the road looking it over.

"What?" she said—squinting as she raised her head—as she brushed the hair out of her face.

"Spoon," he said. "And Benjy—they the main reason you wanna wait till Kansas City?" Seth took a couple steps toward her—Isabel watching him—then looking back down at the map in her hands. "If he's gonna come after us no matter what—no matter when we take off on our own—I just don't see what difference it makes—that's all."

Isabel didn't say anything—standing there in the hot wind—tracing her finger across the laminated sheet of paper. Seth walked over to her and looked down—saw the grid of streets that made up Williston—the jagged blue line that represented the Missouri River.

"That way," he said—pointing toward the railroad tracks—extending one arm while keeping his eyes on the map.

Isabel looked up—turning away from Seth with the map still in her hands—then looked back down and turned the map ninety degrees. Suddenly she bent down and stuffed the map into one of the grocery bags—it's surface shining in the sun as she rolled it up—looking wet to Seth as he wondered what she was doing—wondering still as he watched her grab all the bags and start walking up the gravel embankment—stepping over the train tracks and disappearing over the other side.

Seth waited there by himself on the empty road—turning away from the tracks and the river—wondering what would happen if he walked in the opposite direction—if he walked back into town and started living a normal life again—got a job and found someplace to live—made some new friends and met a normal girl—toying with the idea for just a couple minutes as he stood there alone—then turned back to the train tracks and started hurrying after Isabel—scrambling up the loose gravel—stopping at the top and looking down at the darkened railroad ties—tracing the metal tracks as he slowly raised his head—seeing them come together off in the distance and disappear. He walked down the other side of the gravel embankment into a vacant lot of packed dirt—ran until he caught up to Isabel—walking beside her as they passed a row of concrete grain silos—still beside her as they walked through an empty field next to the levee—tall grass waving in the wind—bare patches of cracked, hard soil where water must've stood for too long.

They walked twenty or thirty yards apart out into the middle of the field—neither of them saying anything—Isabel not even turning her head.

Seth looked around as he felt beads of sweat dripping down his arms and neck—stopped and turned back toward the silos—stood there squinting with no one in sight—no cars or trucks or houses—listening to the wind as he scanned the horizon—no power lines or cornfields or anything else— spinning around after a few minutes to find Isabel about thirty yards away—kneeling down in the tall grass—trying to lift something off the ground—Seth spotting a purple flag behind her feet.

He jogged over to her—took off his backpack and dropped it in the tall grass—squatted down beside her and got his hands underneath the piece of plywood she was trying to lift—helping her slide it out of the way—most of the loose dirt still piled on top. The hole in the ground was shallow this time—shrink-wrapped bundles of cash lined up in one flat layer. Isabel bent down and pulled out the money—stacking it up next to her in a pyramid—then unzipped her backpack and started pulling out the orange blocks of lozenges.

They placed all the blocks they had left in the hole—Isabel arranging them so they stayed below the surface. Then they slid the plywood back—blending the dirt as best they could to hide the edges.

"How much money is it?" Seth said.

"I don't know."

"Looks like a lot."

"It's a big town."

Isabel never looked up from the dirt—still busy making sure the plywood wasn't visible—then picking up the purple flag and stabbing it into the ground—packing all the money into her backpack and walking away.

Seth picked up the grocery bags—then followed a few yards behind her—walking toward the grass-covered levee that stretched out in both directions. After a while Seth stopped and took out a water bottle—drank the whole thing as he watched Isabel start climbing the levee—still watching as she stood at the top and looked to her left and right—shielding her eyes from the sun with her hand—black hair whipping in the wind—grabbing the straps to her backpack before she started descending the other side.

Seth heard something and turned around—saw a train passing along the tracks they'd crossed earlier—two locomotives pulling from the front—hopper cars trailing slowly behind the big engines. Seth watched it for a while—wondering if it was going to Minneapolis or Chicago—if he could catch it and climb onboard—if people ever did that sort of thing anymore. But then he turned back to face the levee before seeing the end of the train—his hair flipping around in the wind—blowing over his eyes and making it hard to see.

A FEW MINUTES LATER HE ARRIVED AT THE TOP OF THE levee—stopped and looked down at the river—spotting the two canoes only fifty yards away—pulled up onto a patch of mud and anchored there. He could see the tarps covering the rest of the ketamine blocks in the middle of the canoes—Benjy and Spoon lying in the shade of some willow brush. He saw Isabel rounding the patch of mud—within twenty yards of them but they hadn't seen her yet.

"OK," Seth said—watching Spoon sit up and wave to Isabel—Benjy waving as well but without even raising his head—Seth watching from the top of the levee as the wind rushed past his ears—as he pulled the cellphone out of his pocket—good reception but there were no missed calls—no messages. "Here we go," he said—taking the pistol Isabel had given him out of his backpack—looking it over before stuffing it down the front of his pants—then tightening his belt—lifting his shirt and letting it fall over the pistol grip.

He descended the levee and made his way to the mud patch and the willow brush—walking in a straight line instead of going around like Isabel had done—straight through the soft, sticky mud—grocery bags slapping against his legs with each step.

"Should've gone around, cap'n," Spoon called out.

Seth looked up and raised his hand in the air—grocery bags coming up near his head—strong wind causing them to vibrate and make a quick snapping sound. He saw them all sitting in the shade—Isabel digging through her backpack and talking to Benjy.

He finally made it to the willow brush and dropped the grocery bags—then kicked his shoes along the weeds and grass—wiping the mud off the soles.

"Bring us some goodies?" Spoon said—already rummaging through all the plastic grocery bags. "Where's the whiskey?" he said—raising his head with a concerned look on his narrow face. "Where's the ice cream?"

"Here," Isabel said—pulling a candy bar from her backpack and throwing it at Spoon—the bar hitting him in the arm and dropping to the ground.

"There it is!" he yelled—opening the wrapper and taking a bite. "Would've preferred the whiskey, but this'll do."

They stayed there in the shade for a while—Seth kicking his shoes across the grass until the mud was all cleaned off—then taking a seat next to Spoon.

"How was your trip into town?" Spoon said—shoving the last bite of the candy bar in his mouth—then wadding up the wrapper and stuffing it in his pocket.

"Alright," Seth said. "How was the river?"

"Just fine in the beginning—stormed the first night but we already had our tents set up. Then when we got close to here the river started spreading out and we got lost a couple times."

"How'd you get lost on a river?"

"It ain't all a river—more like a swamp in some places—hard to tell where the river stops and where the shore begins." Spoon lifted his bare feet for Seth to see. "Had to get out a couple times and pull the damn thing back to deeper water." His pants were wet to the knees—shoes and socks drying in the sun a few feet away.

Seth sat there for a few more minutes—eventually watching Isabel stand up and carry the grocery bags to the canoes—her sandals left in the shady spot where she'd been resting—pants rolled up to above her knees—Seth watching her as she started unpacking the supplies into each canoe—then turning his head to look at Spoon and Benjy—both asleep on their backs now.

Seth got to his feet and slipped off his shoes and socks—rolled up his pants and started off across the mud.

"Hey," he said—walking up to the canoes—his feet sinking into the sand—sun burning the back of his neck.

Isabel finished unloading the grocery bags—then wadded them up and stored them somewhere in the red canoe—turned around and finally looked at Seth.

"What?" she said—squinting with the sun in her face. "Where's the pistol I gave you?"

"Right here." Seth patted the front of his pants.

"Give it to me."

Seth smiled—watching Isabel hold out her hand.

"I'll hold onto it," he said—smiling again as he waited for Isabel to say something—as he studied her face—her hand stretched out toward him. "No."

Isabel pulled the other pistol out from behind her back—pointed it at Seth with a blank expression on her face.

"Give it to me," she said—her voice flat as she lowered her eyes—her hand steady—hair now hanging down behind her head in a long French braid.

Seth took a step back—felt the hot wind running through his hair as he nodded his head—as he looked down at the water—at the two canoes and then back up at the beautiful girl in front of him—wind calming a little as he looked over her head at the levee.

He reached down and lifted his shirt—slowly pulled out the pistol with his thumb and forefinger—then held it up as their eyes met again—Isabel stepping forward—short, careful steps in the wet sand and mud—watching Seth until she grabbed the dangling pistol from his fingers. Then she took a quick step backward and lowered the two pistols—looked downriver as she slipped them both into her pockets.

"We better get going," Isabel said.

"Yeah," Seth said—swallowing hard as he watched her study the river—wondering why she was the way she was.

Isabel walked toward the willow brush and started yelling for Spoon and Benjy to wake up—Seth staying by the canoes—turning and looking out over the river—wind whipping up little clusters of waves on the water's surface. He watched one curl over into a white splash—bubbles and foam spreading out and disappearing—then looked down at the canoes—scrapes running along the sides—mud streaked nearly up to the gunwales. He stayed there for what seemed like a long time—feeling the sun on the back of his neck—then turned around and started walking back through the flat patch of mud.

"You're gonna sink right down to the bottom with those things stuffed in your pants like that," Seth heard Spoon say as he got close.

"Then I won't fall in," Isabel said.

"Oh," Spoon said. "Well that's a great idea—can't believe I didn't think of it myself."

"Shut up."

Spoon was picking up his socks and shoes—Isabel next to him slipping her backpack over her shoulders—Benjy waiting a few steps away—watching and listening but not saying anything.

Seth went and picked up his backpack—checked to make sure the solar charger was still inside—then grabbed his socks and shoes as the other three were already making their way over the mud toward the river.

Seth walked after them but made no effort to catch up— went to the stern of the green canoe and set his shoes and socks and his backpack under the seat—then raised up and saw Isabel coming toward him with a folder.

"Here," she said—holding the folder out for Seth to take. "You and Spoon can take the lead."

"OK," Seth said—taking the folder as Isabel turned and

walked away—opening it and flipping through all the laminated maps and lists—the sun reflecting off the sheets so he turned and held the folder up in front of his face—found three maps with Williston on them and pulled them out—arranging them and then stuffing them back into one of the pockets so they'd all be in the front.

"I'd rather have the pistols if I were you," Spoon said from behind him.

Seth looked over his shoulder. "What do you got?"

"Nothing," Spoon said. "Figure it's better to let y'all do the dirty work."

"Right."

Seth dropped the folder into the canoe—jimmied the rebar anchor out of the ground and shoved it down next to the pile of ketamine blocks—then pushed the canoe out into the water—Spoon hopping into the bow—quickly finding his seat and his paddle—Seth looking over at Isabel—watching her as he walked out into the river—the water soon up to his knees—his hands gripping the green canoe—steadying it before lifting a leg up and over the side.

They paddled out to the main channel and pointed east—Seth studying the maps—trying to figure out exactly where they were. It was still hot and the wind was still blowing—bottom of the canoe scraping rocks and sand in some places—the water brown and cloudy.

Seth saw on the maps how the river suddenly widened into a lake. But to get there they'd have to go through a delta where the main channel was narrow—somehow avoiding all the offshoots that led to dead-ends.

He finally put down the maps and started trying to read the river—keeping an eye on the silted, sandy banks—on little islands that got submerged when the water level was higher—on the plants he saw—tall trees and stands of cattails.

They scraped the bottom a few more times but never

had to get out of the canoe—Seth looking over his shoulder every few minutes to make sure the red canoe was still there—seeing Benjy's red face—squinting against the sun and showing his teeth.

By mid-afternoon they'd made it through to where the river widened—Seth looking down at the thick, curving blue line on the laminated map—tracing it with his finger until he saw 'Lake Sakakawea' written in small letters close to the dam at the end. He put the maps back in the folder and slipped the folder into his backpack—shore being hundreds of yards away now on both sides—picked up his paddle and told Spoon they'd try to stay close to the southern shore— then started paddling through the choppy lake—forgetting to check on the red canoe anymore.

They paddled for another two or three hours—sun behind them now—getting low in the sky. There was no current in the lake—Seth feeling how much of a difference it made— both he and Spoon paddling hard and without speaking to each other—mostly just cliffs to look at along the southern shoreline—few fields of wheat or oats stretching away from the lake—Seth turning his head every hour or so to look at the north shore far off across the rough water—spotting a few homes and a little town.

IT TOOK THEM ANOTHER THREE DAYS OF PADDLING before they were ready to make their next drop—still making their way down Lake Sakakawea—still fighting the sun and the wind every day—waves that sometimes splashed into their canoes—hours of boredom as they tried to keep moving forward through the water.

Now they were camping on the south shore next to a group of grass-covered hills—trees in the ravines between the hills coming all the way down to the lake. Seth sat there alone on the ground in the sunset light—Isabel and Spoon having left a few minutes before—carrying the blocks of ketamine lozenges in their backpacks—Benjy already inside his tent.

Seth sat there and ate his nightly can of soup—not bothering to heat it up—not bothering with a bowl—scooping the chunks of meat and noodles right out of the can. They'd stopped making fires every night and he was too tired and hungry to mess with the little camping stove—eating the unheated soup in a hurry—tipping the can up and drinking the last of the broth as he tried to convince himself he was full.

He faced the hills and leaned back—resting his head on his backpack—looking up at the tops of the hills where he saw Isabel and Spoon emerge from one of the groups of trees—watching them as they walked across the clearing—as they crested one of the hills and then disappeared over the other side. He knew it was too dark to see them after that—they'd be too far away if they had to cross another clearing.

THE NEXT MORNING THE LONG LAKE TURNED TO THE south—rising sun shining in their faces as Seth pulled out the maps—sitting in the stern of the green canoe as Spoon continued paddling from the bow. They passed under a bridge and saw a few cars drive by overhead—then paddled past a large building with a half-full parking lot—Seth flipping through the maps until he discovered it was a casino—looking up and asking Spoon if he thought any of the lozenges wound up there—maybe fished out of a gambler's pocket to calm his nerves—or dissolving slowly inside a waitress's mouth—tucked against her cheek to help her make it through another shift. Spoon shrugged his shoulders and kept paddling—Seth not saying anything else—turning and tucking all the maps back inside the folder—pulling his hat down low over his forehead with one hand as he picked up his paddle with the other.

TWO DAYS LATER SETH WOKE UP IN THE EARLY MORNING to the wind shaking his tent—lying there watching the thin fabric whip in and out—waiting inside his sleeping bag until the sun started coming up. Then he unzipped his tent door and crawled out—stood up and saw Isabel sitting in the red canoe—wearing a sweatshirt with the hood over her head—a puffy vest over that—her legs pulled up inside her sweatshirt—arms wrapped tightly around her knees.

It was too windy to be on the lake so they stayed in camp all day—then spent another night in the same place along Lake Sakakawea—waiting but the wind was even stronger the next morning.

Over two days in camp Seth slept—played cards with Spoon—tried to make better pads for his blistered hands—studied the maps and tried to calculate how long it would take to get through all the lakes and around all the dams—whether they could make it to Kansas City on schedule or not.

It started raining during the second night as Seth ate a can of soup inside his tent—finishing it in just a few minutes—then setting the empty can outside his doorway to catch the rainwater—slipping back inside his sleeping bag as the wind picked up—as flashes of lightning blinked through the thin tent walls—staying awake until most of the lightning and thunder had moved off to the east—smelling the wet earth as he drifted off to sleep—hearing the wind-blown waves as the storm retreated.

He woke up a few hours later—still raining outside but the wind had died down—no lightning or thunder to drown out the water sounds coming from the lake. Seth sat up and listened—his head up against the walls of his tent—able to feel the rain and the cold.

There was a thud off in the distance—maybe a branch falling, he thought—a truck driving down some road they hadn't seen—Isabel shifting around in her sleeping bag.

Seth put on a jacket and left his tent—rain running through his hair as he felt his feet pushing around the wet sand. He clicked on a small flashlight and looked around their little campsite—then pointed the flashlight toward the canoes and saw them floating out in the lake. The water had risen during the night—turning the canoes as they bobbed and banged into each other—two parallel lines where the rebar anchors had been dragged out of the sand.

Seth started running and yelling for the others to help him—dropping the flashlight as he started splashing through the shallows—grabbing the bow of one of the canoes—digging his feet into the sand as he tried to pull it back up onto shore—leaning and pulling with all his strength—wind blowing rain against his body as the flashlight shined out over the water.

Isabel was the first to come out of her tent—running up next to Seth and grabbing the gunwale of the canoe—Seth telling her to keep pulling while he went around to the stern—marching off through the darkness—knees shooting up out of the deeper water as he went—toes digging into the sand as his hands found the stern—then leaning against the canoe—pushing as hard as he could—spinning around after a few steps—pressing his back against the canoe—pushing as little waves splashed against his chest—finally feeling the smooth bottom start to slide up the sandy bank.

Once the canoe was back on solid ground Seth turned around and saw Spoon and Benjy—their hands on the bow—both looking down at him through the light rain. They all took a few deep breaths—then moved to the other canoe and took the same positions—Seth turning around and positioning the point of the stern along his spine—water up to his chest with waves climbing his neck.

There was no wind when the sun came up the next morning—the four of them getting out on the lake as early as they could—sun shining low in a hazy sky—glancing off the water in amber and golden rays. Seth put on a pair of sunglasses and tried not to look up—keeping his eyes on the floor of the canoe as he paddled—only looking up every so often to make sure they were still on the right track—still within sight of the southern shore—still not at the end of the lake.

They paddled all morning and didn't even stop for lunch—the wind picking up early in the afternoon—forcing them to stop for the rest of the day.

That's how it went for the next week or so—paddling out early in the morning with no current to help push them forward—Seth looking for a good campsite around noon— the wind already blowing waves as high as the gunwales of their canoes by that time—whitecaps breaking over and spraying them with windblown mist.

They hadn't had a fire at night since the old man had confronted Spoon and Benjy near Culbertson—staying mostly alone in their tents ever since—Seth sometimes hearing Spoon and Isabel outside—talking and laughing as they ate their cans of soup in the dark—Benjy walking off into the woods by himself some nights—staying away until the others had all fallen asleep—but always back in his tent by morning.

THE NEXT DROP THEY HAD TO MAKE WAS NEAR THE END
of the lake—another five days of mindless paddling before
they got there—just able to set up camp before another
storm swooped in from the west—keeping them in their
tents for a much-needed day of rest—Seth spending most
of the day studying the maps—sitting there with his legs in
his sleeping bag—rain and wind hammering the thin tent
walls all around him—some of the water leaking in through
the seams—a drop hitting his back every few minutes. He
traced his finger over the map in his hands—finding the
dam that created the lake—thin white line with an even
thinner blue line leading south—staring at it for several
minutes before looking up through the little window flap
he had open—trying to see the dam but they were too far
away—trying to think of how they were going to get around
it—how they were going to carry the canoes and the blocks
of ketamine without being noticed.

"Two months," he said as he traced the blue line from
the dam down to Kansas City—shaking his head at the distance they had left to cover—then putting the map down
and looking at his blistered hands—listening to the rain
and the wind pound against his tent. "What the hell am I
doing?"

After a few minutes Seth picked up a protein bar and
took a bite—chewed and closed his eyes. After the protein
bar was gone he lay down and pulled the sleeping bag up
to his chin—keeping his eyes closed as he listened to the
wind whistling outside—rain smacking into puddles near
his head. Then he heard a zipper start to open down by his
feet.

Seth opened his eyes and lifted his head—saw Isabel
sticking her head through the door to his tent—a black rain
jacket on with beads of water dotting its surface—her hair
spilling out of the hood. She climbed into the tent and took
her shoes off—pulled back the hood and looked at Seth.

"You got the maps?" Isabel said—taking her rain jacket off and setting it in the corner of the tent—sitting with her legs crossed beside Seth's knees.

"Yeah." Seth propped himself up on an elbow—watched Isabel as he wondered what kind of visit this was—what she really wanted from him. "We're not gonna make it," he said. "Barely more than a month left to go—no way we make it to Kansas City on time."

"We'll pick up the pace once we get out of this lake."

"There's three more."

Isabel pulled her lower lip into her mouth—turned her head—Seth seeing a few water droplets sparkle in her hair.

"What about the schedule?"

"Supposed to make a drop tomorrow—but we're not gonna make it."

Seth kept looking at Isabel—watching her stare off toward the tent door—her lower lip still sucked into her mouth.

"Can you call him?"

"It only accepts calls," Seth said—picking up the cellphone and raising it in front of him. "Won't call out."

"It's OK," Isabel said—nodding her head now—looking down at Seth. "He'll call. He's still tracking us, right?" Seth nodded. "He'll call—it's not our fault." Isabel kept nodding.

"He doesn't seem like the most understanding person to me," Seth said—then waited but Isabel stayed silent—staring blankly at the tent wall in front of her. "I'll go anywhere you wanna go," Seth continued—almost whispering now. "He won't find us—and if he does we'll be ready."

The rain started coming down harder outside. Seth sat up and listened—wind making the walls of the tent buckle and wave—a cool draught sweeping across his face—Isabel still looking straight ahead—her hair mostly dry but a little frizzy from the rain—cotton pants and shirt creased where she must've been lying on her stomach—her big toe wiggling back and forth.

She turned and opened her mouth to talk but Seth grabbed her before any words came out—or maybe she said something but the rain and the wind drowned it out. He grabbed her arms and pulled her toward him—felt her weaker or maybe just skinnier than the last time he'd held her—pulling her close and falling back—aware that she was crying even before his head hit the sleeping bag.

Some of the water droplets he'd seen in her hair collected and fell onto his neck—holding her on top of him for what seemed like a long time—eventually feeling her pull a hand up to her face—feeling her cheek on his chest—feeling her shake—looking down through her hair as more droplets fell to his neck—as they ran down and disappeared between his skin and the sleeping bag.

At some point it stopped raining—the sun went down and all the insects and frogs came out to call to each other. Isabel was gone when Seth woke up—rolling over and checking the cellphone—resting his head on his arm as he stared at the screen—watching it dim after a minute or so—then go dark a few seconds after that.

15

THE NEXT DAY WAS HOT AND HUMID—SETH STARTING to sweat as he finished his first bottle of water in the stern of the green canoe—the four of them already paddling when the sun came up—already stripped down to short-sleeve shirts—already splashing the first cupped handfuls of river water onto the backs of their necks.

"If we had enough of them things," Spoon said from the bow—watching Seth spread out the solar panel to charge the cellphone. "We could power a little outboard motor."

Seth plugged the charging cord into the phone—then looked up at Spoon—watching the skinny boy as he inspected the stern of the canoe.

"Should be able to mount it easy enough," Spoon said. "Put a battery under the seat."

The sun was shining now—pale yellow as it climbed quickly into the cloudless sky—turning white hot within half an hour of rising.

Seth looked back over his shoulder and saw the red

canoe—saw Benjy squinting and paddling hard—Isabel behind him—her face completely shaded by her hat.

"That would save us a lot of time—putting a motor on each canoe—wouldn't it?" Seth said.

"Save our hands, at least," Spoon said—setting his paddle down on his lap and shaking his gloved hands—making a fist and then stretching out his stiff fingers.

Seth shook his head as he turned to face forward—looking out over the water—up at the hills to their right—across the wide part of the lake to his left. The sun was in his face so he pulled his hat down low—adjusted his gloves and started paddling again.

"We're not gonna make our next drop on time," Seth said—still paddling as Spoon finished stretching his hands—the skinny boy pausing but not turning around—adjusting his gloves and then taking a drink from a water bottle.

Seth let a few minutes go by—surface of the lake finally calm—everything quiet except for the slap of their paddles—sound of water being pushed around.

"There's a dam up here at the end of this lake," he said. "We're gonna have to get out and carry everything around it."

Spoon again stayed silent—paddling from the bow of the green canoe—probably still thinking about the outboard motor, Seth thought—or how to portage all the ketamine around the dam—all their supplies and the canoes—all without attracting too much attention.

They paddled for another two hours—Seth constantly looking for the end of the lake up ahead—eventually spotting the dam running along the horizon—squinting his eyes before setting his paddle in his lap and pulling out the maps—running his index finger over one of the laminated sheets before he looked back up at the shoreline—then back down at the map and thought he knew where they were—close to a marina and a little town—long dock jutting out into the lake—the town's grid of streets adjacent to the dam.

Seth tried to find a way to avoid them both—a hidden spot where they could exit the lake—using the scale on the map to estimate the distances. But every route seemed to be at least two miles down to the river—two miles carrying all their gear—all the ketamine blocks and the canoes.

"How many trips you think it'd take us to carry all this stuff around the dam?" Seth said—keeping his eyes down on the map—talking loud enough for Spoon to hear him.

"Well," Spoon said. "We got maybe fifteen-hundred pounds of ketamine left between the two canoes—three, four-hundred pounds of gear." He was quiet for a moment—stopped paddling as he mumbled to himself. "Maybe five or six trips."

They paddled until noon—the wind never picking up and the lake remaining calm. Seth had finally picked a place on the map to exit the lake and he knew they were getting close—scanning the shoreline as they paddled—checking what he saw against the map.

Then the cellphone started ringing on the tarp in front of him.

"Hello, Seth," the man said.

"Hello."

It was hot with no clouds in the sky—Seth feeling his arms starting to burn in the sun—his sweat-soaked shirt sticking to his back. He sat there with the phone to his ear—watching Spoon set his paddle down in his lap—lift his shirt to wipe his face.

"I have never been able to understand why people allow themselves to harbor certain vulnerabilities—normal people, like you."

Seth didn't say anything—just sat there and waited—twisted around to make sure the red canoe was still behind them.

"For instance, why are people perpetually seeking an escape from reality?"

"I don't—I don't know, sir."

Seth waited—the man taking another long pause—breathing into the phone.

"It's hard," Seth said. "It's hard being alive—I guess."

"Is it?"

"That's how most people feel—I think."

"Well, in order for it to be described as hard or difficult, wouldn't you have to have something to compare it to?"

"I guess you could compare it to being dead."

"But no one alive knows what it's like to be dead."

"Yeah."

There was yet another long pause—Seth seeing the red canoe creeping up on their left—starting to turn his head but then didn't.

"Why do people love each other? It's by far the easiest thing to use against someone."

Seth didn't say anything—sat there and listened to the man breathing into the phone—the red canoe coming closer—soon so close he could hear Spoon and Benjy whispering to each other.

"Ask Isabel for the maps, Seth."

"I have them."

"Good," the man said. "Do you see Forty-Fifth Avenue?"

Seth flipped through the few maps he had on the tarp in front of him—found the   right one and then dragged his index finger back and forth over it—quickly reading all the road names.

"Yeah," he said. "I see it."

"A white pickup is waiting there for you. It's been modified to be twice as tall as it was originally intended to be—springs and shocks replaced—myriad other alterations, I presume—'lifted,' I think is what it's called. Anyway, the driver's name is Marvin and he's an imbecile. He will take you around the dam to a safe place where you can enter the river again."

"OK."

"Do you understand, Seth?"

"Yessir."

"That's good, Seth," the man said. "Do you still have the pistols?"

"Yeah." Seth looked over his shoulder at Isabel—paddle in her lap as she leaned forward trying to listen.

"Good." The man paused—another few seconds of Seth listening to him breathe into the phone. "You know, I'd be very disappointed if you were ever dishonest with me, Seth." The man paused yet again—Seth's forehead starting to sweat as he tried to read the map in his hands—cellphone to his ear as he tried to figure out exactly where they were supposed to exit the lake. "After all," the man continued. "What do we gentlemen have if not our honor?" Seth heard the man move—stand up or sit down—maybe just lean to one side or the other. "Authority and honor, Seth—that's all there is." The man ended the call—Seth holding the phone up in front of him—looking at the screen and seeing the call time before it went black—breathing hard still—sweat dripping off his face—some of the drops hitting the laminated map in his lap.

"What'd he say?" Isabel said.

Seth looked out over the water and then down at the map—not bothering to turn toward Isabel—not bothering to answer her question. After a minute or two he picked up the paddle from his lap—held it above the water and turned toward the red canoe.

"He's got somebody waiting for us not too far away—they're gonna take us around the dam." Seth watched her for a few seconds—paddling now as he watched the red canoe pulling ahead of them.

"Where?" Isabel said.

"Not too far."

Seth started to paddle harder—getting the green canoe back in the lead—steering to the right as he studied the shoreline—groups of trees and grass-covered hills—couple alfalfa fields in the low-lying flat areas.

A HALF HOUR LATER SETH RECOGNIZED A LITTLE BAY from the map—turned the canoe hard to the right as he looked for any sign of the road—glancing back to see the red canoe turning as well—all four of them paddling for the rocky shoreline—cottonwood trees and shrubs clumped together about ten yards from the water.

The front of the green canoe hit the rocks hard—Spoon setting his paddle down—hopping out and grabbing the bow—Seth stepping down into the deeper water—going around to the stern where he started pushing—Spoon pulling at the same time as they moved the canoe a few feet—getting it up onto the rocks and sand—tiny waves rippling up the sides.

"Where's our ride?" Spoon said—walking up out of the lake.

"Around here somewhere." Seth turned and watched the red canoe crash into the rocks—heard the bottom scrape as Isabel stepped out into the knee-deep water. "Stay here," he said to Spoon.

Seth walked toward the trees—up away from the river—walked fast without turning to look back. There were mosquitoes swarming near the shrubs at the base of the trees—hovering there in the shade as Seth walked right through them—then walked on until he saw the white pickup—maybe fifty yards from the river—partially hidden among the thick trees and shrubs.

A man sat asleep in the driver's seat—his head tipped back against the headrest—his mouth open. Seth kept walking—dragging his feet through the dirt to make noise as he approached. When he was close he kicked a rock that hit the front left tire—waking the man who immediately started shaking his head—blinking and straightening his hat. Seth saw sweat stains on the hat—saw that the man's long beard hid his neck and the collar of his T-shirt.

"Hey," the man said—clearing his throat. "Hi."

Seth walked up to the window—put his hand up on the rearview mirror and stood there—looked at the man but didn't say anything at first.

"You Marvin?" he said after a few seconds.

"Yeah." Marvin put his hands on the steering wheel—looked at Seth—then looked past him toward the river—tapping on the steering wheel as he tried to avoid Seth's eyes. "What?" he said.

"Hmm?"

"What is it?"

Seth waited—still watching the stranger. "I was thinking about your pickup—maybe taking it from you." Seth turned his head and looked at the open tailgate—then down the dirt path that led away from the river. "Drive it all the way to California."

"Hey I was just told to give you a ride, man." Marvin raised his hands off the steering wheel. "I don't know nothing else—really don't wanna know nothing else."

There was a pause as Seth continued staring down the dirt path—thick trunks of cottonwood trees—open spaces with little shrubs and bare dirt.

"Guess I'm just tired of being such a pussy," Seth said. "Letting everybody walk all over me."

"Huh?"

"Hey," Isabel yelled from behind Seth—causing him to turn and watch her walking up through the trees—thumbs looped through the straps of her backpack. "Everything OK?"

Seth started walking down toward her—ground sticky and compacted from recent rains—sunlight trickling through the trees but they were both mostly in the shade. He stopped a few feet from Isabel—up the hill from where she stood—looking over her head but unable to see the canoes or the river—then spotting Benjy and Spoon carefully making their way over the rocks at the water's edge.

Seth looked back down and noticed a pistol grip sticking out of Isabel's pocket—lunged toward her and tried to grab it but she turned away from him—blocked his hand and pulled the other pistol out from behind her back. Seth grabbed her arm and pulled her closer to him—felt her fire a shot as his ears started ringing—then shook her arm until she dropped the pistol—grabbed her backpack and threw her to the side.

He turned and spotted the pistol in the exposed roots of a nearby tree—getting to it just as Benjy was running up—raising it and squeezing the trigger just as the two young men were about to collide. Benjy's arms went loose and fell to his sides—his head jerked back and his body started falling forward—Seth watching the stocky boy's knees hit the ground beside him—chest going down as his arms flung out and hit the hard earth—blood already starting to flow onto the dirt.

Seth's ears were still ringing but he could hear people yelling—turning his head to see Isabel getting to her feet—Benjy's body between them—forcing him to hop over it to get to her. She pulled the other pistol out of her pocket and retreated a few steps—raised it as Seth dove down and to the side. He heard a shot go off as he hit the ground—dropping the pistol that'd been in his hand—crawling behind a tree as he heard Isabel fire another round.

When he peeked around the other side of the tree he saw Isabel marching toward him—pistol still raised—backpack gone and a little mud on her arms.

Seth kept the tree between them as Isabel tried to get a clear shot—kept peeking around to see where she was—making two circles around the tree before he saw his chance—coming up behind her and diving for her legs—tripping her and watching her stumble forward—hearing another shot as she twisted around before hitting the ground—as he saw the flash of fire from the barrel.

Seth scurried over and grabbed Isabel's arm—twisted it so the pistol pointed at the tree branches above them—crawled closer as she squeezed off another shot—Seth barely able to hear it now. He climbed on top of her—keeping hold of her arm and wrist with both hands—using his weight as she kicked and tried to squirm free—as she used her free hand to punch at Seth's face but couldn't make good contact. Seth tried to hold her still—tried to pry the pistol from her hand—failed and so he banged her hand on the ground until the pistol popped free.

He reached over and picked it up—Isabel still trying to punch him as he used his other hand to block—leaning back as he straddled her stomach—as he waited for her to exhaust herself—her hands and arms eventually dropping to the ground—her chest filling with air and her ribs pressing against his legs—mouth partway open—strands of her hair sticking to her face.

Seth stood up slowly with the pistol pointed skyward—his other hand ready in case Isabel decided to kick or raise her knee. He took a few steps to the side and glanced down—aware of noises behind him but his ears were still ringing too much to tell what they were. He bent down and picked up the other pistol—tucked it into the waistband of his pants and turned around.

"Dead," he saw Spoon say—reading his lips more than hearing his voice—seeing the skinny boy kneeling over Benjy's body—crying as he repeated the word many times. "He's dead—dead."

The man in the white pickup, Marvin, was standing near the front bumper with the driver's side door left open—looking around as Seth watched him bring a limp hand up to his head—remove his hat as he dropped his eyes to stare at Benjy's body.

"Get him back down to the river," Seth said to Marvin—barely able to hear his own voice—repeating the command in case he'd said it wrong.

Marvin stood there looking at Seth—his hat held gingerly in both hands—plump beads of sweat on his forehead. Seth raised the pistol.

"Alright, man—alright," Marvin said—raising his hands as he started walking toward the body.

"Spoon," Seth said as he turned with the pistol. "Help him."

Spoon was still crying—his hands on Benjy's back. He looked up at Seth—his face red and shaking—glistening with tears. Seth waited—held the pistol out in front of him—looked over his shoulder and saw Isabel still on the ground. When he turned back Spoon was standing up—grabbing Benjy's limp legs.

Marvin grabbed under the stocky boy's armpits and they lifted the body—Seth watching them waddle down through the trees—stopping twice to rest. He followed a few yards behind them—kicking dirt over the drops and jagged lines of blood—checking on Isabel as his hearing gradually returned to normal—seeing her on her back still—lying in the same spot near the pickup.

As they approached the lake Seth turned and jogged back up through the trees—reached inside the white pickup and pulled out the keys.

"I'm not gonna run off," Isabel said.

Seth was starting back down toward Spoon and Marvin—keys rattling against each other in his hand. He stopped and looked down at her—wondered what she was looking at up in the trees—why she wouldn't even raise her head.

"What?"

"Where do you think I'd go?"

"Anywhere," Seth said—turning his head to watch Spoon and Marvin carry the body the last few feet to the rocky shoreline—almost out of sight behind the trunks of several cottonwood trees. "Away from all this."

"Anywhere'd be just as bad—worse, maybe."

Seth watched her for a few more seconds—sunlight moving over her skin in patches as green leaves swayed high above their heads. Then he turned and jogged down to the river—Benjy's body laid out on the rocks just beyond the trees—Spoon and Marvin standing next to it in the shade. They both looked down at the pistol in Seth's hand. He watched them breathing hard with sweat on their foreheads—Spoon's face still red—his eyes still puffy.

"Over here," Seth said—walking around them to a spot a few yards from the canoes—then pointing down at the ground with the pistol. "Dig a hole right here—as deep as you can go."

He stood there in the sun and looked up at them—Spoon staying back in the shade and glaring at him—Marvin walking around with his hands clasped over the top of his head—bill of his hat smashed down over his eyes.

"Marvin," Seth said—raising the pistol. "Did you hear me?"

"Look, man," Marvin said—walking toward Seth. "Just let me go—I won't say nothing—just let me go, man—please."

"Dig the hole, Marvin," Seth said—doing his best to sound calm and confident—to stand his ground as Marvin came closer.

Marvin stopped and looked down at the spot where the hole would be—looked up at the pistol—nodded his head and flapped his arms—then bent down and started moving some of the rocks.

Seth walked back toward the trees—looked down at Benjy's body as he passed it—on his back now with his eyes closed—one of his arms dangling across his stomach.

Seth went over and sat down in the shade—leaned back against a young cottonwood tree. Spoon was still there—still glaring at him.

"You too, Spoon," Seth said—motioning with the pistol.

Spoon waited a moment—looked out over the lake before lifting a hand to his face—rubbing his forehead as he stood up—as he walked out into the sunlight to help dig Benjy's grave.

Seth watched Marvin and Spoon as they did their work—tossing the bigger rocks out of the way—then bending down and scooping up wet sand with the trowels—creating a hole no more than a foot deep before Seth told them to stop. Then he watched them lift Benjy's body and carry it over—Spoon lowering the legs into the hole before going around to help Marvin with the upper body.

They covered Benjy with the wet sand and the rocks—then went to the lake to wash their hands.

"HE WASN'T ALL BAD," ISABEL SAID—STANDING BEHIND Seth with her arms crossed—leaning against a tree a few yards away—both of them watching Spoon and Marvin at the edge of the lake—crouching with their hands in the water. "He'd still be alive if I'd kept the bullets somewhere else—or just thrown everything in the lake."

Seth turned to look at her—studied her face but didn't say anything—noticing the lack of tears—lack of any sign she was sad or angry.

"You were never gonna run off with me after Kansas City," he said. "Were you?"

"There'd be no point—he'd find us eventually." Isabel took a step closer.

"Stay there." Seth stood up and turned to face her—Isabel

taking another couple steps before stopping—looking down at the pistol in his hand—both of them quiet for a few seconds.

"But since we're not even gonna make it to Kansas City," Isabel said—flapping her arms and shaking her head. "Let's just take all the money and fly to Vegas—have some fun before he kills us—stay in the penthouse suite and pretend we're on our honeymoon or whatever." Her face was shaking now—Seth able to see tears forming in her eyes. "I'll even pretend I'm into you—like none of this ever happened and we just met someplace normal—like he'll never be able to find us—whatever you want—whatever you want."

"Stop it," Seth said. "We'll make it—there's still four of us with Marvin."

He turned and saw Spoon and Marvin walking up— moved to the side and motioned for them to come closer— all of them standing in the shade but Seth could tell the sun was starting to set—could tell the temperature had dropped some as a little breeze started blowing through the trees.

"Wait," Marvin said. "What do you mean?"

"You're coming with us," Seth said—turning toward Marvin with the pistol still in his hand—shaking it a little so Marvin knew it was there.

"Look, man, I won't tell nobody, I swear—just let me go. I'll drive you wherever you want—just let me go, man, please."

"That's not the right answer, Marvin." Seth raised the pistol. "There's money in it—you'll get paid once we get there—plus you won't get shot."

Marvin didn't say anything. He'd taken a few steps back while Seth was talking—then stopped at the mention of getting shot—sweat on his round face—his hands still dripping with the river water—breathing hard still—hard enough for Seth to see his chest filling and emptying.

"Let's get everything in the pickup," Seth said—tucking

the pistol into his pocket—then taking the other one out of the waistband of his pants and moving it to his other pocket.

They carried the orange, shrink-wrapped blocks from the canoes to the pickup—Seth keeping his distance from the others—taking his own route up through the trees. Next they loaded their supplies—then headed back down to the lake for the empty canoes—seeing a sailboat pass by—Seth waving and smiling at the people on deck—telling the other three to do the same. Once it was gone they hauled the canoes out of the water—loaded them into the bed of the pickup and tied them down.

"Let's go," Seth said—climbing into the back seat on the driver's side—Isabel stepping up into the passenger's seat and Spoon sitting next to Seth.

Marvin pulled the driver's side door shut and reached for the ignition—started patting his pockets as Seth handed him the keys over his shoulder—then told him to drive to a grocery store.

Seth had his backpack and the duffel bag of cash on the floorboard between his legs—one of the pistols in his right hand—resting sideways on the seat. They drove out to a two-lane highway—Seth watching the sun as it dipped closer to the horizon—watching the pastures and the green fields.

They drove over the dam—lake nearly up to the road on their left—ground dropping off over a cement cliff on their right—Seth barely able to see the thin line of water where the river started again.

They drove on and soon entered Riverdale—Marvin pulling into a grocery store parking lot—leaving the pickup running—his hands on the steering wheel—waiting for whatever came next.

"I'll go," Isabel said—opening the door and climbing down out of the pickup.

Seth shifted in his seat but didn't try to stop her—didn't say anything as the three of them sat there and watched

Isabel cross the parking lot. The store was a one-story metal building—a sign above the glass doors but it was too faded to read. They watched her swing open one of the doors and walk inside.

"He was gonna kill Benjy in Kansas City," Seth said. "He told me." He sat there silent for a few seconds—then turned his head and looked at Spoon.

"If he was planning on killing somebody," Spoon said— still staring out the window. "Then he's gonna kill some- body—Benjy being gone ain't gonna change his mind—just changes which one of us is gonna get it."

"Did you say Kansas City?" Marvin said from the driv- er's seat—looking up at the rearview mirror but Seth kept his eyes on Spoon—ignoring the question—the panic in Marvin's voice.

"If we can make the rest of the drops on time," Seth said. "No more problems—no more delays—I think we'll be fine."

"No," Spoon said—looking at Seth and shaking his head. "We won't."

They sat there and waited—the sun starting to dim as Seth looked out the window at the clouds—watching several birds as they flew between the trees at the edge of the park- ing lot—Isabel eventually coming out of the store with two full grocery bags—climbing up into the pickup as Seth told Marvin to drive them to the river.

16

IT WAS NEARLY DARK BY THE TIME THEY GOT THE canoes loaded—Seth standing off to the side as the other three finished covering the blocks of ketamine with tarps—watching them but mostly looking out across the water—listening to the tiny waves rushing up the sand and slapping against the sides of the canoes—looking up at the sky where the sun had set just minutes before—then down at the river again while there was still a little light left—trees almost black along the opposite shoreline—Seth barely able to see the branches waving in the breeze.

"Let's go," he said—motioning for Isabel to get into the front seat of the red canoe—waiting for her to get settled—then pushing the canoe into the water and holding it steady—raising one of the pistols as he looked back at Marvin and Spoon—forcing them to climb into the green canoe.

Once they were situated they floated out past Isabel—started to drift away in the current—Seth stepping into the stern of the red canoe and sitting down—waiting for it to stop rocking before picking up his paddle—then yelling to Marvin and Spoon to go ahead but to stay close—watching them paddle off down the river as he stuffed both pistols into his backpack—as he slid a heel back and touched the duffel bag.

The moon was bright that night and the sky was clear—the two canoes moving slowly downriver—keeping the shoreline in sight—no one saying anything as they listened to the insects calling to each other—the paddles and the breeze moving through the trees. Seth kept looking up at the stars—watching the moon move across the sky as he paddled just enough to keep pace with the green canoe—keeping them moving until the moon was three quarters of the way across the sky—then found a sandy spot along the right side of the river—directed both canoes toward it as he checked the cellphone for any missed calls.

"Let's get the tents set up," Seth said—stepping out of the red canoe into knee-deep water—both pistols in his pockets again.

They grabbed their camping gear and walked up the little beach—Seth staying behind to anchor the canoes—hammering the pieces of rebar into the sand until they nearly disappeared.

"How's this go?" Marvin said—Benjy's tent spread out on the ground at his feet—poles still folded in his hands—Spoon walking over to help him.

Seth walked up and sat there on the ground—watched them in the dark—last minutes of moonlight helping him see Isabel get into her tent as soon as she got it set up—then zipper the door closed before clicking on a flashlight—Seth listening to her shift around inside her sleeping bag.

Spoon and Marvin finished with their tents soon after—Spoon crawling inside without saying anything—Marvin unrolling Benjy's sleeping bag and searching for the zipper—looking up at Seth once he'd found it.

"Ain't you gonna sleep?" Marvin said.

"I will." Seth sat there—legs crossed in the sand with his backpack and unassembled tent next to him. "Think I'll stay up a while first."

"Oh." Marvin nodded his head—crawled into the tent and zippered the door closed.

Seth yawned and leaned back into the shifting sand— used his rolled up sleeping bag as a pillow—crossed his arms over his chest and looked up at the stars—listening to all the night sounds—the three tents nearby—a flashlight clicking off—crumple of a plastic water bottle—someone shifting around in their sleeping bag.

"Goodnight," Seth said—loud enough for all three to hear.

No one responded.

Seth burrowed deeper into the loose sand—wriggling his body from side to side—feeling the sand come up and cradle his ribs and hips—feeling it cold on his lower back.

The stars twinkled above him as he tried to watch one long enough to see it move across the sky—gave up and then looked for the constellations he knew—Orion's Belt—the Big Dipper and the Little Dipper—finding all three before leaning his head back—looking at the tops of the trees up the steep bank behind their campsite—watching the topmost leaves sway as he listened to the river—to the tiny waves lapping against the sandy shore.

THEY MOVED DOWN THE RIVER THAT WAY FOR THE NEXT week or so—no one saying very much—Seth telling them when and where to stop for lunch—when to stop for the night—where to go to make the drops. The days were hot and windy and the skies stayed clear—the current helping to propel them down the river—helping them get back on schedule.

They stopped in Bismarck, North Dakota to resupply and to make their largest drop yet—then moved on and came to another lake two days later—a Saturday morning when they first set out on Lake Oahe—the current disappearing—shorelines shooting off into the distance—becoming thin green lines at the edges of the lake. They had to paddle hard again—moving the weight of the canoes by themselves.

By noon they started seeing boats on the water—people holding fishing poles in one hand while they waved with the other. Seth kept them far enough away so they wouldn't have to talk to anyone—telling the other three when to slow down—when to speed up—leading them out into the middle of the lake when he spotted boats along the shoreline.

The good weather held and Seth pushed them hard each day—sleeping outside each night by himself—waking up anytime one of them moved around inside their tent—spraying himself with bug spray a few times every night to keep the mosquitoes away.

They ate canned soup in the evenings—protein bars and trail mix and beef jerky during the day. When they ran out of water they stopped and filtered the lake water for an hour or so—taking turns while the others rested—filling up all their bottles again.

They made four drops as they moved down the lake—same routine as all the others—find the purple flag and start digging—take the money and leave the ketamine.

Seth made sure each canoe held the same number of orange, shrink-wrapped blocks after each drop—transferring a few from one canoe to the other—wondering why people were paying so much money for the homemade drugs—what was wrong with them and how the lozenges helped.

"CAN YOU HEAR WHAT THEY'RE SAYING?" SETH SAID—
sweating under the mid-afternoon sun as they neared the
dam at the end of the lake.

Isabel turned from her seat in the bow of the red canoe—looked at him through her sunglasses but didn't say
anything—then turned back around and started paddling
again.

"What are they talking about up there?" Seth stopped
paddling and tried to listen—watching as Marvin and
Spoon talked and laughed up ahead in the green canoe.

"I have no idea," Isabel said—dropping her paddle onto
the gunwales—then dropping her head to her hands.

Seth picked up one of the maps from the floor of the
canoe—held his hand up to block the sun while he studied
it—then looked up at the bare hills and the ravines—the
jagged shoreline.

"We're close," Seth said. "Let's catch up to them." He
dropped the map and started paddling hard—Isabel leaving her paddle to roll back and forth below her knees—her
head still in her hands.

"And then he grabbed the highway patrolman's hat
off the hood of his car," Seth heard Marvin saying as they
approached the green canoe—Spoon sitting there with a
smile on his face. "Put the hat on his head and did some
goofy little dance."

They both laughed—shaking the green canoe as they
held their paddles in their laps. Isabel pulled a handkerchief from her pocket and wiped her face—then opened a
bottle of water as Seth kept paddling—within a few feet of
the green canoe now.

"So y'all surely got arrested, right?" Spoon said.

"Nope," Marvin said. "Turns out he had one of them
dashboard cameras. If he'd arrested us he woulda had to
show everybody the tape as evidence. Then his boss and
everybody woulda seen some drunk idiot dancing around

his patrol car—his own patrolman's hat on." They laughed as Seth kept paddling—smiling at the portion of the story he'd heard.

When Spoon and Marvin noticed the red canoe gaining on them they picked up their paddles—started pulling away as they paddled in unison—forcing Seth to call out and tell them to slow down.

"We're getting close to the dam," Seth said. "Think I found a place where we can get out and haul everything around to where the river starts again."

"This the last lake?" Spoon said—none of them looking at Seth as they paddled—Isabel stopping again to drink from the bottle she kept by her feet—to sit there and look out over the water from behind her sunglasses.

"Nope," Seth said.

They kept paddling—Seth eventually telling Spoon and Marvin to follow him—steering the red canoe closer to shore—checking the map every few minutes.

It was getting late—close to sundown as Seth noticed the temperature dropping—wind blowing harder and gray clouds pushing up in front of them. He looked up and saw the sun shining on the tops of the rounded clouds—watching them expand and flatten against some invisible ceiling.

Then the cellphone started ringing.

"Hello," Seth said—hearing something move on the other end of the line—something slide across a table, maybe—the man staying silent for a long time—Isabel turning around and looking at Seth—sunglasses hanging from the neck of her shirt now.

"Seth," the man finally said—then paused as Seth felt the canoe turning to one side—drifting in the water.

He looked up and saw the spot he'd picked out along the shoreline—checked the laminated map again to be sure. It was a hundred yards away and there was a black pickup parked right at the edge of the lake—someone in the driver's seat with their left arm hanging out the window.

"There will be a large storm in your area very soon, Seth," the man said. "Wind, rain, thunder and lightning."

"Yeah I see it."

"Do you also see a black pickup? There should be a very small, very soft-bodied man driving."

"Yeah—yessir."

"He will take you around the lakes."

"The lakes?" Seth said. "All of them?"

"You know you will never have intercourse with her again—surely you already know that—don't you, Seth?"

"What?"

The wind blew in gusts now—big gray clouds coming together to block out the last few minutes of sunlight—Seth trying to lead the two canoes to the pickup as he listened to the man—as he waited through the long pauses—as he responded to the man's ramblings.

"I used to think there was something wrong with me," the man said. "That I was defective in some fundamental way."

Seth was only able to hear every other word the man said—the canoes bobbing in the rough water—the green canoe passing them as Spoon and Marvin paddled hard for shore—Seth holding the phone with his shoulder—trying to help Isabel paddle while he waited for the man to continue—raindrops smacking against the tarp in front of him.

"Then I thought I was homosexual," the man said. "Convinced myself I liked men instead of women and that was the only issue—but that wasn't true either."

There was another pause as Seth looked up at the sky—seeing a flash of lightning off in the distance—waiting for the thunder to reach them.

"It's actually quite an advantage, I've come to find—not feeling the urge to gesticulate against another human being."

"Yeah," Seth yelled into the phone. "Yessir." He paddled

as best he could—watching Isabel paddle hard in the bow of the canoe as the rain and the wind picked up.

"I suppose it's just another addiction—sex, that is. But when nearly everyone has the same addiction it's not considered an addiction at all—It's normal behavior—natural— perfectly, irrevocably natural—nothing to be ashamed of."

"I guess so."

The front of their canoe hit the rocks along the shore-line—Seth already stepping out into the shallow water—the pistols already in his pockets—his backpack hanging from his shoulders—duffel bag with all the money in it held tightly in one hand. Spoon and Marvin were in front of him—helping Isabel out and holding the canoe steady.

"You see, Seth, it's all just a game—sex, alcohol, tobacco, food, trinkets everyone thinks they need but no one really does—anything that can be exploited by powerful people and not cause the complete collapse of society—it's al-lowed—even encouraged."

"OK," Seth said—walking up the rocky beach now— moving toward the black pickup—the driver standing there by the front tire with his hands in his pockets—wind blow-ing hard against Seth's shirt—soaked through from the rain along with everything else. "So where's this guy taking us?"

"His name is Chad—Chad from Pierre, South Dakota."

"Where's he driving us?"

"Give him the lozenges for the next three drops."

"OK but where the hell are we going?" Seth said—a little too loud—a little too much anger in his voice.

He stopped walking halfway between the canoes and the pickup—stood there in the wind and the rain and closed his eyes—rubbed his forehead as a burst of thunder reached his ears.

"If I choose to keep you in the dark, Seth—you stupid, weak boy—it's because you belong in the dark—understand, Seth?"

Seth nodded—still with his eyes closed. "Yeah," he said. "Yessir."

Seth waited for the man to continue—listened to the storm and the man's slow breathing—then heard the call end. He stuffed the cellphone into his pocket and ran up the riverbank—the other three already carrying the orange blocks to the pickup from the canoes. He tossed his backpack and the duffel bag onto the backseat without acknowledging the driver—Chad—then ran down to grab a load of the lozenges.

Once everything was loaded into the pickup—camping gear soaking wet from the rain—they all crowded into the backseat as Seth opened the passenger's side door—lightning flashing as darkness settled in—Chad waiting for them with his hands on the steering wheel—his eyes black—patches of facial hair on his cheeks and chin. He didn't say anything as they drove off through the rain—canoes sticking out the back of the pickup.

After a while Seth asked him where they were going—watched Chad turn his head and look across the center console—waited for him to answer but he never did—just turned back to the road without saying anything.

Seth eventually stopped trying to get anything out of Chad—sat back and nearly fell asleep as they drove through the storm—keeping his hands pressed down on the pistols in his pockets.

It was dark inside the cab of the pickup—green buttons and gauges glowing along the dash providing just enough light to see Chad's face and features—flashes of lightning briefly illuminating the backseat—Seth twisting his head around to see Isabel asleep behind him—her hair wrapped in a towel—head leaning against the window—Marvin and Spoon both asleep beside her.

Soon they turned onto I-90 and headed east—Seth still forcing himself to stay awake—leaning over and reaching out for the radio controls—trying to turn it on but nothing happened—no sound as he twisted the volume knob—just glowing buttons—digital clock showing all zeros.

It took them four hours to get to Yankton, South Dakota—Seth keeping track of time on the cellphone. It rained for the first three hours but then tapered off to sprinkles and then mist—cool and breezy by the time they reached Yankton—muddy but not raining anymore.

They stopped at a Walmart to buy supplies—Seth going into the store with Marvin—piling boxes of protein bars and beef jerky in their cart—cans of soup and a bottle of sunscreen that Isabel wanted—the empty bottle in Marvin's back pocket so they'd be sure to get the exact same kind. They bought toilet paper and moleskin and a pack of socks for them all to share—deodorant and toothpaste and a box of tampons.

Then Chad drove them through town—turned onto a dirt road—shut off the pickup's headlights and drove on for ten or fifteen minutes. Seth kept one of the maps out on his lap—using the flashlight on the cellphone to check it—finally figuring out where they were—relieved to see they were past all the lakes—downriver a few miles from the final dam.

They were in the river bottoms now—flat, level ground with tall grass on each side of the pickup—probably soybeans or corn in the fields this far south and east, Seth guessed. They were all quiet for a few minutes as they bounced down the dirt road—pickup rattling over the rutted, muddy path—everyone awake and alert—Seth staring out the windshield—waiting to see the river.

Soon Chad found the end of the road and stopped the pickup—shut off the engine and opened his door—triggering the dome light as Seth looked back at Marvin and Spoon—crumbs and dirt in Marvin's beard—Spoon's greasy hair combed over to one side.

Seth stepped out of the pickup and waited for his

eyes to adjust—looking through a stand of willows and cottonwoods—seeing tiny, dull bits of shimmering light on the river's surface—hearing the engine ticking as it cooled beside him. Then he turned and walked to the tailgate of the black pickup—started counting out the ketamine for the next three drops—Chad taking the orange blocks and hiding them under the backseat—still silent as he carefully counted each package—checking a ripped piece of paper he'd pulled from his pocket. The other three took the canoes down to the river and set them on a sandy beach—Seth listening to the insects buzzing as he watched everyone work—as he heard the water swirling around on itself.

For a few minutes they went back and forth carrying loads of supplies and orange shrink-wrapped blocks—Seth eventually pitching in—keeping one hand free in case he needed one of the pistols—watching the other three as they passed by each other—watching Chad as he stood near the tailgate and waited for them to finish.

Once the pickup was empty Chad drove off without saying a word—heading away from the river with his headlights still dark.

They camped on the sandy beach that night—Seth lying down in the middle of the three tents—looking up at the sky—moon glowing through the clouds but he couldn't see any stars—lying there listening to all the night sounds until he fell asleep.

17

"WE'RE ABOUT HALFWAY," SETH SAID—THE FOUR of them sitting together in a circle as the sun came up—Marvin using the camping stove to heat water for coffee.

"But no more lakes, right?" Spoon said—busy cutting moleskin for his hands—not bothering to look up as he spoke.

"Right."

Seth set the map he'd been holding down on the sand— sipped from a bottle of water as he watched Isabel eat one of the protein bars—wearing her jacket against the early morning cold—a hairbrush sticking out of one of the pockets.

The sun was shining on the hills across the river—sparkling as the light bounced off all the wet leaves and grass— not high enough yet to reach them.

"Well thank God for that," Spoon said—now wrapping his hand with athletic tape—shaking his head. "These hands can't take much more paddling."

"We should be ahead of schedule now," Isabel said. "Be

able to rest a little more." She put the last bit of the protein bar in her mouth.

"Yeah," Seth said.

They stayed there through midmorning—Seth walking back into the trees by himself—watching hummingbirds zip around from flower to flower. He sat at the trunk of a tree once he lost sight of the tiny birds—looked out at their campsite—Isabel brushing her hair—Spoon inside his tent with the door left open—Marvin drinking a second cup of coffee at the river's edge—staring out over the water.

Seth stood up after a while and walked back—went over and sat down in the sand next to Marvin.

"You alright?" Seth said after a pause—his head tilted down as he looked at his feet.

"Yeah."

"I didn't mean to get you involved in all this," Seth said—digging an index finger into the sand. "Didn't even mean to get myself involved in it."

"I just thought it'd be no big deal—haul some canoes and gear around the dam for some kids—keep myself from asking any questions." Marvin looked at Seth. "Easy money, right?"

Seth nodded—both of them looking out over the water now—sitting there together for a few minutes without talking.

Eventually Spoon crawled out of his tent—stood up and stretched—then walked out to the water's edge and looked around—Seth turning his head to watch him—turning again to see Isabel still brushing her hair.

"How much money we talking about—if I go all the way to Kansas City?" Marvin said—Seth not answering right away—just as clueless but not wanting to admit it.

"What'd you do before this?"

"Picked up junk."

Seth turned and looked at Marvin. "What?" he said.

"People had junk in their garage or basement or whatever—they'd call me and I'd come pick it up and take it away."

"You make good money?"

Marvin shook his head.

"Well this should pay a lot more than that." Seth turned back to the river—saw Spoon trying to skip rocks over the water. "A whole lot more."

By noon they were paddling downriver—feeling the current pulling them along—the river shallow in some spots but still easy to navigate. They saw more fields than they'd seen around the lakes—more trees and tall grasses along the shore. The sky stayed clear throughout the afternoon—light breeze blowing at their backs—cool enough that none of them were even sweating.

Seth looked around and smiled. "Wish we'd see a mountain lion," he said—trying to get Isabel to talk as she paddled from the bow of the red canoe.

"So you can kill it?" she said.

"I'd only kill it if it tried to kill me first," Seth said—turning toward the sun—using his hand to shade his eyes. "Guess I'd also have to kill it if it came after you."

They paddled on until an hour or so before sundown—Spoon and Marvin laughing in the green canoe as they came ashore—Seth listening to them joke—laughing along as he hammered in the rebar anchors. Then he stood up and watched Isabel grab her things and hop out of the canoe—passing close behind him as he pressed his hands against the pistols in his pockets.

THE NEXT DAY THEY PULLED OUT OF THE RIVER EARLY in the afternoon—choosing a campsite north of Sioux City, Iowa—dragging the canoes up onto a layer of riprap that lined the river—carrying their camping supplies up the bank into a cluster of trees—then waiting for the sun to go down.

Seth left camp alone while the other three rested in the shade—walked through the trees with one of the maps in his hands—eventually coming to the edge of a soybean field— borders seeming to match what the map showed.

"Guess this is it," he said—crossing his arms as he leaned back against a tree. "Looks like home."

A few minutes later Seth walked back to their camp- site—saw Isabel reading a book—Marvin and Spoon telling stories and laughing. He set up his tent for the first time since Marvin joined up with them—crawled inside and took the pistols out of his pockets—set them down and covered them with the duffel bag that held all the money—lay back and used the lumpy bag as a pillow—setting an alarm on the cellphone before falling asleep.

SETH AND ISABEL WALKED OUT INTO THE MIDDLE OF the soybean field that night to make their next drop—Isabel wearing her headlamp but waiting to turn it on—Seth car- rying the ketamine in the two backpacks—a trowel in case they had to dig.

"I can carry one of those," Isabel said as they walked— soybeans nearly waist-high—growing together over the rows of dirt between them.

"It's alright," Seth said—adjusting the straps hooked over his shoulders—carrying the other backpack cradled in front of him.

They walked on through the flat field—moon and the stars providing enough light to see where they were going—making their way to the middle of the field where Seth stopped—pulled out one of the maps he'd brought and studied it—spinning around in a circle—looking up at the trees off in the distance.

"Must be five-hundred acres just in this one field," he said—spending another couple minutes studying the map—making sure he knew where they were before moving on—Isabel walking in the row beside him.

"What do you think he's gonna do once we get to Kansas City?" Isabel said.

Seth looked over at her. "Why're you asking me?" he said. "Thought you knew him better than I did."

"I do," she said. "But you're a crazy white guy—he's definitely a crazy white guy—maybe you have some insight I don't."

Seth turned his head again—made eye contact with her as they kept moving—hearing their legs pushing through the viny tendrils of the thick soybeans—thousands or maybe millions of insect calls.

"If you want my opinion," Isabel continued. "I think he's gonna kill you and Marvin before you even set your paddles down."

"Don't see why he'd do something like that," Seth said— looking up at the stars as they kept walking. "Maybe he'll kill you—maybe all four of us."

"Yeah," Isabel said. "We'll see, I guess."

A few minutes later they came to a clearing—maybe twenty yards across—two small grain bins in one corner— grass and weeds covering the ground all dead and brown— showing tire marks running in all directions. Seth told Isabel to turn on her headlamp—spotlighting some of the marks as they ran in a straight line—wide, jagged indentations from tractor tires—other marks running in circles made by something smaller—a pickup or an SUV.

"Why's all the grass dead?" Isabel said—still scanning the ground with her headlamp.

"Been sprayed with pesticide." Seth moved toward the

grain bins. "These big tire marks must be from the sprayer."

"What about the other ones?"

"Don't know."

Seth walked around to the backside of the grain bins—some gravel on the ground—broken pieces of a concrete slab. One of the bins had a door cut into it—new doorknob that shined even in the light coming off the moon and the stars—shined a blinding white when Isabel came around and pointed her headlamp toward it.

Seth set the backpacks down and pulled out one of the pistols from his pocket—twisted the doorknob and pushed the door open—stepping back as he peered inside the grain bin—raising the pistol as he stared into the darkness.

"What'd you see that on TV or something?" Isabel said—walking past him and through the doorway—her headlamp lighting up the inside. "There it is." She pointed down at a purple flag sticking up from a black trash bag in the middle of the concrete floor.

Seth put the pistol back in his pocket—picked up the two backpacks and walked inside. Isabel shined her light up to the top of the bin—both of them looking up and seeing cobwebs along all the edges—the galvanized metal rusting but there didn't seem to be any holes.

They took the money out of the trash bag—all in twenty-dollar bills—banded together and sealed inside large clear plastic bags. Then Seth dumped the ketamine blocks out of both backpacks—bent down and started transferring them into the black trash bag.

"Freeze," a man's voice commanded from the doorway—Seth turning as he heard a flashlight click on—squinting against the light and lowering his eyes. "Stand up," the voice continued. "Gimme that pistol, young man. And turn that damn light off, little lady."

Seth stood up and turned around—pulled the pistol that was in his left pocket out and held it in front of him—his eyes adjusting to the light—seeing a second figure come forward—walk up to him and take the pistol from his hand before backing away.

"You got any guns on you, honey?" the second figure said—a woman's voice this time.

"No," Isabel said.

"I'm shaking like a leaf, babe," Seth heard the woman say—watching her waddle back to the man through a steady beam of light—holding the pistol down and away from her body.

"It's alright," the man said. "They're gonna behave themselves—ain't that right, you two?" Seth nodded—then glanced over at Isabel—standing there blinking against the light with her hands in the air.

"Now back up against the wall," the man said—taking a step inside the grain bin. "Go on." He motioned with the flashlight.

Seth could see them better now—could tell they were older—the man bald and skinny—tall but hunched over at the shoulders. The woman was short and fat—her hair in tight curls all around her head.

They both walked forward until they reached the pile of lozenges and the plastic bags full of cash—Seth sliding his feet backward—looking at the man's hands—flashlight in his left and a revolver pointed at them in his right.

"That the stuff we're looking for, Mary Ann?" the man said.

"Oh, dear me," the woman said—kneeling down and picking up one of the shrink-wrapped blocks. "I believe so." She looked up at Seth and Isabel. "These the medicine candies?"

"They're lozenges," Seth said.

The man pointed his flashlight down at the lozenges in the woman's hands—keeping the revolver pointed at Seth.

Seth was able to see the man's worn jeans and plaid

shirt—the woman's old polyester pants and cotton T-shirt—dark spots on the man's bald head from the sun.

"This your land?" Seth said.

"What?" the man said.

"Is this your farm?"

"You just stand there and be good, you hear?"

The woman was busy peeling back the shrink wrap—working her small, thick fingers until she was able to get one of the packages out.

"Sure," Seth said—watching the woman set the shrink-wrapped block back down on the ground—then stand up as she tried to open the small package of lozenges. "Beans look good."

"What?" the man said—pointing the flashlight back at Seth.

"Whoever they belong to should have a nice crop," Seth said. "The pods all fill out yet?"

"Just about." The man kept the flashlight pointed at him—Seth squinting and then closing his eyes—able to hear the woman still fiddling with the package. "What's a drug dealer wanna know about soybeans for?"

"Got it," the woman said—Seth opening his eyes just in time to see her pop one of the lozenges into her mouth.

"This isn't my usual line of work," Seth said.

"Oh that's it, baby," the woman said—sucking hard on the lozenge—rattling it against her teeth. "Yeah, that's the right stuff."

"Pack it up—let's get outta here," the man said—tossing an empty duffel bag on the floor near the woman's feet.

"I don't think what you're doing here is a good idea," Seth said.

"I'm sure you don't," the man said—holding the revolver steady—still pointing it at Seth—pointing the flashlight at the woman as she loaded the ketamine and the cash into the duffel bag.

"The man we work for," Seth said—feeling time running out—knowing what would happen if they lost the man's money. "He isn't the sort of person you wanna cross."

"That's a risk we just gotta live with at this point."

Seth watched the woman—her hands shaking—breathing hard as she filled the duffel bag. Then he turned his head to look at Isabel—saw her eyes were closed—watched her take a deep breath.

"You ever shoot anybody with that thing?"

"Don't matter," the man said. "It works and it's loaded and it's pointed right at you."

"I can't let you leave with that money," Seth said.

"I will shoot you," the man said—extending his arm out straight—raising the revolver a few inches.

"Done," the woman said—having a hard time standing up again—putting both hands on her knee as she stumbled forward—taking a couple unsteady steps but staying on her feet.

"Here," the man said—stepping forward and handing the woman the flashlight—then bending down and grabbing the straps of the duffel bag—revolver still held out in his right hand.

"Don't—," Seth said—taking a step forward as he dropped his hands.

"Stop!" the man yelled—his voice echoing off the curved metal walls—causing the woman to jump as she retreated toward the door.

Seth stopped—put his hands up again but didn't step back—glanced over at Isabel but she was staring at the ground—her back against the wall of the grain bin.

"Oh, Bill," the woman said—shuffling backward as the flashlight shook in her hand. "Don't, Bill—let's just go." She reached out for his arm but he was too far in front of her.

The man lifted the duffel bag—leaning to one side so he could get it off the ground—then walked backward until his heels found the doorway—stepped out of the grain bin and took two more steps back.

"Go ahead, Mary Ann," he said—the woman coming forward to shut the door—Seth hearing it lock as the grain bin went dark—then hearing the couple as they hurried away through the small clearing.

Seth walked forward to where he knew the door was—ran his hand along the warm metal—then pulled the second pistol from his pocket—raised it as he stepped back from the doorknob—turned his head and fired one shot. He heard the woman outside scream—heard her mumble a few panicked words to the man—the pair moving away but still close—probably not even out of the little clearing yet, he thought.

Seth pushed the door open and stepped outside—looked around but didn't see where they'd gone—listened and eventually heard them—their feet dragging the ground—the woman still talking but trying to be quiet. He went around the grain bin and saw a flash of light—then heard the gunshot and ducked down—jerked his hands up and retreated a few steps—waited a few seconds before he stepped out and aimed the pistol in their direction—fired as the old man fired the revolver back at him. Then Seth hid behind the grain bin again and waited.

The old couple had nearly made it to the end of the clearing—Seth sticking his head out to watch them—stepping around the grain bin as he saw the woman hurrying down a path that led out of the clearing. She looked back but didn't see him—then turned and said something to the man. Seth looked ahead of them but didn't see anything—trees bordering the field off in the distance—no car or pickup anywhere nearby. He took another few steps away from the grain bin—watching the man stop and lift the bag with both hands and swing it over his shoulder—shift the weight around on his back—then start off again at a stiff jog.

"Where'd they go?" Isabel said—standing near the doorway behind Seth.

"Down that path," Seth said—turning and talking quietly. "I think they gotta go all the way to the trees for whatever they drove out here."

He watched Isabel for a few seconds—stretching her neck and looking out over the field. His eyes had adjusted to the darkness so he could see her well—blue starlight bouncing off the galvanized walls of the grain bin—bouncing off the dead grass and weeds in the clearing.

"Stay here," he said.

"We gotta get that money."

"I know—I'll get it." Seth started backing away from Isabel—pistol held low in one hand—using the other to lift his shirt and wipe his face. "Just stay down in case he starts shooting over here again."

"What're you gonna do?"

"It's at least a quarter mile to those trees," Seth said. "She's not gonna make it—and he's not gonna leave her behind."

He turned and took off running—got to the soybeans and had to lift his feet high with every stride as he crossed the rows—then turned and ran parallel to the path for a few seconds—able to see the shapes of the man and woman in the dark—still ahead of him but not by much. He raised the pistol as he ran and fired—then dove down under the soybeans—hearing the man fire two shots in his direction—the woman screaming now as the man tried to hurry her along.

Seth stayed there below the vines and leaves as he listened to the old couple—wiped his face with his shirt as he waited for his breathing to slow—then stood up and started crossing the rows again—this time heading toward the path—lifting his legs up high—measuring his strides by the rows.

The woman started screaming again as Seth neared the

path—the man turning beside her and raising the revolver—Seth ducking under the soybeans again as he heard another shot ring out over the flat field—waiting only a few seconds before standing up—running again as the old man tried to follow him with the revolver.

"Oh, dear, there he is!" Seth heard the woman yell.

A few seconds later he crossed the path—dove over the first row of soybeans on the other side—the man firing again but Seth was already on the ground—lying there on his back—feeling his heart pumping hard and steady—taking deep breaths as he tried not to make any noise—trying to hear whether the man was coming for him or not.

Instead he heard the woman fall as they tried to continue down the path—heard her scream and heard the dirt slide under her feet—then saw the bright beam of light from the flashlight whip across the field before dropping out of sight.

Seth flipped over and crouched on the balls of his feet—popped his head up above the soybeans—sweat running down his face as he watched the man drop the duffel bag to the ground—hurrying to help the woman up—flashlight near her head illuminating a strip of the dirt path.

He watched as the woman slowly got to her feet—watched as the man tossed the revolver into the field—then heard him ask the woman for the pistol she'd taken from Seth inside the grain bin. She was breathing hard—looking out to where she thought Seth might be—making a wheezing sound with every breath. The man had to yell at her a second time about the pistol before she reached into her pocket and pulled it out—the man snatching it from her hand—then looking down the path in Seth's direction.

"Stop right there, boy!" the man yelled—Seth walking toward them now—his figure barely visible in the dark—walking down the middle of the path—moving fast but relaxed—pistol held down by his side—sweaty and dirty and still taking deep breaths.

The woman screamed and grabbed the man's arm—the man quickly shaking her off—raising the pistol and pointing it at Seth.

Seth didn't say anything—just kept walking with the pistol down by his side—his elbows stinging as he swung his arms with each long stride.

"Shoot him, Bill!" the woman yelled.

"You ain't leaving me many options here," the man said.

Seth was within twenty yards now—still advancing toward the old couple—pistol still pointed at the ground.

The man pulled the trigger—felt the pistol click without firing—pulled the trigger twice more and it clicked each time—then held the pistol in front of his face and looked at it. Seth was within ten yards now.

The man pointed the pistol at him again and pulled the trigger—again the pistol clicked.

The woman screamed—turned and started running down the path—kicking the flashlight as she went—spinning it several times—bright beam of light flashing over the field and path until it stopped.

"Don't bother," Seth said—stopping a few yards in front of the man. "It was empty when I gave it to her."

The man stopped pulling the trigger and the pistol stopped clicking.

"Well, young man," the old man said—letting his arm drop down to his side. "What the hell are you doing with an unloaded pistol in your pocket?"

"Too many people wanna take it from me," Seth said—smiling at the old man.

There was a pause as Seth slowly raised the loaded pistol—his sweaty palm sliding over the grip—the man looking calm as he stared over the barrel and met Seth's eyes—as the insects and frogs kept up their songs—stars and moon giving the two men just enough light to see each other.

"Guess if you're gonna do it, go on and get it over with,"

the old man said. "Just leave her alone." He pointed back over his shoulder with his thumb—the woman still running and screaming. "Please."

Seth adjusted his grip on the pistol—stiffened his arm and looked at the old man for what seemed like a long time.

"Go on," Seth finally said—lowering the pistol—holding it down by his side as he stared at the duffel bag. "Go."

Seth felt a drop of sweat slide into his mouth—tasted the salt—felt his elbows stinging as he waited for the old man to start moving.

The man turned a few seconds later—started walking down the path with his shoulders slumped—the woman somewhere in the trees now. Seth looked up and watched the man until he got to the end of the field—then saw a dome light glowing in the dark as one of them opened a door— heard a second door open and then both of them close. Then he heard an engine start—stood there and watched them drive away.

"Why'd you do that?" Isabel said from behind him—Seth turning around to see her standing in the middle of the path.

"I don't know," Seth said—flapping his arms as he looked out over the field. "Not really sure why I do anything anymore."

Seth went and picked up the duffel bag—tossed it over his shoulder and they walked back to the grain bins—Isabel clicking on her headlamp as they crossed the little clearing again—going through the doorway by herself and picking up their empty backpacks—then standing there in the middle of the cement floor—her light shining on the back wall. Seth waited for her outside—leaning against the doorway—wip-ing sweat from his face with his shirt.

"I thought we were gonna die in here," Isabel said. "I knew it—I knew we were."

"He didn't wanna kill us."

"Every man wants to kill something," Isabel said—still

staring at the back wall. "He comes out here waving a loaded gun around—stealing money and drugs in the middle of the night—doesn't seem any different from the rest of you."

Isabel clicked off her headlamp—turned around but stayed where she was in the middle of the grain bin—the two of them looking at each other through the doorway—Seth barely able to see the outline of Isabel's face.

"Some of us are forced to pull triggers—even though we don't like to," he said—tilting his head back to look up at the stars—adjusting the duffel bag before looking through the doorway again. "That old man would've killed me just now—but he wasn't a bad guy—probably just under water on a loan or something—his wife addicted to drugs—family falling apart and for some reason he thought doing this would fix everything."

Isabel made a noise—something between a cough and a laugh—then cleared her throat and started walking toward the doorway.

"Let's go," she said—passing close by Seth as she left the grain bin—not looking at him, though—not waiting for him as he turned to watch her go—stepping over the dead grass and weeds in the dark.

THEY LEFT THE FIELD AND WALKED BACK TO WHERE they'd set up camp earlier in the day—Seth dropping the duffel bag in front of his tent and sitting down in the dirt— taking his shoes off as he tried to inspect his elbows. Spoon and Marvin were down by the canoes—Isabel talking to them with the two empty backpacks still hooked onto her shoulders—coming up to Seth a few minutes later—her headlamp on and the first aid kit in her hands.

Spoon and Marvin came up soon after Isabel—stood

around while she cleaned and bandaged Seth's elbows—telling them the story of what happened while she worked—telling how the old couple had robbed them and then tried to get away—how Seth had stopped them—had gotten the money back as well as all the ketamine. They both wanted to pack up and start heading downriver immediately—Seth spending several minutes calming them down—telling them the old man wouldn't be back after almost getting himself killed—after almost getting his wife killed—telling them how defeated and tired he'd looked as he walked away toward the trees.

They were all quiet again by the time Isabel finished with Seth's elbows—Seth thanking her as she stood up and walked away toward the canoes. Then Seth opened the duffel bag—pulled out the ketamine blocks and set them on the ground—watched as Spoon and Marvin took them down to the canoes and started stacking them under the tarps.

"How'd this one get opened?" Marvin said—holding up one of the blocks as Isabel turned and shined her headlamp onto the shrink wrap.

"The old lady tried one," Isabel said.

"Did it work?"

"What's it supposed to do?" Seth said—walking down to join them by the canoes.

"It's like a party drug," Spoon said. "Like Ecstasy but it makes you more relaxed than crazy."

"She was pretty hysterical so I guess one wasn't enough," Seth said. "You ever tried it?" He looked up at Spoon.

Spoon shook his head. "Always worried he'd find out somehow."

They were all silent for a few seconds—Isabel's headlamp shining down onto the shredded shrink wrap—her hand sliding inside—pulling out one of the little square containers with the ketamine lozenges stacked tightly together—then reaching back in and pulling out another.

"We'll tell him the lady ran off with a few packs," she

said. "He won't know." Isabel looked around at the three of them—shining her headlamp in Seth's face—forcing him to close his eyes as he nodded his head.

Isabel counted out four lozenges and offered them to Spoon.

"Really should taste my own recipe," Spoon said—taking the lozenges and putting all four in his mouth.

Isabel counted out four lozenges for each of them—then turned off her headlamp as they walked back up into the trees—sitting down in the dark—their mouths so full no one even tried to talk—Seth listening to the lozenges clack together in all their mouths—then lying back on the ground and forgetting about the others—looking up at the tops of the trees—the stars that shined through the branches and the leaves—listening to the river—then finally seeing and hearing other things—things he knew weren't really there.

The stars and the trees started to come back into focus after a while—Seth able to hear the wind moving through the upper branches again—sitting up and looking around—blinking hard as he noticed Spoon and Marvin were gone—then turning his head and seeing Isabel a few feet away—her head resting on the duffel bag—staring up at the sky—smiling—her eyes wet with happy tears.

Seth got up and walked over to Isabel's tent—took out an extra blanket she always had with her and brought it back—laid it over her as carefully as he could—then sat down on the ground again—leaned back against a tree as he watched her and waited.

A while later her eyes started scanning the trees—hands started moving and the smile went away—the ketamine wearing off gradually—her hands folding over her stomach—eyelids closing as she swallowed and cleared her throat.

"Thanks," Isabel said—grabbing the blanket and looking back at Seth.

"You're welcome."

18

THEY SLEPT IN LATE THE NEXT MORNING—SETH waking up in his tent as he heard Marvin and Spoon talking—already warm out as Seth felt sweat coating the inside of his sleeping bag—lying there in his underwear—stretching, yawning and listening for a few minutes.

"It was like blood—just like blood," he heard Marvin say.

"The whole river?" Spoon said.

"Yep—whole river—and it was bright and sunny—little blue cartoon birds flying all around."

"Sounds like a lot more fun than what I seen," Spoon said—Seth still listening—hearing someone open one of the protein bars. "There was this girl running away from me through the woods—naked."

"What?"

"Wasn't even wearing shoes. I chased after her through the woods but never could catch up to her. When I stopped she'd stop and look back at me—shake her ass a little and laugh. Then I'd take off running again and she'd start running too."

"You finally catch her?"

Seth didn't hear Spoon respond—waited but neither of them said anything more.

A minute or two later he heard Isabel unzipping the door of her tent—heard her start walking down toward the canoes as he got out of his sleeping bag—only hearing the wind and the river by the time he slipped on a pair of shorts and a shirt.

THEY ONLY HAD ONE DROP TO MAKE OVER THE NEXT few days—no storms slowing them down—no lakes or dams to deal with—wind out of the south but not blowing too hard—strong, steady current helping them move quickly down the river—Seth constantly checking the maps and the schedule—glad they were finally making good time.

They came to the outskirts of Omaha, Nebraska late one morning—sky filling with clouds—wind starting to blow. They passed by an old battleship and a submarine sitting in a park along the right bank—Marvin and Spoon arguing about how they'd gotten there—Marvin saying they could have made it up the river under their own power—Spoon saying there was no way the river was ever deep enough to float a battleship or a submarine—leading Spoon and Marvin both to stab down with their paddles as far as they could into the muddy water—neither able to touch the bottom.

Seth kept them in the main channel of the river—safe distance from any boats or people on shore. They passed under several bridges—right through downtown Omaha—few people waving at them—taking pictures from a pedestrian bridge—Seth keeping them moving—all of them looking up at the buildings as they passed by—watching the cars going over the bridges—distracted by all the traffic—the noise and energy of the city.

They paddled for another couple hours—wind picking up and the clouds getting lower, slower and darker. Seth checked the map one last time—then looked up and found a decent campsite just as it started to rain—hurrying toward a sandy stretch of shoreline—all four of them hopping out and dragging the canoes up a soft bank into a stand of trees—wind blowing hard now as they started hearing thunder—Seth turning back to see little whitecaps breaking on the river's surface.

They set up their tents and anchored them to the ground—rain already coming down in big drops—wind blowing the branches above them—stripping off green leaves and sending them swirling around the tents—lightning flashing as Seth hammered the last anchor for his tent into the ground—thunder following soon after—shaking his chest as the rain started coming down even harder. He looked around and made sure the other three were in their tents—then climbed inside his own and started taking off his wet clothes.

"Hey," Seth said as someone started unzipping the door to his tent—his wet shirt already in his left hand—reaching for the pistol with his right.

Isabel shoved her head through the small opening she'd made—then unzipped the door the rest of the way and crawled inside—Seth scooting over to make room—quickly closing the door behind her.

"What are you doing?" he said—barely able to hear his own voice over the storm.

Isabel's hair was wet—hanging down loose all around her face—sticking to her cheeks and neck. She sat there and looked at Seth—trying to catch her breath.

"Your tent OK?" Seth yelled—waiting for Isabel to say something but she stayed quiet—breathed—looked at him like she wasn't sure what to say—wasn't sure why she was there—whether she should stay or go.

She leaned forward and kissed him before he could say anything else—her hand coming up around his neck—pulling him down onto his sleeping bag—rain pounding the tent outside—letting up a little as the wind started blowing harder—the tent's thin walls buckling and flapping—the anchors somehow holding throughout the storm.

Isabel fell asleep almost immediately after—her head on Seth's chest—the two of them tight against each other inside the sleeping bag—Seth watching the raindrops pound the tent walls—running his middle finger up and down Isabel's spine—careful not to wake her.

He fell asleep a few minutes later—wind still blowing just as hard as before—rain coming down in those big drops again.

SETH WOKE UP AS ISABEL WAS TRYING TO GET HERSELF out of his sleeping bag—nearly dark outside but not quite—not raining anymore but still cloudy—wind still blowing but weaker now. He reached over and pulled the sleeping bag's zipper halfway down—Isabel sliding out—lying there pulling up her cotton pants.

"What time is it?" Seth said.

"I don't know." Isabel looked at him—smiled and then turned away.

Seth laid his head on his arm and watched her get dressed—Isabel looking at him only once more—smiling before pulling her shirt over her head—then scooting to the end of the tent to find her shoes.

"You gonna barge in on me again tonight?" Seth said—sitting up now—watching her shake her head—her hair still not dry—hanging down around her face. "Please?"

"No," Isabel said. "But I'll go with you tonight."

"Guess that'll have to do."

Isabel unzipped the door and stepped out—started walking toward her tent as Spoon said something to her—Isabel telling him to shut his mouth as she kept walking—Spoon laughing and then everyone was quiet again.

Seth lay there in his sleeping bag—watching raindrops collect and slip down the walls of his tent—having a hard time keeping his eyes open when he heard the cellphone start ringing.

"Hello," Seth said—propping himself up on his elbow—holding the phone up to his ear.

"Hello, Seth," the man said. "You're making excellent time."

"Yeah."

There was a pause—Seth able to hear something in the background—a TV or a radio.

"You sound more assertive, Seth—more like a dog than a puppy." Seth didn't say anything—waited through another long pause before the man continued. "Would you attempt to usurp me, Seth?"

"No."

"Do you know what 'usurp' means?"

"No."

"Well," the man said. "Sadly that does not preclude you from trying to do it."

Seth waited—heard someone walking around outside and leaned forward to look out the door of his tent—looked through the screen and saw Marvin—cans of soup and their bowls in his hands.

"The one she had before you," the man said. "Ricky, I think it was—he wanted to take her away—run away and probably get married—buy her a little house and fill it with little children and all the rest."

"I'm not—" Seth started saying—stopping when the man interrupted him.

"But I knew what he was doing—what he was planning. He was manipulating her—brainwashing her—trying to get her to do something she did not want to do."

Seth stayed quiet—sat there next to the door of his tent and watched Marvin start the little camping stove—watched him open a can of soup and pour it into the pot—clouds starting to clear from the west as the sun was setting—pink lines running along the dark gray sky.

"I get it," Seth said. "I understand."

"Any vice can make you a slave, Seth—and a fool." The man paused yet again—Seth still able to hear something in the background—voices—maybe the sound of an engine. "It's a blessing, really—having the fortitude to resist treasuring anything too dearly."

"What about the money?"

"Oh, well, I'm here, aren't I? I'm breathing in and out—my heart is pumping blood through my veins. I have to do something with my time—challenge myself in some sort of way."

Seth again stayed quiet—several minutes passing as he waited for the man to end the call—eventually holding the phone in front of his face but he saw the call stayed connected—saw the timer still ticking so he put the phone back to his ear.

"You know," the man said. "I find myself almost enjoying our conversations, Seth." The man ended the call—Seth checking the screen again to make sure—then dropping the cellphone onto his sleeping bag.

He watched Marvin eat his bowl of soup—Spoon coming over to where Marvin was sitting soon after he was finished—Isabel coming out of her tent around the same time—wearing a jacket now—Seth able to tell she'd brushed her hair. He lay back down and listened to them talking as the sun disappeared—Spoon heating a can of soup—pouring the soup into a bowl before passing it to Isabel. After a while Seth put on his clothes—then joined them for dinner.

Later that night Seth and Isabel went out with their backpacks full of lozenges—Seth carrying a map in his hands—
pistol in his pocket. They had to walk downriver for half an
hour before they came to the right field—a cornfield about
as big and as flat as all the others along that stretch of the
river—corn's tassels hanging three or four feet above their
heads as they walked through the rows—Seth telling Isabel
to keep her forearms up in front of her face—the splayed-
over leaves brushing against each other in the dark—making
a cutting sound.

They walked through the muddy field until they came to
an old well—covered over by a slab of concrete—purple flag
they always looked for sticking out of the mud next to it. The
wind picked up and all the corn leaves clacked against each
other—Isabel looking all around as the noise increased—
Seth seeing the light from her headlamp shoot from one side
to the other. He grabbed her arm with one hand and pulled
out the pistol with the other—waiting until the wind died
down—until the corn went quiet again and all they could
hear were the insects.

A minute or two later Seth took the trowel from one of
the backpacks and started digging—finding a large metal
box under just a few inches of mud. They pulled it out and
opened it—took out the money and stacked the shrink-
wrapped blocks inside—slid the box back into the hole and
covered it with the mud—then hurried back toward their
camp—Isabel keeping her headlamp on as they made their
way through the dark—Seth grabbing her hand once they
left the cornfield—Isabel refusing to look at him as they
walked—pulling her hand free after a few minutes—refusing to talk or smile as she walked a few feet ahead—scanning
the ground for any obstacles.

THEY HAD MORE GOOD WEATHER OVER THE NEXT FEW days—current strong and the river full—Seth starting to notice water backing up and rushing over submerged wing dams along each bank—first they'd seen as the river quickly grew wider and deeper.

He kept them far away from shore as much as he could—leading the green canoe down the middle of the river—watching for any snags—floating branches or submerged trees—examining the slope of the shoreline—checking for tire tracks or any other sign of activity.

"This is where I grew up," Seth said—sitting down in a thin patch of short grass—stunted and sickly from recent flooding—shading his eyes with his hands and looking around.

"Where the hell are we?" Marvin said.

It was mid-afternoon—sunlight still blinding as it bounced off the brown water—the four of them setting up their tents just a few yards from the river.

An hour or so earlier they'd passed the spot where he first met the man—where he got himself beat with a penny whistle—then was forced to load two dead bodies into Mr. Loomis's pickup.

Seth looked up at the top of the levee—then down at the water—remembering how he'd stood along the river's edge and talked to the man that first night—how sure he'd felt that he was about to die—sure he'd reached the strange end to his short, uneventful life.

"Nebraska," Seth said. "Missouri's across the river. We're about a hundred miles from Kansas City."

He left his tent out on the ground and walked over to the river—sandy shoreline that wasn't too steep—sun still shining on their camp over a tall levee behind him—hot, humid air tempered by a steady breeze—white clouds bubbling up over his head—still small with plenty of blue sky between them.

"That's only what, three days?" Marvin said.

"If the weather's good," Spoon said. "Not too sure about these clouds, though."

Seth watched two birds chasing each other over the water—watched them fly toward the levee on the other side of the river—losing sight of them at some point but still looking in that direction—seeing the tops of cottonwood trees in the landscape beyond.

"You know how to read clouds, Pocahontas?" Spoon said to Isabel—Seth knowing she wouldn't respond—standing there at the water's edge still—listening to them assemble their tents behind him—letting the wind blow through his hair—breathing in as he watched the tops of the trees across the river—their branches swaying—flashing the undersides of their leaves.

"Hey cap'n!" Spoon yelled—causing Seth to turn around. "You know any girls we can get to come out here? My type's thick and desperate—daddy issues a bonus."

"You're disgusting," Isabel said—Seth watching her make a face as she fit her tent poles together—smiling as he walked back up to their camp—shaking his head at Spoon as he sat down in the sand beside his backpack.

"You know any good eating places?" Spoon said. "If we ain't gonna get any women we might as well get some good food for once—sick as hell of these soup cans."

"Yeah," Seth said—pulling several maps out of the folder. "Me too."

Seth found a town on the Nebraska side of the river—place he'd heard about but never been to—only a few miles from their campsite—still early enough to make it back before dark, he thought.

"Anybody wanna go to Rulo?" he said—looking up at the three of them.

"What's there?" Isabel said.

"Yes," Spoon said. "Hell yes we wanna go! Who cares what's there!"

"Think I remember hearing about a restaurant—big enough town to have at least one."

"They better serve beer," Marvin said as he dropped his tent to the ground—then started walking off away from the river—passed Spoon and slapped him on the shoulder. "This way, boss?" he said—turning his head to look at Seth as he pointed—Seth nodding—watching him go from his seat on the ground.

Spoon smiled at him—smiled at Isabel and Seth—then turned and started walking up the levee with Marvin—sandy, packed silt turning to loose dirt at the top—short trees and open ground with patches of grass.

Seth looked up at Isabel—standing beside him now—shading her eyes with her hand as she watched Marvin and Spoon.

"Maybe we should let them go," Seth said. "You and me can stay out here by ourselves."

"Hmmmm," Isabel said—looking away as she tapped her cheek—wearing a white tank-top and shorts—Seth looking down her brown legs—seeing her foot tapping the ground. "Nah," she said—walking away in the same direction as Spoon and Marvin—jogging up the levee without looking back.

"Why not?" Seth said to himself—glancing down at his tent and his rolled up sleeping bag—then raising his head to watch Isabel before she disappeared. "I need a burger." He stood up—hid the canoes and their tents in some willow brush—hid the duffel bag of cash down between some roots and covered it with branches—then started climbing the levee.

SETH CAUGHT UP TO THEM AT THE EDGE OF A SOYBEAN

field—checking the map he'd brought along—guiding them to a gravel road that led straight into Rulo. When they got there Seth checked the cellphone—checked for a signal and then for missed calls—then shoved the phone back into his pocket—tapped his other pocket and felt the pistol.

The town was a handful of brick buildings laid out along two perpendicular streets—surrounded by houses and trailers that gradually thinned out to pastures and fields. The four of them stood in the center of town—examining the storefronts.

"How about that place?" Marvin said—Seth watching him as he tried to sound out the name painted on the brick wall next to the door.

"Ye Ole Tyme Saloon, dummy," Spoon said—walking past them all as he shook his head—crossing the empty street without looking back.

Isabel turned to Seth—made eye contact as she raised her eyebrows and shrugged her shoulders—then started hurrying toward the brick building—Marvin following close behind her—leaving Seth alone on the shaded street corner—trying to fold the laminated map so he could stuff it into his pocket.

"Better get a move on, young fella," Seth heard someone say—turning to see an old man in overalls—sitting on a stack of old tires outside a crumbling brick building. "Your friends are liable to eat up all the food if you don't hurry." The man started laughing—closing his eyes and slapping his knees—rocking back and forth on the tires—Seth noticing there were only a few teeth in the old man's mouth.

It was almost dark inside the restaurant—big windows in the front that faced the street but not much light made it through—few fluorescent light fixtures blinking and buzzing twenty feet above Seth's head as he walked to the back—the three others already standing at a counter—staring up at a menu board.

"I'll do a burger and fries," Marvin said—leaning forward as he spoke to the boy behind the counter. "And three beers."

"Three?" the boy said—looking up at Marvin before jotting his order down on a notepad—then walking it over to the kitchen—Seth watching him drag his right foot along behind him as he went. "Beer's over there." The boy pointed with his pen to a glass door refrigerator.

The rest of them ordered the same thing but with only one beer each—Seth stepping over to the cash register and paying for everyone—then grabbing his beer and walking over to the table where the other three were now sitting.

"Just one beer, Spoon?" Seth said as he sat down.

"The night is young, cap'n."

"We should get back before dark," Isabel said.

Marvin finished his first beer and opened his second—Seth watching him as he took a sip of his own beer—then looking around the restaurant as he felt his stomach turning over—as he smelled the fryer and heard the music in the background—noticing three men sitting together at a table in the far corner—beers on the table but no food.

"You been here before, cap'n?" Spoon said.

"No. I hardly came over to this side of the river."

"I don't blame you if there ain't no women." Spoon stretched his neck and looked around.

The boy who took their orders came over with two plates—setting the first one down in front of Isabel—the second in front of Marvin.

"Hey," Spoon said to him. "There gonna be any ladies in here later on?"

"It's Saturday—couple local girls usually stumble in around ten o'clock."

"We'll have to make ourselves comfortable then," Spoon said—looking around the table and smiling.

"Where are you all from?" the boy said.

"Other side of the river," Seth said—watching the boy as

he nodded his head—as he pulled a ketchup bottle out of a pocket stitched onto his apron—waiting for the other three to answer—waiting still as he set the bottle on the table—then walking away once it was clear they weren't going to respond.

"How much money you guys think we're gonna get once we make it to Kansas City?" Marvin said between bites.

"Probably just enough to get back home—maybe a little extra to go out and get rowdy a couple nights—buy a couple video games," Spoon said.

"You're so full of shit, Spoon," Isabel said—pulling a pickle from underneath her hamburger bun—slipping it into her mouth before starting in on her fries. "How rowdy you think you're gonna get when you always fall asleep after three beers? Remember that time we went to Applebee's in Billings?"

"Well if you'd quit putting sleeping pills in my drinks I'd be able to stay awake longer," Spoon said—causing Isabel to laugh as she bit off the end of a French fry—the two of them arguing back and forth as Isabel ate and Spoon drank.

"He'll give us a good chunk of the money," Seth said—looking across the table at Marvin. "Don't worry about that."

"Then I can go my own way?" Marvin said.

Seth kept looking at him as the boy brought over the other two plates—setting one down in front of Seth and the other in front of Spoon.

"Yeah," Seth said. "Of course."

Marvin leaned back in his chair—weighing Seth's answer as he looked down at his plate—as he looked around the table at Isabel and Spoon—watching them argue and laugh for a little while—then picking up his beer—shrugging his shoulders—smiling and shaking his head as he lifted the can to his lips.

Seth watched him while he drank—watched him finish his second beer and set it down next to the first.

They all ate their food and finished their beers—Seth going to the counter to order another round—bringing the beers back on a tray and setting them down on the table—another group of men coming in at about the same time—taking a table near the entrance—all looking at Seth as he stood there with the tray—none of them moving toward the counter.

"It ain't so much the depth that's the problem," Spoon said—gesturing with an empty can. "It'd work as long as it's under any amount of water."

"I don't think he's gonna go for it," Isabel said—Seth watching her shake her head—noticing her cheeks turning pink—looking at her until she turned and looked back.

Spoon was explaining his plan to put outboard motors on the canoes for their next trip—Isabel arguing with him—Seth nodding whenever one of them looked his way—sitting there keeping an eye on the two groups of men—Marvin drinking beer after beer—staring down at the table.

After another round of beers more people came into the restaurant—one of them putting some money into the jukebox—some ordering food but most just wanted beer—everyone inspecting the four strangers but no one came over.

Eventually Seth stood up from the table and went to the bathroom—coming back just a couple minutes later to find two of the men that had walked in earlier—smiling at each other as they tried talking to Isabel—one of them standing and the other sitting in Seth's chair.

"Hey there," the man said that was sitting down—Seth standing next to him now—giving the two men a chance to be friendly.

"This is my boyfriend," Isabel said. "You're in his seat."

"Boyfriend?" the man standing said.

"You ain't got no boyfriend," the man sitting down said—reaching out slowly with his hand—trying to touch Isabel's face as both men laughed.

Seth hit the man that was standing next to the table—hit him as hard as he could without winding up—then turned back to the man that'd been sitting in his seat but he was too late. The man put his shoulder into Seth's ribs and drove him back against the wall—Seth feeling the air leave his lungs—trying to twist away as they both dropped to the floor—the man on top of him—pinning him down as he raised up and grabbed Seth's throat with one hand—Seth watching him raise his right fist in the air.

"OK," the man said suddenly—both hands up in the air now—showing both palms—getting to his feet and backing away. "Alright—just take it easy."

Seth held the pistol up in front of him—keeping it pointed at the man's head—then sat up and cleared his throat—put his left hand on the ground and started to stand up—laminated map that'd been in his pocket unfolded now—creased and shiny as it slipped off his hip to the floor.

"Let's go," Seth said—standing there with sweat on his forehead—breathing hard as he gripped the pistol—still facing the man as he backed his way toward the table.

Isabel put a hand on Seth's back once he got close—guiding him around the chair that was on the ground—Seth keeping the pistol held out in front of him—keeping an eye on the two men—standing beside each other now with their hands up by their shoulders.

All the other customers gave them a wide berth as they moved toward the door—Isabel gripping the back of Seth's shirt—Spoon staying close beside her as they inched there way over the creaking wood floor—jukebox still playing in the background as they walked out the doorway—turning together but still watching the restaurant.

"It's always something with you two," Spoon said—running beside each other down the dark street—seeing lights on in a few of the homes and trailers—still able to hear the music coming from the restaurant. "Makes me wonder how we got this far."

They ran for another block and then started to walk—blacktop turning into a gravel road—no more buildings or houses. Seth looked up and saw power lines hanging above a drainage ditch—saw the first stars between the lines—the moon already setting.

"Hey," Spoon said. "Where the hell's Marvin?"

Seth stopped and looked around—turned and looked back toward the restaurant.

"You think he ran off?" Isabel said.

"Yeah."

They stood there in the middle of the gravel road—Spoon walking back and forth in the dark—kicking at piles of loose rocks. They heard a dog bark off in the distance—another two or three barking a few seconds later.

"We don't have that far to go," Seth said—Spoon stopping and looking up at him—Isabel standing a few feet away—looking out over the dark fields. "I'll paddle one canoe and you two can take the other."

"It's hard enough with two people," Spoon said.

"We're almost out of ketamine—we'll load what we have left in your canoe."

"He would have killed him anyway—once we got to Kansas City," Isabel said—waving her foot over the rocks in the road—her arms crossed—not bothering to look back at either of them. "Guess we'll be saving his life this way."

"Yeah."

They stood there a while longer—Spoon pacing back and forth again—nodding his head as he kept looking back toward the restaurant—Seth hesitating—wondering if he should go back and try to find Marvin—if it would matter to the man or not so long as they finished the job.

Eventually Seth walked over and wrapped his arm around Isabel's shoulders—turned and the three of them started walking down the gravel road again—Isabel keeping her head turned toward the fields and pastures—no one saying anything as they walked slowly through the dark—loose rocks crunching under their feet.

THEY FOUND THEIR WAY BACK TO CAMP AND STARTED packing everything into the green canoe—lightning off in the distance—too far away for them to hear the thunder. Once they'd finished loading the canoes they stood at the edge of the water—Seth watching the black sky—waiting for the lightning to stretch out across the clouds—listening for the thunder but it never came.

"Think it's coming this way?" Spoon said.

"No," Isabel said—Seth looking down at her—seeing the headlamp strapped to her forehead—her black hair hanging down around her face—turning her head to look up at him—motioning toward the water—then stepping into the stern of the green canoe.

They paddled most of that night—watching the storm in front of them—hearing thunder a few times but it was always far off in the distance—cool breeze at their backs—Seth feeling it move through his hair—keeping up with the green canoe but having to paddle the whole time—current helping to push them downriver—Isabel turning her headlamp on every few minutes—scanning the river for snags.

An hour or so before sunrise Seth heard a gurgling sound to his left—turned just as Isabel was clicking on her headlamp—his paddle raised out of the water and gripped tight—leaning back as he saw the limbs of a submerged tree sticking up out of the water—bubbles sprouting around the dead wood just a few yards from his canoe.

They continued downriver until they found a place to hide the canoes—setting up their tents just before sunrise—Seth checking the maps with the cellphone's

flashlight—remembering the mile marker he'd seen just before they left the river—using it to find their location—only
twenty miles from St. Joseph, Missouri—another day or two
of paddling from there to get to Kansas City.

He put the maps away—laid his head down on his
backpack—checked the cellphone and saw the battery was
almost dead. He could hear Isabel or Spoon moving around
inside their tent—listened and waited for them to settle—
turned the phone's flashlight on again and shined the light
at the door to his tent—sat up and waited a minute or two
longer—then turned the phone off and spread himself out
on top of his sleeping bag—his eyes wide open as he waited
to fall asleep.

19

"HEY," SPOON SAID THE NEXT DAY—STARING UP AT a clear blue sky around noon—Seth sitting beside him—watching a strong wind whip up little waves on the river's brown surface. "Wasn't Jesse James from Missouri?"

"Yeah," Seth said.

The three of them sat shoulder to shoulder in the shade underneath a big cottonwood tree—camping stove on the ground in front of them—their empty bowls and empty soup cans sitting next to it.

"He cause any trouble in your hometown?" Spoon said.

"No," Seth said. "Not that I know of."

Seth closed his eyes—listened to the wind blowing through the trees—smelled something Isabel must've been wearing—some lotion or maybe the soap she'd used that morning.

"Did he just rob banks?" Isabel said.

"Trains too," Seth said. "But they never robbed the passengers—just took what was in the safe." He opened his eyes and looked out over the river—opposite bank lined with riprap—stand of trees and then fields of soybeans and corn.

"Should've done it the other way around," Spoon said. "Robbed the passengers and left the safe."

"Why?" Isabel said.

"Regular folks can't do much about getting robbed—but rich folks," Spoon said—trailing off as he stood up and started stretching his thin body.

Seth and Isabel sat there for a few minutes without saying anything—Seth eating a protein bar—then ripping the wrapper off another one before Isabel snatched it out of his hand—leaned away and took a quick bite—looking back at Seth as they both smiled.

"We're outlaws too," Spoon said—turning to look at them. "More like the mob, I guess—organized crime."

"Yeah we're real organized, Spoon," Isabel said—letting out a little chuckle while she shook her head. "Guess we do have a godfather keeping an eye on us while we do all the work—that's sort of like the mob."

Spoon shrugged his shoulders—kept stretching for a while—then walked off toward the river—turning once to look back at them but didn't stop walking.

Seth watched him make his way over the riprap—watched him kneel down next to the water and pick up some rocks—sunlight shimmering on the river's choppy surface—Spoon standing there alone—sorting the rocks in his hands for a few seconds—then trying to skip them over the brown water—each one impacting a tiny wave—none of them able to make even a single hop.

They had good weather that day and the next as they made there way downriver—meeting several barges moving fast in the opposite direction—steering their canoes to one side or the other to let them pass—Seth always trying to keep them away from the wing dams—safe from any debris submerged in the shallows.

It stayed windy and hot—tall trees lining both sides of the river nearly the entire way. They camped just outside St. Joseph, Missouri at the end of the second day—Seth finding a place close to where they would make their last drop near a casino—setting up their tents in a narrow band of trees between a soybean field and the river.

That night Seth and Isabel left camp together—walked along the river with their backpacks full of lozenges—finding the purple flag just off the casino's parking lot—stuck inside the edge of a round metal manhole cover—Seth sliding the cover out of the way—Isabel pointing her headlamp down into the hole—both of them looking at concrete walls and a stained concrete floor—plastic bag full of money at the bottom—little water puddled around it—Seth climbing down to retrieve the bag of cash—Isabel emptying their backpacks and tossing the ketamine blocks down for him to stack—then helping him out before they covered the hole again.

"Where are you sleeping tonight?" Seth said—walking back through the trees with the money in his backpack—Isabel in front of him—turning her headlamp on whenever she couldn't see the ground.

"Same place I sleep every night."

"Maybe it's my turn to barge in on you in your tent."

"Probably not a good idea."

"Why not?" Seth said—Isabel not stopping—not turning around or saying anything. "We're done with all the drops—gonna be in Kansas City soon—so why the hell not?"

"Let's just focus on getting there," Isabel said. "Staying alive somehow."

"We could go back to that casino—double this money and disappear together," Seth said—waiting for Isabel to surprise him—to go along with his spontaneous plan—waiting but knowing she wouldn't. "I still want to, you know—run away together."

"No you don't," Isabel said without turning around—without stopping. "Not really."

Seth stopped—stood there by the river and watched her keep walking—seeing the light from her headlamp bobbing up and down along the uneven ground—the river to his left just a couple steps away—water splashing up the sandy shoreline. He watched her for a minute or two—gripping the straps of his backpack—feeling the weight of all the cash inside—thinking about her as he watched her walking—thinking about dark bedrooms in Montana—used clothing stores and diners and hotel rooms across the Upper Midwest—grocery stores and dark fields and his crowded tent during thunderstorms—each moment multiplied in his mind—then added together to make something he thought was real—something he thought he could never walk away from.

Seth reached back and pulled a bottle of water from a pouch on the side of his backpack—drank as he hurried to catch up before she was out of sight.

IT TOOK THEM TWO MORE DAYS OF PADDLING TO REACH the outskirts of Kansas City—passing towns along the way—more barges to deal with—highway bridges and a few motorboats. During the second day they started seeing commercial airplanes coming in low—some rising with their noses pointed up into the sky—paddling slowly as they heard the planes screeching through the air.

Seth disconnected the solar charger from the cell-phone—set his paddle in his lap and checked the phone for missed calls—checked the reception and the time as he heard another plane coming in to land.

"So where the hell are we meeting him?" Spoon said.

"I don't know," Seth said—looking up at the sky as he stuffed the cellphone into his pocket.

They paddled on—another hour before they could see Kansas City's skyline—glass and stone buildings rising into the air in front of them—Seth leading in the red canoe—checking the cellphone to make sure the ringer was turned up and the reception was good—scanning the shoreline on each side of the river.

"You can't call him?" Isabel said as they neared downtown—coming up beside Seth in the green canoe.

"No," Seth said—looking toward a riverfront park not too far in front of them—people jogging and sitting on benches—walking their dogs and pushing strollers.

They stared at the big buildings as they drifted toward downtown—Spoon trying to count the windows of the tallest two or three—sound of traffic on the busy streets and highway bridges—glass windows shining in the sun.

Seth checked all the maps again—searching but finding nothing to indicate where they should exit the river—checked the cellphone one more time for text messages but found none—then started stuffing it back into his pocket just as the phone started ringing.

"Hello."

"Hello, Seth."

Seth left his paddle in his lap—Isabel and Spoon grabbing his canoe—the three of them floating together downriver.

"Do you think you're in love, Seth?"

"What?"

"I don't understand it either," the man said. "I understand the desire to procreate, I suppose—at least the utility of it—the overwhelming urge to seek out a desirable mate so that your genes and your species can live on—that makes sense to me."

Seth glanced over at Isabel—squinting against the sun.

"But to call it love—to attach all this emotion to it," the man said after a pause. "It just seems so absurd." He laughed.

Seth looked up at the buildings as they started drifting around a bend—three bridges slowly coming into view ahead of them—a smaller river on their right flowing into the Missouri.

"We're passing through downtown right now," Seth said. "There's bridges ahead of us."

"I know where you are, Seth."

"OK."

"You have my money, Seth. I know where my money is."

"OK—yessir."

Seth felt them spinning together as they drifted with the current—heard Spoon start paddling while Isabel held tight to the gunwale of Seth's canoe—getting them pointed straight downriver again just before they reached the first bridge.

"At the heart of everything a person does," the man said. "Is self-interest—conceit, Seth—pride—we're made more of those things than of water."

Seth pressed the phone to his ear as they passed under the bridge—drifting through a block of shade—deafening sound of the constant traffic over their heads—the noise reverberating off the bridge supports and the water—Seth still waiting—still not saying anything as the current carried them back out into the sunlight.

"No matter the affectations of some people—the pharmaceutical companies—politicians."

"Where should we meet you?"

"I don't want you to get the impression that we are any better, Seth—nor should you deem our actions any worse."

They continued drifting downriver—Spoon using his paddle as a rudder—keeping them from spinning. Soon they were passing under the second bridge—Seth covering his other ear with his cupped hand—trying to keep out the traffic noise as another block of shade overtook the two canoes—the man still silent—Seth barely able to hear him breathing.

"You're one mile from a boat ramp," the man said. "On your right."

"OK," Seth said—waiting for the man to end the call—holding the cellphone out in front of him and looking at the screen—timer still ticking as they neared the third bridge—Seth looking toward shore as he put the phone back up to his ear.

"I must admit," the man said. "You have been surprisingly useful to me, Seth."

Seth heard the man end the call—lowered the cellphone from his ear to his leg—then looked down at the phone's black screen.

"What'd he say?" Spoon said. "Where the hell is he?"

"We're close," Seth said without raising his eyes or turning his head. "Let's go."

The two canoes separated—Seth paddling through the shadow of the third bridge—then turning toward the shoreline—Spoon and Isabel behind him in the green canoe. He was sweating as he looked for the boat ramp—feeling all the blistered places and little cuts on his hands—sitting up straight as he tried to stretch his back—his shoulders sore as he shifted around on the hard plastic seat.

A few minutes later they spotted the man—standing down by the water on the boat ramp—staring at them with his hands on his hips—Seth looking above him at a white pickup in the parking lot—then twisting around to look at Isabel in the green canoe—watching her paddle slowly—leaning to one side so she could see the man—Spoon paddling in front of her with his head down—sunburned and tired—worry showing on his thin face.

Seth turned to face forward again—saw the man was wearing sunglasses—watched him pull off his cowboy hat and wave to them—smile on his pale, shiny face. Seth looked down at the blue tarp covering the duffel bag full of money—stared at it sitting there in front of him at the bottom of the canoe.

"That him?" Spoon said—cheering up suddenly as he started talking about how hungry he was—about all the barbeque places he'd heard there were in Kansas City.

Isabel kept looking at the man—kept paddling but each distracted stroke only skimmed the top of the water—Seth letting the green canoe catch up until they were almost even with him—looking at Isabel until she looked back—wanting to say something to her but not sure what—not sure why or what difference it could make—nodding to her instead—then turning away and paddling the rest of the way to the boat ramp.

"Hello, Seth," the man said.

Seth felt the bow of the canoe scrape against the submerged concrete of the boat ramp—rested his hands on his legs while still holding onto the paddle—pressing his right hand down to feel the pistol in his pocket.

"Hi."

The man stayed where he was on the boat ramp—eventually putting his hat back on—still smiling.

Seth stepped out of the red canoe and stood on the sloping concrete—water halfway up his shins. He turned around and wondered if the man might shoot him—tried not to think about it as he watched Isabel and Spoon in the green canoe—sun shining hot and bright as they kept paddling—trees along the opposite bank showing different shades of dark green—few red brick buildings there within the trees—the three bridges they'd passed under to Seth's left—still able to hear the traffic—to see the cars and trucks.

As the green canoe hit the boat ramp—coming to a hard stop as the bottom scraped across the concrete—Seth heard the man start playing the penny whistle behind him.

"Here," Seth said—offering his hand to help Isabel out of the canoe—the man playing an uptempo song—Isabel watching him—grabbing Seth's hand but not meeting his eyes—Spoon still in his seat—smiling and bobbing his head.

"Thank you, Bertram," the man said once he'd finished the short song—Spoon clapping for a few seconds before hopping out of the canoe. "I just thought you all might have missed it." Seth turned and started walking up the boat ramp—trying hard not to look up at the man. "I wrote that song especially for this occasion, you know."

"Well it's a real nice song," Spoon said.

Seth pulled the red canoe up the boat ramp until it was completely out of the water—then went to the green canoe and helped Spoon drag it out of the water as well. They unloaded their supplies—their tents and sleeping bags and the little cooking stove—the duffel bag full of money—the leftover ketamine lozenges taken from the old couple that had tried to rob them—carrying everything up the boat ramp to the white pickup—the man never moving from his spot above the canoes—spinning around to watch them as they made their way to the parking lot and back.

Once they were finished the man walked up the boat ramp and locked the pickup's camper shell—Seth and Spoon loading the canoes on top and strapping them down—Seth meeting Isabel as he came around the pickup—finding her frozen next to the passenger's side door—her fingers gripping the handle but she hadn't opened it yet—her eyes full of fear, exhaustion and maybe a little regret—Seth knowing he had the same look on his face—his hand slowly reaching into his pocket for the pistol.

"I can take that off your hands, Seth," the man said from behind him.

Seth took his hand out of his pocket when he heard the man's voice—turned around and saw him next to the taillight—sun behind him—his haloed silhouette showing Seth the penny whistle in his right hand.

"All the bad men are gone now, Seth," the man said— stepping forward and holding out his left hand—Seth pulling the pistol from his pocket—holding the grip—feeling the trigger guard as he hesitated—raising the barrel as the man took a step toward him—raising it some more with his arm extended—sliding his finger back as sweat collected above his eyes.

The man took another quick step and grabbed the pistol—grabbed it by the barrel and twisted it out of Seth's hand—then tossed it in the air and caught the grip—stuffing it into the waistband of his pants behind his back.

"Let's go," the man said—the big smile returning to his face—twirling the penny whistle in his right hand as he walked around to the driver's side door.

THEY DROVE SOUTH THROUGH DOWNTOWN AND THEN turned west—Seth watching the businesses and apartment buildings out the window—people walking along the side-walks—few restaurants with tables and chairs set outside. Spoon kept leaning over Seth to look out his window—examining the food on people's plates when they had to stop at a light—staring up at the shiniest buildings—watching a homeless man pet his dog at a bus stop.

They drove on—watching the buildings get shorter and older—most constructed of brick as they left downtown— the road turning several times as they went—Seth rolling down his window as they picked up speed—hearing trains blowing their air horns off in the distance.

Soon they stopped in front of a four-story brick building—Seth able to see plywood covering the windows—an old wooden door—empty, crumbling sidewalks all around them. He turned his head and saw the empty lot across the street—remembering the first time the man had brought him there—had forced him to drive through the night in his blood-soaked clothes—two dead bodies in the bed of Mr. Loomis's pickup.

"Go in and open the roller door, Seth," the man said. "Do you remember where it is?" He turned and looked at Seth in the backseat—Seth nodding as he glanced at the back of Isabel's head—her hair down and her face hidden.

He got out of the pickup and walked over to the door—turned the knob but the door was stuck. He used his fist to bang on the edges—then tried to wiggle it back and forth—pickup already around the corner and out of sight when Seth looked back—all alone as he looked down the street in both directions—as he picked up a piece of the broken sidewalk and started hammering the hinges—several more minutes before he finally forced the door open—then walked inside the unlit building.

He shut the door behind him and stood there in the dark—pulled the cellphone out of his pocket—turned on the flashlight and pointed it toward the ground—walking with the phone held out in front of him—waving it back and forth as he listened to his feet shuffling across the concrete floor.

It took him a few minutes to find the roller door—following the sound of the pickup's idling engine outside as he got closer—finding the chain before stuffing the cellphone back into his pocket—then pulling down on the chain to raise the door.

The light from outside came up Seth's legs as the door opened—lit up his shirt and then he felt it warm on his arms—closing his eyes once the light reached his face. The man pulled the pickup inside—Seth starting to close the door as the taillights cleared the doorway—hearing the pickup driving away from him as he pulled the chain down hand over hand—turning his head just as the yellow headlights came on.

Seth finished closing the door and turned around—pickup out of sight now but he could still hear it—listening as he stood there in the dark—looking back at the big roller door—slivers of daylight coming through the edges. Then he pulled the cellphone out of his pocket again—turned on the flashlight and started walking.

He walked around the dark building for ten or fifteen minutes—using the phone's flashlight to try to find his way—battery almost dead by the time he found the tunnel—stepping from the smooth concrete floor to the broken, uneven ground—walking downhill as he shined the flashlight to the left and right—seeing the walls of rough-cut limestone rising on each side—feeling himself getting deeper into the tunnel—farther below ground.

After a couple minutes he saw a light ahead of him—saw it getting brighter as he continued walking—hearing voices as he got closer—able to see the rough ground now without the light from the cellphone—stuffing it back into his pocket as he started walking faster—then started jogging as his heart rate increased—sweat seeping into his shirt even though it was cool in the cave.

"Seth," the man called out—then paused as his voice echoed around the cave—Seth stopping suddenly at the entrance to the large open space—blinking and looking around but not seeing anyone—hearing the buzzing of the overhead fluorescent lights—looking at the white pickup—the two shipping containers—the hole in the ground and the pile of salt beside it—twice the size it'd been before. "Come join us," the man said—Seth able to tell where his voice was coming from this time.

Seth walked over to the shipping containers—looked inside the first one and saw the three of them sitting together at a plastic table near the back—fluorescent light fixture hanging down over the table on two uneven chains—duffel bag with the money inside sitting on the ground next to the man—his back to Seth but he didn't turn around—Seth waiting near the open door—looking at Isabel—then looking at Spoon.

"Come, Seth," the man said. "Sit down."

Seth walked inside and went around the table to the only empty chair—floor of the shipping container making a hollow sound every time he took a step.

"Bertram was just telling me about Benjamin," the man said—Seth glancing over at Spoon—his head down and his hands in his lap. "How you dealt with him in the same fashion you dealt with the man who tried to sodomize you." Seth turned his head and looked across the table—felt Isabel staring at him as he wiped his index finger across his forehead. "Same as the man you left for dead inside the shipping container next door." The man raised his eyebrows—little smile on his face—without his sunglasses now—his cowboy hat on the table. "Is that accurate, Seth?"

There was a long pause as Seth stared at the plastic table—the man's hat pointed at him—only sound the light fixture buzzing above their heads—all the light fixtures buzzing together out in the open space.

"Yeah," Seth said.

"What?"

"Yessir."

"Are you saying you killed him, Seth? You killed Benjamin?"

"Yessir."

"And you have nothing else to say to me?"

Seth looked up at the man and shook his head.

They were all quiet again—Seth watching the man lean back in his chair—watching his hands raise and come together behind his head.

"Loyalty," the man said. "People are largely a mystery to me—you all know this—but I've always understood loyalty." Seth looked at Spoon—saw him nodding his head—his tan, thin arms crossed over his chest. "I've demanded it—you've given it—and now here we are." The man lifted the bag sitting on the ground next to his chair. "Satchel full of money." He dropped it—then leaned forward over the table. "And you three aren't dead yet."

Seth watched the man's eyes widen—his jaw muscles twist into knots below each red cheek—anger showing on his face for just a moment—then fading quickly as he sat back—that big smile returning as he looked around the table.

"I guess all I'm trying to say," the man started. "Is thank you." He bowed his head—still smiling—fists resting on the table—skin pink and waxy around his knuckles. "Job well done."

They sat there a while longer—the man nodding his head—raising his eyebrows as a thought crossed his mind—Seth turning eventually to look at Isabel—watching her move her fingertips across the plastic table—her head down—hair hanging close around her face—sliding her fingertips in long arcing lines—big circles that always ended up right back in front of her.

"I'll go unload the pickup," the man said—putting his hands on the arms of his chair—still smiling as he looked around the table at each of them. "Stay here—guard my money."

The man stood up and turned toward the door—leaving the duffel bag full of cash on the floor of the shipping container next to his empty chair—pulling the penny whistle from his back pocket as he started walking—Seth seeing the pistol tucked into the waistband of his pants—the man now playing a fast song as he moved toward the open door—kicking one leg out and then the other—then hopping around in a tight circle.

"Let's go," Seth said as he stood up from the table. "Get up." He looked at Isabel and then Spoon. "Go," he said—louder this time as he moved around the table—watching the man take the little step down out of the shipping container—still playing the same song as he stood there for a moment—leaning back and flapping his arms.

Seth looked down at Isabel and Spoon—grabbing Isabel by the arm as she hesitated—half in and half out of her chair—Spoon's eyes darting back and forth between Seth and the man.

Seth looked up again as he started dragging Isabel out of her chair—turning toward the shipping container's open door—seeing that the man wasn't there anymore.

"Wait!" Seth yelled—running now for the large open space before the door started closing—hearing the loud hollow thuds his footsteps made—sounds that blended with Isabel's footsteps behind him.

Seth ran through the open doorway—stopped after taking a few steps on the gritty, uneven floor of the cave— then stood there and looked around—Isabel doing the same beside him—hearing the man still playing the same song on the penny whistle somewhere off in the distance—staying out of sight as the music echoed off the rough-cut limestone walls—fluorescent lights shining down on them from the ceiling—Seth looking at the opening to the tunnel that led up to the surface—then hearing the booming metal sounds of Spoon's footsteps as he ran out of the shipping container behind them.

"What the hell, man?" Spoon said—coming up beside Seth—breathing hard as he waited for an answer—Seth and Isabel both staying quiet—scanning the cave as the man continued with his song.

"There he is," Isabel said—pointing to the other side of the large open space—Seth turning his head to see the man directly across from them—dancing around in the shadows near the wall—then skipping and twirling toward them with the penny whistle held up to his lips.

The three of them stayed close together as the man

approached—then parted so he could pass between them—
Seth able to see sweat running down the man's face—blue
vein bulging from the middle of his high forehead.

They watched the man circle around them a few
times—jumping and spinning as he continued playing the
same song—moving eventually toward the pickup—leaning
back against the tailgate as he blasted out a few final notes—
sweat making his face and neck shine—already soaked into
the collar and the armpits of his shirt.

After his finale he placed his hands on his knees and
bent a little at the waist—breathing hard—the smile gone
now as Seth watched him stare at the ground.

"Thomas Edison played the piano, you know," the man
said. "Al Capone the mandola—no idea how proficient they
were—music obviously just a hobby for them—not their
principal vocation."

There was a long pause as the man's breathing slowed—
as some of the color left his face—never looking up at them
or anywhere else but the ground at his feet.

"You sound real good to me," Spoon said. "Probably better than both of them."

"Thank you, Bertram," the man said—tilting his head
back—looking at Spoon with a grave expression on his face.
"Thank you."

Seth glanced over at Spoon—watched him nod his head
and smile at the man—his hand shaking down by his leg.

"Come over here, Seth," the man said—staring at the
ground again as Seth walked over—still leaning back against
the tailgate—hands still on his knees—his breathing almost
back to normal. "Take this." The man reached into his pocket
and pulled out a key—held it up and Seth took it. "It's for the
other shipping container." Seth turned and looked back—
past Isabel and Spoon to the chain and padlock around the
levers of the closed doors. "Don't worry," the man said. "He's
not there any longer."

The man finally stood up straight—turned without looking at Seth and opened the tailgate—dragged out the duffel bag with the blocks of ketamine inside but didn't lift it—taking a step back instead—motioning to Seth with his right hand—holding the pistol now with his index finger resting on the trigger. Seth went over and lifted the bag off the tailgate—hoisted it onto his shoulder and started walking toward the locked shipping container—the man following close behind him.

Isabel was watching him as he walked past her—Seth noticing she'd pulled her hair back—noticing a few strands still hanging loose around her face—smiling at her but he knew she wouldn't smile back.

Seth got to the door of the shipping container—set the duffel bag on the ground—unlocked the padlock and pulled the chain free from the levers—dropping the chain onto the ground as the man took the padlock and the key from him— Seth then opening one of the doors and swinging it out of the way—levers and hinges squeaking—light shooting into the first few feet of the shipping container—the man motioning with the pistol as he looked at Seth—Seth stepping over to pick up the duffel bag—seeing a dark spot on the inside wall of the shipping container—splatters in all directions—long thick lines trailing down to the floor. He pulled the cellphone out of his pocket so he could use the flashlight to see inside.

"Give me the cellphone," the man said—his soft hand held out—pistol held down by his side but Seth could tell his arm was flexed—another fake smile suddenly forming on his face—mustache trimmed away from his pink lips.

Seth looked down at the pistol—then over at Isabel— her worried eyes locked on his for a moment—then quickly turning with her hands on her hips—stepping slowly away as Seth handed the cellphone to the man—still watching Isabel as the man pulled a small flashlight out of his pock- et—Seth's eyes lingering on the back of Isabel's head—her thick black hair—slender shoulders and arms tanned by the sun. He finally turned toward the man—took the flashlight and stood there with the duffel bag hanging from one hand.

"Where do I put it?"

"All the way in the back," the man said—grinning with a layer of sweat still coating his face.

Seth turned toward the shipping container and clicked on the flashlight—stepped inside and started walking without looking back—seeing shelves against the back wall—two suitcases and a few black trash bags on the bottom shelf—hearing only his own footsteps as he went.

"Do you remember, Seth," the man said from the doorway. "That story I told you about Emperor Claudius and his food taster?"

Seth stopped and turned around. "I remember," he said—clicking the flashlight off—the man standing there with his hand on the edge of the door—all the overhead lights behind him—Seth only able to see his dark silhouette.

"I can't let you become my Halotus, Seth—I'm sure you understand."

Seth heard the man start laughing—thought he could see the whites of his eyes and his teeth but he wasn't sure—took a step toward the door—then another—then saw the man back up and start swinging the door closed.

Seth dropped the duffel bag and started running.

"Wait!" Seth yelled—watching the light shrink toward the door as the opening closed—hearing the hinges and the hollow sound of the metal floor—still running as the light pulled back from the walls of the shipping container—the man hidden behind the closing door now.

Everything went dark as the door banged closed—Seth hearing the latches lock into place—still ten feet or so from the end of the shipping container—stopping and standing there—clicking the flashlight back on—pointing it at the door's rusty metal surface.

"Isabel," Seth heard the man say—then heard the chain being lifted off the ground. "Here—lock it up while Bertram and I retrieve the money."

Seth stepped forward with the flashlight held out in front of him—watching the wide, dim circle of light shrink and brighten as he neared the door—seeing little divots he knew were from the last man locked inside—remembering the desperate gunshots just a few months ago—Seth slamming the doors shut—then leaving the cave while the doomed man cried.

Now it was him inside the shipping container—leaning on the door and listening—hearing Isabel walk over to the man—take the chain and the padlock from his hands—then hearing the man walk away.

"Bertram," the man said near the front of the other shipping container—Seth hearing Spoon hurry forward to meet him—then hearing their quick footsteps on the metal floor as they went inside. "Go to the back wall, Bertram."

"What?" Spoon said. "Wait I—"

"You lied to me, Bertram," the man said—Seth standing there listening—listening also to Isabel on the other side of the metal door—doing something with the chain.

"You lied about Benjamin," the man said.

"No I ain't lying he—" Spoon said—frantically trying to explain.

Seth heard Isabel start rattling the loose chain against the outside of the door—heard one of the latches start squeaking—then saw a thin line of light where the doors came together—gap just wide enough for him to see her black hair—her neck and cheek—her hands dropping the chain to the ground before grabbing the latch again.

Seth could still hear Spoon talking in the other shipping container—Isabel working the latch until she got the door unlocked—hinges squeaking as Seth pushed it open—as he saw her eyes and how hard she was breathing—pushing the door as he tried to listen for the man—careful to make sure Isabel was out of the way.

Seth stepped out onto the rough-cut limestone—turned and ran toward the other shipping container—hearing Spoon and the man suddenly stop talking as he grabbed the edge of the only open door—then hearing the sound of their feet sliding on the metal floor inside.

The door became stuck as Seth started pushing it closed—hinges popping and groaning as he worked the door back and forth—never looking up but hearing footsteps coming toward him—then gunshots as the door finally moved—Seth swinging it around and slamming it closed—grabbing the handles and locking down the two flat levers.

Seth's ears were ringing now—his hands feeling the metal vibrate with every gunshot—then feeling the man slam into the doors from the inside—regroup and hit the metal doors again—Seth hearing him lose his footing—his feet making a sliding sound as Seth stood there watching the doors buckle and shake—watching the vertical bars—making sure the cams were all locked in place. He backed up a couple steps but kept his eyes on the doors—the man firing two more shots before everything went quiet—the ringing in Seth's ears going away after a while—soon able to hear the man laughing—Seth wondering what he'd overlooked—waiting to see if the man was about to escape somehow—taking another couple steps back as the laughing continued.

"Oh, Seth," the man said—sounding amused and a little out of breath. "It appears you've beaten me at my own game." He started laughing again—Seth hearing him lean against the door—tapping it lightly with the pistol. "I've erred, Seth—underestimated you, I suppose—but I'll have you know I'm actually experiencing a fair amount of joy right now—excitement for what's to come."

Seth looked back at Isabel—standing behind him with the chain back in her hands—meeting Seth's eyes for just a moment—then looking past him at the closed doors—taking deep breaths still—taking tiny steps forward as Seth watched her swallow.

"Seth?" the man said. "I didn't shoot you, did I, Seth?"

Seth checked himself—holding his arms out—looking them up and down—then scanning his midsection and his legs.

"No," he said.

"Good."

Seth heard the man start walking back and forth—pacing the width of the shipping container—heard the hollow sound his feet made each time they hit the metal floor—ringing out and echoing off the limestone walls of the cave.

"I appreciate you leaving me all the money, Seth—very gentlemanly of you," the man said—then paused for a while as he continued pacing. "I'm going to enjoy this, Seth—you leaving me in here—me struggling in the darkness—trying to figure out how to escape—the subsequent chase—the retribution."

Seth looked around the large open space—seeing a few of the fluorescent lights starting to blink—looking back at the pickup and the pile of salt—the dark entrance to the tunnel.

"I'm proud of you, Seth," the man said. "You've really come alive."

Seth stared at the closed doors—listening to the man's footsteps—remembering who he'd been before—the scared boy who cowered for hours in the middle of that cornfield—suddenly terrified he might slip back into that life—might lose whoever he'd become.

He watched as Isabel walked past him—watched her walk to the shipping container with the chain rattling in her hands—then heard the man stop pacing back and forth as she got closer—heard him lean against the doors again.

"My Isabel," the man said—tenderness in his voice

seeming almost genuine. "Mine no more." He hit one of the doors from the inside—sound rumbling through the shipping container—echoing through the large open space for what seemed like a long time.

Isabel started wrapping the chain around the levers and the vertical rods—Seth hearing the man slide down the inside of the door—then hearing him start playing a sad song on the penny whistle while Isabel finished with the chain—pulling the padlock from her pocket and locking the ends of the chain together—the man still playing the song as she backed away toward Seth.

They stood there together as the man played on—Isabel starting to cry when Seth tried to wrap his arm around her—leaning away from him—shrugging her shoulders as she stepped forward out of his reach. Seth pulled his arm back and watched her as she stared at the shipping container doors—both of them listening to the sad song.

The man played the penny whistle for several minutes—everything quiet for a while after he finished—buzzing of the overhead lights the only sound inside the cave—Isabel wiping her face with the sleeve of her shirt—Seth still watching her.

"Isabel?" Spoon said—still in the back of the shipping container somewhere—sounding like he was far away.

"Bertram!" the man said. "I nearly forgot about you." Seth heard the man stand up and start walking down the length of the shipping container—double tap of his boots ringing out with each step. "We're going to have fun in here, Bertram—lots and lots of fun."

Seth stepped forward and grabbed Isabel's arm—started pulling her toward the tunnel—the man still marching over the metal floor of the shipping container—both of them listening but only Isabel with her eyes still on the locked doors—hearing the plastic table being slid out of the way—plastic chairs thrown or kicked—Spoon moving around in the back of the shipping container as the man got closer.

Isabel kept looking back—Seth eventually having to grab her around the waist to keep her moving—getting them to the tunnel as they heard Spoon start to scream—the man talking to him in a low voice—Spoon screaming for him to stop—screaming for Isabel and then for Seth.

Seth never looked back—held tight onto Isabel and started walking up the tunnel—light dimming and then disappearing as they got farther from the cave—sounds fading but never going away.

20

"**I**T'S OK," SETH SAID. "WE HAD TO DO IT—YOU KNOW that, right?"

They were walking down the sidewalk a block away from the abandoned factory—day still sunny with a hot breeze blowing against their skin.

"And there's no way he's getting outta there," Seth said—Isabel nodding as they kept walking—going a few blocks without talking—Seth eventually leading Isabel across the street so they could stay in the shade—passing by more abandoned buildings with their windows boarded up—eventually coming to a park where they saw smoke rising into the air.

"You hungry?" Seth said—Isabel glancing over at him— shaking her head as Seth noticed her eyes were still puffy and bloodshot—her lips almost red—cheeks still shiny from a few recent tears.

They turned into the parking lot and saw people standing in line next to a smoker—few folding tables off to the side—the smoker on a trailer behind a red pickup—long enough for two people to work side by side in front of it. Seth and Isabel walked closer—saw two men painting barbeque sauce on big chunks of meat—a woman working the cash register while another scooped side dishes onto plates—then handed people napkins and plastic utensils.

They went to the back of the line and stood there waiting—silent as the rest of the people around them talked and laughed—Seth ordering two plates and four beers once their turn came—one plate with grilled chicken and the other with burnt ends. He paid and took his change—stepping off to the side to count the money he had left in his wallet—enough for a few more beers—maybe another piece of grilled chicken if Isabel wanted it—leaving him broke again by dark, he thought.

When their order was ready Isabel carried the beers and Seth carried the plates—walking out into the park away from all the people—finding a picnic table where they sat down across from each other—Seth watching the trees sway back and forth as they ate—looking out over the grass—an empty playground off in the distance—then a line of trees that ran along the border of the park.

He took another bite of the burnt ends on his plate. "This is pretty great," he said—Isabel keeping her head down as she ate—Seth turning to look at her across the table—waiting for her to say something—wondering where they were going to sleep that night—wishing they'd at least brought their camping gear—then watching as Isabel tipped her head back and finished off one of the beers.

"Yeah," she said. "It's perfect."

Dear reader,

Thank you for reading *The River Snakes*. I spent several years writing this book—late nights and early mornings—stolen daylight hours when most people would say I should've been doing something else—something more productive. I just couldn't help myself. All I wanted to do was find out what happened next—how Seth would respond to new dangers—what violent, unpredictable thing the man might do and how everyone else would react. To be honest, I still can't help myself—still think about the characters in this book nearly every day—Spoon's goofy jokes—Benjy's reflexive anger—but mostly about Isabel—whether she sticks with Seth after the ending you just read—where she goes and how she starts over with nothing.

I'll let you know what I find out.

Please rate/review *The River Snakes* on Amazon or Goodreads or anywhere else. Also, keep an eye on my website, AdamDarby.com, for news on upcoming releases (sequels) or to contact me directly.

Again, thank you for reading,

Adam Darby

Read the first chapter of *mark* on the next pages! It's a horror/suspense novel with a bit of mystery to it. Enjoy!

MARK

CHAPTER ONE

IT WAS NEARLY DARK BY THE TIME THEY EMERGED from the jungle—stepping from the shaded, muddy trail to the dry, firm ground of the tribe's village—small huts surrounding a taller, longer structure at the center of the clearing—all with reed walls and thatched roofs—open ground mostly bare, red-brown dirt—packed by billions of footsteps over thousands of years. Mark stopped when his captors stopped—looked up and saw a full moon rising through the soft sunset colors still visible—pinks, purples and oranges fading fast from east to west—first few stars blinking in the darkest parts of the sky.

The four men spoke to each other—their strange language accompanied by grunts and hand gestures—coming to some sort of consensus after a minute or two—then shoving Mark toward a small hut along the edge of the village. A group of children stopped playing and stared silently as he passed—mouths open—fear and wonder on their little faces. Mark tried to smile at them—tried to put them at ease but he felt too much pain to pretend—too much fear to worry about anyone else being afraid—walking past them with his eyes on the ground—focusing on his pace and not deviating from the path his captors were taking—keeping the wooden spears off his head and away from his sore back.

They kept Mark outside the small hut while two of the men entered and spoke with someone—voices hushed and hurried—one of them much more animated than the others. Mark waited and listened—tried to see inside but it was too dark as he peered through the open doorway.

After a few minutes the two men came out and relayed some brief commands to the other two—all four then working together to force Mark inside the small, unlit hut—pushing and pulling his arms—poking his back with their fire-hardened spears.

Once inside the dank, windowless space—once his eyes had adjusted to the darkness—it was easy to see what they wanted—the task he'd have to complete—his first taste of forced labor just a day after being taken by the tribe.

Light soon began to trickle in from a quickly growing bonfire outside—making shadows on the reed walls and thatched ceiling. A woman was laid out on the floor in the center of the hut—naked with her legs bent at the knees and spread apart—head and face resting back in the shadows—arms stretched out away from her body. Mark looked at her hands in the increasing flickers of light and saw they were covered in ocher paint—smeared as well over her breasts—a line of it going from her neck down to her waist.

Two of the men let go of Mark's arms and backed away. At the same time Mark felt spears poking into the muscles that ran along his spine—nudging him toward an older man he hadn't seen at first—kneeling just on the other side of the woman. They looked at each other and Mark saw dark lines carefully drawn onto the man's face—charcoal tracings along the deep wrinkles in his skin—his hair cut in the same shape as all the other men.

As Mark approached the older man began waving a bundle of smoking leaves and bark over the woman's body—burning specks floating down to her skin but she did not move. Her chest raised, fingers twitched and toes just barely started to curl—but the rest of her stayed firmly in place—determined, Mark thought, to remain—to endure any and all hardships for as long as she had to.

THIS WASN'T MARK'S REAL LIFE—SLAVE TO A prehistoric tribe. It wasn't his life just thirty-six hours ago—before they found him wandering the jungle—the two days he'd spent lost and alone before that—or for all the weeks and months and years of his life leading up to now. This wasn't him—who he really was.

He'd known he was lost soon after leaving the outfitter's camp—had become aware of something following him two days later—something close but never seen—never heard when he stopped to listen. There was something tracking him—hunting him as he tried to find his way back.

Occasionally he would stop and stand as motionless as possible—sweating with every heartbeat pounding up through his head—watching for any movement—waiting to hear another small sound from whatever terrible thing was pursuing him.

Finally the four small men emerged from behind giant trees, tangled vines and broad-leafed jungle plants—surrounding him and slowly closing in. Mark spun around to see each man with a long wooden spear held waist-high—all pointing toward the middle of his body.

The men spoke to each other but never turned their heads or even seemed to blink. Mark slipped and stumbled as he searched for a way to escape the tightening circle—sturdy, shoeless feet of all the men shuffling in unison over the leaf-littered forest floor—working together to keep him corralled—their eyes never leaving him—tips of their spears never dropping or turning away—strips of cloth or animal skin hanging down from coarse rope belts.

As they inched closer Mark put his hands in the air and tried to speak to them—English words and phrases he hoped they would somehow understand. But the four small men did not stop moving toward him until the points of their spears touched his ribs and stomach—two of them poking at the backpack hanging from his shoulders—one even testing the bottle of insect repellant bulging from the front pocket of his pants.

They talked to each other for another minute or two— puzzled glances now traded between them as they decided Mark's fate. Then the circle suddenly broke apart—two of the men marching away single file—the other two slapping at Mark with their spears—hitting his backpack and legs— his arms and swinging for his head.

They walked for hours through the thick jungle—small bodies of the four men moving easily between the trees and dangling vines as Mark struggled to keep up. When he couldn't match their pace they stabbed at him from behind with their spears—tripped and fell and they beat him with the blunt ends of the same long, fire-hardened sticks. When he tried to escape—running off suddenly through the dense vegetation with no idea where he was going—the men would chase after him and have him surrounded within a few minutes—laughing and joking with each other as they closed in—striking him in turns before returning to the trail.

At one point they stopped and ripped Mark's backpack off his shoulders—made him sit in the mud as they inspect- ed its strange contents—pulling things out one by one and passing them around—synthetic sleeping bag and rain jacket and the little metal stove. Once they were through inspecting an item the last man holding it would toss it over his shoulder—discarding Mark's carefully chosen supplies and leaving them to disappear into the jungle—curiosities only useful as amusing distractions during a break in their long march.

They continued their trek into the night and through to the next morning—traversing trails Mark could not distinguish from the rest of the jungle. But he kept moving forward—tired, thirsty and sore from all the beatings—anxious to see their destination—wondering if they were taking him to some deeper, darker, even more untouched place—a cursed part of the forest where primitive tribes killed and ate their enemies and any outsiders they managed to capture. Or maybe they were delivering him back to civilization—deporting him to the outside world where something so weak, so strange and so useless surely belonged.

In the small, dark hut with the woman and the older man, Mark continued stepping forward until the spearpoints finally pulled back from the skin around his spine—flinching to a stop as he heard the blunt ends of the heavy spears tapping down onto the packed-earth floor behind him.

He was at the woman's feet now—looking down into the shadows—the older man wafting smoke into her face from the bundle he held—Mark able to see that her eyes were open—tears on her cheeks with her nostrils flared.

He stood there and watched as the older man bent down and whispered into the woman's ear—bundle held over her abdomen—smoke drifting up across Mark's face. The older man continued talking to the woman for what seemed like a long time—eventually shaking the collection of burning leaves and bark as he spoke—Mark watching more of the gray-white particles breaking away from the bundle—some hanging in the air and rising toward the ceiling—some dancing away and sinking slowly toward the ground.

Once the older man had finished his incantations, Mark felt someone stepping forward from the doorway—rough, small hands grabbing his shoulders from behind—pulling him down to his knees—the other men then coming forward as they all began to chant—the older man standing up slowly—looking down at Mark—staring blankly at him with firelight flickering over his face—the chanting growing louder and louder.

Mark turned his head and looked out the open doorway—the rest of the tribe now dancing around the raging bonfire—chanting in time with the men inside the hut. He turned back and looked down at the woman—her head raised out of the shadows—bloodshot eyes staring up at him—shaky voice chanting along with everyone else.

A few seconds later one of the men pushed Mark down on top of the woman—her head falling back but she kept looking at him—kept dutifully chanting—Mark looking up as the older man began dancing around them in a tightening circle—wafting smoke through the air as he went—the other four men still chanting as they did the same dance.

Mark looked back down at the woman—on his hands and knees with his bottom half between her legs—feeling her smooth skin wrapping around him—her hand squeezing inside the waistband of his pants—ligaments in her neck protruding as she leaned forward—hand still reaching—searching inside the strange garment—still chanting along with everyone else.

When he looked up again at the dancing men, Mark saw spears in their hands and knew what would happen if he fought—if he protested—if he refused to do what they demanded be done.

MARK WOKE UP IN THE MORNING WITH HIS ARMS STILL wrapped around his head. Members of the tribe had rushed into the little hut several times throughout the night to hit him with spears as he slept—waking him suddenly and laughing as he rolled away—laughing even as he screamed and eventually cried against the back wall of the hut. It started several hours after the woman left—after all the dancing and chanting and the smoking bundle of leaves and bark—after the bonfire had slowly burned itself out.

But as he opened his eyes just after the sun had risen above the tallest treetops—as he cautiously raised his head to look around—there were no spears and no one else seemed to be inside the tiny hut—morning light coming in through the open doorway—smoke from the night's fire still hanging in the heavy air. Mark blinked himself awake and turned his head away from the sun—sat up after a minute or two and scooted carefully into the shade—vertebrae popping as he moved—bruises and cuts hurting as his muscles flexed and his skin stretched—his mouth feeling dry as he instinctively began looking around for water.

"Hi," Mark said as he noticed the older man—the witch doctor with the charcoal black lines curving around his wrinkled facesitting in a patch of shade on the other side of the hut—the two of them separated by the angled block of sunlight coming in through the open doorway—staring at each other—the older man not moving—not even blinking his eyes."Hi," Mark said again as he raised a hand to wave—squinting and yawning—scanning the rest of the packed-earth floor—hoping in vain to see something that held water—an ancient clay pot or bowl or even just an upturned leaf. "Water," he said. "Water." Mark cupped his hands and lifted them to his mouth—pantomiming for the motionless older man.

THE RAIN STARTED EARLY IN THE AFTERNOON THAT day—Mark's first full day with the tribe after his first full moon night—not allowed out of the hut until the storm finally arrived—rain pouring down while thunder ricocheted off the thick walls of jungle that surrounded the village.

The older man stayed with him inside the hut all morning—never moving except to turn his head each time Mark ran out the open doorway—then turning again a few minutes later to watch him being shoved back inside by the same four men that had found him wandering the jungle—the failed escape attempts piling up as noon came and went—the beatings—not even able to find something to drink in one of the wettest places on Earth.

Once the rain started, however, Mark ran outside and was surprised when no one came running after him—stopped and stood there waiting for them to come—soaking wet with bare feet squishing into the slick mud—spinning around to peer inside all the huts—seeing columns of small faces staring out at him—smallest children at the bottom—then the adolescents and then a few adult faces at the top.

The rain smacked into his head and body and soaked into the pants he was still wearing—his shirt, shoes and socks having been taken from him the night before—half-naked now as he turned from hut to hut—watching the faces appear and then disappear from the open doorways—eventually spotting a puddle of muddy water near where the bonfire had been—now just a concave circle of gray ash—black and brown pieces of half-burnt wood.

Mark walked over and squatted down—tried to sweep away some of the silt from the puddle—then cupped his hands and submerged them—carefully lifting as much water as he could to his mouth. He drank twice more from the puddle—then looked back up at all the people in the doorways—rain still falling—running cool down his face and back—muddy water collecting in his stomach.

Eventually he stood up and turned toward the largest hut in the center of the village.

"I'm leaving," Mark said—barely able to hear his own voice over the rain—shattering sound of myriad drops slapping into the bare ground and the rooftops—soaking the endless jungle beyond. "Bye, everybody—hell of a party last night." His voice was shaky as he backed away—more faces crowding into the doorways as he got farther from the half-drained puddle—serious faces of men intent on keeping their captive—their soft-bellied slave.

Once he got to the trees Mark turned and started running—navigating a narrow tunnel of tropical vegetation with branches coming together over his head—broad green leaves leaning over in front of him—heavy with the afternoon rain. He smacked them out of his way and tried not to slip on the muddy trail—finally looking back to see several faces running after him—bows held out in front of their strong, slender bodies—bundles of arrows held vertical in angry hands.

Mark ran harder—heart pumping faster and lungs trying to catch up—not worrying as much about slipping or stepping on something sharp with his tender feet—few seconds later feeling a sudden bite in his leg just below his knee—then tumbling down to the mushy, decomposing leaves that lined the forest floor—rolling through thin stalks of jungle underbrush.

Once he came to a stop Mark turned over onto his back and looked down at his leg—blood leaking out with an arrow going through it—something shiny catching his eye at the front end of the lightweight wooden shaft—delicate-looking feathers attached to the back.

"How'd they—" he started saying as the pain suddenly eased—as his eyelids drooped and his hearing faded—reaching to touch the sharpened metal tip as his captors quickly approached—dead leaves clinging to his arms and back—his pants heavy with rain and blood.

Soon Mark felt the young men lifting him off the

ground—raindrops hitting his eyes as he suddenly found it hard to focus—hard to see or hear or even smell anything—to distinguish the waking world from one of dreamed-up terrors.

"I THINK I'VE FIGURED OUT A NAME FOR YOU," MARK said from his back—turning his head a few minutes after he woke up inside the same small hut where he'd spent that morning—where he'd been forced onto a woman the night before. "Splinter," he said—blinking as his eyes tried to focus on the older man sitting across from him in the dark—seeing the man's unblinking eyes and the dark tracings on his face. "Ever heard of the Teenage Mutant Ninja Turtles?" Mark was sitting up now—rubbing his forehead as he looked around and out the open doorway. The rain had stopped and all he could hear were insects and frogs. The moon was up and close to full—making the wet, bare ground outside the hut shine blue. "Didn't think so," he continued—talking to the older man as he looked outside. "There's a group of turtles in New York City—in the sewers. They mutate into ninjas somehow—then they're brought up by a mutant rat who's sort of their leader. Anyway, the rat's name is Splinter."

Nothing about the older man changed—no movements that might have signaled he'd heard sounds coming from his tribe's strange captive—from the tall slave sitting just a few feet across from him. He just kept looking at Mark—kept his hands clasped in his lap.

Mark laughed as he inspected the two wounds now bracketing his leg—pants cut away from his knee down. The arrow with the shiny, sharp tip and stabilizing feathers was gone—thick layer of green paste now covering the holes—dried blood clumped in his leg hairs and there was swelling beneath his skin.

"I guess I'll have to figure out what names to give the other four—the ones who dragged me here. There's Donatello, Leonardo, Raphael and my personal favorite, Michelangelo."

Mark touched the two wounds but couldn't feel the pressure he placed on his leg—moved his hand down toward his ankle and the feeling gradually came back—then wiggled his toes and tried to flex his calf muscle—sending a sharp, sudden pain shooting through his leg—fresh blood leaking through cracks in the green paste. He winced and looked up at Splinter but the expression on the older man's face hadn't changed.

Mark scooted back against the wall and looked around—pushed himself as deep as he could into the corner of the tiny hut—tried to ask for his shirt or a blanket but got no response—then just leaned against the wall and crossed his arms—big smile on his face so the tears wouldn't start—trying to distract himself—wondering if he'd be warmer if he took his wet pants off.

"I guess that woman last night will be April," Mark said. "She gets herself roped into helping the Ninja Turtles all the time. And I guess I'll have to be Casey Jones. He's kind of a screwup but he has fun."

Splinter sat there on the bare ground—never speaking or making any kind of gesture—Mark's silent guard for the night. Mark looked him over carefully—the deep wrinkles of his face—black eyes and lipless mouth. Then he let his eyes wander to the walls of the hut and out the open doorway—Splinter's eyes, meanwhile, never leaving his captive's face.

After some time the darkness and the quiet began to burrow deep into Mark—the solitude and the helplessness—the shock of suddenly realizing he was now a slave to a prehistoric tribe—something insignificant that would likely be discarded soon—left for the jungle to slowly swallow.

So he began to talk—to dream out loud—to pray for yesterday's yesterday and for the chance to turn back—to choose another route—to go where they would not find him.